Mercy Denied

By

Kerry Barnes

Dedication

To My Family

Copyright

Mercy Denied by Kerry Barnes ISBN 978-1-7393019-4-1

This is a work of fiction. Names, characters, places, and incidents either are the product of the author's imagination or are used fictitiously. Any resemblance to actual persons, living or dead, events, or locales is entirely coincidental.

ISBN 978-1-7393019-4-1

Mercy Denied by Kerry Barnes

For more information, address: kerrybarnes999@gmail.com.

Publishers Once Upon A Book

www.authorkerrybarnes.co.uk

Warning

This book contains graphic details of murder, kidnapping, violence and profanities.

Other works by Kerry Barnes

Ruthless

Ruby's Palace

Raw Justice

The Hunted

The Rules

The Choice

Deceit

Cruel Secrets

Wicked Lies

Ugly Truth

Raising A Gangster

Outcast

Voice of Reason

Voice of Rage

Trusted

Taboo

Torment

Nemesis

Malice

Callous

Needs Must book 1 of the Carrie Verne series

Bitter Enemies book 2 of the Carrie Verne series

Broken Bond book 3 of the Carrie Verne series

Mercy Denied book 4 of the Carrie Verne series

Acknowledgements

Once again, I would like to thank my editor, Robert Wood. His insight, skill, and dedication have brought this book to life. From the first draft to the final version, Robert, with his clear understanding of this kind of storytelling, used his sharp editorial eye to lift the entire manuscript.

Working with Robert has felt like a true partnership based on mutual respect and a shared goal of creating the best book possible. He has pushed me when it mattered, but always in a way that respected my voice and vision. His suggestions have made the work stronger. I feel incredibly lucky to work with someone so professional and generous with his time and expertise.

Thank you, Robert, for everything – you've had a more significant impact on this project than you probably realise.

I also want to thank Deryl and the NotRights Book Club members for their generous support since I began writing.

And for all the readers who have taken a chance on reading my books, I am forever grateful.

I want to wish Maz Canny a Happy 70th Birthday x

PROLOGUE

April 2003

Lorraine ran her fingers gently over the smooth wood of the new cot. It wouldn't be long now. A few more weeks and she would be holding the little life growing inside her. She couldn't wait.

Meanwhile accountant Graham Fairweather, her husband, was in his study and doing an inventory of the contents to his safe. There had been a spate of burglaries in the area over the past six months and he had been advised by the local police to be vigilant.

The Fairweathers, both in their early thirties, lived in a stunning Georgian-style house on The Bishops Avenue, Hampstead Heath – better known as Billionaires' Row to some. The imposing wrought iron fence and massive metal gates offered a sense of security. However, the rear boundary wall was only six feet high, which had recently become a concern. With their baby on the way, Graham was determined to have it properly secured.

'Lorraine, darling!' called out Graham, as he left the study. 'Madeleine is finished for the day. Do you need her over the weekend?'

Lorraine sighed and rubbed slow circles over her belly. They didn't need extra help. However, with Graham's inheritance and his professional work, they were wealthy enough to employ a nanny, as well as Madeleine, the housekeeper, and Jim, the gardener.

From the window, she spotted Jim pruning the roses. He held a blossom to his nose, inhaling as if it contained something magical, something only he could sense. She was pleased she had taken him on, but, then again, it was part of her charity work to find employment for ex-addicts.

'Lorraine?' Graham's voice came again, this time louder.

She blinked away her thoughts. 'Yes, love, that would be wonderful. And please tell Madeleine there's a bit extra in the pay packet as a thank you for all her hard work . . . Never mind, darling, I'll come down and tell her myself.'

Lorraine descended the grand winding staircase at a steady pace, with one hand on the polished banister and the other resting protectively on her belly. She smiled warmly at Madeleine Tate, waving for her to wait.

'Maddie, thank you for everything this week. You've been such a help,' she said, embracing the middle-aged woman and pressing a soft kiss to her cheek.

Madeleine smiled. 'Oh, Lorraine, it was nothing. You will need to rest more now and reserve energy for the little one when it arrives. Anyway, if you don't need me, I'll see you bright and early on Monday morning.'

As Madeleine stepped out of the grand entrance, Jim appeared. He wandered inside and wiped the dirt from his boots before stepping on to the wooden floor.

'Miss,' he called, just as Lorraine was heading to the study to fetch his wages.

She turned and found him standing there with a handful of red roses from her garden. They were wrapped in a cloth to protect her from the thorns.

'I picked them for you. They wouldn't have lasted another couple of days. We've got a wind coming our way.'

'Oh, Jim, they're beautiful. Thank you,' she said, softly, inhaling the sweet fragrance.

Graham stepped forward, to relieve the gardener of the flowers. 'Cheers, Jim. I'll put them in some water and fetch your wages,' he said, fussing as always.

'D'you mind if I pick a couple for me missus?'

Lorraine waved a hand. 'Of course not. Go right ahead.'

Jim hesitated. 'Miss, can I show Mia around? So she can see what I do and what I've done?'

Lorraine beamed. She knew how much pride Jim took in his work. 'Of course, Jim.'

As she gazed out towards and beyond the front gates, she spotted Jim's wife Mia hanging around again.

Handing Jim his wages, Graham then pressed the security button to open the main gate to let Madeleine out and allow Mia to come in.

Wishing them a pleasant weekend, Lorraine watched them for a moment before heading across to the kitchen where Graham was filling the vase with water. The moment she entered the room, she stopped dead.

Two big menacing-looking men in black balaclavas stood at the French doors leading out to the rear garden.

It was as if she had stepped into a horror film. A cold fist of fear gripped her throat.

She couldn't move. Couldn't breathe.

With his back to the doors, Graham had no idea they were even there.

Before she could find her voice, the two masked men burst into the house, the French doors smashing against the walls.

Graham instantly spun around, and in doing so, he knocked the vase off the worktop. As soon as it hit the quarry tiled floor, the glass shattered. The sound was like a bomb going off.

Which, in turn, put the two intruders on edge.

Now, not only nervous, the loud noise sent one of the masked gunmen into a temper. He charged at Graham, but clumsily, he lost his footing, slipped on the wet tiles, and fell onto his back.

The gun went off.

Lorraine felt a searing, white-hot pain slice through her body. Her knees buckled. The room tilted.

She hit the floor hard, the agony swallowing her whole.

Somewhere in the distance, she heard Graham shout her name. She tried to speak, but her mouth was filling with something warm, thick, and metallic. She knew it was blood. Instinctively, when her hands ran over her belly, a cold feeling engulfed her entire body, along with a tremor that vibrated through every muscle.

The gunman scrambled to his feet, his balaclava twisted over his eyes. In a panic, he yanked it off.

With her eyes half-closed, she saw him, his face, the man who would be the murderer of not just her but her unborn too.

Graham fell to his knees beside his wife, desperate to will her on to live. Anger surged through his body as he daringly locked eyes with the unmasked gunman. He didn't need to speak, his expressions said it all: hate and horror rolled into one.

'You prick! Now he's seen you!' snarled the second gunman, who had made sure his own mask was tightly in place.

There was no hesitation. A second gunshot rang out.

Graham collapsed, his body crumpling to the ground beside her.

Still barely alive, Lorraine, now absolutely terrified, tried to scream, but only a gurgling rasp left her lips.

The masked man swore under his breath, before ripping his own balaclava off his head. 'Now, let's carry on and do what we were supposed to fucking do,' he spat, before glancing at the cable ties hanging from his partner's pocket. 'Well, Max, you won't be needing those now, will ya? They ain't going anywhere.'

'She's still alive.'

'Well, looking at the amount of blood, I shouldn't think she'll be getting up anytime soon. Leave it, Max. She's gonna die.'

'I'm sorry, Moriarty.'

'Shut up. Let's get this done and quick.'

***

Outside, Jim heard a sharp crack – twice. He knew exactly what those sounds were.

He didn't hesitate. Grabbing Mia's wrist, he yanked her behind the oversized brick barbecue.

'Get off me, Jim! What the fuck are you doing?' she hissed, struggling to break free.

'Shut up, Mia! For fuck's sake, be quiet!' he snapped, gripping her wrist tighter. 'There's someone in the house. That wasn't just plates being dropped. Those were gunshots.'

'Well, we need to get out of here. What if it's burglars? What if they see us? Fuck, fuck—'

Jim clamped a hand over her mouth. 'Shut up, Mia. Just shut the fuck up,' he whispered. 'I don't know if they can see us from the windows.'

A distant wail of sirens made Jim's heart pound harder. His brow lifted. Someone must have called the police.

At that moment, two figures bolted across the lawn. They were both running fast, red-faced, with sweat dripping off their foreheads, desperate to get away.

But not far enough away to realise that he and Mia had had time to get a good, clear look at their faces.

Jim's gut twisted as he glared at Max and then Moriarty Shipley. He wasn't sure if they had seen him. But he had seen them all right. He knew them, and he was fully aware of what they were capable of. And as sure as hell, when he saw the gun in Max's hand, he knew they had shot the Fairweathers.

His grip on Mia tightened.

They wouldn't be safe. Not now. Not ever.

CHAPTER ONE

May 2003

It was an exceptionally warm, sunny morning and Kenny Ruck could feel himself prickling with sweat once he stepped out of the tall, austere prison gates. Shaking hands with the two screws who had followed him on to the pavement, he flashed his famous wink, the kind that said he'd got their backs. Or, more to the point, that they'd be looked after financially.

A keen observer on the street would still have been hard-pressed to spot a transaction going on between one of the officers and Kenny. It all happened so quickly.

For ten long years since being sentenced for armed robbery, he had longed for this day to happen. So, glad to see the back of the place, he gave a final look at the imposing Victorian structure, with its two hundred and thirty foot high chimney dominating the Manchester skyline, before he smiled and then shielded his eyes from the glare of the sun to check where his wife was parked.

There she was, leaning – or was that posing – against her outrageously powerful brand-new BMW X5 with her arms folded under her shockingly large new boobs and showing off her designer sunglasses, which were perched on her head like some footballer's wife.

The stale air of the prison walls seemed to cling to him as he walked across the main road to the SUV that was parked, with its engine running.

He wasn't the same man who had entered the tomblike building. Those last few years had a way of hardening a man. The time had chiselled away at whatever softness he'd once had or what he liked to think he had.

The truth was that no matter how he saw himself, the outside world saw him differently. He was regarded as a ruthless bastard.

In his late forties, he was a known face from North London – well, an ugly face, if you asked anyone. He had a scar that ran from his cheek to his chin, and yet he told everyone that his opponent had come off far worse. At five foot ten, with bulging biceps stretching the fabric of his sleeves and a map of thick veins coating his defined muscles – a result of countless hours spent in the gym – he looked exactly how he wished to be portrayed.

Running his wing like a business was par for the course for a man of his ilk. After all, what else other than his regular workouts did he have to do to while away the years?

As he walked up to the motor, he felt that constant nagging of hate toward his old friends-turned-strangers who'd helped put him behind bars. He didn't know where they'd be, but he intended to find out. This wasn't just some notion about new-found freedom: it was about reclaiming his life, bit by bit. Starting today.

***

It seemed there and then that his life in Manchester Prison, formerly Strangeways, had vanished like a puff of smoke. His time served hadn't been as easy as he'd liked everyone to think, though, mainly because he'd missed watching Tandy, his daughter, grow up while hearing constant rumours about his wife's infidelity.

But all of that was behind him now. He was out today, and first on his list was seeing his wife in the flesh. The others who'd either betrayed him or stuck the knife in while he was down, or, more poignantly, behind bars, he would deal with later.

Their last phone call had been somewhat awkward, to say the least, being filled with cold, uncaring silences. But he knew she'd show up. She would have been fucking stupid not to. He had toyed with the idea of getting everything off his chest as soon as they set off back to London. But now, seeing her like this, he went off that idea.

***

Having raised their daughter without him, it was three years into her husband's sentence when Grace was told that the authorities were transferring him from Brixton Prison to Manchester Prison. It had been a godsend. At least he couldn't demand a visit every week. She found out much later that her husband had pissed off higher-ups in the prison staff by not paying them their 'dues' on time. This was the third time it had happened, and so Kenny was carted off up north. And, of course, he blamed her for not coming up with the readies when he snapped his fingers. But he was beholden to her. She was his lifeline. It was her opportunity to call the shots. And in that first phone call when he had moved to Manchester, she was like the cat that got the cream.

***

A moment flashed in Kenny's mind. It was the time when she delighted in telling him that all prison visits would cease from now on. She had made sure that her reasons were well rehearsed. She told him that after the prison riots in April 1990, she didn't feel it 'appropriate' for their daughter to be brought to Manchester Prison, in case the same thing happened again. It wasn't safe.

For his part, his criminal antenna had worked overtime after that phone call. He went back into his cell and mulled over not only her words but her cocky tone.

That night, alone in his cell, he went over and over the conversation while grinding his teeth and clenching his fists. At first, he agreed with her. That the prison was not an ideal environment for his little princess. Those prison riots had put many wives off coming over to see their loved ones. However, they had taken place well before he entered the prison. It was when she then tried to milk what was a perfectly valid reason by giving him all kinds of other excuses – she was too busy with her beauty business – and she would get lost driving up to Manchester to see him – he went berserk. Shouting and screaming at her, he told her that her beauty business didn't need her presence because it virtually ran itself. And as for getting lost, didn't most cars now have a satnav? He would bet all of his money that her car did!

The next day, while he was doing some bench work in the gym, he came to a realisation. The crafty bitch clearly had an ulterior motive. That was abundantly clear. It was now obvious to her that if she brought his daughter, she might well grass on her. Because sure as hell, Grace had another man or men.

That was a no-no as far as he was concerned. He accepted that she would think that the way he'd treated her in the past was perhaps justification for getting her end away with someone else. But, as far as he was concerned, that didn't give her the right to entertain other men. She knew when she married him that she had to play by his rules. And infidelity wasn't something he would ignore or even forgive.

***

It took Kenny a few moments to process what he was seeing in front of him. Grace was nothing like the sweet, shy girl he'd left behind. Back then, she'd had mousy hair in a neat bob, with barely a swipe of make-up. Now, she had bleached hair cascading down her back, a full face of war paint, a figure-hugging dress, and knee-high boots with heels that made her legs look endless. She looked like one of those dolly birds he used to splash his cash on in the big clubs. The kind who'd drape themselves over him when he sat at the private tables with his pals as he popped the champagne.

Sweat dripped down his neck as his nostrils flared. Grace had never worn heels for him before, nor had she worn a dress like that either. It threw him off his stride.

She watched him come closer, her expression unreadable.

As he closed the distance between them, he could feel her sizing him up, her eyes tracing the lines etched into his face and the rough edge he'd brought back with him. When he was near enough to touch her, he caught a flicker in her gaze. Was it resentment? Regret, perhaps? Or was it fear?

'Grace,' he finally said, lifting his chin, in a sharp acknowledgement.

'Kenny,' she replied, trying desperately to mirror him in her body language and facial expression.

A fleeting thought had her wishing the two of them were back in the past. To a time when they only had to look at each other before they wanted to rip each other's clothes off and go at it like the youngsters they were.

But that was then and this was now. Now, they both had secrets – secrets that probably wouldn't last for much longer, if she wasn't very much mistaken.

Glancing over at him, she wished she could change the past – all of it. If only she had been the dutiful wife and waited for him, she wouldn't feel so terrified now.

'Tandy's at me mum's,' she quickly explained. 'I thought it'd be best if she saw you once you had the chance to settle in a bit. Know what I mean?'

He nodded, not surprised.

He wanted to see his princess. Tandy, his little girl, would be a woman now. His temper was bubbling under the surface just thinking about it. He concluded it was a good idea that she wasn't here, not today, until he had clarified a few things.

They stood looking each other over for what seemed like hours until she finally broke the silence.

'Kenny, there are some things you should know,' she said, having vowed to herself that she would try and be honest. Because with a man like him, you didn't lie if you wanted to keep your kneecaps. She didn't doubt that her husband had eyes everywhere. So what she would admit to, he probably already knew, and he was just waiting for her to say it.

Without speaking, Kenny cocked an eyebrow and pointed to her car with a sharp nod.

The darkness in his gaze made Grace's stomach feel hollow with fear. It was a look that said he was just getting started. He was massive. He'd been big before, but now he was towering over her like a monster truck beside a Ford Fiesta. She felt her throat go dry, a coating of sweat lining her palms. She knew there was no escape from this. She'd come to pick him up, and now she had to see it through.

After tossing his prison sack into the boot, Kenny climbed into the front passenger seat, taking in the rich leather seats and the slick, refined cabin. The gadgets and gizmos seemed to catch him off guard, but he ran a hand over some of them.

'This cost a fucking fortune, didn't it?' he hissed. It was more an accusation than a question.

He knew it did. This was a high-end BMW. And knowing his cars, he was aware that this particular model was capable of producing close on to three hundred and fifty brake horsepower. It clearly had a high specification, what with heated seats all round, air conditioning, a panoramic glass sunroof, and even a TV function, to name just a few of its features.

'On finance, Kenny,' Grace said, keeping her tone flat, knowing full well he was about to go off on one. Bracing herself by gripping the steering wheel tighter, she could almost hear the gears turning in his head.

***

She gunned the BMW and they were off. It was clear she knew where she was going.

'So you're not having any problems getting back home, I see,' he said, caustically.

She glanced across at him, her face devoid of any real expression, relieved to see that he didn't expect her to reply. The sound of him trying to calm his breathing was a dead giveaway, but all she could do was keep driving. Nevertheless, the silence between them was not just like torture: it was eating her alive. She wished she could read his mind; she had to know what those little grasses had whispered in his ear. But she would be stupid if she ever believed she could be one step ahead of him.

Kenny was never one to spill his guts. He liked to take his time and let things simmer, like marinating a good cut of meat – slow and steady, ready to serve. She hated him for it. When he went away, she'd had ten years of freedom. Ten years of imagining he'd rot in there for good. Assuming that parole would never be an option with the number of prison nickings he had for fighting and being involved in drugs and every other contraband you could think of.

However, she knew that she had got a little complacent. And even though he'd apparently received one bad report after another, she was made aware through the grapevine that nothing had ever stuck. Somehow, he'd always seemed to manage to grease the right palms. So then, she'd hoped his money would run out, and he wouldn't have the readies to pay people off. The charges would then stick, parole would be denied, and he would die inside. But that hope had died a death. Here he was, as spiteful as ever, looking as though he was sitting with his bare arse cheeks exposed on a bed of stinging nettles.

Four hours later, they finally pulled up to the house – her home, but his bricks and mortar – and she cut the engine. She only noticed how much her hands were shaking when she took them off the wheel. She'd been stupid to believe that this confident front she'd built up over the years would play out well in front of a man like Kenny. All the work she'd put into herself, the attention from men, the gifts that made her feel like someone – all of it had boosted her confidence. But sitting beside him now, feeling the raw weight of him back in her life, she knew that her front was as fragile as a pane of glass.

'Shall we?' he muttered, gesturing towards the house as if he was doing her a favour in inviting her in.

It didn't look like his home anymore – at least not inside. He wouldn't even recognise it. But he owned it legally. In fact, he owned three houses, one of which her mother was living in, and she couldn't risk her getting turfed out.

As soon as she slipped the key into the lock, he shoved his way past her. Ignoring his rudeness, she headed down the hallway and into the kitchen. The oak kitchen he'd known was long gone. Now, everything was pristine and spotless, with sleek white units and every conceivable appliance known to man.

'Coffee?' she offered, forcing a casual tone, as she skipped past him.

He didn't say anything for a while, too busy snorting cocaine. But a few minutes later, when he turned towards her, she saw the look of twisted fury on his face, which instantly raised her heart rate.

Standing in the middle of the kitchen, Kenny's eyes burned with rage, and a vein throbbed in his neck. What he saw – all the expensive modifications to his home – without so much as a heads-up – boiled his blood.

'Since when the fuck do I drink coffee, eh?' His voice was a snarl. 'You've got the wrong fella, you stupid little tart.'

Holding her breath, Grace gripped the edge of the granite worktop. She knew that look in his eyes better than anyone. If she had the guts, she would stab him right here, right now, in the chest – and then run for her life. But her feet stayed planted, frozen to the floor.

Her life had moved on. His, it was clear, hadn't budged an inch.

'Listen, Kenny, me and you . . .'

He nodded slowly and rhythmically.

He had that look, and it scared the life out of her.

'Ten years, Kenny. Ten fucking years . . .'

His head twisted to an unnatural angle as his lips thinned, and that was the look she hated the most. She felt her stomach churn and her heart race before she felt the sudden grip of his hands around her throat. His nose pressed against hers, and his eyes evoked a sense of fear that sent a chill down her spine.

'You are my fucking *wife*, and I told you, ya dirty cunt, you don't go around showing me up.'

He let go of her throat then, with a harsh shove, but his eyes remained glaring. 'You are my fucking wife, not some ol' bit of skirt. Look at ya,' he spat. 'Your fake tits, all that make-up.' He stopped and laughed before he grabbed the back of her hair with his left hand. With the other, he roughly rubbed his massive hand over her face, which smudged her lipstick and tore her false eyelashes.

She gasped, the moment he let go. But she didn't expect what happened next. Ripping open her blouse, he tore her bra apart to reveal her breasts.

'I'm assuming these were bought outta my fucking money. Am I right?'

Grace held her breath, not able to utter a word. She dared not move because he was right. She *had* bought them out of his money, their savings, and even though she'd paid into the pot with her beauty business, it didn't matter. So far as he was concerned, the money was all his.

Grabbing her breasts, he laughed. 'Nice! Fucking nice,' he said, as he squeezed them, making her flinch.

But she still didn't make a sound, knowing exactly what he would do next.

In a flash, he ripped off her skirt and then her thong. 'It's been a long time, Grace. Fucking ten years. Now, you give me what I want because, believe me, ya slut, you *owe* me. If you behave like a brass, I'll treat you like one. Now, get on the floor!'

'No, please, Kenny, please don't, please.' Tears rolled down her cheeks, but, in her heart, she knew that pleading and begging never worked on a man like Kenny.

He grabbed her hair and forced her head down until she was on all fours on the cold tiles.

'That's it, bitch, you acted like a dog, and now I'll fuck you like one.'

She acknowledged it was useless, and tears wouldn't halt the unavoidable, so she raised her exposed backside and rested her cheeks on the floor.

In seconds, he was on her. His penis rammed mercilessly inside while he dug his fingers deep into her shoulders. Then, as he forced himself deeper and deeper, his hands gripped her hips. He tossed her back and forth like a rag doll, before he flipped her over and pushed her legs up by her head and continued relentlessly. She couldn't look at him. He repulsed her. Biting her lip to stop the screams, she assumed he would finish in a minute. Still, as he kept going and going, throwing her in different positions, she realised the effects from snorting a line of Charlie were already working. Kenny on cocaine was terrifying, and her only way out was to run. As soon as he'd finished, he jumped to his feet and dragged her up as well.

Grace couldn't stand up straight. She found herself wobbling all over the place because he'd torn a muscle in her right leg, which was now causing her unbearable pain.

He then cruelly looked her up and down. 'You look like what you are, an old fucking whore. 'Cos, see, Gracie, I fucking know what you've been up to.' In a flash, he backhanded her, sending her flying towards the kitchen sink. But he didn't stop there. Holding a clump of hair at the back of her head, he rammed her face into the taps before turning them on and filling the sink with cold water.

It took a moment for her to realise what he was about to do. When she did, fear took over. She fought with everything she had, kicking and writhing, her nails scraping against his skin, as she tried to free herself from his grip. 'Please! Please!' she cried, her voice cracking with desperation. 'Kenny, don't do this!'

But it was no use. He simply laughed before he pushed her head under the water.

Unable to breathe, panic set in, compelling her to wriggle and claw as she desperately tried to push her head back against his hand. Finally, when she was all but ready to die, he pulled her head up. She gasped and gasped, panting and still scrapping like a cat dragged out of the river. But as soon as she caught her breath, he plunged her head back under the water again.

He repeated his cruel punishment six times until he finally yanked her away from the sink and threw her down onto the floor.

Too exhausted to move, Grace, nevertheless, felt elated because she was still alive. Her nose throbbed, and for sure there was blood dripping all over the place, but she didn't care. Her hope was that he was heading out of the house.

But, a moment later, when her senses returned to normal, she felt his presence. Heavy, coarse breathing behind her ruined any moment that she was on her own. It seemed that she would be his plaything, a helpless mouse trapped in the claws of a relentless, sick, and twisted cat. He wouldn't stop until the cocaine pumping through his veins finally lost its grip on him. Even then, he wouldn't be sorry. He'd blame her. He'd say she made him do it.

CHAPTER TWO

Three days later

Cas glanced around his study and eyed the oak panels on the walls that dated back a few hundred years. It was an elegant room where the previous owner had spared no expense in making the room extremely comfortable. The red and green leather sofas, though, in contrast, were a relatively recent addition. They were a gift from his local MP.

Casting his mind back many years ago now, he recalled the time he met Andrew Cresswell, or 'Randy Andy' as he was affectionately known. Cresswell, although a bit poncy and la-di-da, was actually a first-class local MP. He would go the extra mile for his constituents whenever he could. However, he had two main flaws. One was his love for betting on the dogs, and the other was enjoying the company of very young women, but not kids.

Andrew invited Cas to his club just off St James's Street, close to his office. Over a three-course gourmet meal, Andrew confided that he was being blackmailed. It wasn't from betting on the dogs this time. A pair of young wannabe gangsters had been making waves in the criminal fraternity that year by carrying out some bold hits on well-heeled older men. And Andrew was one of them. Apparently, he had met a very curvaceous blonde who had given him her number so that they could hook up for sex. He had responded willingly, and when several compromising photos were sent to him, he knew that not only was his career on the line but his marriage to a well-known socialite was too.

Cas, in his wisdom, knew that it would bode very well for him in the future if he helped Andrew, especially if he needed to call in any favours.

The trap was set. Cas, along with Walter Whistler and Dennis the Menace, his most trusted right-hand men, accosted the two blackmailers as the money exchanged hands. For the lovebirds, their time sadly came to an end. A week later, an athlete out on a trail run found them both strung up from the bough of an ancient oak tree in Coombe Wood, about an hour's drive from Wadhurst, where Cas lived. Andrew didn't ask Cas if he had anything to do with it, but he granted him a few favours, and so a valuable friendship was forged.

Cas settled his gaze on the battle-scarred relic he called his desk that had once been smashed to bits. He'd thought about replacing it, but there was something about that item of furniture he couldn't let go. Perhaps it was lessons learned and the number of times he'd sat behind it as an enforcer or The Governor, as he was once called. So he'd called in a carpenter to put it back together. Still, he knew it was time to update everything. If he was honest, he also needed to get a grip on the computer, although it was a proper headache. No matter how many times Billy showed him the basics, nothing seemed to stick. But today wasn't the day for spreadsheets.

Cas's eyes narrowed as he stared at the note in his hand, his stomach churning. It had been five years since Willow's murder, and back then, he wouldn't have batted an eyelid if he'd ended up in the same grave. But time had a funny way of shifting things, and life, as twisted as it was, had carried on. He wasn't the hard-as-nails boss he used to be, but he still had the respect to run his firm and dabble in the 'illegal projects', as he liked to call them – with a cheeky grin, of course.

The old ways were precisely that – old – and even he could see the need to move on. Billy had been a solid teacher, in guiding him towards new ventures and projects – ones Billy likely already had a stake in. Cas chuckled, knowing he'd been conned but not minding one bit. Put simply, he had grown attached to the young man. In fact, to the whole family, which, in some ways, had eased his grief and stopped him from jumping off a bridge. But now he was faced with a dilemma, and for the first time in his life, he was worried. Not for himself, of course, but for the people around him.

He looked at the note once more, and a cold shiver ran through his body as the name Kenny Ruck got stuck in his throat.

Before he could put it in the drawer, Billy stormed into the office. His face was like thunder.

'Billy, what's the matter? You look like you've found a penny and lost a pound.'

Billy stood with his hands on his hips and shook his head.

Cas admired the young man's stature. He was tall and muscular but sleek with it. Today, he was wearing a pinstripe suit that wouldn't look out of place in any fashion catalogue.

'Well, boy, what's up?'

'Right now, Cas, I am not quite sure, but something's wrong. I came to collect the spare keys.'

'To what?'

'The apartments.'

'The apartments? I thought you had a set at the office?'

'Yeah, well, it looks like Bronte has misplaced them.'

Cas stood up with a deep frown. 'What? All of them?'

Billy sighed. 'That's what I said! So, I thought I'd get the spares and have copies made until the apartments are all complete and ready for showing.'

Cas nodded. 'Listen, you can ask me to mind my own business, but do you really trust Bronte?'

Billy stared out of the window. Did he trust Bronte? Clearly, the question had him thinking. Turning back to face Cas, he replied, 'Yes, I do. But I just think she's got a lot on her mind, and maybe she's getting a bit forgetful. Perhaps working for me isn't the ideal job for her. What do you think?'

Cas shrugged. 'Well, she left school at twelve and never studied business or anything, so maybe her employment was more your soppy move. What have I told ya, Billy? See, never think with your dick. Always use your brain.'

Billy lifted his chin in resentment. He didn't like to be told he was wrong, for the simple reason he rarely was. 'Well, I left school early too, Cas.'

With a sharp point of his finger, Cas remarked, 'You are a totally different kinda person. You were a man before you were even outta nappies, ya cocky little fucker, and blessed with brains and a good business head. Now, if you have second thoughts about Bronte working for you, then sack her. Don't let the distraction of a pretty face fuck up your business.'

All this advice was old hat to Billy because not only had he worked that out for himself but he knew that what Cas had just said was true. But he liked to think through all the angles about a problem before reaching a conclusion. He chewed his lip in deep thought. Eventually, he said, 'I thought you knew me better, Cas. As if any bird would get in the way of me making money. But, yeah, maybe I'll have a chat with her.'

'Oh, and, Billy.' Cas turned his mind back to Kenny Ruck. 'Listen, is there anything else you need from the house, the safe, or wherever? Only I'm locking it up for a bit. I want the builders in, so if you need me, call, yeah. Don't come here.'

Billy was about to walk out of the study at that point, having said all he wanted to say. But that last instruction had him turning on his heel. Cas's face said it all.

'Builders?'

'Yeah, builders. Why? Is there something wrong with that?'

'Nothing wrong at all, Cas, but lying definitely is. Cas, you forget I know you.'

'Oi, listen to me, cocky bollocks, I'm a lot older than you, so don't you start telling me about myself, d'you hear me?'

'Fair enough, but are you okay, Cas?'

'Yeah, yeah, of course I am. So why do you need the keys now? What can't wait?'

Billy rolled his eyes. 'It's Ginty. She's been on at me for one of the one-bedders, and she wants a look around.'

'Jesus, well, ain't no surprise there, I suppose. The woman's a fucking nightmare.'

Billy nodded. 'That's true enough. But . . .'

'I know, Billy. She saved yours and Jesse's bacon, but no one does anything for free these days.' He winked.

Billy stared at Cas, wondering where this conversation was heading. 'Well, she was hardly lending us a bag of sugar, was she?'

'No, I guess not, but, truth be told, I owe her, too. After all, Irvin Slade killed my granddaughter, Willow, and Ginty took the blame for his murder, didn't she,' Cas said, with a grin. 'But don't for one minute think she didn't know she would get off.

She's no stranger to the law. She's spent enough years behind bars to know what she could get away with and what she couldn't.'

'True enough.' Billy shrugged. 'Either way, Cas, she came through for us. Look, I know she's a demanding old bat, but letting her rent one of the apartments is a small price to pay, don't ya think?'

Cas nodded and deliberately looked at his wristwatch. 'Yeah, son, of course, it is. Now, the spare keys are in the safe, and just remember, this place will be locked up. I'm going to stay away for a bit. I can't stand the place in a mess. The dust gets down me lungs.'

Something about the eye avoidance put a fleeting thought inside Billy's head that Cas was covering up something. But the reason for that thought disappeared as quickly as it arrived as his mind turned to Bronte. Deciding not to push Cas for answers because it would breach their mutual understanding, which had been built on trust and respect, he picked up his laptop from a side table and walked out of the room.

***

Running slightly later than planned, Billy decided to take a quick trip to the new block of apartments he'd purchased at a steal but which needed a lot of work before they would be habitable. What he found in the basement rocked him. He literally staggered back until rage burned at his throat and sent his mind flying in all directions.

By the time he reached the office, he was more controlled and ready for a serious conversation with Bronte. He had to get to the bottom of what he'd discovered before he blew a fuse.

His train of thought was soon distracted when he saw a black Land Rover parked outside his property management office on the high street between a boutique and an estate agent. He sighed heavily. Those two brothers of Bronte's, Franklin and Archie, were a pain in the backside. They were keen to live the travellers' way and often reminded him that he himself had a travellers' heritage.

Feeling his hackles rising as he opened the door to his office, Billy stopped in his tracks. Sprawled in his swivel chair was Franklin – a chunky man sporting a greasy Elvis quiff, his fingers dripping in gold rings, which looked like knuckledusters. He was swivelling on the chair as if he owned the place.

Meanwhile, Bronte had her hands rummaging through his filing cabinet while Archie lounged in the guest chair and played with his flick knife.

'Here he is,' Franklin said, without a care in the world, not even attempting to get up and off his chair.

Billy put his laptop on the table near the window and then strode over to his desk. He placed his hands palm downwards and shoved his jaw almost in Franklin's face. Giving the man a little wink and a smirk, he almost pictured himself knocking the smug bastard right off the chair with a single backhander.

Feeling the atmosphere heat up, Franklin quickly scrambled to his feet.

Spinning round to face Billy, Bronte's cheeks reddened in the blink of an eye. 'Oh, oh, er, hello, Billy. I, uh, I found the keys! S-Silly me, they were in my bag after all,' she stammered.

Raising an eyebrow, Billy made it clear he wasn't buying a word of it.

Glancing at the open filing cabinet, he stared Bronte down until she looked away, her face now very pale.

'What did you need, Bronte? Maybe I could help,' he said, in a dry tone, which was as cold as ice.

'I was just looking for the plans . . . the drawings of the apartments . . . to show Franklin and Archie.'

Billy turned his gaze to Archie, who was still lounging on the chair, his flick knife in his hand again, idly toying with the blade. The casual attitude was winding him up.

'So why would you be interested in the architectural plans?' Billy asked, gripping the back of the guest chair before spinning it around to face Archie directly.

Archie shot to his feet. 'Oi! What are you doing?'

Billy took a step back, glaring at both brothers in turn. 'More to the fucking point – what are *you* doing? I don't see why either of you would be in my office.' He pointed at Franklin. 'Or sitting at my desk and poking around in my business.'

Bronte cut in, looking flustered. 'No, no, Billy, it's not like that! I was excited and wanted to show them the plans . . . We were waiting for you.'

She glanced at Franklin as if to urge him to speak up.

'Billy, me and Archie want a word.' Franklin jerked his chin at Bronte. 'Go grab some doughnuts from up the road, love. And take ya time.'

Billy stepped around the desk to check his drawers, which were still locked, and powered up his desktop computer. He acted as though Franklin and Archie weren't even there. But inside, he was livid. The thought of sacking Bronte had just become much easier. Especially when he noticed her giving her brother a sly wink as she scurried off.

'So, let's 'ave it, then. What's this little chat you wanted? Go on, impress me.'

Franklin and Archie, who was three inches shorter than his brother, were now taking a stance – legs apart, shoulders squared.

With his hands on his hips, Billy nodded. 'Go on, then.'

'You've been with our Bronte, what, five years now? You know how we feel about her. She's a looker and no mistake. She could have any bloke she wanted. So, let's not fuck about,' said Franklin.

'And? Is that all you've got to say?' Billy replied, utterly unimpressed.

'You know how it is – you bed her, you marry her. Have you forgotten the travellers' way, mate?'

Billy smirked. 'Let's just get a few things clear. First, I ain't ya mate. Never 'ave been, never will be. But, more importantly, I'm not a bloody *gypsy*.'

'Oh, but you are,' Franklin said, with a sneer. 'Your grandad and gran were both travellers, same as your mum, Carrie. So, you know how it works.'

Billy nodded slowly as he looked each brother over. 'Maybe in *your world*. But not in mine. I don't live that life. Neither do my parents. So, if that's what you want for her, take her, and find her a good gypsy lad because let me tell you this: no one tells me who I'll marry.' He pointed at Franklin and then at Archie. 'Not you, and not anyone else.'

'Hold up a minute—' said Archie, trying to jump in.

'No,' Billy snapped, cutting him off. 'I'm not done, you pair of fucking clowns. This is *my* office, *my* business. I won't have anyone thinking they can stroll in and mug me off. I know why you wanted to see those plans. You're after sticking your beaks into my affairs. Be honest, lads. You couldn't care less who marries Bronte, as long as they have money. You're just using her good looks as a bargaining tool. In my eyes, that makes you worse than any fucking pimp.'

Franklin shifted uncomfortably. 'Now, hang on a minute. Why are you getting so trappy?'

'Shut it, Franklin, I haven't finished.' Billy's voice dropped, now cold and steely. 'When Bronte said she'd lost the keys, I knew that was all a load of bollocks. There's been no reason for her to go to the apartments this week. I've got no appointments with any surveyors or architects. No inspections. Those keys shouldn't have left my drawer.'

Archie and Franklin exchanged looks, each hoping the other would come up with a credible excuse.

'So, I thought, why don't I check my apartments myself.' He tapped his chest. 'My apartments – not Bronte's, and not anyone else's. And guess what I found?'

Franklin raised his hand like a schoolboy. 'Look—'

'Shut it, Franklin,' Billy cut in, his patience now worn thin.

'Who do you think you're talking to?' Archie growled, brandishing the flick knife.

Billy's gaze locked on to the blade, and a demonic smile spread across his face. 'You'd better know how to use that thing.' His eyes, cold and menacing, then fixed on Archie.

Archie could feel his spine prickling. They'd been warned about the Murphys – never underestimate them. And he could tell that Billy wasn't even remotely fazed; he was actually spoiling for a fight.

Archie slid the knife back into his pocket.

'That's more like it. Now, turn around and get out of my office.'

Franklin grabbed Archie's jacket and pulled him towards the door.

But just as they reached it, Billy added, 'Oh, by the way, know anyone in the market for a load of weed? Because some thick cunt's set up a marijuana grow in the basement of my apartments.'

With his face contorted with rage, Archie lunged at Billy.

But Billy was faster. In a flash, he landed a punch square across Archie's nose. The crack echoed around the room. Grabbing Archie by the ears, he dragged him across the room and smashed his face onto the desk twice, leaving him slumped on his knees with blood pouring from his nostrils and dripping onto the floor.

Billy turned to Franklin. 'Seen enough, 'ave ya? Now, you get this piece of trash out of my office, you two-bob mug. And if you want to have a go, believe me, I'll split your concrete skull wide open.'

Franklin stood frozen, his brain struggling to process what had just happened. Their little moneymaking scheme with the marijuana grow in the basement of the apartments had seemed perfect. Bronte had the keys, and nobody ever went down there. She had made sure of it.

Utterly fuming, Franklin shoved Archie out of the door. Opening his car door, he pushed Archie inside, as though he was stuffing a duvet cover into a pillow slip.

Standing at the window, Billy stood grinning at the two buffoons.

But Franklin wasn't finished. He stormed back into the office and glared at Billy. 'You fucking know that's our gear.' He wiped the spittle from the corners of his mouth.

With a look of sheer nonchalance, Billy simply shrugged his shoulders. 'I couldn't give a flying shit, mate, whose gear it is. You see, the thing is, someone, as I see it, has taken a right liberty. Those apartments are all legal and above board. However, you and your brother chose to use my building to grow not fucking tomatoes or mushrooms but *marijuana.* And knowing full well my name is on the deeds. So if the Ol' Bill came sniffing around and found that shit in my building,' he said, poking his chest, 'I would be carted off down the cop shop and nicked for intent to supply, which you and I both know I would serve time over. So now, if you think for one minute that you will get the gear back, think on. The pods, the lights, 'ave gotta be worth five grand, and the plants, I'd say, another ten. So, I think fifteen grand for the inconvenience is about right.'

Franklin shook his head. 'No way, no fucking way. They ain't even our plants.'

Billy nodded. 'You're fucking right there, mush, 'cos they're mine now.'

Franklin wiped the sweat away from his brow. 'No, listen to me, Billy. Look, come on, we're practically family. Those plants really ain't mine, right? I gave this geezer—'

Holding up his hand, Billy stepped forward. 'Shut up, Franklin, you don't seem to get it! You put my liberty at risk, and so there are consequences. Now, I won't say another word about it if you spin on your dealer boots and fuck off.'

Franklin could feel the wrath of a demon in Billy's cold, almost mocking eyes, and so he decided that there was no point in arguing. 'You ain't heard the last of this, Billy. Believe me, you ain't.'

Billy watched as Franklin slammed the door of the office and marched to his vehicle. He laughed and shook his head. 'What mugs.'

A few minutes later, Billy heard Bronte enter the property by the back door. An enticing aroma from the freshly made doughnuts pervaded the office and heralded her arrival. Quickly, he rushed over to the front door, locked it, and placed the 'Closed' sign around before she was even in sight.

With a beaming smile, she waltzed in but then stopped dead. 'Oh, oh, where's me bruvvers gone, Billy?'

Placing his hand on her cheek, Billy kissed her forehead. 'Come with me, babe,' he said, giving her a slow wink.

'Did they say anything, Billy?' she asked, in such an eager tone.

He nodded, giving her that smile that always got to her, and slowly, he led her back towards the room at the rear of the property where he held his business meetings. The room could best be described as businesslike without the feminine touch. But what it lacked in plants or vibrant pictures, it more than made up for in functional efficiency by having a modern round table with eight comfy chairs around it and a coffee machine in the corner.

'Billy, what are you thinking?' she giggled, as he locked the door behind them.

'Billy . . .' She drew out his name, pulling him close and kissing his neck.

He stayed quiet, like he always did in these moments, but she thought nothing of it. In a way, she found this pose dead sexy. When he winked at her, her knees practically turned to jelly. He kissed her hard and pushed her onto the table.

'Careful, Billy.'

Sitting up, she gave him a half-smile, not used to him being so forceful. But she thought maybe she could get to like it. However, when he ripped her expensive underwear off, the sting against her skin gave her pause for thought. She said nothing, trying to kiss him again, but he didn't return the kiss. Instead of his usual playful, teasing foreplay, he pushed her down onto the table again, opened her legs, and forced himself inside. She wasn't even ready, and he wasn't gentle.

He wouldn't look at her, his gaze fixed on the blank wall above her head. A chill washed over her. This wasn't Billy – not her Billy, not the Billy she knew, who was always gentle and sweet and who offered whispering soft words when they were together. No, this . . . well, this was different. Very different. This actually hurt. He was rough, hard, and fast, as though he wasn't even seeing her.

'Billy, stop! Please, stop!'

He froze then. Moments later, he climbed off her and zipped up his trousers. Standing there, his expression was distant and cold.

She sat up, feeling shaken and confused. Putting her underwear back on and pulling her skirt down, her hands trembled as she wrapped her arms around herself and tried to process what had just happened.

'Billy . . . what's going on? Why would you even think—' She struggled to find the words, her voice barely a whisper. This wasn't the man she knew, the man who had always treated her with such respect and tenderness.

Billy suddenly realised what he'd done. This wasn't him at all. But he was so enraged that the one woman – apart from his family – whom he trusted with his life – had let him down so severely that he could never stay with her. So he had wanted to punish her. But now, the realisation that he had treated Bronte in such an abominable way brought his senses back into play. It was wrong. Very wrong.

'Billy, what's the matter? What's going on? What did me bruvvers say to you? Look, we don't have to get married. I can wait. I mean—'

'Shut up, Bronte. Just shut up.'

She moved towards him, trying to grip his arms, but he shrugged her off. When her eyes pleaded with him, he looked away.

'Billy, please tell me. What's going on?'

Once again, the less pleasant side of Billy, the almost pragmatic one, had to win over the gentleman he had always tried to be where a female was concerned. He was so upset, so disgusted with Bronte, that he couldn't help himself. Letting out a sarcastic grin, he said, 'Oh, *you* knew exactly what was going on. It's just a pity *I* didn't. So let me tell you something: no one mugs me off *twice*. Now, grab your bag and get the hell out.'

Bronte's face drained of colour and her eyes filled up. 'Billy, I don't know what you're talking about.'

He unlocked the door with a bitter grin. 'Oh, I think you do. And you know what? I might have listened, if you'd just come clean, apologised even. But like the gypsy you are, you're still pleading your innocence.'

She stood straighter now, shaking her head, her eyes pleading with him. But she could tell by his cold expression that he was having none of it.

'I've known you five years, Bronte – five years – and I thought you knew better than to try and play me. But no, you thought you were smarter – or maybe you did what you did because I trusted you with my keys. You took me for a fool. You thought my kindness was a sign of weakness.'

'Oh . . .' It was all she could manage.

'Yeah, *oh*. You risked my liberty, Bronte. And what's sad is that I'd have never done that to you. I really cared about you.'

His voice softened, making her shrink under his gaze.

'I'm so sorry. It wasn't like that—'

'Shut up, Bronte. For once, stop. Now leave, and don't come back.'

She froze, barely able to breathe. 'Are you . . . are you breaking up with me, Billy?'

He laughed. It was a short, hard laugh before he looked her up and down as though she was a piece of shit. 'Did you need that in writing? Of course, I am.'

'But, Billy, we were meant to be . . . I mean, you bedded me—'

'Oh, spare me. So you're playing that card, too, are you? Let me tell you something. I'm not a gypsy. I don't live by that bloody *code*. I never said I'd marry you. If that was your deal, you should've said something upfront. Now, get your bag and go.'

'Please, Billy, don't do this to us . . .'

'Oh, Bronte, *I* didn't do this to us. It was *you* who did. And I'll tell you something else, before you go and fuck up another man's head. I was going to ask you to marry me. On your *birthday*.'

'Oh . . . that's next week,' she said, as tears fell down her cheeks.

For a split second, Billy wanted to hold her and brush them away, but he soon pushed that feeling to one side. 'I was waiting for the ring I'd had specially made for you. It was arriving from Switzerland.'

'Please, Billy, don't do this,' Bronte begged, gripping his shirt. 'Please, Billy! Please!'

'It's done! Now get off me,' he said, as he peeled her fingers from his shirt and stepped back. 'Just go.'

Bronte stared into his eyes. She was hoping to find a slither of hope, some compassion in them, but they were so cold. Knowing that once Billy had made up his mind about something, that was the end of it, and realising she couldn't convince him otherwise, she grabbed her bag and stormed out of the office through the back exit.

Once he'd made a call to Ross, his cousin, Billy closed the meeting room door behind him, slumped down onto a chair, and pressed his hands over his eyes, as he choked back the sob lodged in his throat.

CHAPTER THREE

A sharp knock broke the stillness in the office. Billy brushed away his tears before he cleared his throat. Taking a deep breath, he changed the 'Closed' sign to 'Open' and then unlocked the door and pulled it open. Bracing himself, he rather expected to see Bronte. After all, although she'd stormed off, there was more than a good chance she would return. But if that was the case, he wouldn't let her see him with red eyes. He wouldn't give her that satisfaction. If she thought he was the slightest bit upset, she'd work on him to take her back.

But, as it happened, it wasn't Bronte.

'Jesse!' Relief swept over Billy, and he stepped forward, pulling his brother into a quick hug. He felt the solid muscle under Jesse's shirt and stepped back to give him a once-over. 'Bloody hell, you've been hitting the gym, haven't you? Love the clobber,' he said, as he tapped Jesse's polo shirt with the back of his fingers.

And Jesse did look smart. His usual dark, wayward locks had been cut off and neatly styled into a graduated crop. His shirt and jeans were saying 'old money', but his trainers were modern and fresh. Even his aftershave had a sharp citrus twang to it.

Billy had never known Jesse to take so much pride in his appearance. 'What's it like, all the way up in North London?'

The thought of losing Bronte had now gone out of the window. It was just so good to have his brother here at last because it seemed as though he'd been away for ages.

Jesse grinned, the spark in his eyes brighter than usual. 'Loving it, Billy. But before you start—' He raised a hand to stop Billy jumping in. 'Don't do it by taking the piss or telling me I'm making a mistake again, yeah?'

Shaking his head, Billy winked. 'Nah, not today. Besides, I'm just teasing. Look, Jesse, you've been a constable since the day you turned eighteen. You know I wasn't happy about it back then. It wasn't so much about you being a copper, but more about you not going into business full-time with me. But it's your life.

So, come on, then – spill the beans. How's it going? Are they treating you right?'

Jesse's grin couldn't be any wider. When he was happy, his energy was infectious. 'You won't believe it! DCI Redwood's fast-tracking me on to his team.'

Billy raised his eyebrows. 'No way.' He slapped Jesse on the shoulder. 'That's brilliant, mate. Five years in, and you're already moving up? That's mad. But I'm not really surprised, to tell you the truth. Us Murphys, we like grafting.'

'Tell me about it,' Jesse said, practically bouncing on the balls of his feet. 'Most people wait *over* five years to make the jump, but Redwood's not only got a soft spot for me, but he reckons I'm ready.'

Billy rolled his eyes. 'Bloody hell, Jesse. Let me guess – you've toned down the swearing and dropped the travellers' accent. Right?'

Jesse blushed, his grin turning sheepish. 'Had to, didn't I? Anyway, I thought I'd tell you first, before heading over to Mum's. You know what she's like – she'll be baking a bloody cake and planning a party already.'

Billy laughed. 'And why not, eh? You've done well.'

Jesse hesitated, his grin fading slightly. 'Oh, by the way . . . um, have you had a row with Bronte? Only, I, er, saw her stomping up the road. I beeped, but do you know what she did? She only stuck two fingers up. Maybe she didn't realise it was me.'

Leaning against the desk, Billy's shoulders slumped, and he let out a weary sigh. 'I s'pose I'd better tell you. I've just dumped her, a few minutes ago.'

'*What?*' Jesse's eyes widened. 'Why?'

Billy's jaw tightened. 'She mugged me off – her and her bloody pikey brothers. I'm fucking fuming.'

'What happened?'

'They had a grow – marijuana – in the basement of the apartments. Only Bronte and myself had the keys, Jesse. She knew all about it. She was obviously letting them in. And she was sneaky about it too, and I can't stand sly people.'

Jesse shook his head. Disbelief was written across his face. 'You are joking, mate, ain't ya?' he said, reverting to his old ways of speaking.

Billy's fist clenched at the memory. 'No, unfortunately, it's not a joke. I was that fucking angry, Jesse, I smashed Archie's face onto the desk. He's lucky I didn't rip his fucking ears off.'

Jesse flinched. Billy didn't swear often, and so when he did, it carried weight. 'Billy . . . if the police—'

Billy barked a laugh. 'Police, is it now? Not *filth* or *pigs* anymore? You've changed, Jesse.'

When he saw his brother look downcast at that jibe, his grin faded, and he gave Jesse a hug. 'Sorry, mate. You've caught me in a raw state. No, you're right. If the police got wind of it – and it's on my premises – well, technically ours . . . Er, yeah, that doesn't look good, does it.'

Jesse's face went pale, and he raked a hand through his thick black hair. 'Shit! Shit! The stupid bastards.'

'Stupid?' growled Billy. 'Cor, they are more than stupid, the wankers. Anyway, it's handled. I called Ross. He's clearing out the lot – gear, pods, the works. He'll sell it off, and I told him he can keep the profit.'

Jesse frowned. 'They had a proper grow, then? You've got to get all the light, temperature, and humidity spot on. It's all science. Anyway, those tosspots wouldn't have a clue, would they. The way they talk, I doubt very much if they even went to school. But even so, I can't believe those two meatheads would have the fucking front to do what they did.'

Billy shrugged. 'Well, they did. But Ross'll sort it.'

Jesse nodded and relief settled on his face. He trusted Billy to handle their property business and keep it clean. 'What about you, though? You liked Bronte. A lot, I should add.'

Billy's lips tightened. 'I liked her enough to marry her. But not enough to forgive her. I need a loyal bird who has my back. Someone I can trust. Not a backstabber.' A bitter laugh escaped him. 'You'll laugh at this, though.'

Jesse tilted his head. 'Go on.'

'They came here – her brothers – telling me I had to marry her. The same old gypsy crap. "You bed her, you wed her."'

Jesse's response was typically sharp. 'Billy, they're just after your money. That's all that is.'

Billy grinned, the edge still in his eyes. 'Oh, believe me, I know that. They have no interest in Bronte. They fucking flaunt her pretty face like . . . well, like a whore, I s'pose. Never mind, come on. I'll lock up and head to Mum's with you. Haven't seen her in a few days.'

As Billy locked the office, Jesse stepped back and eyed the sign above the door. 'I love that – *Murphys' Property Management*. It's classy.'

'It'll be even better once I've got the proper staff,' Billy muttered. 'Not just a bimbo with a pretty face.'

'Ouch,' Jesse said, wincing. 'No second chances, then?'

Billy rubbed the back of his neck. 'You know me, Jesse. I don't do second chances.'

Jesse glanced at the pavement, his voice quieter. 'You gave me one.'

Billy paused, and then, once again, he threw an arm around his brother's shoulders. 'That's different. We were kids. I was hurt, yeah, but you were hurting more. And besides . . .' Glancing around, he then lowered his voice. 'You saved my life, Jesse. We're brothers. We'll always have each other's backs.'

Jesse nodded.

Before they headed off, a taxi pulled up outside.

'Oh, fuck, I forgot about Ginty.'

Jesse rolled his eyes. 'What the fuck is she doing 'ere?'

'She's got her eye on one of the apartments.'

Jesse shook his head. 'She's draining, Billy. Proper fucking draining.'

Billy put his finger to his lips. 'Listen, Jesse, it's a small price to pay. Think about it. We could have spent twenty years in the nick if she hadn't taken the rap for killing Danny and Irvin.'

'Yeah, I know, but it's the constant milking it that does my head in.'

'Shush.'

They both stood with their arms folded as they watched with embarrassment. Ginty was dressed in a long black figure-hugging skirt and a T-shirt that showed every roll of fat. With her head inside the cab driver's window, she was arguing with the poor man – and not quietly, either.

'You're a fucking piss-taking wanker. Ten quid! Jesus Christ, mate, I barely sat me arse on the seat before you pulled up, and you want ten quid. I'll give you a fiver, and I won't put a curse on ya! How about that?'

Billy sighed, having seen it all before, several times. Pulling some notes from his pocket, he marched over to the cab and pulled Ginty away from the window.

She tutted and turned to face Billy. 'A right rip-off,' she snapped, before heading towards Jesse.

'It's on the meter, mate, I don't make these prices up.'

'Here you go,' said Billy, shoving a twenty into the cab driver's hand.

'Right, cheers, mate. Oh, er, hang on. I'll give you your change.'

Billy shook his head and muttered, 'I reckon you deserve a tip.'

'Cor, tell me about it.' He looked Billy up and down and then glanced at the office frontage. 'She ain't really related to you, is she?'

Billy lowered his voice. 'We humour her.'

The cab driver laughed before he said, 'Thanks again.'

As soon as he pulled away, Ginty suddenly started acting old and infirm. 'Aw, boys, get me inside, would ya. I'm gasping for a cup o' Rosie Lee. Me stomach thinks me throat's been cut. Got any cakes or a sandwich on the go?'

Jesse rolled his eyes. 'Hello, Ginty.'

'Oi, hang on a fucking minute, Jesse boy, I'm Nan to you. Now, you take me arm and get me inside.'

Billy unlocked the front door and raised his brow at Jesse, who was not amused at all.

Ginty almost fell onto the nearest chair. 'Cor blimey, me bones ache, and me ankles have never been the same ever since that fucking Irvin kept me prisoner,' she said, as she rubbed her legs. 'Billy, put the kettle on, love, would ya.'

Both the men knew that Ginty was playing the 'you owe me' card. Of course, she had been through what was an horrendous ordeal, but that happened almost five years ago. But they knew she would never let them forget about it. It served her nicely, and it was a good way of reminding them that they owed her.

Billy and Jesse had both come to the same conclusion that when Ginty acted all sweet and kind when she offered to take the rap for these men's murders, she must have known she wouldn't get a long sentence, if any at all. She'd lived on the wrong side of the law for long enough to know that the judge wouldn't have locked her up. However, it also meant that she had them kissing her feet and pampering to her every need.

Billy waltzed over to the drinks machine he'd had installed to make any customer feel special. After all, if anyone was willing to buy one of his apartments or wanted his company to manage their properties, he would want them to feel comfortable and to take their time.

Jesse was about to sit at Billy's desk when he spotted blood on the floor. Quickly, he hurried to the small room at the back of the office, which held the vacuum cleaner, clothes, and cleaning sprays. He returned and wiped the floor clean.

'You're like ya muvver, Jesse. She loves to clean,' Ginty said.

'Might as well, while I'm here.'

Billy handed Ginty a cup of tea, which was made just the way she liked it, with three sugars and lots of milk – full cream, of course.

'That was quick, Billy boy. Did it even have time to brew?'

'Yes, it's fine.' When his eyes then shot to the bakery bag on the other desk, he remembered that Bronte had returned from the shops with doughnuts. 'Here you are.' He handed her the paper bag.

Her face lit up. 'Did you get these in especially for me, Billy?'

'Yeah, of course, er . . . listen, I know I said I would take you to see your apartment, but there's a problem. There's no access until next week. I've had builders in, and they haven't finished, so sorry about that—'

'Are you fucking joking? I came all this way, and now I can't see me flat.'

'I can do better than that, Gint . . . I mean Nan.'

Billy opened the filing cabinet and retrieved the file containing images showing how the apartments would look once decorated and furnished. He handed her the one to the apartment she would be living in.

'This, Nan, is better than showing you around a dusty, empty building where the walls are not even plastered yet.'

Ginty snatched the file and pulled out the first picture. It was stunning and modern, with compact furniture, tall lamps, and sleek-looking ornaments strategically placed to give a sense of space and quality.

Of course, what she saw was only an illustration of what might be there. It had been produced using a specific computer program.

'Cor blimey, that's beautiful, proper nice, and I get all this furniture an' all, do I?' she asked, as she took her time looking at each picture.

'I can arrange for the same type of furniture, but, Gin . . . I mean, Nan, those images are to show you what it *could* look like. So what do you think?'

The minute he asked that question, he saw Jesse roll his eyes.

'Well, for starters, I don't like the colour of the kitchen, and I'd need a bigger fridge. I prefer blue in the bathroom. And see this window? I'd want nets up and not blinds. And does the flat have gas central heating? 'Cos I can't get cold, not with me ankles going purple the way they do.'

Billy held up his hands. 'Nan, Nan! Listen, you're going to be living in an *apartment*, not a flat.' Clearly frustrated that the old bat was downgrading what was an expensive piece of real estate, he then modulated his tone. Taking a deep breath, he said, calmly, 'All the finer details will be discussed when the structural work is completed, but I can assure you there will be central heating, with hot and cold running water, and a phone line. So all the basics will most certainly be covered, and, hopefully, so will your rent.'

Ginty shot him a harsh look. 'What? The rent? You said—'

'I said I would adjust your rent enough so that your benefits will cover it.'

Ginty nodded with obvious approval, and a smile crept across her face. 'You're a good boy, you are. Right then . . .' Knowing that she was on to a right winner, her greedy eyes spied the doughnuts once more, and before she got another word out, she clutched one, popped it into her mouth, and wolfed it down faster than a viper eating its prey.

'As I was saying, I can't live in that poxy shit-hole the council gave me. I don't like me neighbours, ya see. They're a right proper bunch of Moaning Minnies.'

Jesse was itching now to get away from Ginty's company. Having no patience with her at all, he rolled his eyes again. 'Listen, I have to dash, and so do you, Billy.' He knew he couldn't leave his brother to put up with Ginty alone because she'd drive him nuts.

Totally ignoring the comment, Ginty rattled on, 'Billy boy, I saw Bronte on the way here, up the road by the roundabout. I thought she was touting for business since she was leaning into a car window with her arse in the air. I didn't realise it was her until we got closer, and she stood up straight. I couldn't see. But to be honest, if it was a fella, she was gabbing to, well, I'm not one for gossiping, and you'll never catch me sticking me nose in, but I wouldn't have that, if I were you, Billy boy. I mean, she's your bird, and dressed like that an' all. Ya can't 'ave her carrying herself in that way, 'cos, no doubt, you'll be getting wed to her, won't ya.'

Billy looked up in the ceiling in despair. Bronte was the last person he wanted to talk about right now. Taking a deep breath to stem his anger, he said, 'Ginty, she's *not* my girlfriend, not now, and she certainly ain't gonna be my wife so—'

'What are you on about?' she said, as she calmly took another doughnut from the bag and took a huge bite out of it. 'You two have been together for years. She's a proper travelling girl and has a pretty face to go with it. She's just right for you, Billy boy. And her family are a good lot. The ol' man still lives on the site and makes his tea on the outside fire.'

'Right,' snapped Billy, as he held his hands up, his anger bubbling away. 'I've been good to you, and I've even said you can have one of the apartments, but one thing I fucking won't have, Ginty, is you telling me how to live my life. I wasn't with

Bronte because she was a good travelling girl. In fact, I would have bloody preferred it if she *hadn't* been. At least then she would have understood loyalty, even if she couldn't fucking spell the word.'

Ginty threw the rest of her half-eaten second doughnut back into the bag. 'You're me grandson. I should have some say in your future, and if I can guide you in the right direction, I will.'

Jesse looked at his brother, knowing that when Billy had had enough, there was no winding him in.

Billy's eyes narrowed as he glared at Ginty. 'Look around you, Ginty! Have a good fucking look!'

Ginty visibly shrank back into her chair.

'All this, all my apartments, my businesses, my top-of-the-range motors, they weren't fucking got through anything remotely illegal. It was done through hard grafting and using my brain. I worked the stock market from the age of fifteen. I ploughed mine and Jesse's money into property, and now I own two blocks of apartments and manage thirty-two properties. I have investors wanting to throw money at me because what I do is make money. And guess what! I've done it all without the help of a fucking traveller, a gypsy, a fucking pikey. So please do *not* tell me Bronte was good for me. In fact, if you must know, she is a sly, underhanded bitch who tried to do me over. Now, understand this: I won't hear another word about who or what is right for me.'

Ginty's mouth froze open, completely stunned that Billy, who had been so accommodating to her over the last five years, had suddenly spoken to her like that.

'I take it you're still hurt then, Billy boy?' she replied, in her most sarcastic tone.

Exasperated, Billy placed his hands on his hips and exhaled a long sigh.

Jesse knew then he had to intervene, or his brother might just put his hands around their grandmother's throat and throttle her. 'Nan, come on, I'll give you a lift home. Billy's got a lot of work on.'

Slowly, Ginty clambered out of the chair, snatched the bag with the rest of the doughnuts, and turned to Billy. 'Oh, and I want a white kitchen, mind. None of that coloured shit. And make sure I get a blue bathroom. I want navy blue.'

'No problem, Nan. No problem at all.'

The door slammed shut behind them, leaving Billy with time to take a few deep breaths and calm himself down. His phone buzzed on the desk, the screen lighting up with a familiar number. It was Bronte. Billy froze, his hand hovering over it. His brain was screaming at him: 'Take the call, take the call.' And he almost did. But then his gaze shifted to the filing cabinet across the room, and he recalled the moment when she'd blindsided him. And just like that, she'd played him for a fool.

A chill swept through him, chasing away the flicker of hesitation. Of course, he'd loved her – it wasn't something he could switch off – but love wasn't enough. Not now. It would take time, but he'd get over her. He had to.

CHAPTER FOUR

Billy turned off his phone, set the burglar alarm, and walked out past the mini meeting room and out by the back door of the building, locking it behind him. The area behind the property was where the bins were kept, but there was sufficient space for Cas or himself to park their cars. He paused and glanced either side as he made his way to his brand-new Audi TT. A prickling sensation crept up his spine – someone was there. For a moment, he thought it might be Bronte because he hadn't answered her call.

Where his office-cum-shop front joined two other premises – one on either side – brick walls separated the properties. But those walls didn't extend all the way to the main back alley. They were there purely to set boundaries. The back alley was only used by the delivery drivers or for the dustcarts.

He froze, scanning both walls until two men stepped into view.

There was no reason for them to be there unless it had something to do with his property specifically.

Billy didn't move. He stood still and watched as the two men approached.

They were older, maybe in their thirties, big men, but sharply dressed – not the usual skanky opportunists. The first man had blond waves that gave him a beachboy look, but his outfit – starched white shirt, jacket, designer jeans, and brown loafers – was far from casual. He looked as though he'd just stepped out of the bathroom, he was so clean.

Billy could even smell the man's aftershave from where he stood.

The other man, who was dark-haired, was just as sleek – wearing black trousers, a fitted black T-shirt, and a gold necklace. He stopped a few steps away, his dark eyes scanning Billy from head to toe. Taking a long drag of his cigarette, he flicked the butt to the ground, twisted it under his foot, and straightened up.

‘So, I’m guessing you’re a Murphy. Billy, is it?’ His voice was calm.

For Billy, the man’s manner was too calm, so he decided not to reply. His attention flicked to the blond man, who flexed his hands. It was a clear signal that he wasn’t here to chew the fat. And they weren’t here for business either.

Although he was in the mood for a fight, these two looked like serious hard cases. The fact that he’d never seen them before was not in doubt. And they weren’t travellers, that much was obvious.

‘And you are?’ asked Billy, who was feeling a little uneasy.

‘Fair question,’ replied the dark-haired man, his voice smooth but carrying an edge. ‘I’m Reece Shipley, and this here’s my brother Dario Shipley.’

Billy’s stomach tightened. He forced himself to nod, keeping his expression neutral. ‘All right. How can I help?’ he asked. Inside, though, his brain was scrambling with all kinds of thoughts.

The Shipleys. The name alone carried weight. Billy had never met any of them, but their reputation had a way of reaching ears whether you wanted to hear about them or not. They were gangsters, pure and simple, but not the street-level kind. Not by any means. No, their operations were vast, illegal, and – by all accounts – profitable. Their tidy firm was ruthless and efficient, with a strict take-no-prisoners approach.

And yet here they were in the flesh. But they must have scoped him out. Their presence was certainly no coincidence.

Billy couldn’t wrap his head around it. Why the hell would two men like Reece and Dario Shipley be bothered with him? From what he’d heard, they’d never got their hands dirty. That was what henchmen were for – foot soldiers carrying out orders without hesitation. But these men didn’t look as though they’d just climbed the ladder of someone else’s scheme. They looked polished, composed, and far more dangerous than the stories behind their success hinted.

Feeling out of his depth, Billy’s heart rate began to soar. Even though the rumours about the Shipleys might have been exaggerated, Reece’s gaze was so cold and fixed that at that point, Billy doubted they were.

'Are you Billy Murphy?' asked Reece.

'Yes, I am, and so, like I asked, how can I help you?'

The two men looked at each other and grinned as though they were sharing a private joke.

When Reece stepped forward, his face beaming, it was so obvious that he was putting on a false front that Billy's temper began to bubble over. He wasn't in the best of moods in any case, and now here he was expected to pussyfoot around two known faces.

Silence. It seemed to prolong the tension. Reece simply stared, obviously trying to intimidate Billy, but this only infuriated him further. He tilted his head to the side and raised a single brow.

'You owe me,' said Reece, still with that annoying grin on his face.

'Oh yeah? How's that, then? Do tell me. Because as far as I last checked, I don't owe anyone a thing. Oh, er . . . yeah, except my mum, for having me.'

Reece laughed and looked at his brother, who was shaking his head.

'Yeah, mate, you fucking definitely do owe me.'

'Right. Look, Reece, I'm not a patient man. I'm very busy, so instead of playing with your words, tell me: what the hell am I supposed to owe you?'

'I've just been told that you fucked up the grow that belonged to us. So we thought we should come and pay you a visit ourselves.'

Billy recalled Franklin warning him that he'd be sorry, but never in his wildest dreams had he considered that the two gypsy boys were mixed up with the likes of the Shipleys. He sighed. Biting his lip in anger, his mind raced to Bronte. Could she have been involved with these men?

The conversation he'd had less than fifteen minutes ago gnawed at him. Ginty had said that she'd seen Bronte leaning into someone's car window. Had the sly bitch set this up with the Shipleys? Was her innocent expression and coy manner all just a front? Had she played him all this time?

'I don't know what you're on about, mate,' he said, doing his best to stay calm.

'You don't want to fuck about with us, Billy Murphy,' Reece growled. 'We don't take kindly to blokes who try to mess with our business.'

Billy didn't like how Reece slid his hand down the back of his trousers. Glancing over his shoulder at the cameras, he hoped to signal that it would all be caught on film if they shot him. But then a dreaded thought struck him. The cameras were remotely linked to the small monitoring room near Cas's office. Cas had said he would be vacating the house because he was having builders in. So did that mean that the cameras might have been switched off?

When Billy turned back to face Reece, the man was still grinning.

'Oh, Billy,' Reece sneered. 'I see you got a bit nervous there. I saw you look at the cameras, and I'm not stupid.'

'Listen, mate, I don't know what you take me for, but a silly cunt ain't it. I don't know you, I've never met you, I don't have anything that fucking belongs to you, and yet here you two are.' He pointed at them both in turn. 'So, yep, of course, I'm checking my cameras are working. See, it looked to me like you may have a weapon tucked down the back of your trousers, and me . . .' He held up his hands. 'I'm unarmed.'

Before Reece or Dario could respond, a sleek-looking Mercedes slowed to a halt by them. It compelled the Shipley brothers to glance over to see who was emerging from the car.

Billy knew exactly who it was and suddenly panicked. He didn't want Dottie getting mixed up in this situation.

Dressed in a stylish navy-blue suit with her reddish blonde hair pulled up in a bun and carrying a smart leather attaché case, Dottie marched towards Billy and politely nodded to the two men.

'Billy, I need to have a meeting.'

When she saw the look on her son's face, she turned and stared at the two men. It was then that she realised they appeared somewhat menacing. Just their stance alone rang alarm bells in her head.

Smiling calmly, she stepped towards them and extended her hand.

'Hi, I'm Dorothy Ellis, and you two are?'

But something inside her stomach tightened. Was she looking into the eyes of someone very familiar, or was it a coincidence?

'We were just having a word with Billy here, weren't we, mate?'

'Sorry, who are you?' she asked, her tone laced with authority.

Reece laughed. 'Not that you need to know, but I'm a gentleman, so I'll tell you. My name's Reece Shipley.'

She now knew exactly who he was. Her hand then recoiled instantly as though his touch was a snake ready to strike.

Reece smirked, sensing her recognition. 'Ah, so you've heard of us. Right, now we've got the introductions out of the way, I was discussing business with Billy. So, if you'd excuse us, Ms Ellis.'

'Sorry, lads, no can do. I've got *urgent* business. Perhaps you could come back tomorrow.'

'What? No, love, we ain't coming back tomorrow.'

Billy was surprised by how Dottie handled them. She was displaying nerves of steel.

Waving her hand dismissively, as if shooing away an annoying wasp, Dottie grabbed Billy's arm and turned him towards the back of the office. Without missing a beat, she glanced back over her shoulder. 'Tomorrow would be better. And use the front entrance next time. The back entrance is for family only.' Her eyes raked over them, cold and calculated. 'And you two? You're definitely *not* family.'

Dario lunged forward, but Reece yanked him back, hissing through gritted teeth, 'Leave it.'

'I fucking wouldn't, if I were you!' snapped Dottie, who was now boiling inside.

Reece held the woman's gaze for a moment longer. Something in her expression told him to leave the matter alone. She knew exactly who they were, and unlike most, she didn't seem the least bothered. For the first time in his life, Reece felt something close to admiration for a woman. Confidence like hers didn't just happen. It came with a backstory – a reason to own it. So now, he'd make it his business to find out exactly who this Dorothy Ellis was.

Still gripping Dario tightly, Reece could feel the tension in his brother's muscles, no doubt from the barely contained fury inside him.

Dario didn't care about consequences: man or woman, it didn't matter to him. If someone pushed him, they'd get hurt and hurt badly.

***

The second they were inside the office, Dottie wiped her brow. 'What are you doing getting mixed up with the Shipleys?'

'You know them, then, Mottie?' Billy asked, intrigued.

Dottie met Billy's eyes. She was at the point of telling him about the woman she met in prison. Her name was Candice Shipley. She murdered her soulmate Billy, the woman her son was named after. However, on this occasion, she decided it was best not to mention her connection with the Shipley family.

'They have a reputation, Billy, but more to the point, what do they want with you?'

Akin to his biological mother in keeping certain information secret, Billy decided to keep what he had learned to himself. He suspected that the likes of the Shipleys wouldn't be turning up in person to iron out a silly dispute over a few grands' worth of marijuana. Their visit to his premises made no sense. The Shipleys had an empire stretching right across North London, so he suspected they were after far more than payment for the grow in the basement. He wasn't happy about the fact that the two brothers came in person, and he knew they would be back. Cas was the best person to get the complete rundown on the Shipleys. Until he had spoken with him, he would stay schtum.

'Mottie, what did you want to talk to me about?'

Dottie knew that her son was as adroit at deflecting a question as she was. 'Never mind that, Billy. Why were the Shipleys here?'

'They were interested in the apartments.'

'Now, you listen to me, Billy. I know you're lying.'

'Leave it, Mottie, please.'

Putting her briefcase onto Billy's desk, she said, 'They'd better not be threatening you, or blackmailing you, or—'

'Mottie, just leave it. I'm fine. Anyway, what did you want?'

He frowned because he could see she now had something eating away at her.

'Are you okay?'

'Me?' She raised her brow. Perching herself on the edge of Billy's desk, she opened her briefcase and pulled out a green manilla file and handed it over to him.

Taking it from her, he placed it on the desk beside her.

'Yeah, I'm all good. I had a call from Peterson. Do you remember that block you wanted to buy? Well, the property developers have pulled out. They couldn't come up with the readies, so Peterson called. It's yours, if you want to go for it. He is fed up with the auctions and the buyers falling short. You know how it is. Their mouths are bigger than their wallets, so they get carried away with the bid and then back out.'

Billy nodded. 'Tell him I'll have another look over them, but he's gonna have to drop the price now.'

'Ever the businessman.' She smiled, but her porcelain face was flushed with concern. 'Billy, are you okay? I'm referring to those two men. I've heard that the family are dangerous.'

'Mottie, listen. It's nothing I can't handle, okay? So stop worrying.'

He glanced at the file. 'Do you have the plans for the Peterson properties? I'll go over them again and check to see if they still grab my attention.'

Dottie stood up and dusted herself down. Grabbing her briefcase, she signalled her readiness to leave.

'I'll email them over to you later. Right, I'll be out of your hair. Let me know if you need me to negotiate. I'm twiddling my thumbs at the moment. All the other businesses are squared up with the accounts, so I'm around if you want me to check over anything.'

'Will do, Mottie,' Billy replied, with a nod.

She smiled, with a fleeting warmth in her expression, before hurrying out through the back door. As soon as she entered the open air, her gaze flicked nervously towards where she had seen the Shipleys' vehicle. The thought of the Shipleys lingering nearby troubled her. Glancing back over her shoulder, she noticed Billy standing there, watching her, his silhouette framed in the doorway. She turned away and walked towards her car.

Sliding into the driver's seat, Dottie started the engine and slowly pulled away, but she didn't go far. Just out of sight, she parked and waited, scanning the area, in case those two men returned. The tension clung to her, and an icy sensation rippled through her chest – not from the cool air or the breeze, but from a memory that refused to fade.

Candice Shipley.

The thought of her struck like a blade, sharp and merciless. That smirk – Candice's cruel, triumphant grin – haunted her even now, twenty years or so later. She could still see that expression as vividly as the day it had happened in the prison canteen.

The room had been filled with noise, yet the moment Candice stabbed Billy, the world went silent for her. Her dearest friend, the one person who had genuinely cared for her, crumpled to the ground as blood pooled around her. She remembered the episode only too well.

***

Glaring at Candice, as they locked eyes, she recalled Candice suddenly looking away.

'You fucking murdered her, you evil bitch. I'll fucking kill you!'

Officer Knight had slapped her hand over her mouth. 'Shut up, Ellis. Please shut up.'

Dottie knew she'd said that because threats such as these were recorded and would go on an inmate's record, making parole so much more complex, and she was well aware that Officer Knight had liked and respected her.

Then, Dottie remembered what Knight had said. 'She's gone, Ellis. Come on, you have to return to your room. You can't do anything now.'

***

The officer was right, of course. But even now, not a single day went by when Dottie wished she'd done it. Wished she'd ended Candice right there and then, smirk and all. Instead, Candice had walked away, leaving behind a wound deeper than any blade could carve.

Her hand trembled on the gearstick as she shook off that memory, her eyes still fixed on the rear of Billy's office. She would wait, just in case, because if Candice's sons were as cold and callous as their mother, then they could quickly return and kill her son in cold blood. After all, she had witnessed that same dark look in Reece's eyes as those of her arch-enemy Candice.

***

Billy leaned back in his chair, now staring at the architect's impression of what this late eighteenth century warehouse he had bought overlooking the Thames might look like when all the renovation work had been completed. Clearly, it had once been a thriving factory. Its red brick exterior and black wrought-iron fire escape gave more than a hint to its industrial past. His mind buzzed with so many ideas. But one stood out: remodel the property into sleek residential units for young, wealthy couples. A sophisticated lobby, perhaps a concierge, and plush hallways leading to compact but modern one-bedroom apartments. This was not a place for families. This was all about style and status. It could be a goldmine.

The shrill ring of the office landline tore his focus away. Billy grabbed the phone. His tone was polite but firm. 'Good afternoon, Murphys' Property Services—'

A deep, gruff voice came on the line. 'Put Cas Ferrier on the phone.'

Billy froze. He pulled the receiver from his ear and stared at it as if the receiver might explain not only who the caller was but the reason for the sudden intrusion. Returning the receiver to his ear, he replied curtly, 'I'm sorry, but you've got the wrong number.'

Cas Ferrier – a silent partner. He rarely came to the office, and his involvement wasn't on any official paperwork. It was all off the books, built on trust. No one who mattered should be calling this number to ask for Cas. And certainly not with *that* tone.

The voice pressed on. 'Is that Billy Murphy?'

'Yes, but like I said, you've got the wrong number for Cas Ferrier.'

The response came sharp and venomous. 'You tell that cunt he can run but he can't hide. I'll find him, and when I do, I'll kill him.'

Billy's patience snapped. This day had been one disaster after another, and now this! His temper flared. 'Get your own fucking secretary! I'm not, and never have been, anyone's fucking messenger service. Now, fuck off!' He slammed the phone down, his chest heaving, as he sucked in sharp breaths.

The realisation hit him almost immediately. He should have asked who the hell was calling. His mind raced as Cas's uneasy expression replayed in his head. 'Builders, my arse, Cas,' he muttered, slamming his hand on the desk. Whoever it was who was after Cas wasn't just trouble, they were fucking dangerous. Cas never ran from anyone, if, of course, that was what he was doing. Usually, it was the other way around.

Billy grabbed his mobile, his fingers madly scrolling through his phone until he found Cas's number. The call went straight to voicemail. Frustration boiled over. 'For fuck's sake,' he hissed, throwing his phone down onto the desk. Whatever was going on was worse than he'd thought – and it was heading straight for them. Was this to do with the Shipleys, or was it someone else?

CHAPTER FIVE

While she waited a further ten minutes to see if either of the Shipley brothers returned to her son's premises, Dottie stared aimlessly out of the windscreen. Casting her mind back again over twenty years ago took her to the time when she was in Holloway Prison.

It wasn't hard to recall that period in her life. It remained imprinted in her memory because it was just a few weeks before her Billy was born. She named him Billy after the death of her best friend and inmate Billy Cardel.

It was 'doughnut day', and she and Billy had walked excitedly into the canteen. Moments later, an altercation started over queue-jumping, and Billy ended up on the floor, having been stabbed in the chest. Her best friend and protector had literally died a death that afternoon.

Candice Shipley. That was the woman.

Dottie already knew that Billy was concerned she might be a target, after telling her that she had been given an ultimatum to release details of where she had hidden her father's stash from a post office robbery carried out by him and her two 'uncles'.

Dottie felt her eyes welling up and blinked the unshed tears away. Billy had confided in her about where she had buried the money, almost as if she'd had a premonition of her own death.

But something didn't add up. How could Candice have had two sons approximately the same ages as the Shipley boys? It didn't make sense. She had served far too long behind bars. Then it hit her like a ton of bricks. Those two men weren't her sons: they were probably her grandsons.

Dottie's stomach churned as the realisation dawned. She had heard of the Shipleys – a notorious gang from North London – but she had never connected the dots. Not until she stared into Reece's eyes and felt that same unshakable gut-wrenching feeling she'd had in the prison canteen all those years ago.

***

Reece slid his key into the lock of his front door. His five-bedroom detached house was his pride and joy. Everything inside had been handpicked by himself. He didn't really have a choice after tipping a pot of pink emulsion over the designer's head while shouting, 'What the fuck do you take me for, eh? This is supposed to be a bachelor pad, not a fucking tart's boudoir. So, take your pastels, shove them up your arse, and fuck off.'

Dario and Reece had purchased what amounted to practically a building site not all that far away from the affluent Little Oak Wood in North London. As all of the properties were off-plan, the brothers had commissioned a builder to build each of them a five-bedroom property, one for their father, and a couple more houses for their uncles and cousins, not forgetting a two-bedroom house for their grandmother, and two others to rent out for investment purposes.

The site was still not complete. As the site manager walked past and offered a friendly acknowledgement, Reece verbally ripped his head off.

'I told you to make sure those fucking workers keep the road clean. There's muck everywhere. Twice in one week, I've had to get me new motor cleaned, and don't think I won't be sending any cleaning bills to you, 'cos believe me, mate, I will!'

Lester Green had been on cloud nine when Reece walked into his office and asked to see the plans for the new development. Of course, he knew who the Shipleys were. As much as he was aware of their financial status, he was also cognizant of how they had accumulated their wealth. It seemed that the brothers were adept at financial wizardry through illegal means, so he reckoned that they were purchasing these properties as part of a well-thought-out money-laundering business. He wasn't bothered, though, one bit: as far as he was concerned, the Shipleys' money was as good as anyone else's. So the fact that they were buying all the properties and adding to them was a gift handed to him on a plate.

'Sorry, Mr Shipley, I'll have a word. Anyway, how are you settling in?' he asked, trying to turn the conversation into something more upbeat.

'Listen, Lester, you don't ask fuck all about me or my family, got it? I do the asking.' He laughed. 'And the fucking telling.

Now, why ain't my alarms working? I told you that by the weekend, I want our houses secured. All alarms, buzzers, cameras, and gates fully operational. But I've just managed to drive almost to my fucking front door without even tapping in a code, so what the fuck's going on?'

Recoiling, Lester stuttered. 'Er . . . well . . . we are fixing that right now. One of our guys accidentally cut through a wire and—'

'A wire? A fucking wire? So tell me, Lester, how in the life of crime, can my security be compromised by a fucking severed wire, 'cos that don't sound too clever to me, does it to you, Lester?'

Feeling totally intimidated, Lester could feel his pale skin redden to the point where it was almost burning his face. 'He's in the hospital, Mr Shipley. He went straight through the armoured cable, and the electric jackhammer shot him ten feet in the air,' he said, hoping to get some sympathy for the lad.

However, it only riled up Reece further. 'And you're telling me this for what, eh? Do I look like I give a flying fuck? My question to you, ya fucking idiot, is why you have employed inexperienced workmen, eh? Are you trying to get a day's collar out of the lad for half the wage and yet charge me full whack?' Stepping forward, he spat, as he approached the hapless, timid-looking man.

'No, no, Mr Shipley, I'd never do that. I'm an honest man.'

Reece laughed. He was joined by Dario, who, having seen the commotion, quickly got out of his car and walked over to give his brother some support.

'That's your problem, Lester,' said Reece. 'Now, get the cable fixed and my security in place.'

Lester didn't have the bottle to tell Reece that it would take a lot longer to sort out all the security, especially when they were still fitting pipework and using heavy machinery to do it. So he nodded and hurried away before Reece or Dario embarrassed him even more.

As soon as Reece was inside his plush new home, he headed for the kitchen, with Dario on his heels.

'Reece, you should have let me give that Billy Murphy a taste of what's to come, in case he doesn't do as we asked. You made me look like a right knob.'

'Dario, listen, you don't need anyone to make you look like a knob. You are more than capable of doing that yourself. Now, we need to get our story straight before Father gets here.'

'Shit! You know he will go off the deep end.'

Reece turned on his new coffee machine and leaned against the kitchen units, arms folded, his eyes narrowed.

'What are you thinking, Reece? Do we tell the old man what happened, or shall we just say we couldn't find the Murphy bloke?'

'Shut up, Dario, you idiot, he's not stupid. Leave me to do the talking. You just do what you do best and say nothing.'

Dario nodded because Reece was the one with the brains. 'Fair enough, Reece, but why didn't you let me show that Murphy prick what he was in for, if he didn't do as we say?'

'Because that woman turned up, that's why.'

'She hardly had a gun in her hand,' Dario said, with a shrug. 'She was probably just some associate, or, I dunno, someone linked to the Murphys' property services. She looked smart, like a businesswoman.'

Reece rolled his eyes. 'For the love of good coffee, you really can't read people, can you?'

Dario frowned. 'I dunno what you mean.'

'I'll educate you, Dario,' Reece said, his voice low and measured, as he leaned in, his eyes fixed on his younger brother. 'This Dorothy Ellis. She wasn't the least bit concerned, not even bothered, in knowing who we are.'

He let the silence hang for a moment, his previous words heavy with implication.

'And, believe me,' he continued, 'the way she pulled her hand back, like I had the fucking plague, told me she knows exactly who we are, anyway. But then, how she looked at us, the way she spoke like we're nothing – like nobodies, pests even – tells me she wasn't intimidated by us. Not one bit.'

Reece's voice hardened as he straightened, his jaw tightening. 'Which means, little brother, she's either got some serious backing or she's one hell of an actress. Either way,' he said, his voice dropping to a menacing whisper, 'I'm going to find out who the fuck she is.'

Before Dario could respond, a loud knock at the front door made Reece jump and spill his coffee all over the new worktop.

'Who the fuck is that?' he snapped, grabbing a paper towel to wipe up the mess.

Dario marched back along the hallway towards the front door and clocked the face of a very impatient-looking man through the glass panel. He opened the door, and before he could greet his father, the man stormed past him straight into the kitchen.

Reece stood ramrod straight as if a sergeant major had just walked in.

'Dad.'

'Well, boy, I saw you pull up, and you didn't think to come over to see me, did ya? What happened, hey? Something went wrong, did it, and now you two need to get your story straight. Is that it?'

He wasn't stupid. The brothers were in the habit of closing ranks to concoct an agreed version, especially if they'd fucked up.

Reece blinked rapidly as if his father was breathing fire, which didn't seem far off the mark. 'No, everything is in hand, okay? Now . . .' He smiled as he saw his father's huge shoulders relax and his face soften. 'Take a seat and have a coffee. I've got this new machine. Honestly, Dad, it's the fucking dog's bollocks.'

Gerard Shipley, the eldest of Candice's sons, pulled a chair out from the table and plonked himself down. He glanced up at Dario. 'And why do you look so fucking sheepish?'

'Do I?'

Gerard waved his hand dismissively. 'How about you tell me exactly what happened, Reece?'

'Like I said, Dad, everything's in order and sorted.' Reece laughed. 'You should've heard Franklin shitting himself on the phone. I could almost smell his fear from miles away, the daft bastard. As if they could ever get away with a marijuana grow in one of the Murphys' apartment blocks.'

'So, the Murphy lad found the grow, eh?'

'Of course, he did. By all accounts, the bloke's no fucking mug. The Penfolds completely underestimated him. And not only that, but Murphy also told them he's selling the weed and even the equipment. Franklin was almost crying when he told me. I said not to worry – he can pay me fifteen grand when he's flush.'

Gerard joined in the laughter. 'I told you they were as thick as compacted pig shit. Their old man's only got half a brain, but you know what gypsies are like. If they think they can get in on a good deal, they'll be all over it – especially if they believe they could be part of the firm. Fucking pikeys. I wouldn't trust them as far as I could throw them. Still, I don't need to. Job done then, yeah?' He raised a questioning brow.

'Well, er, almost—'

Reece felt the atmosphere turning serious. He hated how his father spoke to him – harsh and cold as though he was just another member of the firm. Being his son didn't earn him any special favours. His father was a brutal and unforgiving man, and Reece knew better than most just how hard he was. Like his brother, he'd felt the sting of those vast hands.

As a teenager, that sting had turned into a punch. 'I'm raising men, not fucking silly tarts,' his father would say, anytime they dared shed a tear. It was his favourite saying, which echoed in Reece's mind, whenever his father's temper flared.

Reece understood why his father was so cold towards his sons. While his grandmother, Candice, served time in prison, his father had been raised by a heartless and often cruel man – Harry Shipley. Although Harry had been Candice's loving husband, he'd been a tyrant to his children, especially Gerard, the eldest, the one he suspected wasn't his. What made matters worse was that his grandfather Joe – Candice's father – was an even harder soul. In effect, Gerard had been moulded by two merciless men, and that legacy of brutality and emotional detachment had been passed down to Reece and his brothers.

'Almost? Tell me, boy, you did talk to Billy Murphy, didn't ya? Ya know, Son, like we planned?'

Reece looked at his father. Those eyes were fixed and boring into him.

'So . . .' He looked at Dario.

Dario took it as his cue to join in.

'We got there, but this bird turned up, so we couldn't—'

Gerard leaped up from the table, his chair tipping over and crashing down on the floor.

It made Reece jump.

But Dario just carried on. 'Well, yeah, we were talking to Billy, and I was about to give him a taste of me fists when Reece pulled me away.'

Gerard glared at Reece, his eyes burning with fury. 'You what? You stopped your brother? And why, Reece, would you do that, eh? Because there ain't a world where I could imagine that showing a bit of violence wouldn't fucking work!' He slammed his fist down on the table, which made the mugs rattle.

Reece was fuming with Dario. He'd told him to keep his mouth shut, but there he was, singing like a great big canary. 'Dad, hang on! Dario hasn't told you everything.'

Gerard's eyes ping-ponged between his two sons. 'Go on, and this had better be fucking good.'

'Yeah, we did see Billy,' Reece said, keeping his voice calm. 'And we told him he owed us, just like we planned.' He held up his hands, pre-empting the explosion he could see building behind his father's eyes. After all, as he'd paid a fortune for the designer table and chairs, he had a vested interest in keeping his house in one piece.

'Then this motor pulls up – a brand-spanking-new Mercedes, no fucking less. I didn't know who it was. For all I knew, it could've been the Ol' Bill.'

'Ol' Bill? Fucking Ol' Bill? Are you effing stupid?' Gerard barked, his voice dripping with disdain. 'The filth don't drive around in a brand-new Mercedes.'

Reece nodded, quickly. 'Listen, so this woman gets out, a briefcase under her arm – or whatever it was. So, I thought maybe she was a solicitor, an accountant, or someone important like that.'

Gerard rolled his eyes, his patience wearing thin. 'Are you kidding me? Your mother, before she fucked off, used to walk around like her shit didn't stink, in her little suits with some fancy bag. But the old cow never even had a fucking job.'

Reece's fists clenched under the table. He wanted to punch his father right in the mouth. He'd been fed the same story his whole life that his mother was a whore. But when he finally found out the truth, it was too late. He'd found her in a rotten bedsit, with nothing but a book of photos of her sons, fifty pounds in her bank account, and living off the dole. The poor cow never had another man. She couldn't handle the abuse, so she'd walked out. And come to think of it, he couldn't even recall her wearing any suits. She'd always dressed plainly like a woman trying to disappear into the background.

'Let me finish.'

'This had better be good.'

At that moment, Reece realised how ridiculous what he was about to say would sound. But if he stuttered, it would look as though he was lying. Taking a deep breath, he carried on. 'So, this woman . . . well, she marched straight towards us, and when she looked at me, it was like she already knew who I was.'

Reece braced himself for an explosive backlash, but, instead, he saw a hint of curiosity in his father's face.

Gerard's brows knitted slightly, and his usual harsh expression momentarily softened.

'She put her hand out to shake mine, and when I told her who I was, she pulled it back right away. So, obviously, she knew me. But then, somehow, she turned all cocky, like she wasn't deterred at all. She told us if we needed a meeting, we should use the front entrance, not the back, and, basically, to make an appointment.'

Reece paused, watching his father's reaction, unsure whether he'd just fuelled his father's interest or his wrath.

Gerard remained standing there with his hands resting on his hips and his brow fixed into a frown.

Reece glanced at Dario, who shrugged behind their father's back.

Hearing the jiggling sound of a key in the lock, all three turned to the front door. There was only one other person besides Reece who had a key – Grannie.

The moment she stepped into the hallway, Candice bustled her way to the kitchen. 'Couldn't you fucking wait for me?' she snapped, slapping her son's arm. 'Right, Reece, make us a coffee, love, would ya? Now, how did it go, Reecie?'

Gerard eyed his mother with disdain. 'Mum, couldn't you at least get dressed?'

Candice looked down at her dressing gown and mud-covered slippers. 'Who the fuck are you to tell me what I should and shouldn't wear, eh, boy? Anyway, it's gonna be practically all family in this complex by the time . . .' She glanced at her slippers again, shaking her head. 'It's all finished. And you wanna have a word with Lester about this fucking mud. I've been traipsing it through my new place. I've had to replace my hall rug twice already.'

'Send the bill to him,' Reece said, dismissively. 'He'll pay it.'

'Oi, Reece,' Gerard said, turning back to his mother. 'Don't go off the fucking story. Get to the point where you explain why you stopped your brother from leaving a violent warning . . . that the Murphys will do as they're told. Because now . . .' He winked and laughed. '. . . They owe us.'

'Oh, so did the Murphy boy take the bait?' Candice asked, excitedly, raising an eyebrow.

Gerard glanced back at his mother. 'Well, that's the thing, Mum. This drippy bastard here.' He gestured towards Reece. 'He stopped Dario from giving the bloke a little taste of what would come his way if he didn't do as he was asked.'

Candice, now in her late sixties, still had the grit and gumption of her youth, hardened first by her life on the streets and then even more so by the years she'd spent behind bars – longer than she should have. All of it was done for her sons. But it had been worth every second because she hadn't wanted her kids to go into care. Her sacrifice ensured they stayed together, and that was all that mattered to her.

She adored her sons and her grandsons and was fiercely protective of them. And there wasn't a doubt in anyone's mind – she would do anything for them. Anything at all.

Candice's eyes narrowed and her lips pursed. 'Why, Reecie? Why?'

Before Reece could answer, Gerard intervened again. 'Because some tart turned up and put the wind up him, that's why.' He changed his tone to that of a whiny kid. ''Cos he thought she wasn't afraid of him.'

Candice shot a look at Reece. 'You what? Who the fuck *was* this woman?'

'I don't know who she is, but her last name wasn't Murphy. It was, er, Ellis. Dorothy Ellis.'

Candice stared in shock. Blood drained from her reddened cheeks, and she gripped the back of the chair in front of her. 'Are you sure? What did she look like?'

'Why?' snapped Gerard.

But Candice stared at Reece, ignoring her son. 'What did she look like?' she repeated.

'Tall, slim, with reddish blondish hair and . . .' He glanced at his father, knowing what he was about to say wouldn't bode well. 'Her eyes were a bit kinda—'

'Like a fucking psychopath's?'

Reece nodded. 'You know her, Gran, don't you. Who is she?'

Candice pulled out the chair from under the table and sat down.

Gerard could tell by the look on his mother's face that something serious was about to be revealed. Setting upright the chair he'd knocked over earlier, he also sat down, his expression cautious.

Dario decided he'd said enough. While his brother poured fresh coffee for everyone, he brought them over to the table.

It was Gran who spoke next, and everyone listened. Her history alone commanded respect. As their father and uncles had always said, she deserved to be treated like a queen, certainly after everything she had sacrificed to keep the youngsters away from social services.

Yet, Gerard often wondered if he might have had a better life in care. His upbringing with his father and grandfather certainly wasn't filled with ice cream and jelly or presents under the Christmas tree, for that matter. It was bare-knuckle fighting in the backyard and being pushed through the windows of posh houses to steal the valuables.

The memory of the day the police caught his grandfather, Joe, still haunted him. His legs had been black and blue from the beating with a stick – a punishment for running out of the house with nothing but the jewellery box. His grandfather had ignored his grandson's warnings about there being some kind of alarm inside the property, calling him a chicken and a disgrace to the family. Within minutes, the police had shown up. But his grandfather hadn't heard them. He was too busy swinging the stick and shouting insults.

Gerard could still see it in his mind: the police carting Grandad Joe away while the old man waved his fist and screamed, 'When I get out, I'll have your fucking guts for garters!' But Joe never came out alive. He left prison in a wooden box.

When the prison governor allowed Candice out of Holloway, albeit handcuffed to two officers, to attend her father's funeral, Gerard noticed she didn't seem to cry for him. It made him wonder if she even loved her father. Despite Joe's constant protestations of love for his daughter, had he been cruel to her too?

'So who is this Dorothy Ellis, Mum?' asked Gerard, lowering his harsh tone just for his mother, even though she did get on his nerves on occasion. Like now, for instance, wearing a dressing gown in the late afternoon. It was something he despised, but, then again, she did have the right to live how she pleased.

'Shush a minute, I'm just trying to remember something.' She cupped her mug of coffee in her hands and stared into space. 'And the boy is Billy Murphy, is he? How old is he?'

'He's twenty-one, why?'

Candice began counting back the years on her fingers. 'Twenty-one? So, he was born in 1982, then.'

The room fell silent, all eyes on her, intrigued.

'Billy, you say?' she asked.

'Yeah,' Reece replied. 'Billy Murphy.'

'Not William, just Billy?'

'As far as I know, his name is Billy. Not short for anything.'

Candice sighed and shook her head. 'I'm not sure we should go ahead with the plan.'

'What?' Gerard screeched. 'Look, Mum, we're almost there, right? I'm not letting some tart get in the way. If I have to take her out myself, I will.'

Candice's eyes widened as she shook her head. 'You won't, Gerard. You won't because that woman is one very dangerous bitch. She was friends with Billy Cardel. You remember who Billy Cardel was, don't you?'

Gerard recalled how his mother had been accused of killing Billy Cardel in the prison canteen. She had been highly fortunate to be convicted only for manslaughter, which meant an added tariff. But it was indeed fortunate, in the sense that as far as his mother described the incident at the time, he'd been dead certain she would get a murder conviction. If it hadn't been for the fact that Billy Cardel had been such an aggressive character, he was sure she would still be in prison now.

'And believe me, no one was friends with Billy. She spent most of her prison life in solitary confinement. There was always unrest between us. I ran the prison until she came along. Then I was moved, but she was still there when I returned. When I heard she was friends with this Dottie Ellis, I thought the girl must either be a silly little gofer who Billy could fuck with, or she was one dangerous motherfucking bitch.'

She took a deep breath. 'And I won't forget the look on Dottie's face when I killed Billy. I knew that look, and I knew she would come for me. Fearless she was. So, once they put me in solitary, I asked to be moved out of the prison. They didn't want another death on their hands, and they all knew that she would kill me because she had some kind of bond with Billy. To the point that Billy was going to be her birthing partner. So, anyway, they moved me to HM fucking P Styal.'

The three men hung on to her every word until Reece frowned. 'So what's Billy Murphy got to do with her?'

'Like I said, she was due to give birth in prison when it happened. So, if she gave birth in 1982, and this lad is twenty-one and called Billy, not William, then I guess he's her son.'

Gerard tutted. 'Mum, that was a long time ago. Come on, Holloway was a dangerous place, back then. She was probably just hormonal at the time, being pregnant. And probably a bit loopy.'

'Oh, believe me, Gerard, she was more than a bit loopy. She killed her parents by slitting their throats.'

Reece gasped. 'Fucking seriously?'

Candice nodded. 'In the dead of night, by all accounts. She snuck into their bedroom, and, like I said, cut their throats, I believe. She wasn't sorry for what she did, either. So, Reece, when I said she has the eyes of a psychopath, that's exactly what I meant. And who's to say Billy Murphy doesn't take after her?'

CHAPTER SIX

Grace sat up in bed and hugged herself tightly, feeling not just physically and sexually abused but mentally as well. The last thing she wanted was for Colin, the man she'd been seeing, to show up at her door pretending to be some brave, dreamt-up knight in shining armour. He wasn't. Colin was nothing more than a penpusher who worked for an IT company. Sure enough, he went to the gym on a regular basis, and he had a great body, but he wouldn't know how to throw a punch, let alone defend himself against someone like Kenny.

She had ended it with Colin. She'd made it clear that their relationship was strictly a friends-with-benefits one – nothing more. She'd even told him she'd be picking her husband up from prison soon and warned him not to call or text her again. Kenny hadn't changed one bit. If anything, he'd come back worse than before – crueller, harder, and with an icy coldness in his stare that sent shivers down her spine.

A wave of dread swept over her as she lay there shivering. What if someone told Kenny about Colin? She knew that someone had been blabbing to him about her past relationships. She'd taken every precaution to keep this one hidden, especially from her over-opinionated daughter. She couldn't bear the thought of Kenny finding out. Not now, not ever. The truth is that she had actually fallen in love with Colin, and she despised Kenny. She hated the man for everything he stood for. And worse, as Tandy grew into a woman, she realised that she was so much like her father.

'Get your lazy arse out of bed. Christ, can't a man have a cooked breakfast when he gets out of prison?'

The mere thought of being anywhere near the sink made her whole body tremble, but she had no choice. She was trapped in a loveless marriage and wished, by Christ, that she'd listened to her mother all those years ago. But, of course, she hadn't. And years later, even her own mother had softened towards Kenny, especially after he put her up in one of his houses and brought her flowers every now and then.

He had utterly sucked her mother in with his small gestures. Perhaps she was feeble or perhaps she had yearned for some manly affection. She even called him the son she'd never had. And yet Kenny always referred to her as the old witch – behind her back, of course.

She had hardly slept. Her body ached so much. Kenny was smart; he knew precisely what he was doing. He'd aimed most of the punches at her body, leaving only the bruise above her eye visible where he'd smashed her face into the tap.

Slowly, she hauled herself out of bed, feeling disoriented and nauseous. Swallowing a mouthful of saliva, she took several deep breaths and looked around for her dressing gown and slippers. But she'd hardly stepped more than three paces before the effects of yesterday's beating in the kitchen were all so real. Each one felt like another punch.

All this time, Kenny stared at her, his eyes sharp and unforgiving. 'Look at ya, fucking prancing about in your silky dressing gown. Is that what you wear in the mornings?'

She could feel the anger simmering beneath his words, even without his brain fuelled by cocaine. *Prancing?* she thought. She could barely fucking breathe.

'Dressing like that in front of the postman, the milkman, the neighbours – are ya?'

Grace shook her head quickly. 'I wear this to walk to the bathroom, Kenny, before I get dressed.'

'Sure you fucking do,' he sneered, his lip curling. 'Now, get me a decent bit o' grub, will ya? A proper fry-up. No shit.'

Rifling through the wardrobe, she grabbed a loose tracksuit – nothing too tight. She couldn't even bear the thought of wearing a bra because her body hurt too much. Clutching the clothes, she scurried to the bathroom. The moment she closed the door behind her, she felt as though she could finally breathe.

The mirror, surrounded by its harsh, unforgiving lights, did nothing to hide the state of her bruised body. Slowly, holding the silk dressing gown open, she stared at herself in disbelief. It was no wonder her body hurt so much to breathe. Black-and-purple stripes instead of the black-and-white ones of a zebra lined each rib. She knew then he had broken them – again. When he'd done it before, all the doctor had said at the time was that unless she had punctured a lung, nothing could be done. She had to rest and let her ribs heal on their own.

She could cover the bruise above her forehead with foundation, but she couldn't mask the look in her eyes. She hadn't seen that emptiness in years. The light – the zest for life – it was all gone now.

The banging on the door made her jump out of her skin, and then she heard his excited words.

'Hurry up, Tandy's here.' His tone was shrill, like a kid on Christmas morning receiving the gift they'd always dreamed of.

That was all she needed – her daughter showing up, like a bad penny.

Grace quickly caked her face in make-up, in the hope of masking the damage, and gently slipped on her velour tracksuit. Each step down the stairs felt like a hammer pounding into her ribs. She paused at the bottom and gripped the banister to steady herself before she finally stepped into the hallway.

Her eyes narrowed. Kenny had wrapped his arms tightly around Tandy and was now kissing her cheeks as though she was still a baby. But Tandy wasn't a baby – she was a tall, strikingly attractive woman, with bright-green eyes that flashed deadly lasers and a tongue sharp enough to cut paper.

'Look at you, my baby.' Kenny beamed. 'I'll be fighting off a string of men, no doubt!'

'Dad, I'm a *woman*,' she replied, her voice lilting with affection, as she flicked her long auburn hair over her shoulders. 'Anyway, it's so good to have you home. I said we should throw you a party,' she added, shooting her mother a dirty look. 'But Mother said you wouldn't want that, so I'm sorry if you're disappointed.'

Grace felt Kenny clock the tension between them, and she knew he'd revel in it. His precious daughter, firmly on his side, was just the kind of power play he thrived on.

Instinctively, Grace touched her forehead and felt the bump beneath her make-up. She caught Tandy's gaze flicking to it, but her daughter said nothing. She was too busy praising her father and giggling like a schoolgirl, her voice unnervingly childlike, as she fawned over him.

It turned Grace's stomach. Still, she bit her tongue. The last thing she wanted was another beating. She prayed yesterday's was the last. Because, really, how much more could her body take?

'A party would have been nice, but I guess your mother had other things on her mind.'

Grace remained silent, but she didn't miss the satisfied smug look on her daughter's face. She knew, in that moment, that Tandy would never side with her. She had always been a daddy's girl, and, clearly, she still was. The fights she'd had with her daughter over not visiting her father were endless. Tandy wanted everything her way, and if she didn't get it, she would sulk, row, and even get violent.

'Your mother's going to cook us a right nice fry-up,' Kenny said, grinning.

But Tandy laughed, her tone sharp and mocking. 'Oh, Dad, I don't suppose she's told you, has she? She's turned vegetarian. You could be chowing down on a bean sausage, not a proper pork one.'

Her words were deliberately antagonising, testing her father's allegiance, with a sly grin. And it became evident just how quickly she could get away with blue murder.

Kenny spun around, his jaw tightening to the side.

'You fucking *what*? A vegetarian? Who said? Some new friends of yours talking you into this hippy shit, were they? I'll tell you what, there'd better be a nice rump steak and proper meat sausages on the go. You know I like my meat!'

Grace glared at her daughter, who looked so smug, she wanted to slap her – hard. Instead, she swallowed the urge, turned to Kenny, and said, 'Yes, of course, there is.'

Kenny huffed, satisfied for now. He then flashed a beaming smile at his daughter. 'So, tell me what's been going on. I've missed our regular updates since your mother wouldn't let you come and see me.'

The open-plan kitchen-cum-dining room offered Grace no escape. As Kenny and Tandy settled at the table, she busied herself cooking the fry-up. She didn't want to watch them. She'd rather have been miles away from here. But, unfortunately, there was no avoiding the pair of them.

Grace glanced up to see her daughter place her hand over his. 'It's okay, Dad, we have all the time in the world now. How about we go down the pub this afternoon and see a few of your friends?'

'Hmm, yeah, babes, but maybe another day. I've got some business I need to sort out first,' Kenny said.

Tandy leaned in, and her eyes sparkled with interest. 'Oh yeah? What business is that, Dad?' she asked, eager to get involved in whatever shady dealings he was up to.

Grace wanted to scream, but her head was throbbing, and it hurt even to breathe. So she focused on buttering the toast while not dwelling on their conversation and trying not to look at their spiteful faces.

'Where's our tea?' Kenny suddenly bellowed. 'Fuck me, it's like being back inside, waiting for the smallest of luxuries! All I wanted was a nice brekkie and a decent cup of tea!'

'I'll make it, Dad,' Tandy offered, pushing her chair back to get up.

But before she could leave her chair, Kenny grabbed her arm firmly. 'No daughter of mine is going to be a skivvy. I'm home now, and you, my babes, are going to be treated like the princess you are.'

Tandy smiled and retook her seat, now intent on lapping up all the attention. 'So, what business is it, Dad? Anything I can do to help? I'm kinda bored at the moment.'

Kenny's eyes locked on his daughter's face, and a slow smile crept across his lips. 'You, my princess, can go shopping. See, I've been away for a long time and not been able to spoil my girl. So take a lump of money out of my account – ya mother has the cards – and treat yaself.' He kissed her cheek. 'Look at you, all grown up. I bet people find it hard to say no to you, my princess, don't they?'

Tandy was having a ball. Her father, the villain – a man to be feared – and she, his little princess. She knew he had money tucked away, and she was dead sure it would come to her, and not just by way of the shopping trips either. And it couldn't come soon enough. After all, her mother rarely gave her a penny, always insisting she was old enough to get a job and pay her own way. But with her dad, things would be different. She was banking on it. And no world of work for her. She would do as she pleased. Live a life of Riley.

By the time Grace placed the large plates of breakfast in front of her husband and daughter, she was weak with pain. Barely able to stand up, she mumbled, 'I'm going to the toilet.'

She could hear their laughter and banter echoing from the kitchen as she left the room. This was her chance. Her heart raced as she hurried to the bedroom. Lifting the mattress sent a sharp, searing pain through her ribs, nearly making her collapse, but she pushed through it and retrieved her hidden phone. Clutching it tightly, she rushed to the bathroom and locked the door behind her.

With her hands trembling nineteen to the dozen, she dialled a number. A deep voice answered after the first ring.

'He's home, then,' the voice said, knowingly.

'Cas,' she whispered, her voice cracking. 'I should've listened to you. I know I should now. But I didn't. I knew he was bad, but not this bad, for fuck's sake. He's evil, Cas. Really evil. If I ain't dead by next week, I'll be maimed for sure. I know I will.'

'Oh, girl,' Cas said, softly. 'Has he hurt you?'

'Hurt me? He's broken my ribs, Cas, as well as, well, you can imagine the rest – the disgusting pig. I can't take it. It was so cruel, Cas, so cruel . . . He terrifies me. He literally tossed me around like I was a dog.' Her voice wavered, heavy with resignation. 'It was so . . . so . . . degrading.'

Through the phone, Cas could hear not only her exhaustion but how defeated she sounded. 'Listen to me,' he said, firmly. 'If you can get out, grab some money, your passport, and get over to Cyprus. I've got a villa there. You can stay there. Just get away from him, Grace.'

She sighed deeply, her voice barely audible. 'He sent you a letter, didn't he? Was it a threat?'

'Yeah,' Cas admitted, grimly. 'He warned me. But don't you worry about me. Just get yourself safely away from him.'

'He has a list of people he wants to hurt, and you, I'm afraid, are at the top, Cas. If you thought he was bad before, believe me, he's ten times worse now. He won't just hurt you. He'll go after anyone dear to you, too. The things he's threatened to do to you are outrageous. He is so filled with hate and revenge, Cas. And I believe his threats are not hot air. They're real.'

'Grace,' Cas said, quietly, 'my granddaughter is dead, and I don't speak to my daughter anymore. So—'

'I heard, and I'm so sorry, but listen, Cas,' she said, her voice trembling, 'he's dead set on bringing you down. All I'm saying is, he'll find a way to hurt you, in any way he can. He knows about your business – a fruitful one, by all accounts. A property business, isn't it?'

'Yeah, so?'

'I just thought you should know he's paid people to dig up information about you. That's all. I have to go before he suspects something. But be warned, Cas. He's determined to bring you to your knees, so I suggest you protect everything of any value to you.'

'Grace, love,' Cas said, urgently, 'keep the phone hidden, or, better still, memorise my number. Grab some money and get to the airport. Then call me. I'll give you all the details of where to go. Just get out of there, okay?'

But just as Grace was about to speak, a noise outside the bathroom made her heart stop. She gasped, freezing for a moment, straining to hear. Before she could say goodbye or end the call, the bathroom door exploded inward as though a bomb had gone off.

She had been crouching on the floor beside the bath and speaking to Cas in what she thought was a quiet tone. But, clearly, she hadn't been quiet enough. She hadn't even heard Kenny coming up the stairs.

The door flew off its hinges, smashing into the mirror tiles and shattering them into jagged shards. The sound was so violent, it vibrated through her bones and assaulted her eardrums.

Grace curled tighter against the cold tiles. Her ribs were screaming in pain. She knew what was coming next. She glanced up, her eyes blinking wildly, as Kenny reached down to snatch the phone from her hand.

'Please, Kenny, listen to me—'

'Shut your mouth!' he roared, as he ripped the phone from her trembling hands. His eyes narrowed at seeing the small screen.

Grabbing the phone from his wife, he held it to his ear and hissed in a deep, venomous tone, 'Is that you, Cas? Come on, you fucking two-faced cunt, answer me. Or are you too embarrassed? Well, you can be assured that I'm fucking coming for *you*.'

He yanked the phone away from his ear and stared at the blank screen before smashing it against the wall.

Then, without warning, he lunged forward, grabbed Grace by her arms, and dragged her to her feet. 'You fucking whore,' he spat, while digging his fingers into her arms. 'You sly bitch!'

At that moment, Grace truly believed he was going to kill her. She struggled to catch her breath, but then her eyes caught sight of Tandy, who stood there like a frozen statue, behind her father.

Her daughter. Her only hope. Grace pleaded silently with her eyes, begging Tandy to help. But there was no immediate reaction – just an uncertain hesitation.

It wasn't until Kenny pulled his fist back that Tandy finally stepped forward. She grabbed his arm, her voice sharp. 'No, Dad! Don't. Or else you'll end up back inside, and I don't want that! She ain't worth it.'

Kenny hesitated, his arm still raised, his breathing ragged.

Grace could see the realisation sink in as Tandy's words resonated somewhere in that evil brain of his.

Although relieved by Tandy's intervention to stop the violence, Grace was heartbroken over the reason her daughter gave. It was so clear that Tandy didn't give a shit about her. It was always about her father. He came first in their family, and in her eyes, he could do no wrong. That was the case even when everyone else knew what a bastard he was and how he had crossed a line when he had carried out his last big job.

No villain with a moral compass would ever side with Kenny. Not in a million years. It was only the money-hungry lowlifes who had done so. The likes of Cas and his crew were appalled and refused to stand by him. They did nothing to stop him from going to prison. They had the means. But although they had witnesses who could have come forward and lied to save Kenny, there was no way that would ever have happened. Cas had made it clear that he wouldn't piss on Kenny, if he was on fire.

Finally, Kenny let go of his wife and stormed from the hallway, with Tandy on his heels.

Grace knew then she had to escape. She just had to. Because she was looking at the balled fist of a killer. In fact, she might as well have been looking down the barrel of a gun. Kenny could have her murdered at any time. He knew it, and so did she.

CHAPTER SEVEN

It was the following day when Billy parked up and headed towards his apartment.

'Evening, Mr Murphy.'

Billy was lost in his own thoughts as he entered the main entrance to his complex. 'Oh, er, sorry. Good evening, Clive. Any mail?'

Clive stepped out from behind his desk and handed Billy three letters.

Billy rolled his eyes. 'More junk mail.' He handed them back.

Just as he was about to press the lift button, he paused, spun around, and returned to the desk. 'Clive.'

'Yes, Mr Murphy?'

'Call me Billy. And listen, if Bronte shows up here, stop her, would you?'

'What? Bronte? But—'

The fact that Clive was about to question him made Billy raise a brow and incline his head. The subtle gesture clearly put the fear of God into the man, who immediately clamped his mouth shut and waited.

'Ask her for her keys, but under no circumstances let her in. She's no longer welcome.'

'Of course, Mr . . . er, Billy, er, but . . .'

'That's all, Clive. No buts!'

Billy gave Clive a curt nod and walked away. He was feeling the sharp tug of guilt clenching his throat. He didn't like speaking to people as if he was lording it over them, but he wasn't in the mood for pleasantries.

***

The apartment seemed unnervingly quiet, even though Billy lived alone for most of the time. Perhaps it was the sudden forced mental separation he had tried so hard to impose. In a matter of hours, he had convinced himself that he could shut Bronte out of his mind and move on. But her face, her cheeky smile, and that coy expression of hers kept creeping back in. Anger surged through his thoughts as he wondered if her coquettish countenance was nothing more than an act. *But she couldn't have kept that up for all these years, could she?*

Standing in his lounge, he stared out of the vast floor-to-ceiling windows that stretched the length of the room and framed the stunning London vista. He'd chosen this apartment for himself, not only for its breathtaking views but also because it was the largest unit in the building and it offered a decent room for Jesse as well. This place had been his first major project. It was a vision he'd planted so vividly in his mind that he'd been determined to see it through to its final conclusion. The designer had taken his ideas and laid out what the old building could become after its conversion. The result was perfect. The ground floor exuded class, with a grand entrance hall and on-site security that monitored the property around the clock.

Billy loosened his tie and took a long breath. The space was immaculate, with every surface gleaming with the kind of luxury most people could only dream of. The plush leather sofa, the state-of-the-art Dan D'Agostino sound system, which he'd had imported from the States, and the outstanding view of London and the river all screamed success. He had the business, the Surrey Quays pad, and the lifestyle to go with it. But the one thing he didn't have now was *her*.

Bronte had arrived in his life just at the right time, having lost Willow to that raving nutcase Irvin. It had felt like something out of a dream. Her sweet smile, the way she always seemed to know what to say, how she looked at him like he was her world. She had made him believe in second chances – well, almost. But trust didn't come easily to him. And without it, there was no future for them both.

As Billy tossed his keys onto the granite worktop, he caught sight of Bronte's overnight bag near the sofa. His jaw tightened.

'The fucking cheeky bitch,' he muttered, the words escaping before he could stop them.

Striding towards the bedroom, he fully expected to find her sprawled across his sheets, but the room was untouched, just as he'd left it. She wasn't in the ensuite, either.

Billy stopped outside the second bedroom, his hand hovering over the door handle of Jesse's room. His heart hammered in his chest as memories flooded back. They were of Willow, the unspoken tension between him and Jesse, and, finally, the promises they'd made to move on and never let something like that come between them again.

He clenched his fist, took a deep breath, and opened the door.

It was empty.

The neatly made bed, the few possessions Jesse still kept here, the faint scent of his cologne – it was all untouched.

Billy exhaled, his chest still tight as he closed the door. Jesse was spending most of his time in North London now, but he still held a claim to this place, to this room. That was their deal when they bought the apartment together.

Quickly, his mind returned to his girlfriend – his ex-girlfriend. What was Bronte playing at, by leaving her bag here? His stomach churned as a mix of anger and unease settled in.

Billy grabbed his keys, stormed out of the apartment, and slammed the door behind him. He took the stairs, two at a time, his footsteps echoing in the narrow stairwell, each one fuelled by a simmering rage. Waiting for the lift would have only made him angrier.

When he pushed open the door to the lobby, he found Clive half-asleep.

Clive was leaning back precariously in his chair, his eyes barely focused on the monitors. The moment Billy appeared, Clive jolted upright and nearly toppled over.

'Is everything okay, Mr Murphy?' he asked, nervously, smoothing his uniform.

Clive didn't want to upset Billy. He was a good boss, he paid well, and he wasn't the type to nitpick. But there was no mistaking the tension radiating off him tonight.

Billy ignored the pleasantries. 'Was Bronte here?'

Clive nodded. 'Yes, that's what I was trying to tell you earlier.'

Billy glanced around the lobby. 'Where did she go?'

Clive cleared his throat. 'She went up to the apartment but then came right back down. But she was talking to someone on the phone when she left the building. And then you came in shortly afterwards, Mr Murphy.'

Billy ran a hand through his hair. He nodded absently. 'All right. Listen, if she comes back, you make sure you take her keys, because, Clive, she's no longer welcome here.'

Clive straightened up further, feeling uncomfortable, but obedience was the watchword with this young guy. And he depended heavily on this job.

'Sure thing, Mr Murphy.'

'Right, and actually, Clive, don't let anyone go to my apartment except my family, including Cas. If anyone asks about me, Cas, Bronte, Jesse, or literally anyone I'm associated with, you tell them nothing,' Billy instructed, firmly.

Clive, a man in his fifties, suddenly realised something serious was happening. He nodded, his face tense, as he grasped Billy's words. 'Of course, Mr . . . I mean, Billy.'

Billy gave the man a firm nod before returning to the stairwell. He hurried back to his apartment, grabbed Bronte's overnight case, and left without any hesitation.

***

The drive to the site didn't take long. The caravans loomed in the distance, their shapes familiar yet unyielding, like relics of a life Bronte had never entirely escaped from. Her father's caravan stood in his usual spot; it was flanked by her two brothers' homes on wheels.

Bronte had grown up here, and Billy suspected having never lived in a house, she would have regretted leaving the comforts of his sleek apartment, which must have left their mark. She'd marvelled at the push of a button that brewed coffee and the hum of a dishwasher that saved hours of scrubbing. He could tell that she had warmed to the quiet luxuries – a bubbling pot of pasta carbonara on his stove, with music playing softly in the background, and the sofa that seemed to hug her into relaxation. Compared to that, mucking out horses at dawn must have felt like a distant memory; it was certainly one he knew she wasn't eager to revisit.

Billy remembered how her voice cracked when she admitted she longed to leave her father's home. She wanted out of that life, away from the endless cycle of travellers' expectations. His family had taken to her with open arms and had even encouraged an engagement. His mother, Carrie, especially understood. She had once lived that life, though she'd walked away from the old ways a long time ago.

Billy eased his second car – one of three – this one a Porsche Cayenne with a V8 engine – on to the site, an hour's drive from his apartment and just twenty minutes from his parents' home, its headlights sweeping over the gravel road, as he crawled forward along the dusty lane.

Benny's caravan stood out like a king's throne. It was more prominent than the rest, with a firepit always smouldering out at the front, no matter how inclement the weather.

Billy had been here a handful of times to pick up Bronte. He was often greeted by a circle of gypsy men gathered around the flames, their laughter and low voices blending with the crackle of the fire. Sometimes, the women joined in and began cooking on the open flames, their hands quick and practised. But today, the site was eerily quiet. Although a fire still glowed faintly, no one stood near it.

Billy pulled up outside Benny's caravan and cut the powerful engine, his gaze lingering on the flickering light in the living room window. Benny sat alone inside, slumped in a chair, his figure outlined by the warm glow of the lamps. He looked older now. Perhaps he was worn down by years of hardship, or was the problem that the man was worried about what his sons and his daughter had been up to? Because a man like Benny understood reprisal. But even though he had never lived on the right side of the law, he had always tried to keep the dramas to a minimum.

Billy scrutinised the caravan and then looked for any other movement on the site. But there was no sign of anyone else as far as he could tell.

A sudden, sharp bang on the passenger window jolted him. Billy's head snapped around, his heart racing.

Franklin stood outside, his face twisted with fury, his dark eyes drilling into Billy through the glass.

Billy chuckled at himself for feeling uneasy and laughed even more when the wind caught Franklin's Elvis quiff. It flapped at such a ridiculous angle that he looked more like Daffy Duck than the King himself.

Shaking off his initial nerves, Billy stepped out of the car, opened the rear passenger door, and grabbed the overnight bag.

In one swift motion, he shoved it hard into Franklin's stomach, his eyes never leaving the man. His nostrils flared as he growled, 'You tell your sister to stay the fuck away from me, and she can post her keys back. I'm done with her.'

Franklin staggered slightly, now caught off guard. He was mortified that Billy had the audacity to drive on to their site and start mouthing off. What unnerved him more, though, was that Billy showed no signs of being intimidated whatsoever.

Franklin swallowed hard, his bravado faltering.

Before returning to the driver's seat, Billy jabbed a finger in Franklin's face. 'And you'd best tell the likes of the Shipleys to stay the fuck away from me too. Because let me remind you, it isn't *me* who owes them – it's fucking *you*.'

The blood drained from Franklin's face. 'Shit . . . they paid you a visit, did they, Billy?'

Billy smirked, and then his tone dripped with sarcasm. 'Why do you look so shocked, Franklin? After all, you're the one who told them I'd found your gear in my – I repeat – my property and sold it on. What the hell did you expect? Especially from men like the fucking Shipleys. I know their reputation, and so does everyone else.'

Franklin's mouth opened, but no words came out. He'd assumed the Shipleys would have beaten the life out of Billy. They weren't exactly known for letting people off lightly.

Billy's voice dropped, his fury palpable. 'You know what, Franklin? You really are a piece of work. A proper cunt, aren't you? Well, just so you know, I *was* going to marry Bronte. I had it all planned out – I was going to ask for her hand on her birthday. The ring? That cost me as much as your caravan and your shitty vehicle put together. But you, Archie, and that dumb, backstabbing sister of yours fucked it all up. And then you sent the Shipleys after me? What the hell do you take me for, eh? A right mug?'

Franklin stood there, speechless, his face pale, all bravado completely stripped away.

Billy took a step closer. 'If you or your brother come near me again, believe me, I'll do you serious harm. So take that as a warning – and be grateful you still have your fucking kneecaps intact. See, now, cunt, you've got me so riled up, I'm swearing again, and I fucking hate swearing.'

Franklin held up his hands, his voice shaky. 'Billy, listen! You don't understand. We had no choice. I swear to you on me muvver's life! We didn't!'

Billy's anger flared, and the pressure in his head felt as though it might split his skull. Instantly, he grabbed Franklin's face and dug his fingers deep into his cheeks. Brutally, he squeezed them together until the man's lips puckered grotesquely.

'Your mother's already in her grave, so don't you dare start all that gypsy take oath bollocks,' Billy spat, his voice deadly calm. 'And don't give me that *no-choice* crap. You *always* have a choice. But you, Franklin? You and your ugly fat fucker of a brother made the wrong one.'

Shoving Franklin away, he watched him stumble slightly before he regained his footing. 'Now, fuck off, stay the hell away from me, and make sure your sister gets the message too.'

Billy didn't wait for a reply. He turned sharply, his steps purposeful, as he returned to his SUV.

Franklin stood motionless, now clutching his throbbing face and holding Bronte's bag. He watched silently as Billy reversed at speed along the makeshift drive and out of the site, the tyres crunching over gravel.

The sound of a door creaking open tore Franklin away from the cloud of dust that Billy had left behind. His father, Benny, leaned out. 'Has he gone, Franklin?'

'Yeah, Farver. He's gone.'

Benny waved him inside, his voice low. 'Get in, boy, afore the others start fucking curtain twitching, the nosy bastards.'

Franklin hurried up the steps, the overnight bag still in hand. 'He brought Bronte's bag back,' he muttered. Holding it up, he then dropped it onto the worn sofa.

Benny's face darkened, and his voice rose sharply with anger. 'I fucking knew it. I knew you shouldn't have got involved with the likes of the Shipleys. They're bad news, Franklin – not our kind of people. What the hell's the matter with you, boy, eh? Eh?'

Franklin opened his mouth to speak, but Benny held up a hand. Shaking his head, he sank heavily into his chair, now completely out of breath. 'You're a fool, Franklin. A proper bloody divvy. And now look what you've done. You and Archie, you think you can deal with those gangsters? You're fools! Fools! The pair of you.'

'But—'

'Shut ya mush, Franklin. I told you not to get mixed up with men like that. Because when things go wrong, they go wrong in a big way. You really thought you could get in with those men, didn't ya?' he said, shaking his head. 'Well, now, see what's happened. Our Bronte's lost everything. That little girl has missed out on all that money. That man – Billy – he's rolling in it and going places. Proper wealthy. She could've had it all and maybe even bought her old dad a new caravan, something decent to live out his days in. But no. You and your bruvver have bollocksed it all up!'

Benny's chest heaved as he struggled to catch his breath, his anger momentarily giving way to frustration. His voice was bitter. 'And now I'll probably die in this rickety old thing. And as for our Bronte? She'll end up marrying some traveller who's likely twice her age. She ain't the virgin, is she? Second-hand goods now. You fucked it up for her. And me, I can't forgive you, and I doubt if she ever will, either. She loved him, she did.'

Franklin shifted uncomfortably, but he didn't dare respond.

Benny leaned back, shaking his head in disgust, his muttered words trailing off as he stared at the overnight bag on the sofa.

CHAPTER EIGHT

Jesse arrived home shortly after midnight to find Billy lounging on the white leather sofa with his feet up and going through some paperwork.

'All right, Billy? I thought you were gonna join me at Mum's? That Sunday roast was out of this world.'

Billy glanced up, looking distracted. 'What? Oh, yeah . . . sorry. I got carried away with work. But I'll be over next Sunday. I'm not working over the weekend.'

Jesse wandered into the kitchen and opened the fridge. Staring at the neatly stacked food, he noticed that everything was in its place. It was just how Billy liked it. His brother could be a little OCD at times. The dishwasher could be a bone of contention. Billy wanted everything loaded in the proper way.

'Any beers?' he called out.

'No. You drank the last four.'

Jesse shut the fridge with a sigh and returned to the lounge. Pulling off his jacket, he threw it over the back of the white leather armchair before sitting down. 'You sure you're all right, Billy?'

Billy placed the paperwork on the table and sat up straighter. 'Yeah, of course, I am. Why?'

Rising to his feet, Jesse walked over to the windows and admired the view. 'You've been with Bronte a long time, so surely, it's worth talking with her. Maybe get her side of the story. What d'ya say?'

'I've no need to, so leave it.'

'Listen, you're me bruvver, right?' Jesse sighed heavily, with frustration. 'We had a pact, Billy – me and you against the world. And now you're hiding something from me. I can tell you are, not through my training but because I know you. And we never hide anything from each other, do we?'

'Just leave it, Jesse,' Billy muttered, his voice low.

'Billy, whatever it is, it must be bad, so I wanna know what's going on?'

Jumping to his feet, Billy then paced the room.

'Bronte and her brothers weren't in it alone, all right? They were working with the Shipleys.'

'I'm a bit surprised about that, Billy boy,' Jesse said, as he turned to face his brother, who had stopped pacing the room and was now sprawled out once more on the enormous sofa.

'Well, I can't get my head around it either. Bronte might not be bright in the academic sense, but she's streetwise. She would've known exactly who the Shipleys were before messing with them.'

'Yeah, well, that's a given. Everyone who's anyone knows who that fucking lot are,' Jesse replied. 'Christ, there's a lot of them. Two are on remand, awaiting trial for a double murder, and two are already inside. Even then, there's still plenty of them walking free. They should all be behind bars – all of them – because they're not wired up right. Why Bronte would even look their way, let alone have any dealings with them, God knows.'

Billy shook his head. 'Maybe she likes a bad boy and thought getting in with their kind would be more exciting than being with me.'

And there it was – the real reason Billy was so down, Jesse thought. His brother was jealous.

'Oh, come off it, Billy boy. Bronte loves you. I see the way she stares at you when you're not looking. So, I don't think that's it at all. That's why I reckon you should talk to her.'

'It's clear to me, she never trusted me enough to talk,' Billy shot back. 'No, she just mugged me off, and then she had the fucking cheek to talk her brothers into persuading me to marry her. Well, I'm done. I told her brother earlier to tell her to stay the fuck away from me.' He suddenly stopped talking for a moment and glared at Jesse. 'Did you say *two* of the Shipleys are on remand awaiting trial for a double murder?'

Jesse nodded. 'Yeah. Well, as it happens, Redwood's promoted me to lead investigator. They really thought they were getting away with it.' With raised eyebrows, he smirked. 'Didn't I tell you about it? Shit, no, I didn't. I was going to, but then Ginty rocked up.'

'Oh, right, were you?'

‘Yeah, yeah. So, anyway, these two geezers – Max and Moriarty. What kind of fucking name is Moriarty? Seriously?’ Jesse laughed, shaking his head. ‘Well, anyway, they got pulled in over this double murder – a husband and wife. Poor cow was seven months pregnant, too.’

He paused, his expression darkening, the weight of the statement lingering.

Billy didn’t need to ask to know where Jesse’s thoughts had wandered. It was a silent reminder of Willow – pregnant and murdered, her life stolen in a flash.

‘Go on, Jesse,’ Billy prompted, gently.

‘Sorry, yeah. So, Redwood said he wanted me on his team. He reckons the way I handled those two in the interview room showed I’ve got the makings of a decent detective.’ Jesse gave a small, proud smile. ‘We had enough to charge them, and now they’re awaiting trial.’

‘So are you not bothered that the Shipleys were part of this marijuana grow in the basement of one of our apartments?’

Jesse shook his head. ‘No, not at all. The Shipleys wouldn’t link me to the apartments, and besides, they’re not only organised criminals, they’re chancers too.’

‘Oh, okay, so no link, then?’

‘No, I don’t believe so. They have businesses all over London. They want to fucking run the place and maybe they see the pikeys as little soldier ants. Who knows?’

There was a pause while the two brothers assessed the significance of the Shipley family.

‘Maybe, you’re right,’ said Billy, eventually.

‘Billy, just remember this. Every member of the Shipley family has spent time behind bars at one point or another – even the old girl. What’s her name again? Oh yeah, Candice Shipley. A bit like Ma Barker, she is. Back in the day, people were terrified of her. Hard as nails, a proper nasty piece of work.’

Jesse walked away from admiring the view outside and retook his seat. Removing his shoes and then taking off his polo shirt, he continued, ‘And then there are her sons, and *their* sons. Every man in that family’s bad news. There’s not a good one among them. It’s as if they are trying to outdo each other – a competition to see who can have the longest criminal record. And they're a shameless bunch of wankers. They're forever flaunting their wealth – fucking flashing it about – and no one has yet been able to prove they are laundering it all. The brand-new motors, the houses, the fucking villas, it's a right piss-take. They even own a posh housing development.' He chuckled. 'Well, they all live in close proximity to each other, at least. Like fucking sewer rats!' He looked directly at Billy. 'Do you want me to tell Redwood and pull them in over it? Although you'd best tell Ross to get shot of the plants quickly.'

Billy listened intently, nodding along, to let Jesse know he was paying attention, even though he didn't want to give away his thoughts. He had felt uneasy when Reece and Dario approached him, but he wasn't going to admit that to Jesse. 'I've already done that, mate.'

'Fair enough. The less I'm involved, the better, Billy.'

Deciding to change the subject, Billy asked, 'So, how's Mum and Dad?'

Jesse smiled. 'Same as always. But our Nellie – well, she's gonna be a handful, I'll tell you that much. I've only been away a month, and, cor, I come back, and our little sister is a woman with legs up to her armpits and hair down to her arse. She towers over Mum now, and she's the spitting image of Aunt Dilly. I can't believe she's wearing make-up an' all!'

Billy laughed. 'I know! I saw her last week at Bluewater. She was swanning about the place with her mates like she owned it. Still, at least she's not a loner. I do feel for her sometimes, though, with Charlie forever chaperoning her. The poor girl daren't look at a lad – Char would beat seven bells out of them.'

Jesse laughed, too. 'Well, they've always been close. Like me and you.'

'Yeah, which is a good thing,' Billy replied.

'Mum told me Char got his collar felt – for fighting. And it was over Nellie. Some bloke pinched her backside.'

'They never told me,' Billy said, looking almost hurt.

Jesse paused before replying. 'You don't go around to see them often enough to know what's been going on, and it hurts Mum, you know. She still leaves a place mat out for you at Sunday dinner, just in case you show up. Would it really hurt to go a bit more often? Especially when I'm staying in the North London digs.'

Billy shook his head. 'To be honest, Jesse, I've just been so busy. Between work and Bronte, I haven't had the time.' He sighed heavily. 'Well, without Bronte to consider, I'll be there this coming Sunday for dinner – that's for sure.'

'Great. Well, I'm shattered. I'm hitting the sack,' Jesse said, stretching his arms before heading for his room.

'Me too,' Billy replied, as he watched Jesse saunter into his bedroom and shut the door behind him.

Billy sat for a moment longer, the quiet settling around him. As he got up, he grabbed his phone from the coffee table and scrolled to Cas's number. Pressing the call button, he brought the phone to his ear. It rang and rang before going to voicemail.

'Damn it,' Billy muttered, thoroughly annoyed. The fact that Cas was not answering wasn't unusual in itself, but it never failed to get under his skin, especially now, after hearing some bloke making threats down the phone.

First thing in the morning, he decided, he'd head over to Cas's place and get to the bottom of it. Whatever was going on, he wasn't in the mood for any more secrets.

As he headed for bed, he couldn't shake off the gnawing feeling that things were about to take a turn – and not for the better.

Pushing open his bedroom door, his chest tightened at the sight of Bronte's silk nightdress neatly folded on the bed. It was like a searing needle piercing his ribs. Blindly, he stepped forward and grabbed it, the fabric cool and incredibly soft against his fingers. He could momentarily see her standing there, the silk clinging to her perfect curves and the deep-red colour accentuating her sun-kissed skin and long jet-black hair.

He clenched his jaw. Anger surged, ripping away the lingering tenderness. Instantly, he threw the nightdress into the corner of the bedroom, as if by holding it, he was condoning her behaviour. It landed crumpled on top of an empty box – the same one that had held the perfume he'd bought for her. It was the one she used to dab on her neck with a smile that now felt as though at the time she had really been mocking him.

Billy stood there, staring at the discarded fabric as his stomach churned, the thought sickening him.

Trying to sleep proved to be a no-no. His mind refused to stay still, so wrapped up in his own thoughts – none of which were appealing. The events of the day played out on a relentless loop. The fight with the Penfold brothers was harsh, and perhaps, he had gone over the top. And then ditching Bronte – Christ, the way he'd done it. That wasn't him. That wasn't who he was.

The memory of her lingered, raw and tangled with guilt. Each image stood starkly in his mind as he went over and over how he had belittled her. He'd treated her like shit by fucking her as though she was nothing but a common whore. What the hell was the matter with him? He suspected his brother knew what the problem was. But he hadn't brought the subject up. *Was Jesse still afraid of him, even after all these years?* he wondered. He wished Jesse had said something. At least it might have helped extinguish all the pent-up anger inside him. Instead, he was feeling the way he was because of the way he'd taken out his anger on her. He shouldn't have done that. It made his stomach churn again. He couldn't shake off the look in her eyes when she'd realised what he was doing – what he wasn't saying to her.

The part that really didn't sit right with him, though, was the idea of the Shipleys joining forces with the Penfolds. It made no sense. The Penfolds were gypsies, proud of their independence, never needing anyone to tell them how to run their business, however tiny and illegal that was because they knew it wouldn't carry too much risk of bird. The Shipleys, on the other hand, thrived on control and were rich. They were big-time gangsters, not plastic ones. They supplied the likes of the Eastern Europeans with drugs, so why the hell would both families come together?

He stared at the ceiling, the faint glow of moonlight casting jagged shadows. He could feel it, like a splinter buried too deep to dig out – nagging, persistent, and impossible to ignore. He could see Bronte making eyes at Reece or even at Dario, eager to be a part of their lot.

Just as his body began to surrender to sleep, Cas's face flashed into his mind. The look he'd shown when he mentioned getting the builders in was strained, as though he wasn't telling the whole story. And then there was that menacing phone call.

He had brushed it off at the time, but now, in the dead quiet of the night, it bothered him.

Glancing at the clock on his bedside table, it showed 4:00 a.m. With a sigh, he grabbed his phone and tried Cas again. The ringing seemed to drag on forever before it went to voicemail, the same as before. 'Damn it, Cas,' he muttered, throwing the phone down onto the bed.

Billy lay there fretting as he stared at the ceiling. Cas could handle himself – of that there was no doubt – but something about the whole situation felt off. And he knew himself well enough to admit that he wouldn't rest until he'd got to the bottom of it.

Sleep was a lost cause now. He tossed and turned, his mind restless and his chest tight with unease. When he finally gave up and rolled out of bed, it was 8:00 a.m. He rubbed his face, feeling the kind of heaviness that came after a night of too much booze – even though he hadn't touched a drop.

Dragging himself to the bathroom, he went across to the classy sink with its hands-free sensors, splashed cold water on his face, and stared at his reflection in the mirror. 'Sort it out,' he muttered, under his breath, as if saying it aloud would make it easier.

By the time he was dressed and ready, he had made up his mind. He was going to head to Cas's place first thing to get some answers – whether Cas liked it or not.

Jesse had already left the apartment; he was probably off to see one of his many girlfriends.

Billy inwardly smiled. He was almost wishing he could be more like Jesse. His brother had a way of shrugging off heartbreak. In fact, he never felt heartbroken. He would merely hop from one girl to the next without a care in the world. If one dumped him, he'd laugh it off and move on to the next pretty face, never letting it dent his sunny disposition.

But he, on the other hand, wasn't hardwired in that way. When he fell in love, he did it full-on. First Willow, now Bronte. Both times, it had left him gutted. He could still feel its ache and rawness. Jesse might tease him for being too serious, too invested, but he couldn't help it. When he gave his heart, he gave it completely.

Leaning back against the bathroom door, he let out a long sigh. Maybe Jesse had the right idea. Perhaps adopting a couldn't-care-less approach was the best way to prevent anyone from getting close enough to hurt him. A little thought entered his brain: *stand up for what you believe in – be true to who you are.* After all, there was no point in wishing he was someone he wasn't.

CHAPTER NINE

Deciding to skip breakfast, not that he was hungry, Billy drove straight to Cas's house to find out what the hell was going on.

Once he had negotiated heavy traffic on his way out of the City, he was able to put his foot down on the A21 to Wadhurst. He didn't expect to find Cas there but he had to try since the man wasn't answering his calls. However, a glance up the drive as he entered the property was enough to suspect that Cas wasn't at home. Everything looked very locked up. The shutters on the windows were closed, the two double garages were also shut, and, most unusually, the second set of gates that led to the rear of the house were also closed.

Using his key fob to open the main gates, he drove up the gravel drive and parked directly in front of the main house. He had a key and would have usually knocked first, but, for some reason, he decided to walk straight in. As soon as he opened the door, he felt uneasy, as if someone was watching him. He spun around only to find that no one was there.

'Cas!' he yelled, but there was nothing but silence. Slowly, he walked towards the study, where Cas liked to spend most of his time, now that he was into stocks and shares or his attempt at mastering them. Pricking up his ears, straining to catch the faintest sound, all he could hear was a steady tick-tock from the grandfather clock. He shuddered. He couldn't shake off the feeling that he wasn't alone. But there was no sign of anyone. *Was the place haunted?* he wondered.

Deciding that it was pointless to check out the other rooms in the enormous house, he pushed open the French doors and stepped outside. The wind whipped around his ears like a whispering phantom that sent chills racing down his spine.

When he reached the stables, he found the doors were shut. Cas only had one horse – Goliath, which had been Willow's horse, and he was kept there to simply enjoy the rest of his life.

But where was he? He doubted he would have been left here with the doors closed.

Something was definitely not right. Cas had told him that he was going away because he was having the builders in. But where were they? There were no builders, no building materials either, and the furniture wasn't even covered.

With his gaze fixed on the doors to the stables, their dark silhouette suddenly plucked at his memory. Why on this particular occasion he should feel this was not at all clear to him. After all, it had been many years since he had witnessed Keith's death here in the stables. But he put it down to the way he was feeling. The run-ins with the likes of the Penfolds and the Shipleys and the threatening tones from the voice at the end of a phone had all left him feeling slightly uneasy. And that was not like him at all.

Deciding to check on Goliath's whereabouts, after a brief hesitation, he opened up the stables and went inside. If the huge old horse was in there, then someone would need to release him, especially in this heat.

A sharp scent of hay and damp wood hit him before he saw that the horse was gone.

Hurrying outside, he scanned the fields, desperate to spot any movement, but they were empty of any animals. It seemed that the entire property was deserted.

Panic surged as he spun on his heel and bolted back into the house. He tore through the study, yanking open drawers only to find them gutted, their contents missing. The furniture was all that remained. Everything else of value had been stripped away.

'Shit,' he muttered, under his breath. 'What were you running from, Cas?'

Then he heard it – the sound of breathing behind him. Slow. Deliberate. Someone was in the house – in the study.

Billy didn't move. His eyes flicked across the desk, desperate to find anything that could be used as a weapon. A letter opener, a knife, even a heavy paperweight. But there was nothing. His fingers twitched, and his heart hammered as he forced himself to turn around.

'He was probably running from me.'

The voice was low and gruff, the kind that demanded attention. Billy froze. Was that voice vaguely familiar? Turning round, he faced a man who was built like a bulldozer – with broad shoulders, thick arms, and a chest ready to burst out of his shirt. He wasn't just big: he stood there with the confidence that made it clear he was used to getting his own way.

Swallowing hard, Billy felt the man's eyes boring into him. The tension was oppressive. It felt heavy and suffocating as if the walls themselves were closing in.

Rarely did Billy feel scared of any situation or, indeed, any person. His boxing experience had instilled in him a survival instinct that had come in very handy over the years. But there was something about this man that screamed 'psychopath'. Was it the cold, unforgiving look in his eyes, perhaps? Or was it the memory of facing Irvin Slade for the first time? Now, he was a complete nutter.

Shoving the thought aside, he held his ground and fixed the man with his trademark blank, unflinching stare, telling himself he was just as dangerous – and he hoped even more so. He knew how hard he could hit someone and the damage he could do if it came to a physical fight.

Normally, this would be enough to unnerve anyone. But this bloke didn't flinch. Instead, he grinned, and it wasn't the kind of grin that indicated he was nervous. Quite the opposite. The intruder was enjoying this confrontation.

'Where's Cas?' The man's voice was sharp and demanding.

Billy shrugged casually, but his pulse quickened. 'I have no idea. I came here to find him myself, so if I knew the answer to that, I wouldn't be here, would I . . .?' He let his eyes drag up and down the man, slowly and deliberately. 'Who said you could come in?'

The man laughed. 'The door was open, and, in any case, I don't need a fucking invite. I want a word with the cunt who lives here, so I'll ask you again: where is he?'

Billy shook his head. 'Are you thick or something? I just told you, I don't know where he is.'

'Well, let's get this clear, right? I'm assuming you're Billy Murphy, Cas's business partner.'

The man smirked as though he had a hold over Billy.

But his smirk disappeared when Billy merely stared at him poker-faced.

'I'm here to collect what's owed to me.'

Billy shrugged again. 'Knock yourself out, then. Take a look-see.'

'Where is he likely to be? You're his little rent boy. You must know his habits,' the man spat.

'Like I said, I came here to find him myself. And I take it you were the geezer shouting down the phone. I thought I recognised your voice.'

'Good. That's right an' all. And you, Billy. You are Billy, ain't ya?'

Again, Billy stayed poker-faced, deliberately not answering.

'Well, I take it you're Cas's gofer. You'd best know I'm owed a lot, and I'll be taking what's due.'

The man smirked again and pointed his finger around the room. 'And this lovely manor house? It's mine, for starters. Ten years in the nick – I can see meself living here, like lord of the manor. Ya see, I would've easily made enough money during that fucking time to own all this.'

He pointed at Billy. 'So you tell Cas that I'm coming back, and he'd better have the deeds ready in my name, Kenneth Ruck, or he'll know what happens if he don't. He'll fucking know.'

Turning to walk away, he faltered and spun around. 'And like I say, that's for starters.'

His wink riled up Billy, who shot back, 'I'm not passing on any message because contrary to what you believe, I'm no rent boy or Cas's gofer. So, do your own dirty work! It's got fuck all to do with me!'

He shook his head, trying to keep his cool, but the look on the man's face suggested that a fight might be about to happen.

'You *what*? Do you fucking know who I am?'

'Kenneth. You said your name's Kenneth Ruck, which means fuck all to me. So, if you don't mind, I've got my own business to attend to!'

'You've got balls, I'll give you that. But you'd better understand this: if it's business connected to Cas, then it's *my* business because that cunt owes me a lot. And I will bleed the old man dry. And if it's a joint venture you have with him, then tough tits. See, I don't give a shit. I will take it all as compensation.'

Placing his hands on his hips, Billy grinned. 'I take it you've only just got out of the nick? A long stretch, you said. So that means you've got a probation officer. I bet they've got no idea you're creeping into a man's home uninvited and handing out threats. 'Cos you and I both know they'd have you locked back up in a flash.'

Kenny's eyes widened. 'You don't think I came here without doing some prep, do ya, ya clever cunt? Well, do ya?'

Billy shrugged. 'I don't give a shit.'

Kenny's face twisted in rage, his nostrils flaring, as he glared at Billy. But something about the calmness on the lad's face made him step back. 'You think I'm scared of my probation officer, you prick? I'm no mug. And you, I take it, you're a little grass, are you? I would have thought Cas would have been 'aving it with straight-up men, not little grasses.'

Billy sighed. 'If you think I'm going to sit back and take your insults and threats because you think you're some hard man, then think again. You don't know me. Only *I* fucking know me. Now, fuck off.' His hand hovered over the phone, making it clear that he was ready to make that call.

Kenny wanted to punch Billy in the face, but something stopped him. It was something he'd never seen in anyone before, not least in someone as young as this. Something that tested his kudos. He jabbed a finger in Billy's direction but lowered his irate tone. 'I've been keeping tabs on things, and I know you're Billy Murphy. I know Cas has welcomed you into his firm—'

Billy put his hand up, cutting him off. 'I'll stop you right there, Kenneth. Cas and I are not in together in any firm. You reckon you did your prep? Then, clearly, whoever fed you information got it wrong. I'm not in Cas's firm. Far from it. Not that I need to explain myself to you. But since you've gone to such lengths to find out, I'll put your distorted record straight. I am *not* one of Cas's men. I'm as straight as an arrow, and I've no interest in what Cas or his firm get up to. I own my own legitimate business. I have done for years. So don't tarnish my reputation by suggesting I'm in any fucking firm.'

Kenny clenched his fists, his face twitching, as he struggled to hide his anger. 'You're full of it, ain't ya, Murphy? You might run your little business, but don't think for a second, I won't take you down with Cas, 'cos as far as I'm concerned, anyone, and I mean anyone, who backs that cunt Cas is an enemy of mine.'

Billy stepped forward, his eyes cold and unflinching. 'If you think you can rattle me, you're wrong. I've been through more shit than you could stomach. So, leave me out of your beef with Cas, or you'll find you may have cut off more than you can chew.'

Kenny lunged forward, poking a finger into Billy's chest. 'Is that right? You don't wanna make an enemy of me. Believe me, you don't.'

Billy was raging, now furious that the man had poked him in the chest. However, before he could react, he heard the front door close with a bang. The sound was so loud that it reverberated through the hallway and into the study.

Kenny spun around to see who had barged in and found five men standing there. None of them looked familiar.

Billy stepped back, his survival instincts kicking in. He had no idea what the hell was going on. He had never seen these men before. The aggressive expressions on their faces, combined with their muscular physique, made his heart rate skyrocket.

The tension in the air thickened as the men fanned out, their faces cold and unreadable.

Billy glanced at Kenny, who looked just as stunned, but he quickly masked it with a hardened glare.

'Who the fuck are you?' Kenny demanded.

The man at the front, taller than the others and with a scar slicing down his lip, took a step closer. His shadow loomed over Kenny like a storm cloud. 'It doesn't matter who we are,' he said, his voice low and sharp, cutting through the air. 'What matters is what the fuck are you doing here?'

Before Kenny could answer, the man lunged at him. His hand shot out, clamping around Kenny's throat like a vice. With his other hand, he yanked a gun from his pocket and jammed it hard against Kenny's temple.

'I know who you are,' he hissed. 'And I'm here to give you a little reminder or call it a warning of what happens if you so much as glance in Cas Ferrier's direction. Bold as brass, here you are in his house.' He leaned in closer, his breath hot and sour. 'You cheeky fucker.'

Kenny clawed at the man's hands, his fingers scrabbling, but the grip only tightened.

'Lads, take this lairy cunt to the van,' the man with the scar snapped. 'And put a bag over his ugly mug.'

He shoved Kenny away, letting him crumple to the floor, as though he could have been a heart attack victim, who was now choking and gasping for breath.

Billy's fists curled at his sides, his pulse hammering. Trouble. Big trouble. These men weren't small-time players, and he knew it.

'What do you want?' Billy demanded, his voice hard, daring them to turn their attention to him.

The scar-faced man sneered. 'We're not after you, Billy. It's this prick we want.' He pointed to Kenny, who was sprawled on the floor, red-faced and seething. 'He's a bully. He beat his wife to a pulp. And now he thinks he can threaten Cas.' He let out a short, sharp laugh. 'He crossed a fucking line, he did.'

Billy glanced at Kenny, whose bloodshot eyes burned with hatred. 'I won't let this go. You fucking mark my words, Billy Murphy.'

The scar-faced man snorted. Lashing out with his boot, he slammed it into Kenny's ribs.

Kenny let out a grunt and curled in on himself.

'Shut it, you,' the man snapped, again. He gestured to the two brutes flanking him. 'Get him in the van. This prick needs to be taught a lesson.'

Billy wished he hadn't even bothered going to Cas's house. He felt as though he was on the receiving end of so many threats that it was starting to feel like some kind of nightmare.

Standing there, watching the men drag Kenny – kicking and bucking – through the front door, Billy didn't bother asking who the men were or what they planned to do with him. All he knew was that this wasn't any of his business. He was just about to lock the French doors and make his way home when he heard footsteps behind him.

Spinning around quickly, he groaned. 'Oh, for God's sake, Cas! What the bloody hell is going on, eh?'

Cas waved his hand, dismissively. 'Calm down, Billy. I've got it all in hand. At least you're not hurt. That bastard's a fucking crystal short of a chandelier, I'll tell ya. I'd thought of selling up and moving to Cyprus, but then, of course, I thought about you.'

Billy raised his eyebrows. '*Me?*'

'Yeah, you. See, that Kenny is a dangerous man – a bit fucked up in the head,' he said, twisting a finger into his temple.

'So?'

'Yeah, well, he made threats to hurt you. And I thought, I can't fucking have that, can I? So, anyway, I decided to stay in the country and have a word with the firm.'

'The firm? Cas, I've never seen those men before – they were like five gorillas who had escaped from London Zoo.'

'I'm surprised you didn't recognise them.'

Billy shrugged and shook his head. 'I've never seen them in my life, Cas.'

'Four of them are Walter Whistler's sons, and the tall fucker with the scar is Dennis's son. Keep it in the family, I say.'

'How come I haven't seen them here before, then?'

'Because, son, I don't have their faces seen around my place. My other business . . .' He looked down. 'My naughty business, I keep away from here and away from you.'

Billy sighed. 'And there's me thinking you've gone straight.'

'Oh, leave off, Billy. Anyway, it's all fine. There is nothing for you to worry your handsome little head about. It doesn't interfere with our business.'

Billy rolled his head and tutted. 'I'm going home.'

'Billy,' Cas said, as he grabbed Billy's arm. 'Listen to me, right? I returned because I care about you, although you keep that to yourself. I don't want people believing I've gone soft. That Kenny is dangerous, son. Don't underestimate him. He doesn't care. He hasn't got a moral compass. He'd knock over an old lady if he could nick her purse. I mean, he's a fucking vile human being . . .' Cas looked down, almost in shame. 'I ain't afraid to put a man on his arse, even though I'm older now, but the likes of Kenny Ruck? Well, he's cruel.' He took a deep breath. 'So young Denny, the tall cunt, Dennis's son, he said he would take Kenny for a ride and kick the cockiness out of him.'

'Kenneth said you owe him. So, then, why not pay him what you owe?'

Cas smoothed down his Hawaiian shirt and straightened his back. 'There are some things that don't sit right with me.' He paused and stared out of the window. 'Goliath's at another stable, and my fuckers, I mean heifers, are also at another farm, in case he hurts them.'

'You're changing the subject, Cas. This Kenneth geezer said you owed him.'

Cas went across to his high-backed chair behind his desk.

Billy followed him and sat on the chair across from him.

'Ten years ago, we did this job – a complicated one – and Kenny came on board. Me? I'd never have worked with him, but, as it happens, he knew the bloke with the plans to this vault.'

Billy nodded for Cas to carry on.

'We used two vans – one that Kenny drove and one Keith drove. Kenny had a young lad, Micky, with him. The youngster was only there to load the van and do the grunt work. Me, Keith, and Paddy Pickwick were in the other van. All went well until we heard a police siren.' He sighed heavily as if reliving the ordeal. 'Now, instead of panicking, we drove normally, like you do. We didn't draw attention to ourselves. Kenny, on the other hand, drove off like a fucking nutcase. The back doors of the van weren't locked properly, and young Micky flew out. Well, the poor fucker hit the kerb with his head so hard that he died on impact. And I'll tell ya, he was a right nice kid an' all.'

'Oh shit.' Billy's voice was barely above a whisper.

Cas paused, his eyes locked on nothing. 'Yeah. And here's the kicker. Not only did that bastard not lock the doors, and Micky end up losing his life, but Kenny carried on driving like a lunatic. He swerved around a corner, shot up on to the pavement, and mowed down a little lad who was on his way to Cubs.'

Billy threw his hands to his mouth. 'Jesus. Did he die as well?'

Cas swallowed hard and looked away. 'No, the poor little fella didn't die. He ended up in a wheelchair, though.'

'So that's how Kenny got caught, was it?'

Cas shook his head slowly. 'That bastard didn't stop. Didn't even try to help. He just ran that kid down and carried on, until, eventually, the police chase became a serious affair. Finally, they hemmed him in and dragged him out at gunpoint.'

Billy saw the pain etched on Cas's face. 'And you got away with your stash? That's why he says you owe him?'

Cas shook his head. 'No. He reckons we should've paid off the jury and bribed everyone to get him out. I told him during a visit that I hoped he rotted in hell. Every penny of that money we got – we gave it to the boy's mother, anonymously.'

Billy knew Cas was telling the truth. For all his hard exterior and ruthless reputation, Billy knew that the man had a heart of gold.

'So, anyway, knowing what a ruthless bastard Kenny can be, I thought it best to come and make sure you were okay. I clocked your car along the A21. I guessed you were on your way to mine. And besides, I had young Denny watching ol' Kenny. They followed him here. He won't be making that mistake again in a hurry.'

CHAPTER TEN

A week later

The following Sunday as Billy approached his parents' house, he could smell the roast beef before he even opened the back door. The steam from the veg had misted the windows, and the hiss and crackle of roasting potatoes made his mouth water.

As Carrie spun around, her flushed cheeks glowed, and her smile reached her eyes. 'I'm so glad you came, my big boy.' She turned off the gas under the pan of boiling cauliflower and held open her arms.

Billy naturally walked into them, hugging his mother and leaving the embrace with a gentle kiss on her cheek. 'Smells good, Mum. I've got to say, I do miss your cooking.'

Carrie slapped his arm. 'Well, no one's stopping you from showing your face. Christ, I was beginning to forget what you looked like! In my mind's eye, I still see you as my little boy. But look at ya! Six feet tall and a grown man, a handsome one an' all.'

Before Billy had the chance to ask who was over for dinner – having seen the substantial industrial pots and pans – Charlie breezed in.

'Billy boy!' he said, his face lighting up. 'I thought you'd emigrated.'

Billy ruffled his brother's hair like their mum used to do with him. 'You won't get rid of me that easily. And, little brother, Jesse tells me the police had a word with you.' He raised a brow and stared.

'I had a fight, that's all. Fucking hell, you've had more than me, Billy.'

Carrie poked Charlie in the chest. 'Enough of the language, you. You don't hear your bruvver swearing, now do ya?'

Charlie laughed. 'He's the only one who don't in this family.'

No sooner had he said it than Jesse called out, 'Mum, when's dinner gonna be? Me fucking stomach thinks me throat's been cut.'

'See? Anyway.' He turned to Billy. 'Good to see you, Billy. Sorry to hear about the upset with Bronte.'

Billy rolled his eyes. 'Jesse's got a big mouth.'

Carrie poured hot water and cauliflower through the strainer and turned back to see Billy's face. It was a picture of sadness. 'You are back together though, ain't ya, Billy? In fact, when you called to say you were coming for dinner, I assumed she'd be with you. I've set a table mat for her as well.'

Billy shook his head. 'No. And, Mum, as much as you – and the rest of the family – like her, she wasn't the girl for me.'

'Oh, come on, Billy. We all make mistakes, and part of a good marriage is sometimes letting them go and moving on.'

'Oh yeah, Mum? Has Dad ever mugged you off?'

Carrie used her apron to wipe the perspiration from her face. 'Well . . . no, as it happens. But that don't mean me and him agree on everything.'

Billy gave her a sympathetic, almost patronising smile. 'Mum, she proper mugged me off to the point that I can't trust her.'

'But you two are making a go of it, though, aren't you?'

Billy looked at his mum, his expression hardening.

'No, Mum. I've explained why.'

'Oh, I see . . .' Her eyes narrowed in a look of puzzlement.

'What's up?' asked Billy, sensing there was more to come.

'I saw Benny last night. I was picking your farver up from the pub. The silly sod had way too much to drink. Mind you, your grandfarver had a skinful as well. The pair of them were like two drunken sailors.'

'Mum, what's that got to do with Benny?'

'Sorry, Billy. So I was guiding them into the car and Benny walks past. I said I was sorry to hear about Bronte and Billy's breakup and hoped they could work it out. And he said that he thought you two had because she hadn't come home, and, like me, he thought she'd gone to yours and stayed.'

Billy's eyes widened. 'No, she never stayed, and we never made it up. In fact, virtually the minute after I split up with her,

Ginty saw her with her head in someone's car window. That was over a week ago. Even Ginty thought she was enjoying the chat, so I assumed it was some bloke. Perhaps she went off with whoever he was, but one thing's for damn sure – she ain't with me.'

Carrie nodded and placed a gentle hand on Billy's arm. Her voice softened. 'Are you all right, my boy? I know you liked her a lot.'

Billy exhaled deeply, his shoulders sagging slightly. 'Yeah, Mum, I'll be fine. I've got enough to keep me busy.' But the slight tremor in his voice betrayed his real thoughts.

Before Carrie returned to her cooking, she opened the fridge, pulled out a bottle of cold beer, and handed it to Billy with a small smile. 'I saved it for you, love.'

Billy took the bottle, kissed her cheek again, and wandered into the lounge. The sound of laughter and chattering voices greeted him as he entered to find Jesse, Nellie, and his grandparents, Luanne and Jed.

'Ahh, there's our Billy!' said Luanne, jumping up from her armchair, her arms outstretched. 'Come and give us a hug. And you need to visit more often.'

After hugging her tightly, as Billy pulled away from her, he noticed something for the first time – his grandmother was getting older. The wrinkles spreading to her cheeks were more prominent, and flecks of grey framed the sides of her jet-black hair. Yet even with these signs of age, her looks were still striking. Like all her daughters, she had huge eyes and an olive complexion that gave them a Mediterranean glow. They were Romany gypsies who had left the old ways behind, having traded in caravans for nice houses and discarded some of the traditions – especially those that once restricted the women.

Nellie rose from the sofa and swanned over to Billy, her long hair loose around her face, swaying as she walked.

'Hello, Billy boy,' she said, in a slow, sultry voice, sounding far more womanly than the last time he'd seen her.

He kissed her cheek. 'Too much make-up, Nellie. You're pretty enough not to slap that stuff on.'

'Oh, shut up! Not you an' all. I get it off Charlie all the time.'

Jesse smirked and winked at Billy. 'She's too free-spirited, our Nellie, to even listen.'

'Yep, she's just like her muvver,' said Jed, nursing a beer and with an eye on the football. 'She won't be told, that one. The wild one, I call her.'

Luanne eased herself back into the armchair. 'He's right. You, my beauty, are so much like your muvver was back in the day.'

Sunny waltzed into the room, his presence loud and cheerful as ever. He nudged Billy with a grin. 'I'm sure your mother watered you with Miracle-Gro – you seem to get taller every time I see you. Nice whistle.'

Billy smoothed down his suit jacket and grinned. 'Yeah, I thought I'd make the effort.' With that, he slipped it off and left the lounge to hang it up in the hallway, his mind already drifting back to Bronte and the unanswered questions swirling in his head. Further thoughts spiralled into the dark image of her with another man. He tutted to himself, thinking that it was a good job he'd rid himself of her if she could go off with someone else so soon.

'Billy,' said Jesse, as he joined him. 'Billy, after dinner, can we go to the apartment? I want to talk to you.'

'What about?'

'The Shipleys.'

'What about them?'

Jesse looked over his shoulder. 'Let's enjoy dinner and go back to the apartment to talk.'

Billy saw Charlie helping their mother carry food into the big dining room. It was usually used for Sunday dinner and at Christmas because the table could seat the whole family and more.

He smiled. 'Okay, but are you all right, Jesse?'

'Me? I'm just dandy.' His face beamed, and he gave his signature cheeky wink as if he was up to something. It was a look that most women found charming.

After everyone had finished their dinner and were slowly retiring to the lounge again, Billy scooped up two more crispy potatoes and a Yorkshire pudding onto his plate and poured a generous helping of gravy over the top.

Meanwhile, Jesse swigged his beer and rubbed his belly.

'That's me done for the day. All I need now is a nap,' he said.

Billy looked up. 'I'll finish this, say goodbye to Mum, and meet you back at the apartment.'

Carrie wandered into the dining room and placed her hands on Billy's shoulders. 'Are you sure you don't want chocolate gateaux for afters?'

'No, Mum, not for me. I'm enjoying your roasties.' He put his cheek to her hand. 'I missed this. I think I spent too much time in Bronte's company and neglected the best things in my life – you, Mum, and my family, and the food.'

'Oh, give over, Billy. I've heard how you dine in the best restaurants, spoiling Bronte with lavish meals. I bet you bought her expensive gifts an' all, didn't ya?'

Billy pushed his fork through the gravy, not meeting his mother's eyes. 'That was true. Past tense. I did. I treated her well, Mum.'

Carrie's face hardened, her hands finding her hips. 'Yeah, I know you did, and she fucking repays you like this? Well, fuck her. You can do better, anyway.'

Carefully setting down his knife and fork, Billy's shoulders stiffened, as he looked up at his mother, who dropped onto the chair opposite him.

'I always said she was no good for you.' Her voice was sharp, but her eyes softened when they met his. Before she could say more, Sunny wandered in, wiping his hands on a tea towel.

'No, you never, Carrie. Bloody hell, love, you liked Bronte. You even wanted Billy to have a big lavish wedding.'

Carrie rolled her eyes, at that last remark. 'Well, I want the best for me boys, and obviously, she ain't the best. She didn't go back to Billy's like I thought she would – she fucked off with some other bloke. And come on, Sunny, how long did that take her? What, five sodding minutes? Nah, I'm sorry, but the girl's not who I thought she was, and my Billy boy can do so much better. Look at him, Sunny.'

With a large grin on his face, Sunny couldn't have been more proud of his son. Looking at Carrie, he said, 'Yeah, yeah, Billy's handsome, rich, and could have any bird he wants.'

Although his father was clearly teasing him, Billy laughed. Everyone was used to his mother boasting about her children's talents. And God help anyone who said any different.

'Exactly, Sunny.'

'How's business, Billy?' Sunny asked, leaning against the large oak cabinet, with another easy smile.

'All good, Dad, all good. The apartments should be finished and occupied by Christmas, and then we can start on another project.'

'Good lad,' said Sunny, with a glint of admiration shining in his eyes.

Jesse kissed his mum on the cheek and said, 'I'm off. See you in the week. That is, if I get a day off.'

Smiling softly, Carrie waited for Sunny to leave the room before she turned her attention back to Billy. Her voice dropped as she leaned closer. 'So, I guess we will be seeing more of you, sunshine. Well, at least I hope we will.' She glanced behind her to make sure no one was eavesdropping. 'I think our Nellie needs a word or two. She's getting a little bit too big for her boots. We can all see she's a looker, but she's parading around like she's the queen bee. And I don't want her getting into trouble or getting hurt. So maybe you could bring her into line. She won't listen to me. And you know how girls can be – a little bit of jealousy, and, well, I dread to think. But maybe if she sees more of you, 'cos she does look up to you, Billy.'

She flicked a glance at Jesse as he headed out the door. 'And she looks up to you too, Jesse. She runs poor Charlie ragged because he's another one she won't listen to. And dare I say it but your farver lets her get away with blue fucking murder. His little princess can do no wrong.'

Billy gave a tired smile and nodded. 'I'll make more of an effort. I guess I have let work and . . . Bronte get in the way.'

'Finally, you can see it for yourself, Billy. Anyway, see you back at the apartment,' Jesse said, before he scooted away.

A few minutes later, it was Billy's turn to leave.

Carrie cupped Billy's face and kissed his cheek. 'Now, my boy, don't fret yourself about Bronte. These things happen. You were building a good life for you and the woman you thought was the one. I can't blame you for putting everything into it.' She smiled again. 'You look after yourself, Son. See you soon.'

Just as he was about to leave, Ginty turned up. Barging in like a one-woman tornado, she dragged in two massive carrier bags and had a scowl on her that could curdle milk.

'Carrie Ann, sorry I'm late. That bloody taxi driver took the long way around. You won't believe it, but the cheeky sod's still outside waiting to be paid! Told the greedy cunt he can stick his meter where the sun don't shine before he gets a penny out of me.'

Looking around the kitchen, she spotted Billy and frowned. 'What? No Bronte?'

Billy shook his head. 'No.'

Ginty threw up her hands. 'Dear Lord, what is it with you, Billy boy? Never more than one flaming word comes outta your gob. It's like pulling teeth! If you ever ended up down the nick, no brief would need to tell you twice to say no comment. It's a fucking given.'

It was enough to provoke a response from Billy. Slowly, he cracked a grin and went over and gave her a warm hug. For as much as Ginty could wind him up – and she did, a lot – she could come out with some great lines, and this one was one of her best.

'So, is me dinner in the oven?' Ginty craned her neck around Carrie, eyeing up the massive kitchen range as though it owed her money.

'Yes, Ginty,' Carrie said, with her hands on her hips. 'I dished you up one, with extra Yorkshire puddings.'

Licking her lips like a starving cat, Ginty eyed up the Sunday roast. 'Made 'em yaself, did you, girl?'

Carrie tutted. 'Of course I did.'

Ginty's face lit up as she elbowed Billy. 'Your muvver knows how to cook. I reckon she learned some of that from me.'

Carrie's face twitched as though she'd just sucked on a lemon.

It was a paradox to anyone who knew this family well that there had always been this love-hate relationship between the two women.

Carrie could have reeled off a list as long as one's arm of ways that Ginty had been the world's worst mother-in-law. But that would have totally misrepresented who Ginty – her ex-mother-in-law – was and what she had done for Carrie's family. If it hadn't been for Ginty, arguably, Billy and Jesse may well have been in prison after killing Irvin and Danny Slade.

So the relationship between Carrie and Ginty had always been bitter-sweet.

As for Ginty, she knew that Carrie would have cut her off faster than a bad perm. But when she took the blame for the two men's deaths, she knew that she had played an ace and, boy, was she milking it for all it was worth.

'What you got there, Ginty?' Carrie asked, eyeing up the bags. ''Cos you can sit at me table, but you ain't moving in.'

Ginty shoved the bags onto the kitchen table. 'Now, listen, girl, I had the thief round at mine. He said I could have the lot for fifty quid. Have a gander. It's all the latest designer gear in them there bags. Will do your Nellie a treat.'

'Did I hear my name mentioned?' asked Nellie, who had swanned into the kitchen. But when she saw Ginty standing there, she stopped dead and glared at the woman. 'What are you doing here – again?'

Even Billy didn't like her tone. For all the grief Ginty had caused in the past, she'd never done Nellie any harm. And it was disrespectful to talk to any adult who had been invited into their home.

'Oi, Nellie!' Billy snapped.

Nellie's smart expression vanished, and she suddenly looked more like the young girl she was, rather than a cocky madam.

'Actually,' Ginty said, lowering her voice and looking uncharacteristically sad, 'I got these for you.'

Nellie flicked her long hair over her shoulders and stared at the bags. Part of her itched to dive in, but the other half wrestled with her stance on Ginty. She'd heard the stories and was lately acting as though she was the family's matriarch by thinking she could behave however she pleased, with the support of the others. But now, she'd had her comeuppance.

Glancing back at her brother, she found his eyebrow raised, and she knew she had to apologise.

'Sorry, Ginty.'

Ginty nodded, gently. 'No harm done, love. Anyway, have a look – they're yours if you want them.'

Nellie opened one of the bags and glanced around to see Billy and her mother watching her. She slid out a dress, which she knew all the girls at school would be drooling over. Holding it against her, she knew it would fit like a glove. 'Wow.'

'I thought you might like it.'

It didn't take Nellie long to dive in again and pull out a top. Her eyes widened. 'Shit, these are right nice. Thank you, Ginty.'

'Go on, girl, take them to your room, and have a good try-on.'

Billy clocked how Nellie snatched the bags and scooted off, with not even a gentle kiss on Ginty's cheek or a hug. Not that Nellie and Ginty were related, but it was all about respect, and he worried that his little sister was severely lacking it.

As soon as Nellie was out of sight, Ginty flopped onto a chair at the kitchen table. 'So, you're not back with Bronte, then?'

Billy shook his head. 'No, and I won't be. That's all done and dusted.'

Ginty lifted her chin. 'I saw Benny. I was over at the site, and he thought you two were back together because he said she hadn't come home. Mind you, Billy, if you do get back with Bronte.' She held up her hand. 'I'm not saying you will, but you might wanna bear this in mind. Old Benny wants to see you two married because he reckons you'd buy him a new van – a state-of-the-art one – with all your money. He said, "No husband of my precious daughter would ever let me live out my life in that battered wagon of mine."' She wagged her finger.

Billy shrugged. 'He's got two sons and a daughter who think they know a thing or two about business. They can buy him a new van. They won't be knocking on my door again.'

Ginty suddenly burst out laughing, her face turning pink. 'I heard you nearly took ol' Archie's ears off! That'll teach 'em.'

Billy rolled his eyes. He didn't like his business or his methods being discussed at the family home. His mother was the last person he'd want worrying about him – she'd had enough years of worry to last a lifetime.

Swiftly saying his goodbyes, he hurried out the door before Ginty could say anything else. He knew she was nosy. She probably went to the site to see Benny and find out what was going on with Bronte. Still, as much as he promised to spend more time in the family home, there were a few things niggling him. Top of the list was the issue involving the Shipleys, but running a close second was this threat from Kenneth Ruck. It was probably best to stay away from his parents' place for the time being and concentrate on work.

CHAPTER ELEVEN

'So, what's going on, Jesse?' asked Billy, as he plonked himself on the sofa. Jesse had arrived at their apartment ahead of him and he was halfway through a bottle of beer.

'So, when I said to you that I wasn't worried about the Shipleys . . .' Jesse paused, his brows knitting together.

Billy sat up straight, his attention locked on Jesse. 'Go on, Jesse.'

'I could be wrong, overthinking shit, because I'm trying to work with a detective head on,' Jesse began. 'But when I went into the office, right, Redwood asked me if I was okay taking the lead on the Shipleys. He said he was called on to another case – something to do with a minister getting assaulted, but that's supposed to be confidential. Anyway, I looked around the office, and there was Wesley Jameson, who's been there longer than me and has way more experience, but Redwood's put him under me.'

Billy jumped up, his movements sharp. 'Jesse, you look worried, mate.'

Jesse sighed, his shoulders sagging. 'When we were younger, I always wanted to be a copper.'

Billy nodded, slowly. 'Yeah.'

'Even though I knew some could be bent, I thought, nah, not me. I'll be one of the good guys, one of the decent coppers. But now . . . now, I'm getting paranoid, like I'm watching them instead of watching the bad guys.'

'Watching who?'

'Well, Wesley for starters. He's an okay bloke, but there's something off about him. He looks a nervous wreck, and his phone is never out of his sight. Not just that but when it rings, he jumps, as if the thing fucking bites.'

Billy shrugged as if to say, *so what.*

'And then there's Shona Shaw, right? She's always looking over her shoulder, and when she's at her computer, she has this look, like she's watching something she shouldn't be.'

'Porn?'

Jesse laughed. 'Who knows. But she's another one who doesn't seem quite kosher. She's also sneaking off without telling me where she's going.'

'The shits?'

'Maybe.' Jesse chuckled.

'Hmm,' said Billy. 'Is it just those two you're not sure about?'

'No! There's also Dave Hammond. He's recently been taking his calls outside the office, and when he returns, he comes back kinda flustered. And get this: he's another one who just ups and goes and never lets me know where he's off to.'

'An affair, maybe?'

'Yeah. Could be. D'ya think I'm just being daft?'

'Not at all. But it sounds to me like you're working on a psychiatric ward, not a murder squad,' said Billy, pacing, his hand rubbing the back of his neck as if to massage the tension away.

'Seriously, if you don't feel comfortable, just fucking leave. It's not like you need the money.'

Jesse leaned forward and placed his bottle carefully on the coffee table.

'No, I don't want to leave. I just want you to know – that's all – that there could be something going on.'

Billy stopped pacing abruptly and stared at Jesse, his expression hardening. 'Whoa, hold up a minute. What do you mean? Are you worried that— '

'All right, I'll be honest. See, the more I looked into the Shipleys' case, the more I kept thinking back to what you said about their visit and the small, insignificant grow in the basement. And I kept thinking about the word *insignificant*, and I came to the conclusion that the Shipleys never do anything on such a trivial scale. So why would they work with two pikeys who have no clout whatsoever and have a small grow in your property?'

Billy was nodding, his jaw tightening. 'Listen, Jesse, it's been on my mind for a day or so, especially since you told me you were on the team working on the Shipley case. Of course, it's no coincidence.'

'Fuck! Billy, they're gonna blackmail us, aren't they?'

Billy nodded, his eyes narrowing. 'Those scumbags did this deliberately to get in my face and make me believe I owe them something, and the way to repay it is to get to you.'

Jesse wiped the sweat from his brow. 'Shit.'

'So what would they want? Let's start there,' Billy said, as he sat down and leaned forward, his elbows on his knees.

'You know what, Billy? You ought to have been a copper – you're a heck of a lot smarter than me.'

Billy tutted. 'No, I'm not, Jesse. I've just got an eye for making money, but, obviously, I make mistakes too, like trusting Bronte – the bitch.' He sighed heavily. 'Tell me, what are your thoughts on Redwood? Is he legit, do you think?'

Jesse scratched his head and let out a small laugh. 'Well, let's just say I came into the force as green as a Granny Smith. Even after all that grief in the past, I still thought it was all good cops and bad guys – like the movies. And bent coppers? I figured they were as rare as rocking horse shit. But now, I'm not so sure.'

Billy smirked. 'And Redwood?'

Jesse grinned. 'Sorry. I was kinda rambling, just then. Well, anyway, Redwood's fast-tracked me, and I gotta admit, Billy, I was buzzing at first. But then I thought – hang on – there were way better detectives he could've picked. And now, he's got me leading a case when there's a dozen more qualified than me. So, d'ya think he's setting me up deliberately?'

'Sounds to me like you're doubting yourself. Let's face it, Jesse – you've got a gift, mate. A lot of people lack what you've got. You could charm a confession out of a bloody psychopath. People warm to you. You're not just likeable but you stand out in a room because of your personality.'

Jesse snorted. 'All right, Oprah Winfrey, calm down. Are you trying to make me cry or something?'

Billy laughed. 'Just telling it like it is, Jesse. So maybe Redwood's straight, and the Shipleys got wind of who's running the case. What would they want from you?'

Jesse shrugged, his expression clouded. 'Moriarty and Max are on remand. The case is in three months, so I've got no idea.'

Billy leaned back, rubbing his chin. 'We need to figure this out before those bastards make their next move.'

Jesse bit his bottom lip. Leaning back on the sofa, he shut his eyes and went into deep-thought mode, as though he was about to solve the Da Vinci Code. 'That's another oddity, though. The Shipleys setting up a grow in the basement? I mean, marijuana plants don't grow overnight. How tall were they again?'

Billy frowned, his brows pulling together. 'A good three feet, actually. Jesse, you're fucking right, mate. See, that's the detective in you. I was in the basement only a couple of weeks back, before the plants were there. They couldn't have grown that tall that quick, even with all the gear.'

Hearing some brotherly support, Jesse smiled, leaned back, and crossed his arms. 'Exactly. Unless your name's Jack, and they were magic beans, it's definitely a set-up. They knew you'd get rid of them ASAP because they already know you're as straight as a nun at Sunday Mass.'

Billy sighed. He felt as frustrated as his dad did when trying to assemble IKEA furniture.

'Jesse, when those plants were put in the basement, it wasn't about growing anything. It was about creating a shitstorm to gain some control and use it as leverage.'

'Billy, that family's dangerous, and there are a lot of them. Maybe I should just leave the force – if, of course, we've got it right,' Jesse said, his tone more serious than usual.

Billy snorted. 'Well, we'll soon find out, won't we? Because I bet you, they'll be back, and when they do, I'll have fifteen grand sitting in my office ready to hand over. And if that ain't enough, maybe I'll have to hear them out – or get Cas involved.'

'Cas?' Jesse raised an eyebrow. 'He's getting on a bit, isn't he?'

Billy smirked and winked. 'His firm's suddenly grown legs. Dennis's lad and Walter's four lads are part of Cas's little company, shall we call it. And when I say they're built like brick shithouses, I mean it. Proper units, they are. I don't think Cas has it in him to retire. He likes the risk, the violence, and the power too much.'

Jesse nodded before his expression darkened. 'Why didn't the Shipleys come to me directly?'

Billy shrugged. 'Think about it, Jesse. If they went straight to you, you could nick them. You're still Ol' Bill, and they don't know you. They can't control your reaction. But they know me – probably through that bitch Bronte – and I'm not on the force, am I? And why would I go running to the police, especially after just binning a load of weed out of my basement?'

Jesse flung his arms into the air, the frustration clearly etched on his face. 'It's all very odd, Billy. Redwood putting me on their team was probably around the same time as those fucking plants were planted in the basement. It doesn't sit right. I am beginning to think someone's pulling strings. Or, like I said, I'm being set up.'

Billy's smirk faltered. 'What, seriously? You reckon Redwood's even done this deliberately because he's in with the Shipleys?'

Jesse nodded slowly. 'Maybe. There's something off about all this, Billy. Someone's orchestrating it, and I'm starting to think they're a lot closer to us than we realise.'

'Right then,' said Billy, getting up from the sofa, 'I'm not sitting here twiddling my thumbs. I'm going to pay Franklin, Archie, and Bronte a visit, if she's there. Mum told me today that she bumped into Benny last night, and he told her she hadn't come back.'

Jesse's eyes widened. 'Hang on, Billy! You can't just drive into the fucking gypsy site alone! They'll boil your bones in their bloody great cooking pot!'

Billy rolled his eyes. 'No, they won't. They don't bother me – they're all mouth. But I can't go to bed with all this shit rattling around in my head. I know you can sleep through anything, Jesse, but my brain doesn't have an off switch.' He glanced at his watch. 'It's not too late. I'm sure they're not in their beds just yet. Well, even if they are, I'll fucking wake them up.'

Billy moved to grab his jacket, but Jesse jumped up. 'Wait, I'll get me shoes on!'

'No!' Billy snapped, spinning around. 'You can't. You can't risk your job, and showing up there could cause you problems.'

'Fuck the job, Billy! If you're in danger—'

'I'm not!' Billy tutted, shaking his head. 'I'm not going there tooled up or anything. I'm just going to have a word, that's all.'

Jesse folded his arms, his expression sceptical. 'Yeah, because a *word* with you always goes so smoothly, don't it.'

Billy grinned, already heading for the door. 'Trust me, mate. I'll be back before you've even warmed up the sofa cushions.'

***

The firepit glowed faintly, the embers dying out and casting soft shadows across the quiet site. The pungent smell of horse manure mingled with the sweetness of roast pork in the still air. A couple of dogs barked in the distance, but they were swiftly silenced by sharp commands to belt up.

Billy rapped hard on Benny's door, the sound of his knuckles hitting the door echoing in the silence.

When the old man opened it, there was no defiance in his stance. No folded arms or a demand to know what the hell was going on. His shoulders sagged as he shuffled back to his worn armchair, leaving the door open for Billy to enter.

The moment Billy closed the door behind him, Benny glanced up, his expression darkening. 'Where's Bronte?'

A cold sensation crawled up Billy's spine. 'She ain't with me, Benny. We broke up, but you know that, though, don't you. I came here then, and I reckon you saw me through the window. Besides, I gave Franklin Bronte's bag and told him to give her a message from me, which . . .' He paused, a sardonic grin tugging at his lips. 'I'm sure he told you and half the camp. There was enough curtain twitching going on.'

'Yeah, Billy,' Benny muttered, sitting down in his armchair, his tone laced with suspicion. 'But that was around a week ago. She didn't come home, so I figured you two had made up – a lovers' tiff, they call it. I ran into your muvver last night and told her that.' His face hardened, his voice rising. 'Since you never wed her, like you *should've* done.' He jabbed a gnarled finger in Billy's direction. 'You know our ways, Billy. You know how it works. And I'd bet me life, me little girl was intact before you took her to your bed.'

A pang of guilt needled Billy, but he shoved the thought aside. 'Benny, I bought the ring. I was gonna propose. Not that I'm beholden to your *ways* because, as much as you cling to the old rules, I don't. And I never pretended I did.'

'No, mush, I'll give you that,' Benny conceded, grudgingly. 'Still, five years is a long time to be stringing a girl along.'

'Now, hold up a minute, Benny,' Billy shot back, his voice sharp. 'That ain't the case at all. Like I said, I bought the ring—'

'Words,' Benny snapped, cutting him off. 'Just words. And then you go and dump her like a used rag. My baby girl was born with beauty unmatched in my circles. She could've had her pick of men. But not now, Billy. Not now. You've used her, and now she'll have to settle for whoever's left.'

Billy rolled his eyes, his patience wearing thin. 'Oh, stop it, for fuck's sake. Do you even know what year we're living in? Anyway, forget all that. I want to know what the hell your boys and Bronte were told by the Shipleys?'

Benny's leathery face twisted into a sour scowl, his narrowed eyes gleaming with anger, his lip curling. 'You watch your mouth, lad. Coming into my home, demanding answers – you really do believe you're somethin', don't ya? Well, go and ask the fucking Shipleys yaself. You don't worry me.'

Billy sighed, ignoring the old man's rant. 'I came to ask you where Bronte is, Benny. But it seems you are as clueless as I am.'

Benny pushed himself out of his chair, only to break into a cough that started small but quickly turned into a full-blown fit.

Instantly, Billy was at his side and steadying him back towards his chair. 'I'll get some water.'

Benny waved him off with a weak hand. 'No, get the brandy.'

Turning around, Billy spotted the bottle of brandy. It was on a cabinet nestled between two porcelain shire horses. He hurried over, grabbed the bottle, and poured a generous measure into a chipped cup on the side table beside Benny's armchair.

'Here.' He handed the cup to Benny, helping him by holding it to his mouth.

Benny took two deep gulps, his breath settling, as he wiped his mouth with a threadbare handkerchief.

It was then that Billy's sharp eyes caught the smear of blood before Benny could hide it. 'Can I get you anything else, Benny?'

Benny's fiery glare had softened, his eyes sunken, suddenly looking every bit the old man he tried not to be.

'I get it, Benny. You want to see Bronte settled.'

Benny stared at the handkerchief in his hands, his voice quieter now. 'Yeah, Billy. O' course, I do. Left to her two bruvvers, she'll be in a lion's cage with no way out – the two fucking idiots. It's all their fault, ya know.'

'What is, Benny?' Billy asked, sinking into the armchair opposite.

Benny leaned back, his face drawn. 'Do you want a brandy, Billy?'

Shaking his head, Billy replied, 'Me? No, I'm driving. Tell me, Benny – what's their fault? What happened?'

Benny sighed heavily. Swirling the dregs of the brandy in his cup before meeting Billy's gaze, he said, 'They got her involved with the Shipleys, that's what. Franklin and Archie – they couldn't leave well enough alone. Now, me girl's caught up in their mess, and if she don't come back soon, I fear she won't come back at all.' He closed his eyes and took another deep breath. 'Billy, if she ain't with you, then who's she with, eh?'

For all intents and purposes, Billy wanted to offer his support, to side with Benny, and to play Bronte's knight in shining armour. But the thought of her disloyalty knocked that idea clean out of his mind. Instead, he leaned forward, rested his elbows on his knees, and ignored Benny's question. 'Benny, why did they put those plants in my basement?'

Benny's head bowed, his shoulders slumping under the weight of his admission. 'I suppose it was partly my fault.'

A frown flickered across Billy's forehead. He struggled to believe Benny had anything to do with this mess. After all, the old man wasn't known as a criminal, and he didn't have a reputation for being a hard man or a gangster.

Billy stayed quiet, giving a slight nod to encourage Benny to continue.

'I knew one day I'd leave this place,' Benny began, his voice heavy with regret. 'And with Bronte's dear muvver dead and buried, I drummed it into her head that she should always listen to her bruvvers. Do as they say because they'd always be her protectors – no matter what. Family's family, ya know what I mean?'

Billy nodded. He understood what Benny was saying all too well. His own family was tight-knit, bound together by unshakable loyalty.

‘So, when the opportunity arose to get in with the fucking Shipleys, me dinlo sons jumped at it. I told ’em. Don’t be fucking stupid, I said. The Shipleys are dangerous – there’s a lot of ’em – and I know from the past, and from what I’ve heard, they’re ruthless. They’ve got protection rackets, they run drugs all over the country, and that’s just some of it.’ He sighed and took another long gulp of his brandy. ‘We don’t work that way. Yeah, we’ll steal the odd pound here and there, but nuffin like the Shipleys. But me daft sons thought they knew better. Archie’s eyes were always bigger than his belly.’

Clenching his jaw, Billy stayed silent as Benny continued.

‘I was shook to me bones to hear they’d got me dear little Bronte girl involved. But, then again, maybe I shouldn’t have been. Like I said, I’ve always told her to do as Franklin and Archie said. Family first, no matter what. That’s what I taught her.’ Benny shook his head, his voice breaking. ‘I didn’t think it’d end up like this, Billy. I didn’t think they’d drag her into somethin’ so dangerous. And now I have no idea where she is or who she’s with.’

Again, Billy refused to offer support in searching for Bronte. As far as he was concerned, she was her own free spirit. Forgiveness wasn’t on the table. ‘Did Franklin tell you why they put plants in my basement that were almost fully grown?’

Benny shook his head. ‘No, I don’t understand all that business about growing drugs. Not me thing. I can lay your drive and get you a good price on copper, but other than that, I’m in the dark. You’ll have to talk to Franklin.’

Rising from the armchair, Billy’s movements were sharp with frustration. ‘And she never told you anything about the drugs in the basement? Or anything about my properties?’

Benny’s eyes, round and hollow with sadness, met Billy’s. ‘No, she didn’t, Billy. If she had, I would’ve talked her out of it. I wanted to see her wed . . . to you, Billy boy.’

Billy’s nostrils flared, his voice rising. ‘What, because you think I’d buy you a new van to live out your life in? Is that it?’

To Billy’s surprise, Benny grinned. ‘If you took me daughter away and gave her a good life, I’d go to me grave a happy mush.’

Tapping his foot, Billy stared at Benny, but the old man didn’t look fazed. Instead, his grin widened as though he was savouring the memory of some private joke. 'I always said, whoever my gal married, they'd better be rich enough to buy me a new van – a modern one. But that was more in hope and just me joking than anything else.'

Billy stared at him, the tension in his shoulders easing slightly. He shook his head, his voice quieter now. 'What a shame, Benny. What a fucking shame.'

Benny's grin faded, and for a moment, there was nothing but the sound of the firepit crackling faintly outside. A sinking feeling of dread overcame him, knowing that Billy had well and truly washed his hands of his beautiful daughter.

CHAPTER TWELVE

Billy had been gone five minutes – literally five minutes – when Jesse decided it was a bad mistake to let his brother potentially walk into a rats' nest on his own.

Looking for his shoes, he muttered to himself about how Billy always thought he could handle everything alone when a sharp rap at the door stopped him in his tracks.

'Forgot your keys, have you, ya numpty?' Jesse called, yanking the door open. But it wasn't Billy.

Instead, it was Dottie, her face a mixture of worry and determination.

Jesse peered over her shoulder, half expecting to see Spud, but she was alone.

'Mottie?' he said, stepping aside. 'What's up?'

Brushing past him as she walked into the apartment, Dottie headed straight for the kitchen. Her movements were brisk and focused as though she was on a mission, but that was her all over.

'Where's Billy, love?' she asked, grabbing a glass and filling it with water.

Jesse leaned against the doorframe. 'I'm just about to head over to the pikey site where Bronte lives. He's gone there alone, and the Penfolds aren't exactly happy with him, right now. He told me to stay here, but I've got a bad feeling about this.'

Dottie turned to face him, her expression sharpening.

'So he's gone on his own?' she asked, drinking the water in one go and then setting the empty glass down with a decisive thud.

Jesse nodded. Reaching for his jacket and pulling it on, he said, 'He's gone, and I'm not waiting around for him to get himself into trouble.'

Her eyes darted to the knife block on the worktop.

Jesse barely noticed as she slid one out and tucked it down the back of her trousers. She was already behind him when he left the apartment. Both of them skipped past Clive, who was half-asleep at his station, as usual, and headed for Jesse's car.

Once they were inside, Jesse wasted no time tearing down the road. The tyres screeched as he rounded a corner and shot her a sideways glance.

'All right, Mottie, what's the deal? Why are you here? What's going on?'

Dottie hesitated, the worry in her eyes deepening.

'I wanted to talk to Billy about something that's been playing on my mind,' she admitted, finally.

Jesse raised an eyebrow, still watching the road. 'Oh yeah? What's that, then?'

She bit her lip, clearly debating whether to say more.

'Jesse, has Billy told you about the visit he had from the Shipleys?' she asked.

Jesse's grip tightened on the steering wheel. 'Yeah, he mentioned it. We were talking about it just before he decided to head over to Bronte's to find out what the hell was really going on. Billy realised the plants were fully grown before being put in the basement. So he knew that something dodgy was going on. He believed the Shipleys were setting him up.'

Dottie frowned, processing his words. 'That makes no sense. Why would anyone risk transporting fully grown marijuana plants? Firstly, if they're growing nicely somewhere, why move them? Growing them requires an almost sterile environment. Transporting them risks leaving a trail – a distinctive smell, tongues wagging . . . Secondly, if fully grown, they'd be cut, dried, and bagged up ready for distribution.'

Jesse couldn't help but chuckle at the level of detail she knew. 'Grow them yourself, do you, Mottie?'

She smirked. 'Me? No. But they used to talk about it in prison.' Her face darkened. 'So, anyway, if someone planted a fully grown batch, then they're not using the basement to grow the plants. I think you're right. They're setting Billy up.'

'Well, here's the other thing, Mottie. Not only have I been given the lead investigator role, but I've also been promoted to detective sergeant. And there's something else I wanted to tell ya.'

Dottie's mouth fell open. 'Don't tell me you're on a case involving the Shipleys?'

'Spot on,' Jesse replied, his grin laced with mischief and tension. 'You know about the Shipley case?'

'Oh, come on, Jesse, who doesn't. It has been all over the news. Fucking scumbags. Dirty, rotten, filthy scumbags, the fucking Shipleys.'

Although the words were spat out through gritted teeth, Jesse's amusement faded when he realised she knew the Shipley family.

'How?' he asked, his tone sharp.

'How what?'

'How do you know the Shipleys? Tell me, in case it's linked. I need to know everything about them.'

Dottie stared ahead for a moment, her jaw tightening, as a memory flashed through her mind. The day Candice Shipley gripped her throat . . . She blinked, forcing the vision away.

'Okay,' she said, her voice faltering. 'Billy was named after a dear, dear friend of mine.'

When her voice cracked, Jesse glanced at her.

'Hey, Mottie, are you okay?'

She nodded, biting her lip to stop the tears from threatening to spill. Crying wasn't something she did. Not ever.

'Candice Shipley killed my friend Billy in cold blood right in front of me,' she whispered.

'Oh Jesus, I'm so sorry, Mottie.' A cold feeling ripped through him, and his hands gripped the wheel tighter. 'I . . . I've got a bad feeling about this, Mottie.'

Dottie saw the blood drain from Jesse's face. Whether it was from what she had just revealed or his own instincts were kicking in, it didn't matter. If she had to drive the car herself like Lewis Hamilton to get to her son quicker, she'd do it in a heartbeat. 'I'm calling Spud and James to meet us there. Just in case.'

***

As Billy stepped out of Benny's caravan, the faint scent of stale tobacco and grease lingered in the air behind him. He had only taken two steps towards his car when a wave of cheap aftershave hit his nostrils. It was followed by the sound of rushing air filling his ears.

The unexpected crack of metal against his skull was brutal, reverberating through his head like a thunderclap. Instantly, he dropped to his knees, the ground beneath him tilting as if the world itself had lost its balance. Pain flared hot and sharp at the base of his skull, but there was no time to register it fully. A second blaze of pain, this time across his back, sent him sprawling to the ground, face-first into the dirt.

A high-pitched ringing sound consumed his ears. It drowned out the muffled voices that swirled around him. He could only make out fragments of words that felt like echoes bouncing in his skull. Desperate to fight back, his mind screamed to move, but his limbs felt like lead.

However, moments later, his instincts kicked in, and a primal surge of adrenaline forced his brain to focus. Fight! Fight! Despite momentarily losing his vision, he tenaciously clawed at the dirt and attempted to turn over, so he could identify his attackers. But the pain was excruciating, making it almost impossible for him to move even a muscle. Nevertheless, at least he could be thankful that it was a reminder that he was still alive, and as long as he was, he could fight back.

Then came the blow from a man's boot. It slammed into his ribs with a force that stole the breath from his lungs, leaving him gasping like a fish on dry land. His mind fought against the growing darkness, desperate to stay conscious. If he blacked out, he knew he'd wake up in a shallow grave – if he woke up at all.

With a monumental effort, he managed to get on his back. At that point, he knew who his attackers were. Because even though his vision was still blurred, there was no mistaking the faces.

Archie stood there, his face red with fury, veins bulging in his neck, as if he was about to explode.

Franklin wasn't far behind, his quick, darting eyes gleaming with a manic light. He laughed as he danced around, throwing jabs into the air like a boxer warming up for a fight.

Two other men loomed behind them. Both wore stained vests that clung to their sweaty rotund bodies. They showed off more fat than muscle, but their hands were the size of shovels. They laughed along with Franklin, their laughter loud and forced, as if they were making a point. The sound grating in Billy's ears felt like nails screeching on a chalkboard.

Billy's stomach churned. He knew what was coming, and it wouldn't be pretty. The odds were stacked against him, and every second he stayed on the ground was another second closer to a beating he might not walk away from. But now, the flames of his rage flickered through him.

'You're a dead man, Billy Murphy,' spat Archie. He drew his leg back, aiming another kick at Billy's ribs.

But, somehow, Billy managed to fill his lungs and focus his vision. The moment Archie lashed out, Billy grabbed his foot, and with one skilful move, he twisted Archie's leg sideways.

Archie toppled over with a yelp of pain while clutching his knee. The whiff of alcohol confirmed he had been drinking.

Billy scrambled to his feet, every nerve alive with a jolt of raw urgency. But he could feel warm blood trickling down his neck, and he knew he was in trouble. With his back pressed against the car door, he tugged at the handle, only to find it locked. His plan to get inside and mow them down with the car was dashed.

He was still raging, but his energy was slipping away fast.

Franklin, who was grinning like a madman, charged at him with a balled fist.

Summoning every ounce of strength, Billy swung a right hook.

It landed smack bang on Franklin's chin. Instantly, he stumbled from the impact, his shocked expression conveying to Billy that he had never expected such force. His excitable laughter diminished instantly.

The two more prominent men were stunned by Franklin's momentary fall. Never in their wildest dreams had they expected Billy to stand up after the beating he had taken. Nonetheless, not wanting to come across as cowards, they charged forward. Their heavy steps shook the ground as they prepared to jump in, their shouts blending with Franklin's curses.

Billy braced himself, knowing the real fight was only just beginning. And being realistic, he knew he wouldn't win. He was seriously injured, and it was four against one.

***

Meanwhile, Jesse turned into the site, his heart hammering in his chest. The light spilled from the open doors of the caravans, and the growing crowd near Benny's told him something was very wrong. His combat impulse spiked as he fished out a small but heavy cosh from beside his driver's seat. Detective or not, he was always ready.

Jumping out of the car, his heart nearly stopped when he saw four men surrounding Billy. Two of them were dragging him away while Franklin and Archie continually booted him on the ground. The sight sent a jolt of uncontrollable rage through him; nothing had ever sent him so incensed before. It wasn't the red mist: it was a complete wipeout. Every muscle and sinew burned with ferocity.

'You cunts!' Jesse roared, charging towards them.

Before Archie could even grasp who was coming, Jesse swung the cosh with all his strength, smashing it hard against Archie's head. The man crumpled to the ground without even faltering.

Jesse didn't stop. He ran at Franklin before a fly kick sent him off his feet and sprawling on the ground. It was followed by a number of brutal blows from the cosh.

'You cunts! You fucking cunts!' Jesse screamed, his voice hoarse with malice. He raised the cosh again, ready to strike, when a man's massive boot slammed into his back and sent him crashing forward.

The two larger men had jumped in. But with so much adrenaline coursing through his body, Jesse was quick to get to his feet.

However, then came a voice. It was so sharp and shrill that it cut through the chaos.

'Stop, or I'll slit his throat!'

The command froze everyone in place. Jesse, Franklin, and the two big men all turned towards the source of the threat.

Gripping Benny by the collar, Dottie pressed a knife firmly against his throat.

Benny's face was pale, his eyes wide with terror.

'Get the fuck away from him,' Dottie snarled, her voice cold and deadly.

The man who was dragging Billy released his grip and stepped back, his hands raised.

Franklin, who was still stunned, managed, nevertheless, to rise to his feet and let out a bark of laughter. 'Oh, fuck off. She won't slit his throat, the silly tart.'

But Benny was shaking all over. Raising his hands, he shouted across to his son, 'Shut it, Franklin, you fucking fool. She *will* slit my throat.'

'You hurt my farver, and I'll cut the cunt right out of ya,' Franklin snarled, his voice gritty and venomous.

Jesse hurried to his brother's side, his breath catching, once he had caught sight of all the blood staining Billy's shirt and his motionless body. His heart sank as his worst fear seemed to have been realised. It was as though hot talons were clawing at his chest. Tears streamed down his face as he dropped to his knees, slid his arm under Billy's lifeless body, and pulled his brother towards him.

'Don't die on me, Billy. Come on, Billy boy, come on. Please wake up,' Jesse pleaded, his voice cracking. The tears fell like waterfalls. They splashed onto Billy's shirt as he cradled him in his arms.

'Is he dead?' Dottie's voice cracked, now on the verge of hysteria. 'Jesse, is he? Is he?' she screamed, pressing the knife harder against Benny's throat. The blade glinted in the dim light, her knuckles white as she gripped the handle.

Franklin staggered, his face pale, before doubling over and vomiting onto the ground. Slowly, he got up, raised his hands, and took cautious steps towards the woman. 'Please, don't muller him,' he said, his tone shaky. He now realised that he needed to treat her with more respect. One false move and his father wouldn't live another second.

Jesse clutched Billy tighter, rocking him as his voice broke. 'Billy, please don't leave me. Please!'

A faint groan escaped from Billy's lips. 'I'm not dead, Numbnuts,' came the weak, raspy reply.

Jesse froze, disbelief washing over him. Then, relief surged through his body like a tidal wave. 'He's alive, Mottie! He's alive!' he shouted, his tears mixed with a crooked smile of hope.

The tension crackled like a live wire, the bravado of the men faltering under the weight of Dottie's icy resolve. For a moment, everything seemed to stand still.

That was until the screeching of tyres tore through the silence. Another car had just arrived. It skidded to a halt and kicked up dust. Out stepped a man with a fifty-inch chest, with a crowbar gripped tightly in his hand. Beside him was another man, a giant of a bloke. Both of them built like mountains moved with the kind of authority that made everyone stop and stare.

One of Franklin's sidekicks muttered under his breath, 'Oh shit.'

Franklin recognised them instantly. His stomach churned, his legs turned to jelly, and a warm trickle of urine ran down his leg.

'Spud, Billy needs a hospital!' Jesse's voice cracked with desperation.

Spud didn't hesitate. He hurried towards Jesse and Billy, the crowbar still in hand, his eyes darting between the point of danger and the injured.

Dottie pulled the knife away from Benny's neck.

Benny staggered back, coughing and clutching his throat; his relief was palpable.

But Dottie didn't even glance at him. She bolted towards Billy, with tears streaming down her cheeks.

Franklin's eyes shifted to the second man, James Murphy. He was Billy and Jesse's uncle. The name alone was enough to make men flinch. And now here he was standing like a fucking immovable tank and casually swinging a baseball bat.

As soon as James locked eyes with Franklin, he grinned slowly and menacingly.

'You fucked up, Franklin. Big mistake, four on one, yeah? Well, let's even the score, shall we?'

Before Franklin could react, James's bat cracked him square on the chin. His legs gave way, and he crumpled to the ground like a sack of hot shit.

James didn't stop. He turned first towards Spud, who was trying to lift Billy, but then his sharp gaze scanned the chaos.

Archie was already out cold on the ground.

However, one of Franklin's friends, a bigger man, who realised the odds were against him, turned to make a run for it.

It was a bad idea. James hurled the bat like a javelin. It slammed into the man's back, right between the shoulder blades, sending him sprawling face-first into the dirt.

Before the man could get to his feet, James strode over and booted him hard up the arse, the impact sharp enough to splinter his tailbone.

The thug let out a strangled cry, momentarily paralysed.

James leaned in, his voice low and deadly. 'Move, and I'll crush you like a bloody beetle.'

He swooped down and retrieved his bat with an air of disgust. 'You dirty scumbag – four on one. Well, I'll be back, and I'll take each and every one of you out of the game.'

Without wasting another second, James hurried over to Spud and Jesse, who, between them, were struggling to carry Billy towards James's Range Rover.

James didn't hesitate. Using his arms like a forklift truck, he scooped Billy up effortlessly and carried him, before gently laying his nephew on the back seat, careful not to jostle him too much.

Jesse hurriedly climbed into the front seat, his face streaked with tears.

Spud rummaged through Billy's jacket and fished out his car keys, muttering something about not letting the gypsies nick the motor. 'I'll meet you at the hospital,' Spud said to Dottie, before reaching over to Jesse for his keys and handing those to her.

Dottie nodded. She then glanced at Billy's pale face. Her stomach churned at the sight of the blood seeping through his clothes. Holding Jesse's keys tightly, she turned to James. 'I'll follow you.'

All the while, her mind was racing, she gripped the tiny silver cross that an old friend had given her before she went to prison, a necklace she treasured and saw as her piece of hope. *Please let him be okay. He's alive. He's alive.* She repeated the words like a mantra, in trying to drown out the terrifying image of all that blood.

As the cars pulled away from the gypsy site and the residents hurried back into their caravans, Dottie's eyes filled with tears. Her son had been through so much in his life. All he had ever wanted was a successful business and a good wife. The thought tightened in her chest while she gripped the steering wheel.

Just as her mind was racing with so many what-if scenarios, she caught sight of a young woman stepping out of a taxi. It was Bronte. For a split second, she considered pulling over to ask what the hell was going on. But then her focus immediately snapped back to the road. Billy was all that mattered now. She had to get him to the hospital.

The hospital wasn't very far away, but it seemed as though the journey was taking an eternity. With her heart pounding, she said a silent prayer: *Please, God, please don't let Billy die.*

The prayer echoed over and over in her mind as she tried to push away the dread threatening to consume her.

CHAPTER THIRTEEN

Dottie remained on James's tail as if an invisible umbilical cord connected her to Billy to keep him alive. She had done everything in her power to protect her son – even going as far as murdering her parents and Albert Carson, Billy's uncle. Today had been no different. If those gypsies hadn't let go of Billy, she would have slit Benny's throat without a second thought.

James was hurtling through the streets as though he was in charge of the ambulance himself. Within minutes, he drove straight up to the A&E entrance.

Dottie had managed to stay close behind, and she pulled in directly behind him. As soon as she jumped out, she heard Jesse's panicked screams piercing the air.

'Quick! Help! Someone, help!' Jesse bellowed. His voice was shrill with desperation.

Two hospital staff, alerted by the commotion, hurried over. They then went back inside the building, pulled a gurney from the corridor inside, and took it outside, where James eased Billy onto it.

A doctor, who had been tending to a patient in the back of an ambulance, ran over, drawn by Jesse's cries.

Wasting no time, the doctor shone a penlight into Billy's eyes and listened to his chest. His expression tightened, and he barked orders to the staff. It spurred a sudden, frantic rush to get Billy inside the building.

Dottie stood like a block of ice, her hands clasped over her mouth, her heart hammering so hard, it felt as though it was about to burst at any moment. When her legs began to tremble, threatening to give way, she felt a strong arm around her shoulders.

'Come on, babe. Let's park the cars,' Spud said softly, his voice a steadying force. 'Billy's in good hands.'

Tears welled in her eyes as she stammered, 'W-What if . . . if—'

Spud pulled her closer, holding her tightly. 'He won't die, Dottie. He won't. That boy is made of steel, like his mother.' He kissed her forehead. 'Don't forget he has your genes.'

She pulled away, and then hastily wiping her tears, her mind went on autopilot. Quickly, she manoeuvred the car out of the ambulance entrance and into the public car park. The walk back to A&E was short, but now, with her legs feeling like jelly, which prevented her from running, the distance seemed to stretch endlessly.

Having already parked Billy's car, Spud was waiting for her at the entrance. She paused momentarily to catch her breath and looked at him. Another tear trickled down her cheek.

Spud had always been there for her – the rock, the voice of reason – not just for her but for the boys, for Carrie, and for the whole family. And yet, he had never once asked for anything in return.

Dottie gripped his arm tightly, her emotions overwhelming her.

A sudden flicker of concern furrowed his brow as he looked into her eyes.

She whispered in a quiet voice, 'I love you, Spud. You do know that, don't you?'

He gave her a reassuring wink. 'Always, my girl. Always.'

***

Once inside the heart of A&E, Dottie was immediately struck by the overpowering smell of antiseptic mingled with unmistakable body odours emanating from fear. The chaos hit her, and her eyes darted about, now desperate to find Billy. As she hurried along one corridor after another, the sounds of a distressed child screaming, an old man groaning in pain, and the metallic clanging of equipment punctuated the air. The sheer mania about the place made her feel small, insignificant, and very vulnerable.

Darting from cubicle to cubicle, her eyes flitted from the frenzy of nurses to the doctors hard at work. The atmosphere was almost oppressive with urgency. What Dottie hadn't realised was that a multi-car road traffic accident had brought a flood of casualties into the department.

The aftermath was carnage. She came across a gurney, which had been left abandoned in the corridor, with blood dripping from it and forming a pool on the floor. A cold shiver ran through her. Clasping her hands tightly together, she whispered a silent prayer that it wasn't Billy's blood.

Suddenly, she focused on the high-pitched hysteria of Jesse's voice.

'Get off me! Let go of me!' he yelled, as he flung his arms everywhere, in a vain attempt to break free.

But James had a hold of him, and since he was so much bigger, Jesse stood no chance of freeing himself.

Dottie's gaze darted towards a cubicle where a doctor hurriedly tried to close the curtains.

At the same time, James struggled to hold back a now hysterical Jesse.

Every hair on her body stood on end. A sick and almost macabre feeling gripped her stomach as she rushed towards the curtain. She knew from the panic that Billy wasn't okay at all.

Jesse had already fallen to his knees, his hands covering his face as inconsolable sobs racked his body.

Dottie was torn between rushing to comfort him and pulling open that curtain.

The decision was made for her.

Spud stepped forward, scooped Jesse off the floor, and held him tightly.

Jesse clung to him, his chest heaving with grief, as Spud murmured quiet reassurances.

Dottie's eyes locked on the curtain. Her heart pounded so hard, it felt as though it might burst out of her chest. She had to open it. She had to see Billy.

But before she could reach it, the curtain was pulled open abruptly, and a nurse hurried out. The sight inside froze Dottie to the spot.

A tube protruding from Billy's chest was connected to a bottle rapidly filling with blood.

Dottie's eyes momentarily shifted to the two doctors, who worked with precision and set up machines, cannulas, and drips almost in tandem. However, to her, the room seemed a blur: her focus was solely on her son.

One of the doctors, Lloyd Cummins, a boyish-looking man in his early forties with oversized black-rimmed glasses, glanced up and offered a genuine reassuring smile.

'Are you his mum?' he asked.

Dottie nodded, unable to speak.

'It looks worse than it is,' he said, gently. 'He's got a broken rib that punctured his lung, but he's stable. We're draining the blood so he can breathe properly before he can go into surgery.'

Dottie's eyes swept over Billy's battered body, taking in every bruise, every cut. When her voice finally returned, it was trembling with fear and confusion. 'Why isn't he already in surgery? Why is he still here, surrounded by other patients? And what's the deal with all that commotion outside?'

The doctor sighed, wiping his brow with the back of his gloved hand. 'There was a serious accident on the motorway,' he explained. 'It's stretched our resources. But, please, don't be alarmed. Your son is stable now, and as soon as the surgeon is ready, we'll get him into the operating theatre.'

Dottie's knees wavered, but she gritted her teeth and forced herself to stay strong. She nodded, her eyes now fixed on Billy, as if willing him to hold on just a little longer.

Suddenly, a nurse gripped Dottie's shoulders and literally moved her aside. 'Doctor Cummins, they're ready for him now.'

Doctor Cummins nodded sharply. 'Great, let's get him to surgery.' He glanced back at Dottie and gave her another smile of reassurance.

Before she could say a word, they had disengaged the brakes and were wheeling Billy out of the cubicle, the drips and drains moving with him.

Jesse hurried to the bed, his sobs raw and desperate. 'Don't let him die! Just don't let him die!' he cried, his tear-filled eyes pleading with the medical staff.

Doctor Cummins handed the IV stand to the nurse and then stepped back to grab Jesse's arms. 'Listen to me,' he said, with a calm but steady voice. 'He's out of the woods. I'm guessing you're his brother?'

Jesse nodded quickly, clinging to the doctor's every word, his tear-streaked face searching the man's expression for any hint of hope.

'He's going into surgery now. There's still a journey ahead, but we'll know more, once we've scanned him and sorted out that offending rib. But let me tell you this – he's got a strong heart. And when there's a strong heart, there's a strong will.'

Jesse nodded again as though those words were his lifeline. The tears didn't stop streaming down his face, but there was something new in his expression now – a flicker of hope.

'Now, let us do our job, and maybe you should go and get a coffee.' He grinned and winked. 'Or a brandy, perhaps?'

'Thank you, Doc. Thank you,' said Jesse.

Doctor Cummins glanced at the two huge men standing protectively with Billy's mother. The first thought that crossed his mind was simple: whoever had assaulted Billy wouldn't stand a chance if those two got hold of them.

Just as he turned to follow Billy's gurney to the operating theatre, the doors swung open.

Paramedics wheeled in two men who were laid out on stretchers. They were closely followed by what seemed like half a gypsy site. Another man in a hospital wheelchair was pushed by a beautiful woman with hair down to her backside and eyes like pools of chocolate.

Doctor Cummins, often mistaken for a junior, due to his youthful appearance, was, in fact, a highly respected registrar in the A&E department. His experience had taught him to spot the signs instantly – the accent, the heavy jewellery, the distinct style of clothing, and, above all else, the attitude.

As the crowd spilled in behind the paramedics, he knew how this was likely to go. When a gypsy came in, the whole family did as well, and so it rarely meant a quiet night.

Concluding that Billy was likely to be in the theatre by now, Doctor Cummins turned his attention to the two men who had just been wheeled in. As he approached, the tension seemed to rise. So much so, that, with the gypsies huddled together in one corner and Billy's family facing them, it looked like a Mexican standoff.

Unexpectedly, and to Doctor Cummins's horror, Billy's brother – the same young man he had just consoled moments earlier – was like a man possessed. He flew at the man in the wheelchair before anyone could react and gripped the sides of the chair.

His voice was venomous as he hissed into the man's face, 'If me bruvver dies, I'm coming for you, Franklin, you cunt! You won't need a fucking hospital. You'll need a coffin.'

The man in the wheelchair suddenly looked down, squinting, as if Billy's brother's breath would burn him alive.

A woman who was standing beside the wheelchair turned white and threw her hands over her mouth, her eyes wide with fear.

Jesse spun around to face her, his rage unrelenting. He jabbed a finger into her chest, his voice rising. 'And you, you fucking shit-stirring bitch! This is all your fault!'

She stumbled back, but Jesse followed her, poking her again, his voice a dangerous growl. 'If my Billy dies, I'll make your life a living hell!'

The room seemed to hold its breath as everyone froze, completely stunned by the ferocity of his words.

Luckily, Doctor Cummins knew how to handle the situation. He hurriedly rounded up two of the porters to usher the gypsies to one end of A&E. Then, he accompanied Billy's family to the room that was usually reserved for grieving relatives.

James had a hold of Jesse's shirt and whispered in his ear, 'Leave it, Jesse, or we'll all get nicked. You'll lose your job, and if anything ever happens to those pikeys, you'll be the first person they drag to the police station.'

'Fuck the force, fuck everything. This is war.'

Doctor Cummins followed them in. Right away, he noticed the blood the second Billy's brother turned his back. 'Sorry, I don't know your name,' he said, tapping him on the shoulder.

Jesse spun around. 'I'm Jesse Murphy.'

'Hmmm, I think you need to be seen,' Cummins replied.

'Oi, the cheek of it, I'm not mental – I'm angry,' Jesse shot back.

Doctor Cummins shook his head. 'No, I am referring to the back of your head. It's bleeding. I can see the wound – it needs stitches. Let's get you sorted, but not here in A&E. I'll get a nurse to assist. I must go. As I was telling your mother, there's been a bad accident, so we're stretched to full capacity.'

As Jesse glanced at Dottie, guilt suddenly washed over him. She looked as white as a ghost. He realised he hadn't even thought to console her, having been too caught up in his own anger and grief.

Suddenly, he walked towards her and held out his arms. At that moment, they both broke down and clung to each other as fresh tears fell.

The moment the nurse trundled in with a tray of instruments ready to stitch Jesse's head, James decided he needed some fresh air. So he left Jesse with Dottie and Spud. He felt it only right that he should let Carrie and Sunny know what was happening. His brother would be livid if, God forbid, anything happened to Billy, and they were the last to know.

Deciding to make the call outside, he took a few deep breaths in the cool night air.

It only took two rings for Carrie to answer his call. When he explained where he was and why he was there, she bombarded him with questions.

Suddenly, he heard his brother's voice. 'James, what's gone on?'

Evidently, Sunny had taken the phone from her. And now, Carrie was in the background demanding the phone before he told her to shut up.

James explained what had happened, and he knew that was enough to have them hot-footing it up to the hospital. What he hadn't anticipated was how quickly they'd arrive.

Just as he was about to go back inside, he spotted Bronte pacing the car park, a large plume of smoke escaping her lips. As he approached, she glanced up and nervously stepped back. It made him feel uncomfortable. For all his size and reputation, he had never hurt a woman. And he would never do so, as a rule. But some rules had to be broken. Those detestable gypsies were the exception.

'James – I mean, Mr Murphy . . .'

James frowned. 'It's James. Why would you say Mr Murphy?'

'Sorry, James. I just know I'm not in the family's good books. Is Billy going to be all right?'

He paused, staring into her eyes, which were full of tears. 'We don't know yet, but I think he will. He's strong.'

As he glanced towards the A&E entrance, his jaw tightened. 'I can't say the same for your family, though, Bronte. Four men against one?' His blood simmered just at the mention of it.

Bronte's face flushed and more tears began to fall heavily down her cheeks. Quickly, she wiped them away.

James could tell she was ashamed. Her gaze met his briefly.

But the moment it did, she looked away, and to avoid any awkwardness, she fidgeted with a tissue in her fingers. 'I'm sorry. So sorry,' she whispered, before she scuttled away, her long black hair catching in the wind and swirling around her.

For a fleeting moment, James felt sorry for her. But then his mind snapped back to the sight of his nephew lying there half-dead, having been kicked and dragged across the dirt-covered track by those gypsies. He imagined them tying Billy's legs to one horse and his arms to another, pulling him apart as if they were reenacting a scene from the medieval past.

That image wouldn't leave his mind. It wasn't often these days that his blood pressure rose – but this was one of them, and now, it was at boiling point.

***

Five minutes later, having had time to calm himself down, James headed back inside. He was determined to find a vending machine where he could get himself a coffee or at least some water. He wandered along the maze of corridors before he finally gave up and asked a passing nurse for help. She pointed him towards A&E. With a resigned sigh, he turned around and made his way back to the family room.

As he approached the emergency ward, the quiet hum of the corridors gave way to an angry commotion. It was enough to wake the dead. A group of travellers had gathered, their voices raised in protest, as they demanded attention for their injured men. One woman, with her long braid swaying down to her hips, was in a nurse's face spitting insults at her.

James considered stepping in, but he decided against it. Better to stay focused on his task. That resolve shattered when he heard a familiar voice, raw and desperate, cut through the commotion.

‘Please, would you tell me where me son Billy Murphy is?’

He spun around to see Carrie, breathless and distraught, with Sunny close on her heels.

Before James could respond, the woman with the braid turned from the nurse and jabbed an accusatory finger in Carrie’s direction.

‘You’d better hope your boy doesn’t come out of here alive after what he did to my Henry,’ she snarled.

James immediately stepped between them and pushed the woman back.

But Carrie darted around him. She knew the woman from her younger days and was in her face in an instant, her voice trembling with anger.

‘Oh yeah? Believe me, Maggie, I’ll have you and your fucking sisters, if you talk about me boy like that again!’ Carrie’s sharp eyes scanned the crowd of half a dozen travellers standing nearby. ‘What are you lot staring at? Want some, do ya?’

Her defiant tone sent them scattering, their gazes darting elsewhere.

Maggie, however, wasn’t so easily cowed.

Carrie turned back to her, her voice cracking with emotion. ‘If my Billy—’

Sunny gripped her arm and pulled her back gently. ‘Come on, Carrie. Let’s leave these cunts to themselves,’ he muttered, shooting Maggie a look of utter disgust.

Realising who she had just mouthed off to, Maggie seemed to shrink into herself, her earlier bravado fading.

James leaned in close to her, his voice low and harsh. ‘It was me who beat up your lad. No doubt about it. And if he’s not disabled, I’m coming back. I’ll burn your fucking site to the ground. Now, reel your ugly neck in and fuck off.’

His words hung in the air like a threat too real to ignore.

Maggie’s face went pale as James turned away and guided Carrie and Sunny away from the fray.

The family room wasn’t far away, and as soon as Carrie opened the door, Jesse flew at her. It was at that moment she knew whatever had happened to Billy was serious. She had never seen Jesse so distraught. His eyes were swollen from crying.

Carrie felt like crying herself, but she knew she had to stay strong for Jesse. She hugged him tightly, and over his shoulder, she saw Dottie in tears. Dottie never cried. It was then that she felt her whole body turn to ice.

'Where is he now?' she asked, her voice quaking.

'He's in surgery,' Jesse replied. 'But the doctors said he was stable before they took him in. They didn't say it was life-threatening.'

Carrie nodded and took a deep breath to steady herself before Sunny stepped forward and embraced her.

He tried to hold back his tears, but a few escaped before he briskly wiped the rest away.

'So, what happened?' he asked.

Jesse, who had just flopped down onto a chair, was about to explain when Doctor Cummins walked in with a look of surprise at seeing even more family members.

'This room is really just for family,' Doctor Cummins said, as a nurse entered behind him with a tray of hot drinks.

'I'm Billy's mum,' Carrie replied, her eyes locked on the doctor, searching for answers.

'Oh.' Doctor Cummins glanced at Dottie, frowning slightly.

'We're both his mums,' Dottie added, firmly, by way of an explanation.

Deciding not to press the matter further, the doctor nodded. 'Right, okay. So, Billy's out of surgery and doing well. I wouldn't say he's ready for a photoshoot,' he said, with a small grin, 'but he's breathing on his own. The scans show no internal injuries, just lots of bruising and soft tissue damage, and the offending rib is now where it needs to be. I appreciate it all sounds bad, but he will be as right as rain soon. He's still groggy, but he has opened his eyes. I think he'll be ready for visitors tomorrow.'

Filled with relief, Jesse sprang up and threw his arms around the doctor. 'Thank you! Thank you!' he said, suddenly pulling back, as happy tears streamed down his face.

Doctor Cummins smiled, with genuine warmth. 'You're welcome, but it wasn't me. It was the surgeon. He's a good one. Anyway, I see that there's coffee if anyone needs it.'

Carrie stepped forward, her voice trembling with hope. 'Please, can I see me boy now?'

Doctor Cummins hesitated for a moment, noting her distinct accent, but quickly smiled. 'I don't see why not, but only for a few minutes, though. He needs to rest.'

He turned to Jesse. 'There's one issue. Will Billy need security?' He gestured over his shoulder, clearly referring to the travellers causing a scene in A&E.

Jesse chewed his lip while he considered the matter. 'I'll sit with him, if that's okay.'

'Good. I was hoping one of you would,' Doctor Cummins said, nodding in approval. 'It can get messy with police in and out. They may have to be called later, but for now, the officers in the hospital are still dealing with the motorway incident.' He turned his attention back to Carrie. 'Give it an hour and I'll be back. Billy is in recovery, so we have to wait a while.' He could see the panic on her face. 'It's okay. As soon as he is on the ward, I will see to it that he's placed in a separate room. I will either come myself or send someone to bring you up.'

Carrie smiled, although her heart was breaking. 'Thank you' was all she managed to say.

CHAPTER FOURTEEN

It was four o'clock on the following Monday morning. The blind was drawn and the room was eerily quiet. Everyone had left Billy's bedside, safe in the knowledge that he was in good hands. Jesse, however, remained slumped in the padded chair. His head throbbed, and his back ached. The charge of energy that had surged through his body earlier, acting as a temporary painkiller, had now faded, which had left him utterly drained. Despite his exhaustion, he dared not sleep because the fear of one of those gypsies coming back for revenge was enough to keep him awake.

Occasionally, Billy opened his eyes, muttered a few words, and drifted back to sleep.

Doctor Cummins popped in several times throughout the night to reassure Jesse that Billy's condition was perfectly normal. The prognosis was good, and he should make a full recovery.

It was all well and good, but, in reality, Jesse saw that what those gypsies had done to his brother was a right liberty. It was probably rage mixed with fear that was really keeping him awake – although barely.

Letting his eyes close momentarily, Jesse intended only to rest them. However, when the door creaked open, his instant reaction was to jolt upright. His heart pounded as he scrambled out of the chair. Half-asleep and on high alert, he prepared himself for trouble.

But instead of a threat, he saw Bronte standing there. She was looking like a shadow of her former self. Not only were her eyes red and puffy, but her face was as pale as a sea pearl. She looked fragile, almost broken. Even so, his first instinct was to lash out by giving her a piece of his mind.

Before he could speak, Spud appeared behind her.

'I was coming to take over for a few hours,' Spud said, calmly. 'I wanted to let you get some kip. But I found young Bronte outside.' Glancing between them, he continued, 'And before you go off your head, Jesse, just let her talk.'

Tired and still reeling from what the gypsies had done to his brother, Jesse curled his lip in disdain.

'Talk? Really? And why should I, eh, Spud? That rat is the reason me bruvver ended up here!' He jabbed a finger in Billy's direction.

Billy's head was heavily bandaged, and there were cables and drips connected to machines, which beeped softly.

'Look at the state of him! Fucking look!'

He glared at Bronte with pure hatred. 'And where were you, eh? Hiding in one of those shit pits you lot call caravans, were ya? Waiting for them to finish him off, were ya?'

Spud quickly stepped in between Jesse and Bronte. 'Now, hold it, right there, Jesse. Bronte wasn't there, all right? Dottie told me she saw Bronte getting out of a taxi just as she was leaving the site. So she didn't know what happened. Christ, Jesse!'

Jesse slumped back into his chair with a frustrated sigh. 'Well, Billy told her to fuck off out of his life, so what's she doing here, then?'

Now thoroughly exasperated by Jesse's childish reaction to seeing Bronte, Spud threw his hands up. 'Jesse, will you shut it, boy? For Christ's sake, Bronte was with your brother for *years*! Just because she did something to piss him off doesn't mean she doesn't love him. Look at her, Jesse. Just bloody look at her!'

Reluctantly, Jesse turned his attention to Bronte. His shoulders sagged as he took in her appearance. There were brown rings under her sunken eyes, her cheeks were tear-stained, and she just looked so washed out and heartbroken with it all. Much like himself.

'Please, Jesse,' Bronte begged, her voice trembling. 'Please, let me see Billy. Just for a moment.' Another tear slipped down her cheek as she wiped her runny nose with her sleeve.

Begrudgingly, Jesse nodded. He realised he couldn't say or do anything to make her feel worse than she already did. Rising from his chair, he pushed it closer to Billy's bedside. 'Here you are,' he said, flatly.

Bronte gave him a small, grateful smile. 'Thank you, Jesse.'

Spud flicked his hand, motioning for Jesse to leave the room, but Jesse lingered in the doorway and watched. Despite everything, he'd always thought Bronte was among the sweetest, most genuine women he knew. And he knew his brother had felt the same way. So her underhanded move was a shock to both of them.

Bronte gently took Billy's hand and lifted it to her lips. She kissed it softly, her tears falling onto his skin. 'Oh, Billy. Whatever you think of me, I want you to know I love you with all my heart. I never meant to hurt you. I never meant to cause you no harm. I didn't . . .' Her voice broke as she lowered her head and rested her cheek against his hand. 'Oh, Billy, what have I done? What have I done? I'm so sorry.'

Jesse was about to leave when he noticed Billy's eyes flutter and open. He stepped forward, ready to tell Bronte not to take any of Billy's groggy murmurs seriously – it was just the anaesthetic.

But Billy's eyes locked on to those of Bronte's. His gaze darkened; it was sharp and focused. He yanked his hand away, his voice cutting through the room, clear and cold.

'Fuck off, Bronte. Fuck off.'

'Billy, please, just listen—'

Sensing the tension, Spud stepped forward. 'Come on, Bronte, love. He needs his rest. You can talk to him when he's back home because nothing you say will make sense.'

Slowly, Bronte rose from the chair, her body shaking. Without another word, she walked out of the room.

The moment she was outside, she broke into a run, her cries echoing down the corridor, which left a haunting trail behind her.

***

While Billy slept, Spud and Jesse sat in silence, each preoccupied with the fight at the pikey site and the scenes at the hospital.

Jesse shook his head as he looked at Spud. 'She hurt Billy – badly. Scarred his heart. And you know me bruvver – he's loyal, faithful, no matter how many women throw themselves at him. For her to go behind his back . . . He feels so betrayed, Spud. He won't forgive her, and she knows it.'

Spud sighed, his expression thoughtful. 'But we all make mistakes, Jesse. You know that as well as anyone, don't you?'

'I know,' Jesse admitted, knowing exactly what Spud was getting at. He had shown just as much disloyalty to his brother as

Bronte had. The saying people in glasshouses shouldn't throw stones came to mind. 'But men like Billy, who put everything into a relationship, don't forgive easily. I don't know what exactly went on at the site. All I know – the same as you – is that her bruvvers and their scummy mates were beating the fuck out of Billy.'

A groggy voice broke through their conversation.

'Jesse.'

Both men instantly turned and hurried to Billy's bedside. His eyes were open now, though dark and clouded with pain.

'Are you all right, Billy? Can I get you anything?' Jesse asked, leaning over him anxiously.

Billy's gaze flickered between them, his voice rough but commanding. 'Just get me home.'

'Yeah, yeah,' Jesse replied, quickly. 'All in good time, Billy. All in good time.'

'I need to get out of here *now*, Jesse,' Billy insisted.

'Billy, mate, you won't even be able to stand up. Just rest until the doctor says you can go home.'

'What do you mean, I can't stand? Have they cut off my legs?'

Jesse couldn't help but smile at that quip. 'No, you silly sod. They operated on your chest. You've got a drain in, and the doctor reckons it'll be a few days before you can leave. So shut up and rest. No one's going anywhere, and in case you're worried, we're doing shifts, so you're never alone.'

Billy's eyes softened, though his frustration remained. 'Shifts, eh? I don't need babysitting.'

'Tough luck,' Jesse shot back, with a grin. 'You've got us, whether you like it or not. Now sleep, Billy. We'll sort everything else out later.'

Billy grunted as his eyelids drooped.

***

Deciding that Jesse needed to go home and get some much-needed sleep as well, Spud had taken over the bedside vigil. By midday the following day, he struggled himself to keep his eyes open. He yawned, glanced at his watch, and hoped Sunny would be here soon to take over his shift.

The door creaked open, and Spud looked up expecting to find Sunny there. Instead, he was surprised to see Cas entering the room. He was wearing one of his signature colourful shirts.

'Cas.' Spud nodded. He stood up and stretched his aching legs.

'Hello, Spud,' Cas replied, extending his hand for a firm handshake. 'How's the wounded soldier?'

'Lucky, mate, fucking lucky. It was fucking nasty, Cas. Proper nasty,' Spud said, grimly, with a shake of his head. 'I reckon they were gonna kill him. In fact, the way they were dragging him away, I thought he *was* dead.'

Cas's eyes widened. 'Seriously?

'Yeah. Jesse told me Billy had an argument with Archie and Franklin Penfold a while ago. Anyway, last night, Billy went to the site to have a word with Bronte – to find out why she had fully grown marijuana plants stashed in his basement and why she and her brothers had got involved with the Shipleys. But, meanwhile, Dottie went over to Billy's because she was concerned about the Shipleys. She phoned me and James to meet her and Jesse at the site. Apparently, Jesse had a bad feeling that Billy was going to get in a fight. By the time we got there, all hell had broken loose.'

Cas looked as cool as a cucumber on the outside, but inside, he was seething. His gaze lingered on Billy's bruised face and the bottle beside his bed steadily filling with blood from the drain. His throat tightened.

'And the cunts that did this?' Cas asked, his voice low and clipped.

Spud leaned against the wall, his arms crossed. 'Franklin and Archie Penfold and two other thugs from the pikey site. They were all in here, having their fucking wounds attended to. But, apparently, according to the doctors, they've all been discharged.' Spud paused, before he said, stonily, 'Lucky, really. Jesse's fuming. I don't think he'd have been able to contain himself if they were still here. He wants them hurt bad – real bad.'

Cas nodded slowly, like a bobbing dog, but inside his head, his mind was a storm of violent thoughts. What he wouldn't do to those gypsies if he got his hands on them. His fists clenched at his sides, but he forced himself to focus. There was something even more pressing on his mind.

'Spud,' said Cas, his voice quieter now, but sharp, nevertheless. 'Has anyone been sniffing around? Anyone trying to see Billy?'

Spud frowned. 'Who do you mean, Cas?'

'Like a big ugly cunt named Kenny Ruck. He's got a scar running from his cheek to his chin.'

Spud shook his head, his brows knitting together. 'No, not that I've seen. But, then again, I've only been here a few hours. Who's this Kenny bloke, and what does he want with Billy?'

Letting out a heavy sigh, Cas leaned back as though the weight of the world had just dropped onto his shoulders. 'The bastard recently got out of the nick after a ten-stretch. He's convinced I owe him something. Wants what he *thinks* he's owed. And since I own a chunk of Billy's business, he's got his sights set on that as well. And anyone who knows me has a good idea that . . . well, Billy's like a son to me. So, he'll do whatever it takes to get at me through him.'

Folding his arms, his lips tightening, Spud glanced at Billy, who was lying so still and vulnerable. 'Are you fucking kidding me?'

Cas let out a hollow laugh. 'Do I look like I'm kidding? I tried to deal with it. I brought in five of the biggest lads I know – proper bruisers. I've known them since they were kids, except I reckon they came out of the womb wearing steel-toe-capped boots and swinging metal bars. A right handful they are.'

'And?' Spud pressed.

Cas rubbed his temples in frustration. 'And they grabbed Kenny and threw him in the back of a van for a *friendly chat*. I thought that'd be the end of it.'

Spud leaned forward, now intrigued. 'So, what happened?'

'The bastard only went and escaped,' Cas said, shaking his head, as though he still couldn't believe it. 'Turns out Kenny's got a talent for running. I mean, I knew he was a rat, but I didn't think he'd actually move like one. Apparently, he's spent half his time in prison on the treadmill. My lads might be built like buses, but they sure as hell ain't running a marathon anytime soon.

Meanwhile, Kenny thinks he's bloody Jesse Owens. Legs like pistons, apparently.'

Spud couldn't help but laugh, though, at the wit of Cas.

'So let me get this straight. We've got a track-and-field nutter, who is built like a thug but is as fast as a greyhound, sniffing around Billy. Is that about the size of it?'

'Exactly,' Cas muttered, testily. 'Now I've got to figure out how to deal with the bastard before he rears his ugly head again.'

Spud smirked. 'Maybe, next time, bring lads who can run *and* swing a bat.'

Cas rolled his eyes. 'Thanks for the advice, Usain Bolt. If you've got any sprinters handy, let me know.'

Spud chuckled again, but his gaze flicked back to Billy. 'That lad can't handle more fucking grief.'

'No, no, poor bastard,' Cas chewed his bottom lip. 'What were you saying about the Shipleys?'

'Why, do you know 'em?'

Cas threw his head back and barked a sharp laugh. 'Seriously? O' course I know the poxy family. Who fucking don't! So, what about them?'

'Well, that's why Billy finished it with Bronte and had words with Archie and Franklin. That's why he's ended up here.'

'Go back a bit, Spud. Tell me, why did he end it with Bronte?'

Spud shrugged. 'Like I said, he found a load of fully grown marijuana plants in the basement of those new apartments. The only person with the key was Bronte.'

Cas's eyes widened. 'Ohhh, so *that's* why Billy came asking me for the spare set. He said he wasn't sure if it was a good idea for Bronte to be working with him. Should've known something dodgy was going on. Anyway, carry on.'

'Well, after that, he got a visit from two of the Shipleys – Reece and Dario. Do you know them?'

Cas nodded, menacingly. 'Yep. They are a pair of ruthless bastards. But, then again, the whole family's rotten. Moriarty and Max got nicked for a double murder – a pregnant woman, no less – and there's no way those two were innocent. The lot of them are a right evil bunch of cunts. Even the old lady's done a long stretch. I think it's Reece and Dario's grandmother. Though I've gotta admit, I can't picture her as a sweet old granny with a purple rinse and knitting needles. Unless, of course, she's shoving them in someone's chest.'

Spud snorted, but Cas carried on. 'I'll tell ya, there ain't many faces out there that give me the willies, but the likes of those Shipleys and Kenny Ruck do. That psycho has me sleeping with a shooter under my pillow. I digress. So what do the Shipleys want?'

Spud shrugged again. 'You know Billy, he keeps things close to his chest. I don't have the full picture.'

'Yeah, cagey little fucker, ain't he,' Cas muttered.

A voice piped up from the bed. 'Hey, Cas, I might have my eyes closed, but I can still bloody hear you.'

Pushing past Spud, Cas stood over Billy and peered down at him like a dad checking his kid's homework. 'You all right, son?'

Billy cracked open one eye and gawped at how close Cas's face was. 'Christ, Cas, how much garlic have you had for breakfast? Back up a bit, will ya?'

Realising he'd been practically breathing all over Billy, Cas quickly straightened up. 'Sorry, Billy. Just checking to see if you're still with us.'

Billy groaned and wheezed. 'Well, I'm not ready for bagpipe lessons, but I'm alive, ain't I, and I'm not fucking deaf.'

Cas let out a chuckle. 'Good. I wouldn't want to finish you off. Imagine it, death by garlic breath.'

Unexpectedly, the door swung open, and Cas nearly jumped out of his skin.

Spud and Billy both noticed Cas's plight and exchanged amused glances.

'Hello, Doc,' Cas said, straightening his jacket and eyeing the man from head to toe. 'So is Billy all right? No lasting effects?'

Doctor Cummins smiled politely and then glanced at Billy. Silently, he sought permission to speak about Billy's condition.

Billy grinned and tried to sit up, but only to find the movement too painful. He winced and then sank back onto his pillows. 'Doc, they're fine – they're more like family than friends.'

Doctor Cummins nodded and turned to Cas. He was momentarily bemused by the man's eclectic attire. 'Well, Billy is through the worst of it. He suffered a punctured lung, but, thanks to his family getting him here in time, we managed to drain the fluid and stabilise him. He's healing well and should be back to normal in a few days. He does have extensive bruising. He's a bit . . . mottled, shall we say. So he needs rest, good food, and gentle exercise. Nothing strenuous.'

'Thanks, Doc,' Cas said, stepping back to let the man do his doctorly business, whatever that involved.

Cas flicked his head towards Spud. 'Come on, let's grab a coffee. I think we need a chat. Maybe a family meeting or something.'

Once the men were outside the room, Cas glanced over his shoulder and said to Spud, 'I'm worried about Billy. He's looking pretty vulnerable right now.'

As they approached the hospital café, Cas continued with his concern. 'Will he be all right for a minute?'

'Well, the doc's in there with him,' Spud replied, his hands stuffed in his pockets.

Traipsing through the hospital in silence, they eventually reached the café. Cas got to the counter first and ordered two coffees while Spud claimed a small table tucked into the corner of the eating area.

As soon as Cas returned, he glanced around and said, 'I've been thinking about what you told me. You know, about the Shipleys having full-grown marijuana plants in that basement. Nah.' He shook his head. 'It doesn't add up.'

Spud nodded. 'Well, that's what I thought, and so did Billy. That's why he went to see Bronte to find out what the blazes was going on. Because as I said, the Shipleys paid Billy a visit. They said that because he had got rid of the plants, he now owed them. But, at that point, Dottie arrived with some business for Billy. She told the two Shipley lads to come back during office hours.'

Cas chuckled. 'She's got a way about her, that one, hasn't she?'

'She has,' Spud replied, though his eyes suddenly darted to something across the room – or, rather, nothing at all.

Cas noticed the eye movement. He lowered his coffee cup and gave Spud a pointed look. 'All right, come on. Spit it out.'

Spud hesitated before leaning in. 'When Dottie got home, it was late, and I knew something was on her mind. Anyway, she told me that when the Shipleys turned up at the office, she thought she recognised one of the lads. Something about the look in his eyes. And when he said his name, that sealed it – she knew exactly who they were related to. Candice Shipley.'

Cas nodded slowly, piecing it together. 'Yeah, that's the old bat – Ol' Ma Barker. So, how does Dottie know her?'

Spud shifted uncomfortably. 'Candice killed her mate in prison. A proper close mate. Billy's even named after her.'

Cas's mouth fell open. 'Shit. Now that's really hitting too close to home. Christ, if Dottie thinks the Shipleys are gonna hurt Billy, there's no telling what she'll do. That woman's a one-woman fucking army, when she's set on something.'

Spud nodded solemnly. 'Billy doesn't know yet, but you're right. Dottie hates that Candice with a passion. So, as you can imagine, I feel like I'm not just keeping an eye on Billy for his safety – I'm keeping an eye on Dottie for what *she's* capable of doing. I love her, you know. I don't want her going back inside.'

Cas offered Spud a nervous smile. 'Well, she's a lovely woman. You know I knew her when she and my Tara were kids, right? But . . . can I ask you something personal?'

Spud shrugged. 'Yeah, go on.'

Looking slightly sheepish, Cas cleared his throat. 'Is Dottie a bit, er . . .?'

'Psycho?' Spud cut in, raising an eyebrow.

'Yeah,' Cas admitted, grinning. 'But I mean that in the nicest possible way.'

'My Dottie's a funny soul. She loves the family, as in the Murphys, dearly. She will do anything for them. It stems from when she agreed to give up Billy for adoption to Carrie and Sunny. And how they brought her into the family fold. And if needs must, Dottie will do what it takes to protect the lot of them. Outsiders aren't important. There's no doubt about it, Cas, Dottie is the calm before the chaos, so, yeah, describing her as a psycho, is fair, I suppose.'

Cas sipped his coffee, paused for a moment to look at Spud, and gave him a little wink. ‘She likes me though, eh?’

Spud chuckled. ‘Ha! Yes, Cas, she likes you a lot, mate. Don’t worry, you’re safe.’

CHAPTER FIFTEEN

Billy opened his eyes expecting to see Cas, Spud, or even Jesse. Instead, to his horror, Reece Shipley stood by the foot of his bed. He was dressed in black as though he was trying to replicate some kind of cat burglar. Everything about the man, from his sharp clothes to his calculated stance and the smirk etched across his face, reeked of a sickly sleekness.

Reece carried himself like a predator who had already caught his prey, and Billy knew he'd met his match. Stuck in a hospital bed, battered and barely mobile, he had no choice but to hear him out.

Reece smirked. 'Took a beating, I see. So Billy boy, that is what they call you, ain't it: *Billy boy*? I thought I'd come personally to offer my get-well wishes.' His tone was mocking, and he deliberately tilted his head and eyed Billy as a scientist might inspect a specimen. 'Gotta say, I'm surprised you survived. From what I heard, you were done for.'

Billy stared at him. He wasn't about to give Reece the satisfaction of a reaction. Instead, he studied the man knowing full well that the Shipleys' interest in him wasn't born out of charity.

'I have to say, Billy,' Reece continued, as he slowly paced the room, 'I was taken aback when I heard how your little mob handled the gyppos. Got yourself quite the firm, haven't ya?'

Billy's lips curled into a faint smile. There was a flicker of a defiant spark in his eyes. Even bruised and broken, he still had his trademark cocky glint, which had clearly got up Reece's nose.

'Did you bring me any grapes?'

Not amused, Reece's smirk faded into a grimace. He darted forward, leaning dangerously close now to Billy's face. 'Right, here's the thing. You owe me,' he growled. 'Like I said, those plants belonged to me. And I'm sure you've asked around, and you know exactly who I am by now.'

Billy chuckled. 'Yeah, I've got the measure of who you are.'

‘Good,’ Reece replied, straightening up. ‘So, we understand each other. You need to fix the mess you caused me.’

Billy tilted his head. ‘Mess?’

‘Yeah, mess. Those plants in your basement. I had a buyer lined up. Now they’re gone, and I’m out of a lot of money. By my book, that makes you in debt to my family, and it’s time to pay up.’

Billy saw precisely where this was heading. His smile remained fixed, but now it was his turn to lean forward, as much as his battered body would allow. ‘All right, no worries. Look, I’ll pay you what you would’ve got on the streets. Let’s say . . . twenty grand? Even though my guy reckons you’d be lucky to pull ten. But, hey, I’m a fair man, as I’m sure you’ve heard.’

Reece eyed Billy suspiciously.

‘So,’ Billy continued, smoothly, ‘stop by the office in a couple of days, and I’ll have the pound notes ready for you.’

Reece stared at him, his expression unreadable, but Billy could sense the gears turning. The Shipleys weren’t used to being negotiated with, especially not by someone who was laid up in a hospital bed.

But Billy wasn’t about to let them think he was weak.

‘Ha! See, you’re a businessman, Billy, so you must know all about interest,’ Reece said, his smirk returning.

Billy nodded. ‘That’s why I said I’ll pay you twenty grand. Fair’s fucking fair.’

However, Reece tutted and shook his head. ‘Nah, mate. The interest has gone up. And with all the messing about, the rate’s climbed by the fucking minute. So now, you owe me a hundred grand.’

‘Really?’ said Billy, sarcastically.

As Reece leaned forward, again his gold chain swung into Billy’s face. ‘Now it’s two hundred grand,’ Reece whispered.

Even though Billy’s body was aching as the painkillers started to wear off, he still managed to let out a fake laugh. ‘Let me tell you something about me, shall I? I’m not stupid, so don’t insult my intelligence. What do you really want?’ He exhaled sharply, his irritation creeping through. ‘Not that I don’t already have a clue.’

Reece threw back his shoulders. 'Your brother,' he said, slowly, letting the words hang in the air. 'He's a copper. In fact, he's on the murder squad – or so I'm informed.'

Billy felt his stomach do somersaults, although his face betrayed nothing. 'Is he?' he replied, casually, despite the wave of nausea rising in him.

'Don't play fucking games, Billy. You know he is, and you also know he's working on a case involving my two brothers.'

Billy shrugged. 'Sounds like a *you* problem to me.'

Jabbing a finger towards Billy, Reece's eyes darkened. 'Don't act like you don't know what your brother does. I do my homework, and you two are close – fucking close. So, let's cut the crap. Forget the money you owe me.'

Billy raised an eyebrow but he stayed silent and let Reece continue.

'I need a favour from your brother,' Reece said, holding up his thumb and forefinger to demonstrate a tiny measure. 'A small favour. And the debt? Well, it'll be cleared.'

'Great, Reece. Then go and talk to my brother,' Billy replied, his voice defiant, despite the sickness draining his energy and making him feel washed out.

But Reece's expression suddenly shifted. To Billy, who was already feeling rough and now lightheaded, it was as though he was staring at something demonic – pure evil. Of course, Reece wasn't a demon, not in the physical sense of the word, but his presence carried the weight of menace.

Without warning, Reece lunged forward and ripped the cannula from the back of Billy's hand. The movement was brutal. It tore the skin and sent a spray of blood across the bed.

Billy clutched his hand. 'Arrgghh!'

But before he could do anything, Reece turned his attention to the tube that was draining the blood from his lungs. He gripped the tube and yanked it out in one cruel motion.

The pain was instantly excruciating. Far worse, even, than a moment ago. Billy's vision blurred as he fought back the rising nausea. And his lungs felt as though they were on fire as he fought to breathe.

'Don't get fucking funny with me, Billy,' Reece growled. 'Your brother, being a copper, won't listen to me.' He paused.

Tapping his lip thoughtfully with his forefinger, he continued. 'But since I happen to possess a certain level of intelligence myself, I took a close butcher's at you. Seems to me that if Jesse won't listen to me, he'll fucking well listen to *you.*'

Billy swallowed hard, the effort to suppress his nausea making the pain even worse. His body throbbed, and every muscle screamed in agony.

Reece leaned in closer. 'Now, you've had a taste of what I can do. Look at you. You're probably lying in your own shit by now.'

'You what? You orchestrated this? You're a fucking coward. You couldn't even do your own dirty work. Afraid I might rearrange your pretty face for you, were you?'

'You don't bother me, Billy, but I hate dirt, and I hate pikey sites. So nope. I let them do the scrapping.'

'I hope you paid them well enough to cover the cost of their own fucking funerals.'

Reece grinned, mockingly, but what he said next gave Billy pause for thought.

'Oh, this was just a taster, Billy. Next time, it won't be a couple of bare-knuckle useless didicoys. It'll be my firm, and it won't be you in that bed. It'll be one of your nearest and dearest.'

Reece moved back fractionally from Billy's face. But it wasn't enough. As he was about to stand up straight, he suddenly froze to the spot.

Billy heaved.

To Reece's horror, the contents of Billy's stomach erupted in a violent projectile stream that splattered across his chest. The mustard-coloured vomit coated his designer black T-shirt in thick slushy streaks. It was sufficient to make him gasp as if someone had thrown iced water over him.

'You *cunt*!' Reece snarled, as he stared in disgust at what had been an expensive shirt. 'You fucking dirty—'

Suddenly, the door opened, and a nurse walked in. She was young and blonde, and her ponytail bounced lightly as she entered cheerfully, completely unaware of the chaos inside.

'Oh dear, dear me,' she said, with a polite smile. 'Let's get you cleaned up, Billy. Sorry, I'm late with your painkillers . . .'

Her voice trailed off as her eyes took in the scene. There was blood dripping onto the floor, the chest tube lay discarded like a snake by the bed, the bed sheets were soaked in blood, and when she looked at her patient, she saw that Billy's hands were also covered in blood.

Her gaze then snapped to the visitor as she pieced together what might have happened.

Reece was already pointing at Billy. 'I'll send a message with the details,' he muttered, before adding a cocky smirk.

The nurse's composure hardened. 'I'm afraid I will have to ask you to leave while I clean this mess up.'

Reece sneered, turned on his heel, and walked out, the door slamming shut behind him.

As soon as Reece was gone, Billy grabbed her arm, his hand trembling. 'Don't let him back in,' he said, hoarsely.

The nurse glanced over her shoulder nervously. 'Did he do this?' she asked, her voice quiet but firm. 'I can call security.'

Feeling very weak, Billy merely shook his head. 'Please . . . can I just have something for the pain?'

The nurse hesitated. A moment later, she began to work, her practised movements swift and focused. She gave Billy a dose of morphine to knock him out while she replaced the drain and the cannula.

***

Reece hurried along the corridor, with his sole focus now on finding the toilets. He didn't notice the dishevelled man heading his way because he was too preoccupied with escaping the vile stench of vomit that clung to him like a curse.

He suffered terribly from emetophobia – the overwhelming fear of vomiting. The very thought of being sick terrified him. Even witnessing someone else throwing up was enough to make him heave, and now, with the foul mess coating his T-shirt and clinging to his skin, his legs felt like jelly.

Bursting into the men's toilets, his breathing laboured, he tore his T-shirt off in one swift motion. He then dumped it into the sink. Once he'd turned on the tap, he scrubbed at the fabric desperately, as if washing away the smell and stains might somehow relieve the growing panic in his chest.

A sudden glance up at the mirror above the sink caused his stomach to lurch again. His eyes widened when he spotted chunks of vomit tangled in his hair. His lips curled in disgust, and without a second thought, he turned on the tap to the adjacent sink and shoved his head under the stream of cold water.

The icy rush helped momentarily, but his stomach's rising nausea betrayed him. His body heaved involuntarily as the thought of the vomit – on his T-shirt, in his hair – threatened to overwhelm him completely.

'Fuck me, I thought it was you, Reece,' came a voice from the doorway.

Reece looked up in the mirror. He had to take a few deep breaths before he could focus on the man speaking. The nauseous feeling finally subsided. Standing there, with his wet hair dripping down his bare chest, he tilted his head trying to place the familiar face. It took him a moment. It had been two years since they had last met, and that was in Manchester Prison. But then, the penny dropped, and his face lit up.

'Well, fuck me. Kenny! So they finally let you out, eh?' He held out his hand.

Kenny grabbed it with a firm shake, his grin wide. 'Good to see you, Reece. How's the family?'

Reece combed his wet hair with his fingers, with the water dripping onto the floor. 'So, you ain't heard about Max and Moriarty, then?'

Kenny's grin faltered slightly, and he rolled his head. 'Fuck me, of course I've heard about 'em. They're awaiting trial, yeah? They're looking at a very long bird, mate. Every cunt and his mother's talking about it. So what are you doing here? Don't tell me it's ol' Candice?'

Shaking his head, Reece then laughed. 'Nah, me gran's as fit as a fiddle. She'd still launch a shoe at me if I got mouthy. No, no, just a bit of business with some bloke called Billy—'

'Murphy, by any chance?' Kenny cut in, his tone sharp.

Reece paused, unsure whether to divulge that information. 'Why d'you ask?'

Kenny let out a dry laugh. ''Cos, Reecie, mate, I'm after the prick meself. More now than ever.'

'Oh yeah? What for?'

Kenny's grin faded.

'Reece, you know better than to ask me questions like that,' he said, his tone carrying a subtle warning. However, he suddenly hesitated, carefully weighing his words because he knew he was pushing his luck. As much as he could probably take on Reece in a straight fight, he didn't have the kind of backing to take on the Shipleys – and he knew whose side he'd rather be on. Still, his curiosity was piqued. He wondered how the Shipleys' involvement with Billy might affect his own plans.

Reece smirked. Sensing Kenny's internal struggle, he decided to say nothing. Instead, he left the tension hanging in the air between them.

Kenny sighed. 'Billy Murphy is part of Cas Ferrier's firm.'

Reece nodded. After wringing out his T-shirt, he walked to the hand dryer.

'Go on, mate. I'm all ears,' he said, motioning for Kenny to continue.

With the sound of the hand dryer working at its maximum, Kenny was forced to raise his voice. 'Cas owes me a lot. He set his men on me, but I scarpered – I wasn't hanging around for a good hiding. But I'm not standing for that. So, I followed the old bastard here and took a wild guess. I asked at reception where Billy Murphy was. Who else would Cas be visiting? From what I hear, Billy's like a son to him.'

The hand dryer clicked off, and Reece straightened up, his T-shirt still damp but passably wearable. He looked at Kenny, his expression calculating. 'So, you've done your homework?'

'Yeah,' Kenny replied, with a shrug. 'There's still a few druggies about who'd sell their own mother for a pound. So, yeah, I'm here to give Cas a warning – to pay up and back the fuck off me.'

Crossing his arms, Reece leaned against the wall and frowned. 'We never venture south of the river as a rule – a mutual agreement between him and my father, the miserable bastard.'

Kenny laughed, his posture loosening slightly. 'I spent many a day playing snooker with your old man in Brixton Prison. You lot were nippers back then. You were getting nicked for nicking half of Marks & Spencer out the back door. Used to make me laugh. But I hear you're all doing well now – own a private housing development, if I'm not wrong.'

Reece smirked and puffed out his chest with pride. 'Yeah. I like to keep my family close.'

Kenny nodded, but his chest tightened as the words left his mouth. The realisation hit him like a cold wave. He might have just walked straight into a hornet's nest. He hesitated, his throat dry, before asking cautiously, 'Reece, about Billy . . . Are you—'

Reece patted Kenny's arm. 'Friends with Billy Murphy?'

Kenny's eyes widened. 'Yeah.'

'No, mate. I'm here to sort out a favour he owes me,' replied Reece, casually.

Once again, Kenny's interest was sparked. 'A favour?'

Reece tapped the side of his nose with a knowing smirk. 'A *little* favour. But I reckon the prick isn't feeling cooperative. And you know me and my family, Kenny. If someone doesn't want to play ball, we always find a way to make them see things our way. You know what I mean?'

Kenny nodded, although his mind was already racing with his own ideas. 'Reece, listen. I think me and you could work together. Can I ask – is your aim financial?'

Reece's signature sly grin spread across his face. 'Nah, Kenny. But I'm guessing yours is.'

Kenny nodded. 'Yeah, and I do believe we could help each other out.'

'Oh, do you now?' Reece asked, as he looked Kenny up and down.

Kenny pressed on. 'How about we meet tomorrow and have a proper chat? I'd love to see your old man again. Me and him had a good few laughs back in the day. And your gran, Candice – now, that woman is something else. Hard as nails. There's nothing fucking fake about her.'

Reece chuckled but he didn't let up his calculating stare. 'Yeah, all right, but do yourself a favour first, mate – have a bath or something. You look rough.'

Kenny felt his face redden. It was part embarrassment and part anger. 'Yeah, well, I had to stay low.'

'And make sure Cas isn't following you,' Reece continued. 'Because we all know his reputation. In fact, I'm fucking surprised you're chasing him for money. If it were me, I'd let that debt go. Especially if he's got a tidy little firm backing him.'

Kenny's jaw tightened, his frustration clear, but he didn't react.

'See, Kenny, we all thought the old man Cas had retired,' Reece went on, his voice thoughtful. 'Turns out, he's still in the game – and that makes him dangerous. That man's got years of experience and keeps his cards so close to his chest that none of us even know if he's up to anything. That's what makes Cas Ferrier a threat. And you?' Reece leaned in slightly, tapping Kenny lightly on the chest. 'Well, you might've underestimated him.'

Kenny's fists clenched by his sides, but, again, he forced himself to stay calm.

'Anyway,' Reece said, with a shrug, 'yeah, I'm sure my ol' man would enjoy a catch-up. If you've got something to put on the table that benefits us both, we'd love to hear it.'

With that, Reece gave Kenny a final once-over and walked off.

Reece's ability to belittle someone left Kenny stewing in his own thoughts.

CHAPTER SIXTEEN

Three weeks had passed, and no one had heard from Kenny Ruck or the Shipleys. Billy had vague memories of Reece's visit, and it left a bitter taste in his mouth for two reasons. Firstly, he found the visit cowardly. Secondly, it was a diabolical liberty to cause further pain to someone already in a vulnerable position.

Straightaway, he decided that he would never ever mention the visit to Cas or Spud. He knew full well that they should have been safeguarding him – well, Spud should have, at least. But, even so, he didn't want the incident to cause a rift between himself and them or for them to feel guilty.

But perhaps the visit had been overegged in his mind. Because although he had recalled Reece saying that he would be in touch with the details of the favour he was calling in, there hadn't, as yet, been a message in any shape or form. So he assumed now that the Shipleys had decided to leave the matter well alone.

His recovery had been quick, thanks to the good work done by Doctor Cummins and his team. The doctor had told him that his speedy recovery was in part due to his fitness. That was a fair point. He was a regular at the gym. And he looked after his diet pretty well. With one notable exception. His mother could always tempt him with the odd cake when he made the occasional visit home.

Today was the day he had a meeting with the building inspector – a right fussy bastard. So, he had to go armed with all the relevant paperwork, which was proving to be a chore to find. It made him realise just how much he had relied on Bronte. Without the final signature, none of the apartments could be occupied. And it hadn't helped that there had been delays brought about by a shortage of some materials. But, eventually, he was at the stage, after plenty of back-and-forth meetings, to get the building signed off. All he needed now was the final approval. Then, he'd be good to go.

However, his first task of the day was to advertise for an assistant. He quickly wrote up a notice, printed it out, and stuck it on the window for anyone passing by to see.

Once he reached the new development block, he noticed the designers had been in and had added the final touches. He looked around one of the finished apartments. It was done to such a high standard that, for a moment, he wished Bronte was there to see the final look. But he quickly brushed that thought aside.

The inspector's name was Thomas Bradford. His dress sense resembled that of an undertaker on his way to direct a funeral.

Bradford didn't even glance at Billy. He was too busy rifling through his file. 'So, Mr Murphy, I'm pleased to inform you that we – my team and I' – he said, pretentiously –'have carried out the final checks, and you have been signed off.'

'You mean the apartments, I take it?'

'Yes, obviously. That's what I just said,' snapped Bradford.

Ignoring Bradford's tone, Billy beamed and held out his hand.

Bradford's handshake was firm, but Billy caught the grimace on the inspector's face. He knew why. The way the man had constantly put him, the owner, in his place, with his incessant attention to detail and condescending remarks, suggested more than a touch of sour grapes. Clearly, Bradford was jealous and somewhat irritated by having to deal with someone as young as he was.

But when Bradford came out with the following audacious comment: 'Amazing how much money drugs make these days,' it was the last straw, as far as Billy was concerned.

Billy's reply was sharp. 'I wouldn't know. I've never taken any, and I've never sold any. And I'd like to believe that you, as a professional, are not suggesting otherwise.'

Bradford shifted nervously, clearly caught off guard.

As soon as the file was handed to Billy, Bradford left. At once, the bad energy in the room left with him.

After finally locking up, Billy returned to the office. The place felt cold, dull, and lifeless. It was just him, his computer, and a fan of newly printed catalogues showcasing the apartments. The quiet was unsettling until the door suddenly opened.

Billy looked up to see a young woman step in. She had blonde hair swept up in a bun, flawless skin, and was dressed impeccably in a satin blouse and a black skirt that flattered her figure perfectly. He couldn't help but jump up from his chair. A broad smile instantly spread across his face.

'Hi, how can I help you?' he asked, eagerly.

She paused, her lips curling into a sultry smile. 'Your apartments,' she began, her voice as smooth as velvet. 'I was just glancing at the pictures in the window. They look perfect for what I'm looking for. But every time I pass, the office is closed. However, finally, you're open, I see.'

Billy nodded. 'Yes, Miss . . .?'

Extending her hand, the woman replied, 'Phoebe. My name is Phoebe Langstone.'

'Pleased to meet you, Phoebe. I'm Billy Murphy, the property developer. Take a seat. Would you like tea? Coffee?'

'No, I'm fine, thank you,' she replied, easing onto the chair. 'I'm interested in the apartments. Are they all taken?'

'I, er . . . can show you some layouts and tell you which ones are still available.'

Billy hurried over to the filing cabinet. After a few anxious minutes fumbling through all the files, he finally found the correct folder, which contained the relevant brochures. It was then that he regretted no longer having an assistant to take on the administration. Bronte usually handled the filing, and now he realised how much he had relied on her.

Before he could present them, the phone rang. 'Sorry, excuse me, I need to take this.'

He moved to the other desk. It was where Bronte worked. She had all the necessary office materials – landline, computer, and diaries – to hand.

When he answered the call, there was silence. Now suspicious, he put the phone down immediately and returned to Phoebe, who was already flicking through the various brochures.

'Do you have a photo of the gardens? It mentions a rooftop terrace,' she asked. She realised then that he was distracted for some reason.

Billy blinked. He knew the photos had come in, but he had no idea where they were. Before he could respond, the phone rang again. Frustrated, he answered, only for the caller to hang up once more.

'Looks like you *do* need that assistant,' Phoebe said, chuckling, pointing towards the sign in the window.

Feeling flustered and far less professional than usual, Billy sighed. 'You're right. My assistant left, so you'll have to bear with me.'

'She left?'

Billy was rifling through the filing cabinet again, trying to locate the garden file, when he turned to face her. 'Do you know anyone who can handle an office, book appointments, and—'

'Yes,' she interrupted, confidently. 'Me, actually. I've been looking for a reason to leave my current job. I don't like the senior manager and would rather work for a smaller company like this.'

Billy frowned slightly. 'A *smaller* company?' he asked, a touch offended. 'My business is hardly small. I own—' He stopped himself, realising his pride was getting the better of him. That wasn't who he was.

'Sorry, no, you misunderstood,' Phoebe said, quickly. 'I work for a large insurance company. I'd *love* the chance to work somewhere where my role varies – like filing.' She nodded at the cabinets. 'Or even showing potential clients the apartments. But I guess that's up to you. I only have to give a week's notice because they owe me three weeks' holiday.' She laughed. 'Sorry, I've been a bit presumptuous, haven't I? I'm sure you already have an agency handling the recruitment. If so, I'd love to have their details so I can apply for the position.'

Billy was still taking her in. Struggling to get his brain in gear, he couldn't help the fact that his mind was more focused on her looks than the business at hand.

'Well?' she prompted, her eyes playful, yet steady.

'I'll tell you what,' Billy said, finally. 'Are you busy now?'

She shook her head.

'Great. How about I show you the apartments, and we can discuss what I'm looking for – and what you're looking for – at the same time? How does that sound?'

'I'd like that very much,' Phoebe replied, with a smile playing on her lips.

Billy nodded, finally feeling more in control, though he couldn't ignore how she'd caught him unawares.

By the time he'd finished showing her around one of the apartments, Billy felt overwhelmingly attracted to her. She'd paid him subtle compliments throughout, each one boosting his ego. Not that he was touched by compliments as a rule; he found them irritating.

What stood out for him was her genuine interest in the business. She asked insightful questions, listened intently, and easily grasped the finer details. Concluding that she would be more of an asset than a hindrance, Billy acted impulsively, by offering her the job on the spot, subject to references.

As she smiled and accepted, Billy couldn't help but feel a strange mixture of excitement and curiosity about what this new chapter might bring. Bronte had fleetingly weaved into his mind, but, again, he brushed thoughts of her away.

When they returned to the office, Billy was surprised to find Cas in the back room. He was overseeing an engineer who was rigging up cameras. 'What's all this?' Billy asked, standing with his hands on his hips and staring up at the man on the ladder.

Cas turned around and grinned. 'You can't be too careful these days, Billy.' Then his eyes shifted past Billy and landed on the young woman. 'New client, Billy?'

Momentarily caught unawares, Billy turned to her. 'Oh, Cas, this is Phoebe. She's going to be my new personal assistant.'

Cas let out a sudden laugh. 'A PA, no less,' he said, stepping away from the engineer to take a good look at her.

'Well,' Cas said with a smirk, 'so, you'll be around the office, then? I suppose it'll brighten things up around here.'

'And you are?' she asked, politely, maintaining her poise.

'Cas Ferrier. But you can call me Cas.'

She smiled and shook his hand. 'And may I ask, are you employed here or . . . ?'

'Employed?' he repeated, sounding almost offended. 'No, no, not me. I'm . . . an investor, shall we say.' He gave her a sharp look before turning to Billy, who was staring at Phoebe, his eyes glazed over with something more than admiration.

Cas cleared his throat and pulled Billy's attention back to the matters at hand. 'Billy, these new state-of-the-art cameras are linked to . . .' He hesitated, glancing briefly at Phoebe. 'Well, let's just say they're linked up.'

'Do we really need them?' Phoebe asked, suddenly.

Both men looked at each other.

Raising an eyebrow and surprised by her boldness, Cas remarked, 'Blimey, girl, how long have you been working here?' His tone told her he wasn't amused.

'Sorry, I'm not used to being filmed, that's all. It's kind of new to me,' she replied, evenly, although her face reddened at his directness.

'Hmm,' Cas muttered, eyeing her carefully. 'Well, get used it, doll. Anyway, I'll be off, Billy.'

With that, Cas gave Billy a nod and walked out, leaving an unusual tension in the room.

A few minutes later, the engineer left, having completed the work.

'Sorry, Billy, I didn't mean to offend anyone.'

'It's fine,' Billy replied, with a reassuring smile. 'Hey, why don't we go out for lunch? I'll close up for the day, and you can tell me all about yourself.'

Phoebe giggled like a schoolgirl, her eyes sparkling and her lips curling into something more than flirtatious. 'I'd love to,' she said.

As Billy held open the door to his Audi TT, she slid in and admired the sleek interior. 'This is nice, Billy.'

'It is,' he said, sliding into the driver's seat. 'I have a few, actually, for business purposes, mainly. But this one's for pleasure.'

Unexpectedly, Phoebe found herself not only very attracted to Billy but also drawn to the way he carried himself. He had a confidence about him – clean-cut, polished, and self-assured. Her gaze lingered on him momentarily, and she noticed faint yellow bruises on his cheek. Her interest flickered, but she kept it to herself.

Before she knew it, they were seated in a private booth at a restaurant twenty minutes away from the office. The atmosphere was intimate, and it was clear from the way the staff pampered Billy that he was someone who was well respected. They treated him like royalty, attending to his every need with a level of attention she wasn't used to.

For all her confidence, Phoebe felt slightly out of her depth, but she couldn't deny the thrill of it all. She knew she was attractive, but being out with someone like Billy in a setting like this was entirely new to her. As she sat across from him and watched how he carried himself with quiet authority and ease, she wondered if this was a life she could enjoy. Of course, she would. Her imagination ran wild with the thoughts of designer handbags, beauty treatments, and being wined and dined in only the best places.

And better still, Billy wasn't someone she'd kick out of bed, that was for sure. In fact, he was very handsome. There was something about him. Whether it was his charm, or the way he exuded confidence without trying too hard, or even that air of mystery that lingered around him, she knew he was the man for her.

She could feel herself being drawn in, despite her usual caution when meeting people for the first time. His allure was undeniable, and the more she watched him, the more she saw him as a future partner. Noticing a piece of lint on his black T-shirt, she gently plucked it away, her fingers brushing lightly against him. As her eyes lifted to meet his, she held the connection just long enough to let him know – without a word – that she liked him.

For a moment, Billy felt flattered but then came the twinge of discomfort. She wasn't the first girl to flirt with him, and while he'd always chalked up his lack of response to being a loyal man – faithful to Bronte – he began to wonder if it was something else. Maybe he just didn't like women making the first move. Still, there was no denying she was more than pretty – she was downright sexy.

Deciding that he wanted her to work harder to keep his attention, he let her take the initiative. She was obviously good at flirting, and he had no desire to stop her. Instead, he allowed her to push her personality to the limit. But, occasionally, he pretended to be distracted to see just how hard she would work to keep him interested in her. Her efforts, he concluded, were impressive, to say the least.

But, with ease, he continued to play that game. He was reeling her in without her even realising it. It seemed to him that she was so focused on trying to win him over that she hadn't stopped to consider who was indeed in control.

After a couple of glasses of wine and an expensive meal of lobster thermidor followed by a crème brûlée – the chef's own recipe – they were ready to head back to the office. However, when Billy suggested she could start work next Monday, at nine sharp, if, of course, the references came back in time, her expression suddenly changed, and she looked dejected.

Billy frowned. Leaning forward slightly, he said, 'Sorry, was there something else?'

Gripping her bag with both hands, she shifted awkwardly. 'I, er, thought maybe we could spend the afternoon together. I really enjoyed the meal, and I think we both enjoyed each other's company. So I . . .' Her voice trailed off.

All the way through lunch, Billy couldn't get enough of her, or so it seemed to Phoebe. Slowly rising from the table, she deliberately swivelled from the hips up to achieve the desired effect of managing to look both coy and seductive at the same time.

But then came the shocker.

Billy hesitated, his polite smile faltering. 'Sorry, Phoebe, I would love to, but it's all come as a surprise, and I haven't had a chance to rearrange my diary. I do have a lot on. But I will call you as soon as the references come in, and, hopefully, I will receive them before Monday. Like I said, the job's yours, if you want it.'

Her face hardened, the warmth draining from her features. Anger swept up her spine like a jolt of electricity. She wasn't used to being brushed off – as she saw it – certainly not by a man. When she'd flirted before, they'd been all over her, barely able to get enough.

But Billy . . . he wasn't dancing to her tune, and that left her reeling. After all, she hadn't gone there with the intention of being so attracted to the man, and now here she was, wanting more, and now, here he was, practically telling her to get lost. Nonetheless, she knew she couldn't force the issue, so she smiled sweetly instead. 'Monday morning it is, then.' She lifted her fingers, showing they were crossed.

Billy drove them back to the office for Phoebe to collect her car, but instead of saying goodbye, she followed him into the office. However, he sat at his desk and pretended to focus on his laptop.

'Oh, okay, I'll see you on Monday,' she said, awkwardly.

'Yep, see you soon,' he replied. His eyes only lifted away from the laptop when he heard the door close. Through the window, he saw her heading towards a red car, her walk more of a determined march – a strut, almost. It struck him as slightly amusing, and he concluded that she was either used to getting her own way or simply enjoyed power walking.

Still, he couldn't deny that he found her attractive, but in an entirely different way from how he'd felt about Bronte. This connection felt fresh, daring, and almost thrilling in its newness. With Bronte, everything had been comfortable – sex with her was soft, gentle, and loving. On the other hand, Phoebe stirred something sharper, an emotion that somehow he couldn't quite name.

He sighed, annoyed with himself for thinking about Bronte again. But, then again, he consoled himself with the thought that comparing both girls was probably expected. After all, Bronte had been a considerable part of his life.

As soon as Phoebe tore off in her motor, he clocked another car parked facing the office. It was a taxi and in it was Bronte. He could see her staring straight at him. Pretending that he hadn't seen her, he sat at his desk and reviewed his emails.

The door opened, and Bronte stood there with a shopping bag and a face so white she looked ill.

'I came by to give you some of your things back. I thought I'd wait until you were out of hospital.' She held up the bag.

Billy felt a flicker of guilt for her, but he was already pursuing someone new – albeit only after a few hours.

'Billy, can I ask you something?' Bronte said, softly, her voice carrying a slight gypsy burr. It differed from Phoebe's crisp, enunciated tone.

'Go on, but be quick. I'm busy,' he replied, his tone colder than intended.

Bronte's eyes teared up. He'd never spoken to her like that before. There had always been a smile, a wink, or a sweet word. Now, it was as though they were strangers. 'That woman who just left here,' she said, hesitantly.

Billy nodded, shutting his laptop with a snap. 'Oh, yes, Phoebe. What about her?'

'Are you . . . er, I mean, is she . . .?'

Billy rose abruptly from his chair. 'Bronte, whatever she is,' he said, firmly, 'it is nothing to do with you. Now, you can leave the bag on the desk, and if there's anything here of yours, please collect it. Don't ever leave your stuff at mine – like your overnight bag – because you won't be staying overnight again. And I'll have my keys back, please.' He held out his hand, his expression unreadable.

Swallowing hard, her voice broke down. 'I-I didn't leave me overnight bag deliberately. I only left it there the morning we broke up, and then I went back to collect it and me other stuff, but . . .' She hesitated and then her cheeks flushed with emotion. 'You made it clear you didn't want me, so I rushed out of the apartment because me friend called me in a state, and so I forgot me bag.'

Billy shrugged, exaggeratedly, his expression sharp. 'It doesn't matter. I returned it to your brother – your *cunt* of a brother. So you and your family stay the fuck away.'

Tears streamed down her cheeks. 'I'm so sorry, Billy. Please, forgive me.'

He pointed to the door, his voice unyielding. 'Just go, Bronte. And don't come back.'

She lingered for a moment, her voice trembling. 'Is she your girlfriend, Billy? Is she?'

A sudden, sharp pain shot through his chest – a reminder of the beating he'd taken. It made him glare at her, the irritation drowning out the part of him that might have softened. 'I'm working on it, Bronte. So spin on your heels and fuck off.'

Her face crumpled, and she nodded slowly. Shoulders hunched, she turned and walked out of the office.

Billy turned away, unable to watch her leave.

The look on her face had been enough to make him want to pull her back, hold her, and apologise. But he stood firm, his fists resting on the desk, his eyes fixed on the closed laptop. He told himself it was for the best, but the weight in his chest told a very different story.

CHAPTER SEVENTEEN

Jesse stared at the images of the Shipley clan on his computer screen. However, as soon as Chief Inspector Redwood stormed into the room, Jesse instantly swivelled on his chair to face him. The man was tall and broad-shouldered, with a deep, authoritative voice that commanded attention. Jesse had always admired the man's vocal control and the way he articulated every word with crisp precision. Even his accent was so different from his own. With mousy brown hair swept back and clean-shaven, his face was unremarkable. However, his towering presence made him impossible to overlook.

'May I have everyone's attention, please,' said Redwood, sighing heavily, as he rubbed his forehead with his thumb, a habit of his. 'As we know, Wesley Jameson was on the missing list. He had an argument with his wife before he stormed out. But his domestic issue is unrelated to this situation.' He hesitated, briefly, before he delivered the final blow. 'Now, he's no longer missing. His body was pulled out of the Thames in the early hours of this morning.'

'Was he murdered?' Jesse asked, eagerly.

Redwood sighed, rubbing his forehead again. 'It appears so. I was there when they hauled him out, and I can tell you now, he didn't look as if he had just gone for a stroll and fallen in. The post-mortem will give us a clearer picture, but there's no doubt – someone put him there.'

A young officer, Melanie Sykes, suddenly teared up. Everyone knew that she and Wesley were close. Some even thought they were having an affair.

Redwood, a man with no sentiment, didn't pull his punches. He turned his sharp gaze on her.

'Did you see him the night he stormed out of the marital home?'

Her face flushed. 'Me, Gov? No, I didn't.'

'Right, we need to turn our attention to who did this, and this now takes top priority. He was one of us, a good officer.'

Jesse glanced around the room. Every officer's facial expression was one of sheer devastation. Then he studied Melanie.

She suddenly bowed her head and covered her face before turning away to stare out of the vast windows overlooking London.

Although Jesse was as stunned about the death of Wesley Jameson as anyone, he noticed that none of the other officers attempted to comfort her. That didn't sit right with him. Not at all. Not even Shona, the officer he guessed to be Melanie's age. In fact, she snuck away shortly after the governor had left. He wondered if anyone was having an affair, maybe it was Shona and Redwood. He had clocked the way she followed Redwood around.

Jumping up from his chair, he hurried to Melanie's side and put an arm around her shoulders.

'Shall we go for a coffee? Get out of here for a bit?'

Silently sobbing, Melanie couldn't offer a response.

Jesse pulled her into his arms and murmured, 'Come on, Mel, let's grab a drink.'

He led her out of the office without so much as a glance at the others. *Fuck them*, he thought. Heartless bastards.

When they reached the canteen, Jesse steered her to a corner booth. 'You sit there, Mel. I'll grab the coffee.' He snatched a napkin from the adjacent table and shoved it into her hands. 'Go on, love, have a good cry. You'll feel better after. Sod them lot upstairs.'

When he returned with the drinks, he sat opposite her and took her hand. 'I'm sorry, Mel. I know you were close.'

She suddenly peered up. 'We were close, yeah, but we were just mates, that's all. I never slept with him – he's married – but I . . . I . . .'

'I get it, Mel,' Jesse said, gently. 'You can love someone without sleeping with them. Anyway, it's no one's business other than yours.'

She studied him briefly before murmuring, 'You're not like the others, Jesse, are you?'

Jesse let out a sharp laugh. 'No, I fucking ain't. Leaving you standing there like that? Heartless pricks.'

She chuckled, softly. 'No, I mean . . . well, you don't suck up to anyone. You're so laid-back, it's like you don't give a shit. But you get results. It's like . . . you think like a criminal. It's almost as if you might have been one, in another life!'

Jesse flashed his lopsided grin and winked. 'Nice one, Mel. Well, I guess to catch a criminal, you have to think like one. And, anyway, I won't suck up to anybody. It's not who I am. I do this job because I want to make a difference – not because I need the money.'

'Obviously.'

'Mel, listen, I'm not asking as a copper but as a mate. Do you have any idea who would've done this?'

Her face flushed again, and she looked down at her hands that were clasped on the table.

She didn't have to say a word – Jesse could see it written all over her face. She was clearly devastated.

'No,' she said, in a flat voice.

But Jesse was like a dog with a bone now. He leaned in. 'Mel, listen, I'm not the bad guy here, all right? I'm a good person. Believe me, when—'

Suddenly, she looked up and tilted her head. 'But are you, Jesse? Are you really? Because everyone knows you've been in a fight. The bruises were obvious, but you've never let on about it, have you? But people are talking, you know.'

Leaning back on his seat, Jesse smirked. 'Good. Let the fuckers talk. I don't care. It wasn't a police matter. But I see how you just changed the subject.'

She stared into her coffee, her fingers wrapped tightly around the cup. 'I don't know who would hurt Wesley,' she muttered, before she quickly looked away.

Jesse watched her closely. 'Did you ever see him with the Shipleys?'

The moment the name left his lips, he caught it. It was the slight dilation of her pupils, the flicker of fear, that alerted him.

'You did, didn't you?'

Melanie's whole demeanour shifted. Her eyes darkened, and her expression hardened, as if she'd just flipped a switch.

'Do you even know how dangerous the Shipleys are?' she hissed, quietly. 'I mean, Redwood put you on this team, which,

Jesse, I have to tell you, has got everyone's back up – including Wesley's. He wasn't happy because Redwood's taken a liking to you and fast-tracked you to head up this case, when Wesley . . .' She paused. 'Well, when he'd already done all the groundwork.'

Jesse frowned. 'What are you getting at?'

Melanie let out a weary sigh. 'I think Redwood brought you on board because you don't know the Shipleys' history. Maybe he saw you as a fresh pair of eyes, or perhaps he thought you might see things from a different angle – a *no-fucks-given* attitude that he felt was needed. But it wasn't fair on Wesley. He'd spent years trying to arrest the Shipleys. He knew them inside and out. But, suddenly, he was pushed to the back seat while you got the lead.'

Jesse nodded. 'I agree. Totally, Mel.'

'You do?'

'Yeah. I was blown away myself. Thrilled but shocked. The way I see it, if Wesley wasn't skinny-dipping in the Thames, then the only people who would want him dead would be the Shipleys. If that's the case, he must have had something on them.'

Melanie wiped another stray tear from her cheek and shook her head. 'But why kill him? What difference would that make to the case? Max and Moriarty don't stand a chance of walking free. We've got the gun, the witnesses . . . The list goes on.'

Before Jesse could even taste his coffee, Officer Witchell, a rotund man in his fifties, came hurrying over. 'Jesse, the governor wants you in his office. Now.'

'What's all that about?' Melanie asked, swiftly, but she was met with a sneer.

'The governor asked for Jesse, not you.'

***

Although Jesse knocked hard, he didn't wait for an answer. Pushing the door open, he strode in.

Standing with his hands clasped behind his back, Redwood's expression looked grim. 'There's been two major developments that have just *bloody* come to light.' He held up a file. 'We have a serious problem,' he said, tightly. 'When you shot off with Officer . . . er, whatever her name is—'

'Melanie Sykes, Gov,' Jesse said, quickly, trying to placate the governor's mood.

'Max Shipley's team – yes, his fucking team of defence barristers, and that bloody solicitor Wallace Bear – God, I detest that man. He brought this to me in person, with a smug grin on his face too.' He slapped the file clearly labelled 'ballistics report' with the back of his hand.

Jesse shook his head in confusion. He wondered where his boss was going with this conversation. 'I guess he's just doing his job, Gov.'

Redwood shot him a glare. 'His job? *His job?*' he spat. 'The man's as bent as the rest of them. Have you seen what he drives?'

'Well, I do have the same car, Gov.'

Redwood's irritation deepened. 'Yes, but we looked into your finances. Your wealth is accounted for.'

Jesse smiled, inwardly, because he knew they had. It was par for the course when an officer had money. And he hadn't hidden the fact that he owned a Rolex, valuable property, and flash cars.

'But, Jesse, Wallace Bear doesn't have that kind of money. Still, I digress.' Redwood cleared his throat. 'As I was saying, there have been two recent developments. Max Shipley's team put in a request a few days ago. They wanted the bullets allegedly fired from his gun to be tested by their own ballistics expert.'

Jesse nodded.

'Well,' Redwood said, grimly, pointing to the file, their expert's report came back, and the bullets didn't match the gun.'

Jesse frowned. 'But, Gov, one of the bullets was retrieved from the female victim's body.'

'Yes, yes, spare me the gory details,' Redwood snapped. 'But their specialists have now confirmed otherwise.'

Jesse stiffened. '*What?* But our ballistics report confirmed it *was* a match. As I understand it, it's like a fingerprint. Once a bullet is fired, the imperfections inside the barrel leave unique markings.'

Redwood exhaled, sharply. Rubbing his forehead with his thumb, he fixed Jesse with a stern look.

'Someone swapped the bullets for another set.'

A heavy silence fell between them as Jesse absorbed what Redwood was saying.

'Gov, they have a camera facing the evidence storage unit and a check-in and check-out record. I'll go down and request it. We'll get a better idea of who tampered with the evidence.'

Slowly, Redwood shook his head. 'No need. I've already a very good idea who switched the bullets – because the original bullets were found on . . .' He held up his finger. 'No, sorry, *in* Wesley himself.'

Jesse's heart seemed to go into freefall. 'Shit . . . he was *shot*?'

Redwood shook his head again. 'No, Jesse. He swallowed them.'

Jesse's brows furrowed. 'How do you know?'

'Because his post-mortem took priority. The man was a copper. Charlotte Holmes, our forensic pathologist, called literally minutes ago with the news. The same time Wallace Bear handed me the report.'

'Oh, right. How did he die, Gov?'

'He was beaten to death. Apparently, there wasn't so much as a penny between his bruises. His chest was crushed, and his skull was caved in. They used some kind of blunt axe or a heavy tool.' He sighed.

'The Shipleys?'

'Of course, the bloody Shipleys,' Redwood muttered. 'But we have no witnesses, no evidence. Once again, those violent, evil scumbags walk free. That's the problem. They're too well known in the underworld. No one dares turn Queen's evidence. Not even the low-life druggies will grass. There's not one of those Shipleys who hasn't been through the interview rooms or on our radar – not one damn bastard. And most of them walk away scot-fucking-free.' He suddenly banged his fists on the desk. 'Those animals have their own fucking army. And now they're even building their own little estate.' He huffed. 'I wouldn't be surprised if they build a damn fortress.'

Jesse watched as his boss, who was now smouldering with anger, clenched his jaw and curled his fingers into fists.

'But one day,' Redwood muttered, 'I'll fucking have them.'

The swearing shocked Jesse. He'd never heard Redwood cuss before, and it sounded strange coming from him. But, then again, years of trying to bring the Shipleys to justice had clearly turned into his life's work – a personal mission to take them down.

'So now you've heard the latest developments, I need you to nail these bastards.'

'Gov, may I ask . . . why me? Why did you put me on the team? And in charge?'

Redwood took a deep breath and sat down on his plush high-backed chair. Before speaking, he checked the door to ensure no one was lingering outside.

'Jesse, I know your background. I know who you're in business with. I know about Cas Ferrier and your uncles.'

Jesse nodded, that cheeky glint clearly showing in his eyes. 'Go on.'

'There's one word that comes up when people mention the Murphys. Fearless. Sometimes, they throw in ruthless, too. And when I watch you, Jesse, you've got this way about you – this charm – but more than that, it's like nothing ever rattles you. Everything just rolls off your back.' Redwood leaned forward. 'I never see fear or concern in your eyes. You just get on with things. Unlike some of the others on the team, who struggle with stress.' He held up his hands. 'I'm not knocking them – they all do a good job, and this job is stressful. But you? You're unfazed.'

'So you did your background check on me and mine?'

'Of course, I bloody did. The Murphys have history. And Cas? Well, he certainly does.' Redwood laughed. 'Cas is a different breed. He did us a favour a while back – brought a bent copper to justice. He also helped us put . . .' He hesitated.

'My biological dad, the tosser, behind bars?' Jesse smirked. 'It's all right. I can talk about him.'

Redwood nodded. 'See? Nothing fazes you, does it. You tell it like it is. You're straightforward. And most of all, Jesse, you're no idiot. We need your knowledge and attitude if we're ever going to take down the Shipleys.'

'And Wesley?'

Redwood sighed. 'Look, Wesley was weak. That's why I put you in charge. I suspected he couldn't really handle the Shipleys. He'd been on their case for years and had never secured any significant charges. They always seemed to be one step ahead. But I get the feeling they won't with you.'

'Yeah, but maybe they get away with crimes because, as you just implied, they've got a team of lawyers. Let's face it, Joe Public just gets the one drippy duty solicitor, if they're lucky.'

'Or maybe the Shipleys were blackmailing Wesley. Or lining his pockets. I don't know, but it's concerning.'

Jesse thought about Billy's run-in with the Shipleys, but he decided to keep his mouth shut about that as well as the presence of all those marijuana plants in the basement of the new building. It seemed that the Shipley family had been very cunning. They knew he wouldn't tell his superiors about something like that. But the Shipleys had one thing over him, though. That was for sure. And now the situation had only got a whole lot worse. Shortly after Billy had landed in the hospital, a parcel arrived at the apartment. Inside were photos of him. He had gone to the basement to check that Ross had removed all the plants and the equipment, only to find Ross still in the throes of it. Naturally, he gave his cousin a hand. But, unbeknown to him, the Shipleys had set up concealed cameras. They had him. Enough evidence to slap an 'intent to supply' charge on him, which could quickly put him behind bars.

But it could implicate himself too, thought Jesse.

Since then, there had been no communication. No threats. No visits. Nothing.

It was as though the Shipleys had backed off.

'So what now, Gov?'

'The witnesses. One of them is getting restless. Says he can't handle being in the safe house. He says he's going stir-crazy.'

But Jesse's mind was still on Wesley. He frowned. 'Sorry, Gov, going back to Wesley. If you reckon he switched the bullets with another pair that was not a match for the Shipleys' gun, why would the Shipleys kill him?'

'Who knows? Maybe he was going to hand them the bullets, but then, he changed his mind and swallowed them instead. He had a row with his wife – a nasty one, by her accounts. We're not privy to what was going through his head.'

'So it's possible the Shipleys met with him to get the bullets. But if he swallowed them. . .' Jesse's expression darkened. 'My God, if they knew he swallowed them, they'd have cut him open, wouldn't they?'

Redwood's face paled. He hesitated, and then he smiled nervously.

'Between us, Jesse . . . they did.'

Jesse's stomach tightened.

'He wasn't just beaten to death,' Redwood continued. 'He was cut open. But whoever did it – the butcher – was probably disturbed before they found what they were looking for. Then again . . .' He swallowed hard. 'The insides of his body are a mess. You have to know what you're doing.'

'Fuck a duck, that's gross,' Jesse muttered, forgetting for a moment who he was sitting in front of.

'Gross?' Redwood shot him a look. 'It's damn well inhumane. I wish I could round up every last one of them and—' He stopped himself, exhaling sharply.

Jesse cleared his throat. 'So, if we have the bullets back in our possession, then we've still got enough evidence to make the charges stick, surely?' He huffed. 'That is, as long as the witnesses keep their cool.'

Redwood sighed. 'It's not as simple as that. The bullets would have secured a conviction, but the problem is they were removed from the evidence room. Their lawyers know the judge will rule that the bullets used to kill the Fairweathers will be inadmissible.'

'Oh, I see. That certainly puts a different slant on things, Gov, doesn't it.'

Redwood nodded. 'So, Jesse, forget about the bullets. They're likely to be irrelevant now. We have a more pressing issue. The witnesses. As I said, the male witness is getting restless. What I want you to do is get over to the safe house and turn on the charm. We cannot afford to lose them as well. Everything now hinges on their appearance in court.'

Jesse nodded. He was on his feet in a jiffy.

'You'll have to slip out the back in an unmarked car,' Redwood continued, as he unlocked his desk drawer. He pulled out a folded piece of paper and handed it to Jesse. 'That's the address. Memorise it. You're going alone. Tell no one.'

Jesse's eyes flicked over the address before handing back the note.

Redwood's voice dropped lower. 'After what they did to Wesley, we must take special precautions. Be extra vigilant.'

As Jesse left Redwood's office with the address he was given, he realised that Redwood had answered his question about his suitability to head up this team. He would prove to everyone he was more than up to the job.

CHAPTER EIGHTEEN

Jesse glanced up at the clock. *Bollocks*, he thought. He would hit rush hour. Still, a direct order was something he couldn't ignore. Grabbing his jacket from the back of his chair, he noticed Melanie waiting for him near his desk.

'All right, love? Oops, sorry, habit. Can't call you *love* anymore. Anyway, how are you doing, Mel?'

Although she smiled, the smile didn't quite reach her eyes. 'I'll be fine, I suppose. I'm going to keep busy with the case and try to take my mind off things. All I want now is for the people responsible to be caught.'

'Yes, we all do.' Jesse slid his arms into his jacket and grabbed his keys. 'Must go, Mel. Keep your chin up.'

Shona shuffled her way over, her auburn fringe sticking to her forehead. 'Where are you off to? Have you got a lead?'

He shook his head. 'Other business.'

'What business?'

He tapped the side of his nose. 'Not yours, Shona.'

He turned to leave, but when she suddenly grabbed his arm, he stopped dead. Her expression had changed. She appeared intense, almost determined.

'Jesse, we all want these bastards caught. I can help, you know. I *want* to help. I liked Wesley. He was a good 'un'.' Shona's face flushed.

'Was he?' Jesse snapped, absolutely furious. 'I'll tell you what he was. He was a bloody traitor. The bastard tampered with the bullets!'

'What!' she shrieked, which was echoed by Melanie.

Jesse lowered his voice to a calmer pitch and said, 'Nevertheless, Shona, I'll leave no stone unturned. I'll find who killed Wesley. If it's linked to that poor pregnant woman's murder, I won't stop until they're behind bars.'

But Melanie suddenly looked away, ashen-faced.

Shona stepped back, as if she'd seen something in his eyes – something that told her that this case wasn't just a work-related matter for him. *Had he experienced something like this before in his private life?* she wondered. It wouldn't surprise her if he had.

Of course, she had no idea about Willow Price. The girl who was murdered while three months pregnant with Jesse's child.

As soon as Jesse left the Serious Incident Room, he glanced over his shoulder. No one was following him. But David was glaring at Shona as if they had some shared interest.

Jesse was now on edge. The thought of cutting open a man's guts to find bullets was enough to give anyone the wobbles.

It made sense now. The reason the Shipleys hadn't been near Billy, and they hadn't made any more threats, wasn't because they'd backed off. They'd clearly been too busy dealing with Wesley and the sabotaged bullets.

It made him consider if the Shipleys had threatened someone close to Wesley. Forced his hand, perhaps? It would explain why Wesley had swapped the bullets for two random ones.

Deep in thought, he wondered if he had missed any obvious signs that pointed towards Wesley working with the Shipleys. And, more importantly, who else might the Shipleys have in their back pockets?

Doubt had been weaving in and out of Jesse's mind all day, and now it felt as though a noose was being tightened around his neck. As he drove along the back roads in what looked like an average rep's car, heading for Dorking, the journey gave him some peace of mind. He wouldn't be recognised, for one. And, more importantly, it gave him time to think about Billy.

If the Shipleys really wanted to get to him, they'd use his brother to do it. It stood to reason.

But it was a worry. What if Billy, being Billy, tried to handle the Shipleys alone? He wouldn't put it past his brother to do just that because as much as they were so close, Billy could be a lone wolf at times.

It made him consider chucking in the towel. He could handle himself, and he was really enjoying his job, but he couldn't risk his family getting hurt. Or worse.

As soon as he'd spoken to the family in the safe house, he'd head back and talk to Billy.

Perhaps property development wasn't so boring after all.

***

The little cottage was nestled in a small, quaint, and quiet wooded area, miles away from the nearest village. It wasn't Jesse's ideal home, but for a romantic getaway, it would be perfect. He crawled slowly along the narrow driveway, which branched off the main road, and manoeuvred through a tight, overgrown lane. The dense trees and bushes made it feel almost hidden from the world. When the path opened up, the cottage came into full view, and Jesse immediately noticed the police car parked to the side.

As soon as he got out of his vehicle, the cottage door swung open, and an officer appeared. He was looking both flustered and unimpressed.

Jesse held up his ID with a casual smirk. 'Jesse Murphy. The governor sent me along to have a word. Apparently, one of the witnesses is getting cold feet.'

The officer let out a heavy sigh and glanced back towards the house. 'You'd best come in. I've tried, but Jim Davenport, the fella in question, has already packed his bags, and as for the wife, Mia, well, she . . .' He leaned in closer and lowered his voice. 'I reckon she's champing at the bit to get out of here. I can see they might be husband and wife, but she's a nightmare. I reckon, she's been stubbed more times than Stevie Wonder's big toe. She was flirting with me only an hour ago, and he was ready to have her by the throat.' The officer shook his head. 'Anyway, detective, since you're here now, I'll get off.'

'Whoa, mate, you're the handler. I'm not here to take over. I just need a quick word with them, that's all.'

'Oh, for pity's sake,' the officer muttered. 'Well, I'm having a fag. You do your best before they kill each other.'

Jesse nodded, patted the dishevelled-looking officer on the shoulder, and stepped inside. The living room was small, with heavy blackout curtains and exposed wooden beams. It was in cosy contrast to the tension lingering in the air.

Mia, who was possibly in her late twenties, although it was hard to guess, sat stiffly on one side of the room, while her husband, who was clearly older, stood rigidly holding a suitcase.

The moment Jesse stepped into the room, they both froze, their eyes locked on him in suspicion. The man's expression shifted from stunned to wary, but Jesse flashed his warrant card and gave him a cheeky grin.

'Relax. I'm a detective on the case. How about we all sit down and have a nice little chat?'

Mia immediately sat down opposite him, her gaze never leaving his face. She was almost trancelike, her bulbous eyes just staring.

Jesse noticed it right away – and so did her husband.

Jim gripped the handle of his suitcase tightly. 'I'm not staying. Not with *her*. Fucking hell, she's like a dog on heat. She's always eyeing up the officers. It's embarrassing.'

'Mr Davenport,' Jesse said, keeping his tone calm, 'can I call you Jim?'

The man let out a heavy sigh. 'Yeah, if you must.' The man's voice was laced with a hiss as he whistled through his missing front tooth.

'Jim, listen, I get it. This is a tough situation, mate. I'd find it hard, too.' Jesse gestured around the small living room. 'This place. It's poky. It's got that old feel to it.' He grinned slightly. 'Bit like something out of *Hansel and Gretel*.'

Jesse made his remarks deliberately, knowing full well that the Davenports lived in a cramped top-floor flat in an old Victorian house. When he'd looked over it a few weeks ago, it was apparent they didn't have much. And she – well, she wasn't exactly house-proud. But one thing was clear: this little cottage was like a five-star hotel compared to their poxy, flea-ridden place.

'And I understand that being in each other's pockets twenty-four-seven would drive you around the bend. Especially if, like me, you fancy a nice pint in the local with your mates.'

Jim was steadily warming to Jesse – he spoke like one of his own. 'Well, yes, it's hard, er . . .'

'Jesse. Jesse Murphy,' Jesse added, with a casual nod. 'Call me Jesse. And I know it is.'

His gaze shifted to Mia, who was still staring at him and making him feel hot under the collar. In fact, her drooling made him feel sick. She wasn't exactly subtle about it, either.

Jesse had seen this kind of situation before. It was obvious, she had already checked out of the marriage. He'd bet money that the two of them would go their separate ways, once this was over.

And by the look of her, she had lived a desperate life, certainly not a healthy one.

Mia gave a slow nod.

'She hates this as much as you do. Right?' said Jesse.

Jim turned to his wife and eyed her with resentment. 'Yes, we both want out, don't we, Mia?'

She folded her arms. 'Yeah. To tell ya the truth, I can't stand the fucking sight of him right now, and he can't stand the sight of me. Let alone share a bed. I'd rather sleep in the fucking woods.'

Jesse wanted to laugh, but this wasn't the time and place.

'So, tell me,' Jesse said, straightening up, 'is the reason you two want to leave the safe house just because you aren't getting on?'

Jim gave a curt nod. 'No, detective. It's *her* – the tramp – she has a secret phone. She was keeping the fact from me.'

Jesse's eyes flickered with interest but also concern. 'You *what*? You know you can't bring a phone here – they'll trace you.'

A tear suddenly slipped down Mia's cheek. 'I'm going insane in here with him. I just wanted to talk to someone else.'

Jim let out a bitter laugh. 'Yeah, she'd rather talk to *anyone* but me. And . . .' He lowered his voice. 'She is seeing someone else. I know she is, and I reckon she was before we got caught up in all this bollocks.'

Jesse turned sharply towards Mia. 'Is that true?'

Mia shot an angry glance at Jim before shifting her attention back to Jesse. 'Yeah. But I'm *not* seeing him now, am I? Clearly, I'm fucking stuck here in the arsehole end of nowhere.'

'I get it. I do.' Jesse's eyes ping-ponged between Jim and Mia. 'The thing is, right, as much as you two aren't getting along—' He held up a hand before Jim could start hollering again. 'You're both making a huge difference. To society. Jointly.'

Jim scoffed, but Jesse pressed on.

'Tell me, what keeps you both in North London? Your flat? What is it? Family? Friends?'

They exchanged a look, and then they shook their heads.

Jesse thought back again to the state of their flat. It was part of a run-down Victorian house. The damp walls, the peeling paint. Then, he looked at them. Their clothes were tatty, and their skin was greasy. In fact, Mia had terrible skin and a few missing teeth. And as for Jim, he wasn't exactly a Brad Pitt lookalike.

'Being in a witness protection programme does have its benefits, you know.'

Jim snorted. 'How the fuck do you work that out?'

'You get relocated. New identities. They even find you jobs.'

'I thought they were telling us a load of old flannel. They made it sound too good to be true.'

'Yes, it's not perfect, but it's a fresh start, as long as you stick to the plan. And the cottage is part of the plan.'

Mia looked away. She seemed to Jesse to be chewing the inside of her chapped lip. That was when he noticed her fingernails – or what was left of them – because they were bitten down to the quick. And as he studied her more closely, he saw her bounce her leg restlessly. She was craving for something. Not necessarily for drugs, but for a fix of some kind. Maybe alcohol.

He then looked at Jim. His sunken cheeks from the absence of any back teeth, as well as the gap in the front, weren't from old age. He was actually quite young.

Jesse's eyes then drifted to Jim's arms, where he spotted faint track marks. A further observation saw him consider the bulging veins on his skinny bare legs, which were poking out of his oversized faded shorts. The realisation hit him fast. Without thinking, he blurted out the obvious question.

'Are you an ex-heroin addict?'

Jim hesitated at first, and then he nodded. 'Yeah. What's that got to do with it?'

Jesse didn't answer. He turned to Mia. 'And you?'

She nodded but looked down in shame.

'Did you meet in a programme? Rehab?'

Jim shook his head. 'No, we met before.' His tone had changed. Clearly, he seemed intrigued now, wondering where Jesse was going with this.

'That's probably why you're both struggling,' Jesse said. 'You were different people before rehab. And now, off the drugs, or whatever else you were on, you're seeing the world through different eyes. One of the biggest dangers for you two is this: you might trigger each other's cravings, especially in a situation like this. And I get it. I do. It must be hard.'

'It *is* fucking hard.'

He looked at Mia, who was now staring out of the small leaded light window.

'Mia, was it a boyfriend you were phoning or a dealer?'

Mia's face turned bright red. 'No! It was just a fella.'

But Jesse knew she was lying. 'Mia, you aren't having an affair, are you? It was your dealer you were calling, wasn't it?'

Before she could answer, Jim turned to her and exploded. 'Are you fucking mental or what?' He threw his hands in the air. 'We don't even have money for drugs! How the fuck were you gonna pay for 'em?'

That was it. Jesse had heard enough. He jumped up, his patience snapping. 'Are you two even *hearing* yourselves? *For fuck's sake!* Jim, Mia – do you have any idea how *serious* this is?' He glared between them. His voice was now at fever pitch. 'I can't believe you're sitting here worrying about *how* you'd pay for drugs! That thought shouldn't have even *entered* your tiny fucking minds!'

'You can't speak to us like that!' Mia snapped, suddenly acting as if she was thoroughly offended.

'Seems to me, Mia, I *have* to talk to you in a language you fucking understand. Because, evidently, you haven't been listening to anyone else about how dangerous this gang is. Yes, a *gang*, Mia! A fucking *gang*. A group of very *evil* men. Fuck the drugs. You won't have a *head* if you carry on fucking arsing about.'

Ignoring Jesse, Jim jabbed a finger at her. 'You were seriously calling a dealer? Who, Mia? *Who?*'

She looked down, her voice barely above a whisper. 'Northern Brett.'

Jim's face twisted with rage. '*Where* would you get the money for Brett? Selling your arse to him, are you? Back on the game, yeah?'

Mia's eyes gave it away. She glanced towards the sideboard, and as Jesse followed her gaze, he noticed a thin layer of dust on the surface – probably a week's worth – but, more importantly, a clear ring outline where something had once been. He knew then. She had something to sell. And that *something* didn't belong to her.

Shaking his head in disappointment, Jesse glared at Mia. 'Right, Mia, you need to be *honest* with me. Because if you're not, you'll be risking *all* our lives. Now, did you give this Brett geezer this address?'

She hesitated, chewing her lip. 'Listen, I'm not that stupid. I trust Brett. Believe me, he's as safe as houses. He won't—'

'He's a fucking *dealer*, Mia! A fucking *dealer*! They're *not* as safe as houses!' Jesse threw his hands up in the air in frustration, his temper barely held in check. 'For fuck's sake . . . Right, you two – *wait here.*'

Storming out of the front door, he found the officer hunched over his phone.

At the sound of Jesse's footsteps, the officer straightened up immediately.

'Everything all right?'

'No, it ain't all right! Fuck me! You're their handler. You had *one* job – watch those two soap-dodgers in there! Well, guess what? She's only given her fucking *dealer* this address.'

The officer's mouth dropped open. 'Oh, shit.'

'Yeah, mate – *oh, fucking shit!* Get them in the car and get them *out* of here. *Now.*'

'But – I'm off duty in fifteen minutes.'

Jesse's hands flew into the air. 'I don't give a flying fuck! You could be *dead* in fifteen minutes if you're still here! Jesus.' He jabbed a finger at the officer. 'Now, get on the radio – tell them you need backup.'

Without waiting for a response, Jesse hurried back inside, where he found Jim holding Mia in a tight embrace.

'Right, fucking *Dumb and Dumber* – get your arses in the car.'

Mia blinked. 'Shall I pack my stuff?'

Jesse gaped at her. 'Tell me this: are you deliberately acting like a fool, or is this just for show? Because let me tell you, love, I am not at the fucking theatre right now! So get in that car before we *all* get fucking shot, or worse!'

***

Jesse followed the police car as it pulled out of the driveway and on to the main road. His eyes continually glanced to the rear-view mirror to scan for any suspicious vehicles. Nothing looked out of place. Still, he decided to follow the police car all the way to the police station out of town and make sure that no one was tailing them. They'd need a new safe house and fast.

Once parked outside the station, Jesse pulled out his phone and dialled Redwood's secretary. 'Put me through to Chief Inspector Redwood,' he said, and, surprisingly, she gave him the governor's private number.

It rang twice before Redwood answered. 'Murphy!'

'Gov, we've got a problem. Those two witnesses? They're ex-druggies. And she was on the blower to her dealer. The stupid cow gave the man the safe house address.'

'*No!*' Redwood's voice sharpened. 'Where are they now?'

'Gov, they're at the station. I followed them to make sure no one was on their tail, and I *think* they're okay, for now. But they need proper round-the-clock protection. They're a handful. A few crayons short of a masterpiece and very volatile.'

'Ex-druggies*?*' Redwood muttered. 'I'm wondering if they're even reliable witnesses. The defence team will have a field day tearing them apart on the stand.'

'Well, they will if she gets her hands on any gear. I suggest bringing in a counsellor – or at least a protection officer who's got experience dealing with addicts. Someone who knows the pitfalls of withdrawal and relapse . . . She looked ready to shove *anything* in her arm. And he looks ready to put a shovel through her head.'

Redwood exhaled sharply. 'That's all we need, but hey, listen, good work, Jesse. Good work.'

'Cheers, Gov.'

'Thanks for the update. And don't worry: the officer in charge of the safe house will be reprimanded for this mess. Anyway, at least you're safe, and so are the witnesses.'

In the background, Jesse heard a woman's voice.

'I must go. Thanks again,' Redwood said, abruptly, before hanging up.

Jesse glanced back at the police station and watched as the backup team pulled in behind his car. As the doors swung open and the officers stepped out, he shook his head.

Two of them looked as though they'd barely made it out of school. Their uniforms were too crisp, and their faces were fresh with inexperience. The other two, stepping out of the second vehicle, didn't inspire much confidence either. One of them tripped over his own feet and, in the process, accidentally shoved his partner, who barely managed to stay upright.

Jesse couldn't believe what he was seeing.

'What have we here? A Laurel and Hardy show? God help those witnesses.'

CHAPTER NINETEEN

Ginty slammed the taxi door shut and threw the ten-pound note through the driver's window. 'And I hope you *choke* on it! Fucking daylight *robbery*!'

She hitched her heavy fake designer Burberry bag over her arm and stomped towards the property office. Just as she reached for the door handle, she paused.

An attractive blonde girl was sitting in what had once been Bronte's chair. Ginty eyed her for a moment. The girl looked up and spotted her. Then, instead of offering a polite smile, she curled her lip in mild disdain and returned her focus on the laptop.

Ginty shoved the door open, stood on the threshold, and locked eyes with her. 'And who the *fuck* are you?' she asked, with her arms folded across her chest.

The blonde girl barely looked up. 'Actually, I should be the one asking that question, shouldn't I?'

'Oh, cocky little *madam*, I see.' Ginty tilted her head and studied her. 'And what exactly are you doing in Bronte's chair?'

The girl stood up, her posture straight, her body language unbothered. 'Bronte no longer works here. *I* do. So, I'll ask you again: who are you, and how can I help?' The last part, though, was dripping with forced politeness. She could see she was making the fat woman's blood boil. Her face was as red as a beetroot.

Ginty looked at the girl – the sheer arrogance of her – and replied, 'Cor, girl, when my Billy finds out you were less than polite to me, he'll have your guts for garters.'

The girl's expression didn't flicker. Not even close. 'I highly *doubt* that. I'm his *personal assistant*. And again: who are you?'

Ginty squared her shoulders. 'I'm his grandmuvver.'

Phoebe's eyes widened slightly. The next word left her mouth before she could stop it. '*Really?*'

'What the fuck do you mean – really?' Ginty's expression darkened. 'What are ya saying? That I *don't* look like his grandmuvver?'

Phoebe let her gaze drop to the fake Burberry bag, the dress that belonged on a much younger woman, and the all-over box-dye hair, which had been scraped back too tightly. The large gold hoops swinging from her ears, the layers of gaudy gold chains, and, most of all, that thick Romany accent made her question whether this woman had lost the plot if she genuinely thought she was related to Billy. *Surely*, she thought, *this woman was lying*. Because Billy – who was always immaculate, who always spoke with authority and charm, and who was clearly very rich – could never be related to this rough-looking woman.

Phoebe arched her brow, her doubt evident. 'So you're Billy's grandmother. Is that correct?'

'Do your ears work, or is your fucking brain on strike?' Ginty growled.

Before Phoebe could respond, Ginty walked across to Billy's desk, launched her bag onto it, and began rooting through the contents, muttering under her breath as she did so. Within seconds, she had yanked out her phone and immediately phoned Billy.

As the phone rang, she glared at Phoebe, her expression fierce and unyielding.

That was when Phoebe realised this wasn't some kind of joke. This big gold-clad gypsy woman was dead serious. She wasn't just putting on a show.

Phoebe opened her mouth to apologise, but by now, Ginty was barking into the phone before she could even get a word out.

'Finally, Billy boy! What's the point of having a mobile if it ain't on ya person? Anyway, never mind, I'm in the office, and this hoity-toity slip of a girl—'

'Phoebe?'

'*Who?*' Ginty barked.

'Phoebe, Nan. She's my new assistant.'

'Well, she needs some *fucking* manners. She's been looking me up and down like I was a bit o' dogshit. And . . .' She lowered her voice and turned her face away from the girl for a moment. 'She ain't as pretty as Bronte. Not for love or money, she ain't.'

'She's my assistant, Nan, that's all.'

Glancing across to Phoebe and now thoroughly enjoying the uncomfortable expression creeping across the girl's face, she gave her a sarcastic grin and turned her back on her again.

'When are you back, Billy boy? I wanted to measure up for the curtains. I'm really *not* into these fancy designs. You know me, I'm all about making a home look like a home, not like a clinical *lavatory*.'

'Lavatory? Don't you mean laboratory?'

'Yeah, *that's* it. So, when are you back?'

'Look, I'll be a while, but Phoebe can take you there.'

Ginty's eyes locked on to Phoebe, who stiffened slightly at hearing her name being mentioned.

'Put Phoebe on, would you?'

Phoebe could barely hide her smug expression as she took the phone from Ginty. Before Billy could say a word, she quickly said, 'I'm so sorry, Billy, I had no idea you were expecting your grandmother. I would have made her a coffee, and, obviously, I, uh . . .'

'No harm done, Phoebe. Please show her the apartment. And yes, if she needs a drink, sort that for her.'

'Yes, of course. Er, when will you be in?'

'I don't know yet. Why?'

'Oh, I just wondered, that's all.'

'To be honest, Phoebe, I only keep a diary for meetings, which I showed you how to access on your computer. Look, it's only your second day. You'll get used to it.'

'Yes, I'm sure I will. Okay, I'll lock up and show your granny around the apartments.'

'Great, thank you.'

Ginty grinned, triumphantly, feeling on top of the moon.

'Right, now that's sorted, I'll have a cup of tea, three sugars, please,' she said, still smirking. 'And there should be some of those chocolate biscuits in that bottom drawer, there.'

Phoebe wanted to shoot her a bitch face but she decided against it. Best to keep Billy's family onside. Still, she couldn't shake a deflated feeling creeping on. Billy had been so attentive in their conversations, even agreeing to another lunch date. But now? Now, he felt distant. Cold, in fact.

With a heavy sigh, Phoebe walked across to the drinks machine and made Ginty a cup of tea. Just as she was about to take it over to her, the back door swung open.

A tall woman wearing a navy-blue linen suit strode into the office, having carelessly let the door bang shut behind her. She looked every inch a businesswoman, with her reddish hair swept up into a loose bun and an attaché case tucked under her arm.

Dottie's sharp eyes immediately landed on Ginty. And by God, she wanted to roll them. But every time she thought about sneering at the woman, she forced herself to swallow any saliva down. Because at the end of the day, the boys were *free*. And they could have been rotting in prison if it hadn't been for Ginty.

'Ginty. What a nice surprise to see you here,' Dottie said, keeping up the pretence of respect, even though, deep down, she still found it difficult to shake off the past. But, mentally, she had to acknowledge that Ginty had changed. She was now one of the family's biggest supporters. And if Carrie – after everything Ginty had put her through – could tolerate her, then, surely, she could.

After all, it was very apparent that Ginty loved the boys. She even cared about Nellie and Charlie. And when she thought about it like that, well, there was a lot to be said for giving her a measure of respect. Even if giving her the love to go with it was pushing the envelope a stretch too far.

Ginty beamed. Then, immediately, she turned to glare at Phoebe. 'Seems our Billy boy's gone and got himself a new secretary, Dottie.'

'I'm actually his *PA*,' Phoebe corrected, somewhat haughtily, as she glanced at the woman, whose entire aura screamed authority.

'And you are?' Dottie asked, her tone polite but firm.

'Phoebe Langstone. I started yesterday. And, er, you are?'

'Dorothy Ellis,' she replied, smoothly. 'But you can call me Ms Ellis.'

Phoebe nodded. 'I noticed you came in through the back door. Do you work *for* the company?' Her tone was more measured this time. Having already botched her introduction with Ginty, she wasn't about to make the same mistake twice.

Dottie's lips curled ever so slightly. 'I work *with* Billy. Not *for* him.'

Phoebe, now thoroughly perplexed, decided not to ask any more questions. She was still finding her feet in this business. What with going through endless files, property records, and accounting details, the job was beginning to suffocate her. To the extent that she felt she was being pushed from pillar to post. Although there was no way she would admit that to those present or even her boss! She had naïvely assumed that everything would be clear-cut. That every investor and property owner would be neatly recorded.

But the deeper she dug, the murkier things became – to the untrained eye.

'I'm sure you haven't totally got to grips with everything yet, but I need the *Stevens* file. They're the landscaping company. I think I've missed an invoice. Would you be a charm and get it for me?' Dottie said, almost dismissively, as she walked over to the coffee machine and poured herself a strong black coffee. Then, for good measure, she poured a second cup with added milk and sugar. Taking a slow sip, she placed the other cup on the side cabinet before glancing at Billy's assistant. 'So, what's your background, Phoebe?'

Phoebe felt a wave of sheer panic. What the hell was happening? She had no idea where the Stevens file was. Rushing through the files on the computer, she barely looked up as she answered.

'Oh, er, yeah, um . . . I worked for an insurance company for a few years. I didn't like the manager there, and then this job came up, and I thought it'd be a great opportunity.'

Leaning casually against the cabinet, with both hands wrapped around her cup, Dottie watched the girl as a cat would a mouse, whiling its time, ready for the kill.

'I didn't know Billy had put out an advert for a PA.'

Across the room, Ginty sat back sipping her tea and munching loudly on her biscuit, now thoroughly enjoying her visit. Dottie had Phoebe squirming, and it was fun to watch.

'Well, he put a notice in the window. Clearly, he needed someone. I mean, he was in a bit of a flap.'

Dottie's brow lifted. 'A flap? That doesn't sound like our Billy.'

Phoebe faltered under the older woman's sharp gaze. 'Maybe it's not typical of him, but when I came to view the apartments, he definitely seemed flustered. The phone wouldn't stop ringing, and he couldn't find any files. Anyway, I fancied a change of career . . .' She shrugged. 'And, well, the rest is history.'

'Hmm.' Dottie took another sip, her gaze unreadable. 'And what are your qualifications?'

Now openly amused, Ginty let out a hearty chuckle, as she dunked her biscuit into her tea. She had taken an instant dislike to the girl. Only now, she decided, she wouldn't even try hiding the fact.

Still frantically searching the system, Phoebe finally found the Stevens file. It was listed under Stevens, of course. Letting out a sigh of relief, she turned to face Dottie. But then, something inside her snapped.

Who *was* this woman? And what gave her the right to interrogate her like this? She wasn't used to being questioned or ordered about. Not even Billy had treated her like that. With her frustration reaching a flashpoint, she sniggered, 'Sorry, but who exactly *are* you? Head of HR, perhaps? Billy gave *me* the job, and not once has he said he had to get anyone else's approval for me to work here.'

Dottie pushed herself away from the cabinet and placed the cup of coffee on the side.

Ginty laughed. 'Oh dear, girl, that's well and truly fucked it. A word of warning: Dottie is the last person you wanna piss off, believe me.'

Phoebe looked at Billy's grandmother and then at Ms Ellis.

The woman was staring at her with a look that could peel wallpaper.

'Phoebe, I already told you. I don't work for Billy. I work *with* Billy.'

Before Phoebe could respond, the back door swung open again.

This time, a full-figured woman with thick cascading waves of black hair hurried in.

Dottie had been expecting her sooner than this. Without hesitation, she handed her a cup of coffee.

'You're late, Carrie.'

'Don't I fucking know it.' Carrie sighed, as she blew a strand of hair from her face.

'Sunny ran off with my keys. Took me bleedin' ages to realise they were gone. So I had to drive the old shitter. For fuck's sake, the fucking thing clangs and clunks like it's ready for the breaker's yard. I . . .' Stopping in mid-rant, she looked around. 'Oh, hello, Ginty.' Then her gaze swept the office. 'Where's our Billy boy?'

Phoebe knew instantly that this woman was yet another family member. She didn't bear much resemblance to Billy, but one thing was certain – she was beautiful. With flawless skin, striking eyes, and very long lashes, she found herself feeling a little envious.

'He's not here, Carrie Ann, but,' said Ginty, who was still sprawled out in one of the customers' chairs as though she owned the place, and who was now lazily pointing towards Phoebe, 'he's only gone and got himself a new secretary.'

Carrie's sharp eyes suddenly locked on to the girl.

Phoebe could feel herself out of her depth. The dynamics in the room were working against her.

She had always been the one in control – the leader of her pack at school – the girl no one dared mess with. Because not only was she pretty, but she could handle herself. She knew she could turn the boys' heads and knew exactly how to use that to her advantage. But for the first time in her life, she felt uneasy. It was as if she'd just walked into the middle of a pack of wolves.

This wasn't just a group of women. This was a unit, a family, and she was the outsider being given the full treatment.

Carrie's gaze swept over Phoebe, now assessing the woman to see if she measured up to what she felt her son needed. 'Billy boy never said . . . So you're Bronte's replacement, are you?' She tilted her head slightly, her eyes narrowing with interest. 'Pretty girl, ain't ya.'

The smile that followed wasn't exactly warm. Phoebe's eyes flashed with annoyance when she understood the subtext of what this woman was getting at.

‘I’m a qualified personal assistant,’ she hurriedly stated, with some air of importance.

But the second the words left her mouth, she realised how pathetic they sounded, as she was left scrambling for legitimacy in a world of older and clearly more confident women.

Carrie chuckled. ‘I bet you are, darlin’. I bet you are.’

Turning away, dismissively, Carrie faced Dottie instead and grinned. ‘Dot, I’ve got the table decorations organised. I tell ya, that silly tart we use for the balloons don’t know her head from her arsehole. Anyway, it’s all done and—’

‘Good, I’ve got the list from the caterers, and Billy’s sorting out the other stuff.’

Phoebe listened intently before she asked, ‘Is someone getting married?’

Carrie’s and Dottie’s glares in unison, couldn’t have felt more humiliating if they had tried. It wasn’t so much that she felt pushed out. It was as if a steel wall existed around this whole family – or whatever they were.

Swallowing her discomfort, Phoebe returned to the computer and pressed the print key for Ms Ellis’s requested invoice. Just as the printer whirred to life, a movement outside caught her eye.

Billy.

Her heart pounded as she watched him pull up outside the office. When he stepped out of his car, he looked as sharp as ever. Then, as he moved to the boot, she noticed something that made her breathing speed up a notch – a bouquet. No, not just any bouquet. It was the most enormous, most extravagant arrangement she had ever seen.

Her heart raced.

As he walked towards the office, the massive array of flowers nearly swallowed his face. It was impossible to see his expression. *No man has ever spoiled me like this*, she thought. It was the kind of grand gesture that she would have expected from an A-list movie star.

Phoebe quickly looked down at her screen pretending not to notice, but, inside, she was thrilled. This would surely put a spanner in the works for the three witches from Eastwick.

But the second he stepped inside the building, Billy did something she hadn’t expected.

He separated the bunch.

There were three individual bouquets, all equally stunning. And without so much as a hello, he walked straight past her and towards the two younger women, who, oddly enough, didn't seem in the least surprised. Each of them took a bouquet as if this was normal.

Phoebe's heart sank.

The flowers weren't for her at all.

They were for them.

Ginty sat up straighter, a huge smile spreading across her face. 'One for me, Billy boy, is there?'

Billy turned to Ginty and handed her the last bouquet. Then, without glancing at Phoebe, he focused on his mothers.

'So, Mum, what do you reckon? And you, Mottie? Will these do?'

The penny dropped.

The dark-haired woman was his mother.

But then . . . why was he calling the other woman Mottie? She'd clearly heard this Ginty woman call her Dottie.

'So this florist can supply the tables and rose arch on the day, can they?' Carrie asked, with a beaming smile.

'Yeah, and as fresh as these, I hope,' Dottie said, now studying the bouquets in detail.

'Yes,' Billy replied.

Carrie's eyes flicked between the three bouquets in turn. 'I think the pink. What about you, Dottie? Or do you think the peach?'

Dottie's gaze drifted towards the peach bouquet, but before she answered, she looked at Ginty, who was admiring hers with quiet affection.

'Yeah, definitely the pink.' Ginty nodded. There was a rare softness in her voice, as she stroked the delicate petals. 'Luanne's always loved pink.'

'Oi, you daft mare, getting all sentimental,' Carrie teased. 'You've had your birthday bash – I'm not sure I've even recovered from that hangover yet.'

She laughed, and Ginty grinned, clearly enjoying the moment.

'Right, me boy,' Carrie said, wrapping Billy in a quick hug, 'we're off shopping – gotta look the bee's knees, ya know.'

Dottie playfully rolled her eyes.

Ginty slurped the last of her tea. 'Shopping? What, for a proper rigout for the party?'

Carrie nodded. 'Yeah. Why? D'ya want a lift home?'

Ginty sighed, dramatically. 'I just wish I had someone to help *me* pick out a dress. Never know what looks good on me these days.'

'Mirrors don't lie,' said Dottie, teasingly.

'Lucky they don't laugh either,' replied Carrie, before giving her ex-mother-in-law a hearty chuckle.

'Fuck off, you cheeky mare,' Ginty said, joining in with the laughter.

'I'm sorry, Ginty. Listen, you know I'm joking. And I'm not being nasty, but I reckon you *could* do with a bit of wardrobe advice.'

Ginty looked down at her dress. 'Well, o' course, I could. I've worn the same style since I was a looker with an hourglass figure. I've lost me shape a bit, and now I ain't got a clue what suits me.'

'Come on, then, Cinderella. You *shall* go to the ball.'

Ginty didn't need asking twice. She was off the chair in an instant, eager to follow Carrie and Dottie towards the back door.

Billy smiled and kissed Dottie on the cheek before turning to Ginty.

She pulled him into a tight hug. 'You're a good boy, Billy.'

He gave her a good-natured smirk. Then, pulling a few notes from his pocket, he shoved them into her hand. 'Get yourself a nice dress.'

Ginty kissed his cheek. 'Thanks, Billy. I'll try to look my best – on my life, I will.'

'I know you will.' Billy chuckled. 'And leave the flowers. I'll put them in water while you shop. I know how long those two can be when they're out spending. I'll drop the flowers around later.'

Dottie hurried back inside, snatched the invoice from the printer, and pushed it into her briefcase. 'I'm meeting the accountant tomorrow, Billy.'

Billy winked. 'Good, let's see what the old man can save us.'

The minute the back door closed behind them, Billy turned his attention to Phoebe, who looked thoroughly deflated.

'Are you getting to grips with the files?'

She nodded, but she could feel a lump in the back of her throat. She suddenly felt so dejected, but she knew that there was no reason to be. She hardly knew Billy, and yet here she was craving for his attention. She even felt jealous of his mother, Ms Ellis, and the grandmother getting it all.

'Yes, er, that Ms Ellis asked for an invoice from the Stevens file.'

Billy perched himself on the edge of his desk. 'Yes?' He inclined his head.

'Should I have given it to her? I mean, she wouldn't say who she was. Only that she worked with you, not for you.'

'That's right. She works with me. Right, so let me explain something. My company exists because I have a lot of support from my family.'

'How is Ms Ellis actually family?'

The question clearly came out all wrong. Phoebe winced. 'Sorry, I mean, may I ask? I just, er, sorry, Billy, I just wanted to understand the set-up, that's all.'

Billy's expression remained unreadable. 'Ms Ellis is my mother. Everyone calls her Dottie, but my brother and I call her Mottie as in *mother* Dottie.'

Phoebe frowned slightly. 'But you called that other lady—'

Billy had been patient, but now, his tone cooled. 'They both are.'

'How?' The word slipped out before she could stop it.

The moment the question left her lips, she realised her mistake. Billy's demeanour shifted. She had jumped in too fast and dived straight into waters she should have tested first.

Billy was not a man to be rushed for information.

'Phoebe,' Billy said, sharply, as he stood up. This time, his tone suddenly had a cutting edge to it. 'My family is rather private. Ms Ellis helps run the finances. She handles some of our clients, brings new business, and scouts profitable properties. She does the negotiating. I also have other family members involved in the firm. Let's call them shareholders.'

His gaze locked on to hers, steady and unwavering. 'One of them is my brother. Another is my father. And then there's a silent partner – Cas Ferrier. You met him the other day. Unless he's in a suit, he usually wears loud shirts as if he's just stepped off a plane from Hawaii. But, regardless, Cas is like family and must be treated as such.'

Then, he added, with finality, 'And that's all you need to know – from a PA's point of view.'

The last comment stuck in her throat. And she was now wondering if she hated him or was being drawn into his world of mystery and intrigue because, without a doubt, she was sexually attracted to him.

Staring at the computer screen, Phoebe was in a daze. She couldn't focus on anything. Not now. Not when she was obsessed with her own thoughts on what had just happened. She thought she had him in the palm of her hand. That lunch. It had all gone so well. He had been so attentive and kind and shown that he was very much attracted to her. But this morning? Well, it was a fucking disaster.

She consoled herself with the idea that work and pleasure didn't mix in Billy's world.

CHAPTER TWENTY

As five o'clock approached, Billy glanced at Phoebe. She was still buried in the office filing system, which earlier she'd said was chaotic. He watched her for a moment, concerned that it was taking her so long to get to grips with it all. Because he was well aware that Bronte had found the system very easy to use.

'Phoebe, would you draft a letter for me, please?'

She looked up suddenly, almost like a deer caught in the headlights, but she nodded and opened up a new file on her computer. 'I . . . er, never really sent letters. It was more . . .'

'It's fine. No worries.'

Leaning back in his chair, his hands resting in his lap, he began dictating a letter to a fictitious client. He deliberately used long-winded phrasing, slipping in formalities she might second-guess. He ended it with *Best Wishes*, despite it being a formal business letter, knowing full well it should have been *Yours Sincerely.*

As he spoke, he observed her closely. She looked flustered. Her face was slightly flushed and her eyes were darting over the screen. He wondered if that could be how she reacted under pressure. Once he'd finished dictating the letter, he asked her to print it.

She did as he asked and nervously handed him the letter.

Billy took it into the back meeting room where he scanned the letter. There were mistakes. Lots of them. The worst ones were glaring spelling errors. *Why hadn't she tried the computer spell check?* But there were others. The address was on the wrong side, and the date was misplaced. But worst of all, she had ended the letter exactly as he'd dictated – without questioning it.

Tapping his lip with his forefinger, he sat deep in thought. *Something was off.*

He had already checked her references. Her company had sent them within a couple of days of receiving the request. The glowing replies from the insurance company were exceptional.

They had described Phoebe as a highly valued employee. A company of that size wouldn't fabricate a report like that. Surely, she had done the job she claimed to have had or they would have corrected the requested references.

He brushed the thoughts aside. Maybe he was just overthinking. She was probably nervous and maybe English wasn't her strength. Or perhaps she dealt more with accounts, numbers being more her thing. And if he *wasn't* overthinking it – well, he would deal with that later. Besides, he'd already done something he probably shouldn't have. He'd taken her out to lunch.

Returning to the front office, he cast her a glance. There was no denying it – Phoebe was a good-looking girl. In fact, he fancied the pants off her.

'Do you have to get off home, Phoebe?'

She turned to face him, her lips curving slightly. 'Why? Do you have something better in mind?'

Billy smirked and nodded slowly. 'How about dinner? I just need to drop the flowers off at my nan's, then we could grab a bite to eat – if you fancy it?'

Inside, she wanted to tell him to go fuck himself. But, God, he was attractive.

And despite how he and his family had treated her – so dismissively – she yearned for his attention. Whatever that looked like.

'That would be lovely.' She fluttered her eyelashes, giving him the big come-on.

The restaurant Billy chose was another one of those places where the staff knew him. The second he stepped inside, they were all over him. Greeting him like an old friend, they led him straight to a prime table away from the riff-raff.

Phoebe felt it again – that thrill, that rush – being with someone who mattered and commanded attention without even trying. Not being fussed over because the man was a feared gangster but because he was respected. It was like being with a celebrity.

Billy barely glanced at the menu before ordering champagne. The waiters hovered at their table, all eager to impress and fuss over him like royalty.

He could have used this dinner date to question her – to dig into her past job or interrogate her about that bullshit letter, which was riddled with mistakes. But he didn't.

Tonight, he wanted to take it easy. A night away from work. And if he was honest, he just wanted to sit back and enjoy her pretty face.

'So, tell me about your hobbies, Phoebe.'

And that's when it hit her. She didn't actually have any.

She wasn't interested in anything. Apart from flicking through hair and make-up magazines and obsessing over surgical enhancements, she conceded she was probably a crushing bore. No deep passions. Nothing real or interesting about her.

Which was a diabolical shame. Because as she looked at Billy – who sat there so self-assured and in control – she knew what he was about. He was into women with substance. Women with depth.

At first, she panicked. But then she thought about his ex, Bronte, who Billy had mentioned was a gypsy. To her that suggested Bronte was no academic.

'I like to swim,' she said, because everyone liked to swim, didn't they? And, technically, she did. But that was only when she was on holiday.

'That's great. I like a woman who takes her health and exercise seriously. I like to box and train.'

Phoebe smiled and nodded, but inside, she knew the truth – she *hated* exercise. The only reason she ever stepped foot near a gym was to use the sunbeds. The thought of a treadmill made her stomach turn.

'I can tell.' She reached out and squeezed his right bicep. Before he knew it, she was flashing him her famous come-to-bed eyes.

He played into it immediately.

Although Billy started the conversation to get to know her, the initiative quickly turned – as it always did – with her in control. She had a knack for steering things towards flirting, teasing, and all the sexual innuendos she could come up with.

Once they'd finished their meal, Billy gently stroked the back of her hand. 'What do you want to do now?' he asked.

She reached across the table and ran a manicured fake fingernail down his chest, her voice dripping with suggestion. 'Well, Billy Murphy, I think we should really get to know each other, don't you?'

She licked her lips, let out a sweet giggle, and fluttered her lashes again.

Billy grinned. If this wasn't the biggest come-on he'd ever experienced, then he didn't know jack shit.

'My place for coffee?'

Her eyes lit up. 'I'd love to.'

'Great, I'm just going to make a phone call.'

'I'll meet you by the car,' Phoebe replied, the excitement clear in her voice.

As Billy stepped outside into the cool night air, his eyes immediately locked on to a car parked directly behind his own. Inside, he recognised a face he wasn't happy to see.

The man got out and strode towards him, with a larger guy marching close behind.

Billy felt his temper flare. After what this prick had done to him in the hospital, just *seeing* him again made his blood boil. He wanted to punch the smarmy bastard's face in. But he was on a date and outside one of his favourite restaurants.

'How did you know I was here?' he snapped.

'I have eyes and ears everywhere, Billy Murphy. Now, listen up. It's been a few weeks now, and your debt is climbing, but you can settle it *today*. I'm giving you a chance to pay up – all I need is an address from your brother.'

Billy clocked the rapid way Reece spoke while almost dancing on the spot. Clearly, he was fired up on cocaine.

'Like I told you, Reece. Ask him yourself.'

'Nah, mate, that's not how this is gonna fucking work.' Reece's voice dropped lower. '*You* will ask him for the address.' He poked a finger near Billy's face. 'Or believe me, things are gonna get *fucking ugly*. So, do we have a deal?'

Billy looked him up and down and then glared at Dario, the lump who was standing behind him. 'No, we don't have a deal. So fuck off. You're ruining my otherwise pleasant evening.'

Reece's eyes nearly popped out of his head. 'Are you some kind of stupid cunt?'

'No, I'm not stupid, but what makes you think my brother would do *you* a favour just because I ask him to? That's not how it works between me and him. You're wasting your breath.'

Reece smirked. 'Oh, I know you two better than you think. I've done my research. And I *do* believe he'll do as you say – because if *you* take my threat seriously, then *he* will. As I understand it, he listens to your advice.'

'You're mistaken, Reece. Now, I've got a tart waiting to suck my dick, so fuck off.'

'What?'

Billy had already turned to walk away but he spun back. 'I said I've got a tart ready to suck my dick.'

He could see Reece's expression momentarily turn sour. 'Who?'

With his hands now on his hips and his head tilted to the side, Billy narrowed his eyes. 'What the fuck has that got to do with you?'

'You really think you're hard, don't you, Billy?' Reece laughed. 'Well, like I said, the pikeys *battered* you, and that was just for *fun*. But what happens next? *That* won't be for shits and giggles. That'll be a *warning*.' He winked, knowing it would rile Billy up. 'Think it over. You've been told. What comes next is on *you*.'

Billy took a step closer, his voice low and cold. 'If you so much as *look* at my family, I'll come for you, Reece. Make no mistake about it.'

Dario stepped forward, his bulk towering over Billy, but Reece held up a hand to stop him. 'Leave him. Let him think it over.'

Billy's eyes stayed locked unwaveringly on Reece. 'You don't put the shits up me.' He glared at Dario. 'And neither the fuck do you.'

Reece chuckled. 'Just think about it, Billy. And call this number when your brother gives you the address.' He shoved a piece of paper into Billy's hand. 'You've got two hours.'

Billy barely glanced at it before dropping it onto the pavement and grinding his shoe over it.

'I'd pick that paper up and memorise that number if I were you. Two hours, Billy.'

As Reece and his brother returned to their car, Phoebe crept up behind Billy. 'I'll wait in the car, shall I?'

Billy was still watching the brothers walk away. 'What? Yeah, sure,' he muttered, handing her the keys.

Reece glanced over his shoulder and smirked, but his expression shifted, the second he clapped eyes on Phoebe.

'Jealous cunt,' Billy mumbled, under his breath. As much as he didn't have much respect for Phoebe – because she had practically thrown herself at him – he wasn't blind. She had the kind of face and figure that could stop traffic.

As Reece's car tore off, Billy's eyes narrowed. There was a man in the back seat. It was too dark to make out his face, but he was craning his neck and staring straight at him.

Phoebe clicked the key fob, and the flash of Billy's car lights snapped him back to the here and now. Hurrying behind her, he grabbed the keys without a word and didn't bother holding the passenger door open for her. His head was a mess, and rage was bubbling under the surface. He should have taken Phoebe back to the office, seen her off, and called it a night. But she was all over him again, rubbing his leg, and putting on that sickly, sweet voice that grated on him.

Still, it had been weeks since he'd had sex, and Phoebe wasn't the kind of girl you'd kick out of bed in a hurry.

As he drove towards his apartment block, he remembered why he'd stepped outside the restaurant in the first place. It was to let Jesse know he was bringing someone home. But, it was midweek, and Jesse would probably be at his flat in North London, where he usually stayed a few nights a week.

Phoebe clambered out the moment they pulled up, eager to see where he lived. Stepping into the lobby, her eyes flicked to the security guard. The place reeked of money. It was sleek and high-end. Not somewhere just anyone could afford to live. Having never dated a man who breathed sophistication and walked with so much confidence without being cocky, she knew that this was the life for her.

But what really blew her mind was when the security guard jumped up from his desk, nodded at Billy, and greeted him respectfully. 'Evening, Boss.'

'Everything all right, Clive?'

'Yes, quiet night.' He chuckled. 'That lady in number three was a bit tipsy, but I saw her safely to her apartment.'

'Good man.'

Phoebe was taking it all in. For a moment, she could see herself living here. Although she had been raised around money, it was new money. Not the old wealth that came from good breeding and education.

Phoebe's only issue was that Billy wasn't holding her hand or putting his arm around her. In fact, he didn't introduce her to the security, and for a second, she felt like a prostitute, not a significant part of Billy's life. It grated on her, but she thought it best to work on Billy, maybe by taking it slowly.

'So you own the whole building?'

Billy pushed the lift button. 'Yes.' That was all he said.

'Wow, it's beautiful. Do you own it on your own?'

'No.'

'Oh, who else owns it?'

Billy sighed and faced her. 'Why?'

'Why what?' she replied, looking baffled.

'Why the interest in who owns what? I thought you were coming back to mine for a coffee, not a guided tour on property ownership.'

Phoebe felt him slipping through her net. 'Sorry,' she said, shaking her head. 'I guess I'm just shocked that you own so much at such a young age. I admire you. That's all I was trying to say.'

Billy wasn't stupid. He could read people, and she was spewing out such a whole load of bullshit, it was embarrassing. She certainly wasn't asking out of admiration. At this precise moment, she was probably calculating his exact net worth.

'Anyway, it's a beautiful building. You've got an eye for design.'

She slipped her hand into his. For a moment, he flinched. Then, he let her hold it. It felt wrong, like jamming the wrong jigsaw piece into a puzzle. The only hand that had ever slotted perfectly into his was Bronte's, but he pushed that thought aside. It was time to move on. He gave Phoebe's hand a squeeze just as the lift doors opened.

Even inside the lift, Phoebe's eyes widened. Everything shone like glass. There were no fingerprints, no smudges. Billy obviously kept this place immaculate, just like himself.

When the lift stopped, and the doors slid open, she beamed. The soft carpets and the modern lighting built into the floor looked like something from a property on *Grand Designs*. She watched as Billy unlocked his front door, then waved his arm, letting her enter first.

The apartment even smelled new. As she stepped into the sumptuous lounge, her breathing hitched up a notch. The view across London was insane. She'd never seen anything like it. Thousands of twinkling lights stretched before her, and the floor-to-ceiling windows made it feel as though she was staring at a massive TV screen. Except she wasn't: this was real.

'Coffee?'

Phoebe turned, her eyes still fixed on the view.

'No. I thought maybe something stronger. Perhaps a vodka, or a glass of wine?'

'Oh, right. Okay.' Billy decided then and there that she definitely wanted more than a friendly chat.

He opened the glass-fronted cabinet and pulled out a bottle of Châteauneuf-du-Pape. He stared at the label, unsure whether it was any good. All he knew was that it cost a lot of money and was there for when he had guests. Shrugging his shoulders, he poured a generous measure for her and a smaller one for himself before returning to the lounge.

'Here.' He handed her the glass.

She took it gracefully, holding it by the stem, as she had watched a wine expert do. *What was the word? Som . . . sommelier – that was it.*

Still, any air of sophistication vanished as she knocked back a large gulp – not sipping it, not even tasting it. Just downing it.

'Is it all right?' Billy asked, waiting for the verdict.

Looking puzzled, she said, 'Yeah . . . wine's wine, isn't it?' She suddenly took another swig.

Billy set his own glass aside. So much for enjoying an expensive drink together.

He watched as she drained hers and then turned her attention to him. Before he could react, she forced him onto the sofa and straddled him. He didn't bother to push her off. Her hands roamed his body with confidence. This was no shy, innocent girl. She knew exactly how to handle a man – how to get him aroused.

With practised ease, she unbuttoned her own shirt to reveal her perky breasts and then climbed off him to remove her skirt. Dropping to her knees, she reached for his belt and unbuttoned his trousers with swift, knowing fingers.

There was nothing classy or sweet about her. She was rushed, forceful, and experienced.

As she grabbed him, he groaned, and she smiled sweetly before taking him in her mouth, teasing him.

But he wasn't in the mood for slow, drawn-out games. She hadn't been gentle, so he decided he wouldn't be either. In a flash, he flipped her over and thrust inside her. He didn't really want to look at her face. As pretty as she was, he was finding himself less and less attracted to her. It felt as though the real Phoebe was coming out now, and if all she wanted was sex, then that's precisely what she'd get.

'Slowly, Billy . . . slowly,' she murmured, trying to glance back at him over her shoulder.

But he didn't slow down. He moved harder, rougher, pressing her face into the cushion. She turned her head to the side to breathe, but he kept going – silent, relentless. No words. No groans. Just action.

She tried to turn over, wanting to see his face, but he held her down and gripped her hair. Suddenly, she wasn't enjoying it anymore.

'Stop, Billy. Stop!' she yelled.

Instantly, he pulled away.

She lay there for a moment, trying to catch her breath, her legs slowly drawing together as she turned onto her back.

But Billy was gone.

She swallowed hard, still feeling sore. She'd expected rough sex and would have even enjoyed it. But it wasn't the forcefulness that had shaken her. It was the coldness. The complete lack of feeling. That was what hurt the most.

Trying to smooth her hair, she glanced at the floor, her eyes locking on to her crumpled knickers and skirt. A sick feeling curled in her stomach. She felt dirty and used in a way no man had ever made her feel before. And she sure as hell wasn't about to let Billy Murphy be the first. Not without some comeback.

Her hands shook as she pulled on her clothes, the sting of humiliation burning beneath her skin. Snatching up Billy's glass of wine, she downed it in one go, not even bothering to taste it. She just needed something – anything – to numb the knot in her chest. Wiping her mouth with the back of her hand, she then swallowed the bitter lump in her throat.

Her bag was on the chair. She could grab it, storm out, demand the security guard call her a taxi, and leave this whole thing behind. That was what any self-respecting woman would do. This experience made her question herself. What exactly was she? Was she just a PA or potentially a rich man's wife?

But then her eyes were drawn back to the view – a glittering and endless world of power and wealth wrapped in a skyline. Her gaze swept over the plush furniture, the designer touches, and the kind of life she would want for herself. Walking out now would be foolish.

So, instead, she inhaled sharply, squared her shoulders, and made a decision. She wasn't going anywhere.

CHAPTER TWENTY-ONE

Breathing heavily, Billy shut his bedroom door. He then pulled on a pair of tracksuit bottoms and a clean T-shirt.

When he stepped back into the lounge, Phoebe was already dressed and smiling nervously. He felt it again then – that strange, uncomfortable feeling gnawing at his gut. She'd told him to stop, and he had. Immediately. No hesitation. But now, doubt was creeping in. *Had he overstepped the mark or pushed her too far?* he wondered.

His mind was working overtime, his thoughts totally conflicted. Now they were taking him to his ex-girlfriend. To that day with Bronte. The way he'd had sex with her in such a cold, detached manner before telling her that their relationship was over. It was something that he regretted doing. Massively. He was not that kind of person. No one should treat another human being like that. He and Bronte had invested five years of their young lives in being a couple.

Maybe he shouldn't have been so rough with Phoebe either.

The truth was, he wasn't good at reading women. This was despite being surrounded by them – both his mums, his aunts, and his grandmother, Luanne. All of them were kind, loving, and strong. And yet here he was, second-guessing everything.

First, there was Willow, someone he had totally misunderstood. But there were solid reasons for that, as he learned at Keith Purdey's funeral when he was handed Willow's diary. Thinking back to that day, he recalled Bronte telling him she wanted to get to know him.

And he certainly should have seen the signs with Bronte, but he'd been so in love with her that when he caught her betraying him, his emotions just flipped. Even now, he struggled to get his head around how she'd sneakily allowed the Shipleys to put the marijuana plants in the basement of his property complex. He wondered for a moment if he should have given Bronte time to explain her reasons. Maybe he had it all wrong. Who knew?

Similarly, with Phoebe, he'd assumed she was the kind of woman who wanted sex rough and raw. But it seemed now that she didn't.

Now, he was struggling with how wrong his actions had been again.

Phoebe looked up at him. 'Shall I make us a coffee?'

Billy had expected her to leave. Instead, she was still here and offering a semblance of normality. He shook his head, not trusting himself to speak. Then, he bent down, grabbed his phone, walked straight back to his bedroom, and shut the door behind him.

The tension in his chest tightened. It had been two hours since the Shipleys had made their threat, and now the weight of it was settling on his shoulders. His hands were unsteady as he dialled his father's number. What the hell was going on with him? Instead of sorting out the Shipley business, he'd let his dick control events.

Sunny answered almost immediately. 'Hello, Son. Everything all right? Bit late – I was just about to get in the bath before heading off to bed.'

'Dad, listen,' Billy said, keeping his voice low. 'I've been threatened.' He sighed. 'I won't go into the details, but I just need to know if everyone is home and safe?'

There was a pause. His father's tone changed. 'Who has threatened you, Billy?'

Billy ran a hand over his head. 'The Shipleys. They want an address from Jesse. I basically told them to go fuck themselves. They said I had two hours to get an address.' He sighed, heavily. 'But I don't know if it's just talk or if they mean it.'

'The Shipleys don't make empty threats,' Sunny muttered, his voice dropping into something darker, something serious. 'Jesus, Billy, why the hell didn't you call me sooner?'

Billy swallowed, his stomach in knots. 'Dad, is everyone home?'

'Yeah. Nellie's on her phone, Charlie's watching a late-night film, and your mum's designing your nan's birthday cake.' He paused. 'Well, I'm fucking glad now, I've got the cameras installed and set up.'

'Cameras?'

'Yeah. Cas got a good deal with some security firm. They came around the other day and installed them. I thought I might as well keep up with the times.' He paused again. 'Anyway, don't worry about us. I'll make sure no bastard gets in here. I'll keep an ear out. What about you?'

'I'm at the apartment. Clive's on duty and the place is locked down.' Billy hesitated. 'I'm sorry, Dad. I don't want you worrying about it. The flash bastard was probably acting hard by throwing his family name around. Because this Reece Shipley looks like I could snap him in half, and his brother looks as though he doesn't have the brains to hit a target.' No sooner had he said that than he wondered who he was trying to kid.

Sunny let out a slow breath. 'It don't take a lot of muscle to fire a shooter, Son. Better to be safe than sorry. The Shipleys are a fucking nightmare of a family. I've never dealt with them personally, but their name alone carries weight. You make sure you're safe.'

Billy tightened his grip on the phone. 'I will, and you, Dad, secure the house and keep our Nellie in.'

'What are you gonna do, Billy? Because I could round up the family and pay the Shipleys a visit, although I'd need a few others because the Shipleys are a big firm. And Jesse tells me he's on that Shipley double murder case.'

Billy's jaw clenched. 'Dad, don't worry. I'll call Jesse. I'll sort it.'

He ended the call. Staring at his phone for a long moment, his pulse felt as though it was working like a jackhammer. Decisions, decisions. The obvious first step was to take Phoebe back to her car as soon as possible. He didn't want her caught up in any crossfire. Slipping his feet into his trainers, he opened the bedroom door and walked into the kitchen to find her making two coffees. Right away, it irritated him; she clearly hadn't listened.

'I didn't want any coffee. I thought I made that clear. Look, I think it's best if I drive you back to my office so you can pick up your car.'

He noticed her face suddenly take on a sad expression. Her lips parted, but no words came out, and her eyes looked glassy.

'Phoebe, I'm sorry about earlier, okay? And I think we should remain work colleagues, nothing more.'

Seeing the hurt in her eyes, Billy felt yet another pang of guilt. Just because he wasn't keen on her anymore, it didn't mean he wanted to upset her.

'I'm sorry. My mistake, not yours,' he added, as he ran his hands over the back of his neck. 'You're a nice person, and I think I probably took advantage of you. That's not who I am, Phoebe.'

Gently, she touched his cheek, smiling softly, trying to mask her disappointment.

'No, Billy, it's me who should be sorry. I imagined our time together differently from how you saw it. I assumed too much.' She let out a small, shaky laugh. 'Look, we can start again. I can talk you through what I like, and you, tiger, can tell me what you like. Besides, we enjoy each other's company, don't we?' Her voice was hopeful, trying to sound casual – anything but desperate.

Billy took a step back.

Her hand immediately fell away. At that point, something shifted between them.

'No, Phoebe, it's not even that.'

He hesitated, his eyes sweeping over her, searching for the right words. But even now, hearing her talk about sex, as though it was a transaction, something to negotiate, brought on a surge of anger in the pit of his stomach, before he managed to suppress it.

'I'm not looking for a relationship with any long-term aspirations. I'm sorry, if I gave you that idea.'

Her expression faltered, but she clung to the hope in her voice. 'But, Billy, we get along really well. If you just let me show you how good it can be, I think you'll change your mind.' She reached for his arm.

He pulled away, sharply. 'Show me? Show me how good what could be? Sex? Is that what you think makes a relationship work?' His voice rose, frustration creeping into his tone. 'Good fucking sex?'

'Billy, no, stop. Please, that's not what I meant. I just . . . I thought, me and you . . . well, we're good together.'

He took yet another step back, this time running a hand through his hair. 'Me and you? Bloody hell, Phoebe, I've only known you for five minutes. There is *no* me and you. I think I should call you a taxi to take you back to the office.'

'Is that it, then, Billy?'

Now tired of the conversation, in fact, tired of everything, he said, 'Is what it? There was never anything to begin with. Jesus, look.' He sighed. 'I've got a lot going on. If you don't mind, I'll call Clive, and he'll organise a taxi for you.'

She stepped forward, tears brimming in her eyes. 'But, Billy, I really like you. Can't you even give me a chance?'

'Christ, woman, don't you ever stop? I said I'm sorry. I made a mistake! And now I think I made a mistake in hiring you. Please, just leave.'

Phoebe's breath caught in her throat, and she suddenly backed down. 'Okay, okay . . . but please let me keep my job. I've already packed in my old one.'

With a heavy sigh, Billy nodded. 'Fine. But it's time you left.'

He reached for the intercom to call Clive, but the receiver blared into life before he could touch it. He frowned and picked it up, only to hear the alarm in the voice at the other end of the phone. The words tumbled out in a frantic rush, barely understandable – except for one.

Bronte.

Billy didn't ask questions. The urgency in Clive's voice was enough. His stomach lurched, and he bolted out of the apartment.

Phoebe, who was caught off guard, scrambled after him. She wasn't going to be left hanging.

Billy didn't wait for the lift – he flew down the stairs, clearing three at a time, his heartbeat pounding in his ears. The second he hit the lobby, he gasped.

Clive was crouched over a lifeless body.

Beside him lay a hessian sack, and there, bound at the wrists with rope and silver tape covering her mouth, was Bronte. If Clive hadn't mentioned the name Bronte, Billy would never have recognised her.

'No! No!' Billy's roar ripped through the lobby as he lunged towards her, his hands shaking. Kneeling next to her, he peeled the tape away from her bruised lips.

'I've called an ambulance, Mr Murphy. They're on their way.' Clive was almost choking in anguish. For a grown man, he looked utterly lost, his face streaked with tears. 'A van. A grey van pulled up. I heard it screech to a stop. As I looked up, I saw some blokes open up the side of the van and throw her out. I didn't get the number plate. It all happened so fast, Mr Murphy.'

In desperation, Billy's fingers clumsily fumbled with the knots at her wrists. When the rope finally came loose, he gathered Bronte into his lap and cradled her battered head against his chest.

'Talk to me, Bronte. Come on, baby girl.' He suddenly let his heritage accent come through to match that of Bronte's. 'Open your eyes. I'm here, Bronte. It's me, Billy – your Billy boy. Please, stay with us.' His voice cracked and his body shook, as he rocked her, raw and unfiltered emotion spilling out of him. He'd only cried like this once. It was the day when he learned that Willow had been murdered.

But this time it felt different, somehow. He couldn't bear to see Bronte, his sweet Bronte, so hurt.

Clive stood helpless watching his boss – the cold, unshakable man – plead through his tears.

Finally, Bronte's swollen eyelids fluttered, just barely opening.

'Billy . . .' she whispered, her voice fragile.

'I'm here, Bronte.' He moved a lock of hair that had stuck to her cheek from the congealed blood. 'I've got you. I'm not letting go. Who did this, babe?'

She swallowed, struggling to find her breath. 'I . . . I don't know.' Her voice was barely audible. 'I'm sorry, Billy. I didn't mean to hurt you. I thought . . .'

'Shh, Bronte. It's all right,' he murmured, his jaw tightening, as he took in the full extent of her injuries. Her beautiful face was bruised and swollen. Her lips were split and bloodied. But there was a bump on her head as well as a nasty gash. Someone had done a right number on her. And all this time he had thought the Shipleys would try to go after his own family. Not once had it occurred to him that they would go after Bronte instead.

The rage inside him began to erupt. It was as violent as it was unforgiving. But the anger was chiefly aimed at himself. He should have given her the chance to explain. But he hadn't. Maybe his pride – his stupid pride – was hurt more than anything.

Whoever did this . . .They were already dead as far as he was concerned.

'The ambulance is coming, Bronte. You're going to be all right. I promise you, you'll be all right.'

Her gaze remained locked on Billy, her breathing shallow. 'I thought . . . I thought I could spoil you for a change, with the money they would give me. I was stupid . . . I'm sorry. I just didn't think.'

'Stop. Baby, listen to me. It doesn't matter. It's okay. We just need to get you to the hospital.' His voice was soft, urgent. 'I'm here. I'm not going anywhere—'

He stopped.

Her eyes fluttered. Then they closed.

'Bronte? Bronte!' His voice broke, with panic flooding every inch of him. 'Don't you leave me! Come on, stay awake! Bronte, please, stay with me!'

Clive dropped to the floor beside them. With his fingers pressing against her wrist and then her throat, he finally put his ear to her chest and listened.

'She's not breathing, Mr Murphy. I'm so sorry.'

The blood drained from Billy's face. He suddenly turned ice-cold, and every nerve in his body hurt.

'Where the fucking hell is that ambulance?' he roared, his hands trembling, as he shook Bronte's limp body. 'Don't you fucking die on me! Come on!'

Clive pulled her away from Billy. Placing her flat on the ground before starting chest compressions, his hands then pressed hard and fast against her ribcage.

'That's it, Clive! Bring her back to me! Don't let her die!' Billy's voice cracked, with desperation thick in his throat.

As the distant wail of sirens sliced through the night, Billy prayed they were for Bronte. Leaning back on his haunches, tears ran in rapids down his face, blurring his vision, as he watched Clive breathe into Bronte's mouth.

And then, out of the corner of his eye, he saw Phoebe standing there with her arms folded, a look of irritation and impatience on her face.

The ambulance screeched to a stop outside. The paramedics rushed in, where they immediately took over from Clive.

Billy barely breathed as he watched them at work. His entire world hinged on one moment. One answer.

And then he heard it.

'We've got a pulse.'

Hope.

Phoebe grabbed Billy's arm as the paramedics lifted Bronte onto the stretcher. 'Let them do their job. She's in good hands.'

Billy ripped his arm away from her. 'I'm going with her.'

'But, Billy, she's not your problem. She's your ex.'

His eyes snapped to hers, wide with disbelief and anger.

'You fucking what?' His voice was dangerously low. 'Who the fuck are you to tell me anything? Now, get out of my face before I *really* lose it.'

Phoebe's mouth opened, and then it closed. She had gone too far, and she knew it. But fury bubbled inside her, twisting into something ugly. Watching Billy crying, begging, and pleading, and breaking down over *that* girl stirred something dark and bitter inside her.

That *pikey* girl.

Phoebe hated her. And now she hated Billy too.

He'd turned his back on her.

Fuck you, Billy Murphy.

CHAPTER TWENTY-TWO

Phoebe stared as the ambulance tore off down the street with its blue lights flashing.

As soon as it disappeared from sight, Clive wiped his eyes and leaned against the desk. The shock of it all had knocked the wind right out of him.

'Can I organise a ride home for you, Miss?'

Phoebe glared at Clive, her eyes twitching with barely contained rage.

'*No!*' she snapped. 'I need to get back to Billy's apartment. I left my bag and my shoes.' She pointed to her bare feet.

Clive nodded. 'I'll take you there, Miss.'

She held out her hand. 'I am quite capable of letting myself in. Keys, please.'

Clive didn't like her tone one bit. 'Sorry, no can do.' As far as he was concerned, this woman was of no real significance. The women who mattered in Billy's life already had their own keys. Ignoring her demands, he gestured for her to follow him as he walked to the lift.

'What is it? Don't you trust me?' she sneered. 'I'm sure Billy will have a few words to say about that.' She looked him up and down, her lip curling. 'What are you, anyway? A security guard? A cleaner? What?'

The lift doors opened, and they stepped inside.

Clive, who had now recovered from the shock of seeing Bronte flung from a van battered and beaten, turned to Phoebe with sarcasm written all over his face.

'Oh, so we're just going to ignore reality today? All right, then!' he said, smirking.

'What?' she snapped, again curling her lip at him in disgust.

Clive shook his head and exhaled sharply. 'Mr Murphy is a good man. He treats everyone with the respect they deserve. He didn't introduce you to me, yet I know every woman in his life. And if he wanted you in his home unaccompanied, you'd already have your own key. So get off that high horse of yours, accept my offer, grab your bag and shoes, and take a taxi home.'

He wiped his hand over his mouth as if the whole situation had left a bitter taste. His words were crystal clear, but he wasn't finished. 'I can't believe what I saw down there. You stood there as though nothing had happened. That poor girl was brutally attacked. Christ, she even stopped breathing.' He took a deep breath and shook his head. 'Lordy, Lordy . . . have you no compassion?'

Phoebe's eyes darkened, her lips now curling into something between a sneer and a smirk. 'What? For a *pikey*?'

Clive's glare could have burned through steel. 'Pikey?'

The word hung in the air, thick and ugly.

For the first time in her life, Phoebe's confidence wavered. A flush of colour crept up her neck, and she looked away from him, clearly embarrassed.

The lift doors opened, and Clive strode ahead, leaving her to catch up. He unlocked the door, stepped inside, and then he turned back and slammed it shut in her face.

A few moments later, he reappeared holding her shoes and bag. Without a word, he shoved them into her arms.

'Here,' he said, flatly, his expression unreadable. Then, tilting his head, he added, 'You have a phone?'

Phoebe stood frozen, horrified that this security guard had spoken to her in such a dismissive manner. 'Yes, why?'

'Good. Then you can call your own cab, and I suggest you wait outside.' He crossed his arms, his voice steady but firm. 'I heard how Mr Murphy spoke to you, and let me tell you – he never talks like that. In fact, I don't think I've ever heard him swear.'

Phoebe's nostrils flared. 'You'll lose your job over this. I'll make sure of it.'

Clive simply nodded, a slow smirk playing on his lips. 'If I lose my job over how I treated you, then Mr Murphy isn't the man I thought he was. So knock yourself out, sweetie.'

Phoebe didn't wait for the lift. She stormed down the stairs, with Clive right on her heels.

The moment they reached the lobby, they could see more flashing blue lights reflecting off the glass doors.

Four burly officers in flak jackets stepped inside, their radios buzzing and beeping. As they looked around, their presence commanded immediate attention.

One officer raised a hand and stopped Phoebe before she could stomp her way out of the building.

Clive, though, approached two of the officers with a welcoming nod.

'You just missed the ambulance,' he said. 'They've taken the girl to the hospital.'

'Was it you who called emergency services?' asked one of the officers.

Clive nodded. 'Yeah, right away. The poor girl stopped breathing. Those men flung her from a van.' As he relayed the details, his sharp eyes caught Phoebe trying to sidestep past the officers.

But one of them blocked her path.

'We need a statement.'

'I wasn't here,' she said, dismissively, folding her arms.

Clive turned his head to her, a scowl on his face. 'Yeah, you were. You were here after those men threw the girl out of the van. You were here when I gave her mouth-to-mouth.' He glanced at the officer, who clearly had no intention of letting her leave just yet.

While Clive continued assisting the police, Phoebe stood rigidly, impatiently reciting what she had seen. Her tone was completely devoid of any concern or compassion.

The officer taking notes glanced up from his notebook. 'Do you know the young lady?'

Phoebe shook her head. 'No. All I know is she's Billy Murphy's ex-girlfriend.'

The officer frowned. 'And who is Billy Murphy?'

Clive overheard the officer and stepped in. 'Billy Murphy owns these apartments and lives here. Bronte Penfold was his girlfriend, but, sadly, they broke up a few weeks ago.'

'And where is Mr Murphy now?'

Clive called over. 'He's in the ambulance with Bronte.'

The officer gave Phoebe a knowing look, now beginning to piece everything together.

'So he left. You're still here. I see.'

Phoebe shot him a glare. 'Can I go now, officer?'

The officer ignored her attitude and jotted something down. 'To your knowledge, does Ms Penfold or Mr Murphy have any enemies? Anyone who would want to harm her?'

Phoebe shrugged. 'I don't know. Probably. But I wouldn't know who. I work for Billy, and I don't know Bronte.' She sighed, dramatically. 'Now, may I go?'

The officer glanced at his colleague before nodding. 'Yes, you may. But I'll need your address if we need to contact you.'

Phoebe rolled her eyes. 'Oh, for heaven's sake . . . I suppose so.' She rattled off an address in a bored tone, tossed her head, and strode out of the building without so much as a goodbye.

***

The nearest hospital was King's College London, and as soon as the ambulance screeched to a halt outside A&E, the medics were already waiting. The back doors were flung open, and they surged forward, ready to take over.

Billy's heart pounded so hard it made him feel sick. Not only was his stomach in knots, but his head was spinning too. He had spent the entire ride watching, waiting, and praying as the paramedics worked on Bronte, their voices calm but urgent, their hands moving fast to keep her alive.

As soon as they wheeled her out of the ambulance, the medics rushed her through the double doors, where she was swallowed up by the bright, sterile chaos of the emergency ward.

Billy tried to follow. He'd barely taken two steps before a nurse put a hand on his chest and stopped him. 'You'll have to wait here.'

His breathing became sharp and shallow as he watched the nurses insert IV lines and call out numbers while pushing tubes into her battered body. Machines beeped. Someone shouted for a consultant. Within seconds, Bronte was gone again – through another set of doors and straight into surgery.

It all happened so fast.

Billy stood frozen to the spot in the corridor, his whole body buzzing as if he'd just been electrocuted. His hands were shaking. There was nothing he could do. Nothing at all.

He felt helpless. Useless.

Yanking out his phone from his pocket, he dialled Jesse. The second his brother answered, his voice groggy with sleep, Billy broke down.

'Billy? What's wrong?'

Billy tried to speak, but the words were stuck in his throat. A strangled breath left his lips, and before he knew it, hot, bitter, and uncontrollable tears rolled down his cheeks.

'J-Jesse, I'm at the hospital . . . Bronte . . . She's been taken—'

'Whoa, wait a minute! Which hospital? Why is Bronte there?'

'It's the Shipleys!' Billy's voice cracked under the strain of the moment. 'They tried to fucking murder her. Jesse, they wanted to *kill* her.'

'What? Where are you?' Jesse was wide awake now.

'I'm at King's. She's in surgery, Jesse. I don't even know if she's gonna make it.' His breathing went up a notch and his chest felt tight. He wiped his face, but the tears wouldn't stop. 'They tied her up, Jesse. The cunts beat her half to death and threw her from a fucking van outside the apartments. Just dumped her there. Like she was nothing. Jesse, she's in a bad way. How could anyone hurt her like that, the fucking cowards!'

Listening quietly, Jesse inhaled sharply. He could almost feel his brother's pain.

'Jesus Christ!' he said, his voice low and laced with utter horror. 'I'm on my way over to you now.'

The line went dead.

Billy lowered the phone and stared at it as though it wasn't real. Nothing felt real. The hospital walls seemed to merge into nothing around him. Even the sound of the hospital chaos faded into the background.

And beyond those doors, Bronte was fighting for her life.

***

All the time Billy paced the corridor, he hoped someone would tell him what was happening, but no one did. Then he saw Jesse, who had evidently thrown on a tracksuit in a rush and not even bothered to comb his hair.

He ran towards Billy and flung his arms around him.

'I'm here, Billy.'

Holding his brother in a tight embrace, Jesse could feel the emotion pouring out of him. 'Come on, there's nothing you can do just hanging around in the corridor.'

'They haven't even come out to tell me what's happening.'

'Listen, why do you think that's the case? It's obvious, Billy. They're all caring for Bronte. She'll be in good hands. Let's step out for a minute, all right? The police will be here soon, I promise you that. They'll want to question you, so let's get a coffee and talk.'

With a final glance across to the double doors, to see if one of the medical staff might come over to see him, Billy realised then that it would be some time before he was given an up-to-date assessment of Bronte's condition.

Jesse was right. Better to go and find a place where he could calm down and think about what he would tell the police.

***

The canteen was quiet. A few doctors were sipping their coffee, and a couple of patients in wheelchairs were hanging about.

Billy ordered two coffees, paid the cashier, and placed one in front of Jesse.

'Right, so what happened?'

Billy took a sip to steady himself. Then, with his mind clear, he went over everything – from taking Phoebe to the restaurant to where he was now.

'Billy,' Jesse said, staring at his brother, 'you should have called me sooner.'

Billy shot him an angry look. 'Don't you think I fucking know that now? I was wrong, okay? Fucking wrong. I called home, and everyone was safe indoors. Dad has security cameras up. I didn't think they'd go for Bronte. In fact, I thought they were empty threats.' He shook his head, his frustration evident. 'I told Reece if he wanted an address, then ask you.'

Jesse sighed. 'They don't have me in their back pocket, Billy. There's a lot of them – granted – the firm's big and dangerous. But the witnesses have been moved, and not even I know where they are. They have a senior handler to go through.'

'So, I don't get why they didn't come to you. I mean, they had me beaten up.'

Jesse frowned. '*What?*'

Billy let out an exhausted sigh. 'When I was in the hospital, Reece paid me a visit. He told me that he had me beaten up, and I guess if the pikeys had killed me, they would've used that to get to you. But I didn't die, did I? And Reece said tonight that I had two hours, and I guess I shouldn't have ignored it, but I did. And now Bronte's in the operating room fighting for her life.'

Jesse nodded, the tears in his eyes welling up. 'Billy . . . are you asking for the address?'

Billy shrugged. 'I am proud that you're a detective. You always wanted to be a copper, ever since we found that body in the newt pond . . .'

Jesse exhaled, sharply. 'I get it. My job's not worth anyone's life.'

Billy's eyes darkened. 'All my life, Jesse, I wanted to be on the straight and narrow. I wanted to use what I had to make money, and I did – yeah, I did. The stock market and the properties are all above board. And you, a copper. And look at us, Jesse. Look where we've come from. Our dad and our uncles aren't exactly straight, are they? Even Dottie killed her parents. But we were encouraged to live a straight life.'

Jesse chewed his lip as he listened to his brother – always the voice of reason.

'I worked hard, Jesse. Day and night, long hours to build the business from scratch, when I could have used the money to import a load of drugs to get a bunch of dealers to triple my money overnight or open up a load of barber shops and get into money laundering. But I never did, did I. I never did anything like that.'

'And that should make you proud, Billy.'

'Proud? It made me and you *targets*. Imagine if we had our own firm, if you weren't a copper, and we ran around with shooters, threatening people, acting like bullies—'

'Like the Shipleys?'

'Exactly. They wouldn't come on our turf, would they?'

Jesse shook his head. 'We are who we are, though, Billy, although . . .' He grinned. 'But having said that, there's another side to you. You're so much like Mottie.'

Billy smiled for the first time in what seemed like a lifetime. 'Maybe, but, I will kill them, Jesse.'

'And I'll be with you,' Jesse sighed. 'They know you and me are close. The thing with the Shipleys is they do their deep digging. They find out everything there is to know. They got to one of our coppers and tried to make him switch a piece of evidence. And I knew the bloke. That would've taken some doing. So they know if they hurt you, it would hurt me.'

'Jesse, Reece said that you would listen to me.'

'Well, he'd be right, then. I always have.'

'Then listen now, Jesse. It's war. Fuck doing the right thing. I'm going to find who hurt Bronte, and I'm gonna skin them alive.'

'If they hurt Bronte, who's next, Billy? The Shipleys are determined to get Max and Moriarty off that murder charge.'

'Jesse, why aren't the police keeping the Shipleys under surveillance?'

'Because, dear bruvver, there's always someone inside feeding them information, that's why. They were under surveillance for a while, but keeping a whole family and a firm under constant watch would cost a fortune. The governor had to pull the plug on it because, in all that time, not one of them has put a foot wrong – not even a petty theft. They knew they were being watched. They were always one step ahead.'

'So, Jesse, why are they targeting you now? Or rather, through me?'

'Because somehow, they know I'm leading the case, and Redwood gave me the address. The old address now. They've been moved again. They never give that kind of information to a copper – it's always handled through a middleman. As I said, I don't know the new address, but they won't know that. But, anyway, Redwood trusted me. I know you're angry, but we need to think things through. For starters, I don't want our family becoming a target.'

'They can all go on holiday – all of them,' Billy said, his mind ticking over. 'Hang on . . . I know where they can go. Cas's villa in Cyprus. No one knows about that except a handful of people.'

'Is it big enough to cater for the whole family, though? Nan, Grandad, our aunts, and cousins?'

Billy nodded. 'Yep, it's huge.'

'Right, you talk to Cas. I'll speak to Dad. We need to let him know he has to be ready to get the family out of the country and somewhere safe.'

Billy nodded, his eyes still dark, as if something cold, calculated, and dangerous had taken over.

'Are you sure about this, Billy?'

'I have never been more sure of anything in my life.'

Jesse held his gaze for a moment, then he nodded. 'When the police question you, don't mention the Shipleys.'

Billy snorted. 'I'm not that stupid.'

'No, Billy boy, you ain't.'

'I need to find out how Bronte is, and I swear to God, if she doesn't . . . if she doesn't make it, I will go through all of them.'

Jesse nodded. 'Then call Cas. I'll call Dad. I'll be waiting here, Billy.'

***

Billy arrived outside the theatres and was immediately approached by the same nurse who had stopped him from entering the emergency ward.

Nurse Hallie, a round, dimple-faced woman, who was full of warmth, said, 'She's okay.'

'Thank God,' Billy replied, exhaling loudly and leaning against the wall.

Hallie shook her head. 'No, thank the surgeon. Bronte suffered a clot on her brain that was caused by the injuries. She's in ICU but . . .' She held up her hands before he could panic. 'She will be fine. Give it an hour or so, and you can go and see her. The police are here somewhere. I know they want to speak to you.'

Billy nodded. 'Of course. I'll be about.'

She smiled, tapped his arm, and hurried off.

Billy immediately glanced around. The police were the last people he wanted to see right now. He needed air. Without hesitation, he stepped outside, inhaling deeply as the cool night breeze soothed his tear-stained face and reddened eyes.

Pulling his phone from his back pocket, he dialled Cas's number.

It rang twice before Cas answered, his voice groggy. 'What the fuck, Billy? Do you know what time it is? Actually . . . what is the time? I fucking swear, I need glasses. I can't even see my alarm clock.'

'Cas, I need your help.'

'Go on, son.'

'Your place in Cyprus, is it vacant?'

'Well, Billy, I'm not in it, so, yeah, it's vacant. Why? Fancy a holiday?'

'I need my entire family out of the country.'

'You what? Where are you, Billy?'

'I'm at King's College Hospital. Bronte's been beaten nearly to death, and I need my family safe before the Shipleys strike again.'

'Fucking hell, Billy. Give me an hour, and I'll meet you there.'

'Cas, can my family use your villa?'

'Well, of course they can, soppy bollocks.'

CHAPTER TWENTY-THREE

Cas arrived at King's College Hospital within the hour. Five minutes later, he had made his way to Bronte's room.

When he entered the room and he saw Billy reach across to his ex-girlfriend and hold her hand as though it was made of thin glass, it made Cas's eyes glisten. He was witnessing a very touching moment.

Moments later, he sat down beside Billy. Neither man said a word to each other.

Then Billy explained to Cas why the Shipleys attacked Bronte, owning up to the fact that he'd completely ruled them out in hurting her if he didn't give them the address of the witnesses to the Fairbrothers' murders.

'I'm glad you didn't mention the Shipleys to the Ol' Bill,' said Cas, quietly, as he broke the silence. 'Because believe me, son, they'll have an alibi and not one of 'em will get pulled in for questioning. They've been getting away with blue bloody murder for years. I gotta be honest, though, they ain't ever trod on my toes. It was also an unspoken agreement 'cos if they'd tried to do that, I would've annihilated the lot of 'em.'

Billy let out a slow breath before he turned to Cas. He clocked the man's tracksuit attire, which was unusual for him.

'I guess you would,' Billy said. 'But they've trampled all over my toes, though. It was those bastards who paid Bronte's brothers and their little muggy mates to do me over. They nearly finished me and all, Cas.'

Cas tapped Billy's leg. 'I know, mate. I know.' He glanced around, and then he leaned in. 'Billy . . . I ain't letting this go because those fuckwits obviously *have* been doing their due diligence, and they would know fucking well enough that me and you are linked. So it makes me wonder – why ain't they had a word with me yet? Unless in their tiny naïve little minds, they foolishly believe I'm old and past it. See, that's where Kenny Ruck went wrong, the daft prick. I doubt he'll underestimate me again. He's staying low. Not even Grace, his missus, has heard from him, the fucking coward.'

Billy smirked. 'But you are getting on a bit, Cas.'

'Fuck off, Billy,' Cas shot back. 'I said I was jacking it all in, going straight, just looking after me livestock. But the truth is, it's as boring as shit. There's only so much I can do with cattle. Anyway, I've rounded up a firm – you met some of 'em. They're a handful and no mistake. Sweet lads, but it stands to reason they're hard. They're the sons of proper tasty geezers, they are. Hard, fast, and fucking dangerous, too. My old firm. Back in the good old days when men were men, and rats didn't get rewarded: they got buried.' He scratched his chin, and then his eyes narrowed. 'Speaking of rats, I still need to find that Kenny Ruck and take him out of the picture. And then, I wanna have a word with the Shipleys. Because like it or not, never mind what they did to you, they crossed a line with me.'

Billy inclined his head. 'Well, yeah, I suppose they did.'

Cas shook his head. 'No, see, they grew their plants in what is *almost* my fucking building. As I am an investor and your silent partner, ain't that right?'

Billy nodded. 'Yeah, so?'

'So, Billy, if they think they can demand a favour from you over that debt when the cheeky bastards were growing their little operation without *my permission.*' He poked himself in the chest. 'And on property that's practically half mine, then they've crossed a *dodgy fuckin' line.*'

Billy frowned. 'So?'

Cas grinned, but there was nothing friendly about his expression. 'So only *I* grow plants in *my* backyard. If they wanna run the North London patch, then that's fine. But step on to *my* manor?' He shook his head, his voice dropping to a growl. 'Nahhh. Nahhh. I ain't having that.'

Billy was taking it all in as he watched Cas's expression change. The man was unbelievable. Now well into his sixties, he looked far younger, despite an aversion to any form of physical exercise. Here he was, like a dog with a bone.

'I might be old, but I'm alive, and they've taken a right fucking liberty,' Cas growled. 'Forget this bollocks about the address. The cockroaches have gone too far, and I ain't fucking happy about it. So, I'm taking off some unsavoury heads.'

Billy watched as the old gangster came out in Cas. His tone dropped, deep and dark, his face deadpan and serious. That look alone would make any man sit up and listen.

'Cas, where are you staying?'

'At the manor house, why?'

'Because it was practically empty the last time I was there.'

'Yeah, I've had the builders in. The place looks lovely now – all fresh and new.' He smirked before his expression suddenly darkened again.

Billy remembered that look. He'd first seen it when he was only twelve years old and he'd got caught up in some business he shouldn't have.

'They used to call me *The Governor*, Billy. Well, I'm reclaiming my title. *Now.* Part of me was gonna just fuck off. I hate looking over me shoulder, especially for the likes of Kenny Ruck. And then I thought, no, fuck it. I ain't that old or cowardly. And, besides, the old house needed a fresh coat of paint and a redo of the old orangery. I moved out because of the mess, but I ain't running from no cunt.'

He leaned in again and lowered his voice. 'I've got a couple of shooters in my car. One of 'em's got your name on it.'

Billy's eyes widened. 'A gun? Tell me you're joking, Cas?'

'Nah, I ain't. With the Shipleys, you're gonna need one. Now – do you wanna stay at mine?'

Billy shook his head. 'No, I'll stick to my apartment. It's secure enough. And I'm not scared of those Shipleys, Cas. I'm angry. Raging, in fact. I'd *love* for Reece or Dario to knock at my door.' He clenched his fists, his jaw tight. 'I'll hurt them, Cas. I'll hurt them so badly they'll wish they were dead.'

***

Jesse had finally convinced his father to book the tickets to Cyprus so the family could fly out as soon as possible. Of course, it had been met with resistance, but after enough pushing, his father had relented. The moment he agreed, Jesse let out a deep sigh of relief, the weight on his chest easing just enough for him to focus on what he needed to do next.

As he headed straight for the ICU, his pulse quickened. But when he reached Bronte's room, his stomach tightened into a knot. There were two officers standing outside, their presence impossible to ignore.

Jesse clenched his jaw and steadied himself. Of course, they had a reason to be here. But he wasn't sure whether they were protecting Bronte or keeping an eye on her visitors. Either way, it could cause him a problem.

Exhaling slowly, he squared his shoulders and walked forward.

One of the officers turned to face him head-on, and Jesse's heart almost stopped. Shit!

Jacob Kerns. Of all people, it would have to be him.

He had recently transferred from the station where Jesse worked to the South East to be closer to his ageing parents. A solid, broad-shouldered man in his early forties, he had this uncanny way of gazing at someone long enough to assess their real intentions. Standing outside the room in his crisp uniform, his stance was casual but alert. He was someone who didn't need to exert effort to command authority.

When his eyes met Jesse's, a wide patronising grin spread across his face as he extended a hand.

'Well, look at you. If it ain't Jesse Murphy.'

Forcing a smile, Jesse clasped it. 'Jacob, mate. Good to see you.'

Kerns's dark eyes swept over him, an approving nod coming just before the inevitable comment. 'Being a detective suits you. And I heard you've been promoted. So you're working under Redwood now. Is that right?'

Heat crept up Jesse's neck, not from pride but discomfort. Praise was one thing, but this situation was something else entirely.

With his arms folded across his chest, Kerns tilted his head slightly. 'Leading the Shipley case, I hear? You got lucky there.' He sniggered. 'Or is it a case of being unlucky?'

A forced smirk masked the unease. 'Well, someone's gotta lock up the criminals. So it might as well be me.'

Kerns gave a low chuckle, but it was very brief. A quick flick of his head towards Bronte's room shifted the tone. 'We've got a possible attempted murder. A young woman was thrown from a moving van.'

Biting his lip, Jesse racked his brain for the next move. Before he could land one, a frown deepened on the older man's face.

'Shit, Jesse,' he whispered. 'Billy Murphy. Is he your brother?'

The gut punch landed hard. There was no dodging the question.

A tight nod. 'Yeah . . . I'm just checking on him. Bronte is, well, was his girlfriend.'

Kerns's gaze sharpened as his instincts clearly kicked in. 'We're waiting for her to wake up,' he said, slowly, lifting a questioning eyebrow. 'Any clue as to what happened?'

Jesse was on it without any hesitation. 'Nothing at the moment. We're waiting, just like you, to find out why anyone would do this to her.' Keeping his voice steady took some effort, especially as sweat was beginning to pour off him. 'She's a good girl, Bronte.'

Kerns, though, wasn't convinced by Jesse's response. That much was clear.

But this was a game Jesse couldn't afford to lose.

'I might be way off here, mate,' Kerns said, his eyes remaining sharp, 'but if he's your brother, and she's his ex – though by the looks of things, he still has feelings for her because he hasn't left her side yet – is this connected to the Shipleys?'

Jesse was surprised by that question. Why would Kerns jump to that conclusion? But now that it was out there, he had to think fast.

'I have no idea,' he said, smoothly. 'All we know is Bronte was pushed out of a van onto the pavement and it happened outside Billy's apartment.'

Kerns jutted his jaw. 'Looks like you've got your hands full, mate. We can stay here and wait to question her, if you like. Or do you want to do that when she comes around? She's more likely to open up to you if you know her.'

Jesse gave a firm nod. 'Thanks, Jacob. I'll put a report in and get it over to you. If there's any link to the Shipleys, it'll have to be handled through our station.'

Kerns held up his hands. 'Rather you than me, mate. The Shipleys . . .' He shook his head. 'I won't miss trying to nick them. They're one nasty family. And, Jesse, I really hope you secure that double murder conviction. At least that'll be two down and probably another fifteen to go. They've always seemed like lice to me, forever crawling out of the woodwork.'

Jesse forced a smirk, but inside, his stomach was giving him gyp. He needed to get out of this conversation before Kerns asked any more probing questions.

'Okay, Jacob, you and your colleague might as well get off. Like I said, I'll get a statement over to you as soon as.'

Kerns gave Jesse a sharp nod, and then he flicked his head towards the other officer.

But just as Jesse reached for the door handle, Kerns suddenly spun around and curled his finger.

'Jesse, a word.'

Jesse's pulse kicked up a notch. 'Yeah, mate. What is it?'

'There's another bloke in with Billy – Cas Ferrier.'

Jesse nodded, keeping his expression unreadable.

'He's a known face,' Kerns said, watching Jesse closely. 'You do know that, don't you?'

Letting out a short laugh, Jesse shrugged. 'Face ain't the word, Jacob. Cas is a farmer now – he gave up the old gangster life years ago. Soft ol' bastard, these days.'

Kerns narrowed his eyes, weighing the response. 'So, how do you know him?'

'He . . . helped arrest a bent copper we knew.'

That answer seemed to satisfy Kerns – for now. With a slow nod, he straightened up. 'All right. Well, I hope your brother's ex recovers well.'

Dying to get out of that conversation, Jesse couldn't stop the beads of sweat appearing on his forehead. He was convinced Kerns would make a comment about it.

But the moment passed. Kerns went on his way with his colleague.

Sighing with relief, Jesse stepped inside the room and found a tissue to mop his brow.

'That copper out there only fucking knows me,' he muttered.

Cas rose from his chair, his arms folded. 'Take a seat, Jesse. Did he join the fucking dots?'

Biting his lip, Jesse nodded. 'Yeah, he asked if her assault was connected to the Shipleys. I said I didn't know. But he's thorough. I reckon he'll make a few calls to his boss, and you know what that means.' Running a hand through his hair, he scoffed. 'He was all smiles, congratulating me for making detective, but I could smell the jealousy coming off him. Anyway, forget him. Dad's sorting out the tickets for Cyprus.'

Billy smiled at Cas. 'Nice one, Cas. I feel much better, knowing they'll be out of the country.'

Cas suddenly slapped his leg. 'Oh, shit! I forgot – they'll have company. An old friend of mine, Grace, is out there keeping out of the way of Kenny Ruck, her husband. But it's only her. She won't get in the way.'

Jesse waved a dismissive hand. 'Mum and Nan will make her feel welcome. You know what they're like.'

'Yeah . . .' Cas nodded, but his expression darkened. 'She could probably do with a friend right now. Poor cow can't come home until I fix her problem.'

'Can I help, Cas?' asked Jesse, looking concerned.

'No, son, this problem needs burying, not nicking.'

Jesse laughed. He had always enjoyed Cas's no-nonsense approach to life. Strangely, he found him a breath of fresh air.

'Jesse, do you think you can sit with Bronte?' asked Billy. 'I need to let her ol' man know she's here.'

'Billy, are you fucking kidding me? The last time you were at the gypsy site, they nearly killed you.'

Cas tapped Jesse's back. 'I'll go with him.'

'But, uh . . .'

'If you so much as hint I'm past my sell-by date, I'll swing for ya.' Cas laughed. 'Anyway,' he said, cracking his knuckles, 'I've got a tool in the motor they won't argue with.'

Jesse held up a hand. 'I don't wanna fucking know, Cas.'

He suddenly shoved his fingers in his ears to prove his point, by exaggerating his refusal to listen.

But Cas wasn't having it. Cocking his finger like a gun, his expression darkened.

'I'm not fucking about anymore.' His gaze flicked towards Bronte. 'She might've been a bit ditsy at times, but that girl right there didn't fucking deserve this.'

A nod was all Jesse could manage. Glancing at Bronte, he felt a cold shiver run through him.

'How long will she be out? Have the doctors said anything yet?'

Billy rose from his chair and stretched his stiff back. 'They've sedated her. Want to keep her under for another few hours.' He rolled his shoulders and sighed. 'Look, I'm heading to the site. Will you—'

'Of course, I'll be all right. I'm not going anywhere,' Jesse cut in. 'You let Benny know where his daughter is. But watch your back.'

***

As Cas bowled his way to his car as though he owned the entire car park, his presence as commanding as ever, he was talking nineteen to the dozen, as usual.

Billy, however, wasn't in the mood for any chit-chat. Switching on his phone, it lit up with hundreds of messages. Most of them were from his mother.

He knew he had to call her back. The second he dialled her number and explained what had been going on over the last twenty-four hours, he expected a barrage of frantic questions would hit him all at once.

And they did.

'Mum – Mum, stop! Please, just listen.' Taking a deep breath, he gripped the car door handle. 'Bronte is in the hospital. She was savagely beaten up and thrown from a van. And before any other member of this family gets hurt, I want you all gone – out of here, in a safe place.'

'But Billy, what about you? And dear Bronte? How am I meant to enjoy Cyprus knowing my sons are in danger?'

'Mum, please. Just hear me out. Bronte's going to be fine. If we go with you, we'll only have to return one day and face the same music. Let me deal with it. Cas and his, er . . . well, his associates, are with me. And, come on, let's face it – Jesse's a copper now. So, please, let me focus on Bronte and sort out this issue.'

'Issue!' Carrie screeched down the phone. 'It's hardly just an *issue*, Billy!'

Billy had had enough. 'Mum, stop! Just do me one favour – make sure my family is safe in another fucking country!' He didn't like to shout or speak to his mother like that, but his patience was at an end.

There was a brief moment of silence.

Carrie could sense the anger and the frustration in her eldest son's voice. And in that moment, she knew she had no choice but to do as he asked.

'Okay, my boy,' she said, in a softer tone, this time. 'But I need you to call me every hour, so I can at least have some peace of mind.'

CHAPTER TWENTY-FOUR

It was six o'clock in the morning when Candice wrapped her hands around a hot cup of tea. Her gaze shifted between Reece and Dario before she finally settled on Gerard.

'So, go on, Mum. What the fuck's going on? You called us over at this ungodly hour, you look like death warmed up, so spit it out.'

Candice turned her eyes back to Reece. 'Are all the cameras on this site wired up now?'

He frowned. 'Well, there are a few more problems. They're being sorted now. Some stupid builders had cut through them again. Apparently, they should have been the last thing to be installed. There's been too much pipework, digging and drilling. Why, Gran? What's going on?'

'She was here.'

'Who?' Reece glanced at his father.

Gearard's expression suggested that he was full of doubt, as if his mother had lost the plot.

A storm gathered in her eyes. 'Don't you fucking look at me like that, boy. I'm telling you, Dorothy Ellis was here. She was looking through *my* window.'

Gerard frowned. 'What?'

'I was asleep. I must've heard a noise, and when I woke up, there she was. She was staring right at me. By the time I turned the light on and steadied meself, the bitch had gone.'

Gerard's concern quickly shifted to scepticism. 'Mum, I think you need to see a doctor. Your bedroom's upstairs. So, what you're telling me is that this Dorothy Ellis has wings an' all? Or does she just happen to carry a fucking ladder in her handbag?'

Candice slammed her cup down on the kitchen table so hard that the handle broke off in her hand. Jumping up, she jabbed a finger in Gerard's direction. 'Don't you ever talk to me like that again, you saucy cunt. I'm not going fucking mad!' Wiping her mouth with the back of her hand, she said, 'You dare treat me like I'm senile! I've got more brains than you useless lot put together.'

'Mum—' Gerard softened his tone, now sensing her fury.

'Don't you dare, Gerard!' she snapped, before sitting down again. 'I wasn't sleeping upstairs, you idiot! I was on the sofa, and she was right there, at the window. Now, check the cameras. They'll confirm she was here.'

Shooting a glance at Reece, Gerard's jaw tightened. 'The cameras ain't out of action again, are they? Fuck me, it was only around a month ago when the last prick, who, by the way, nearly blew himself up, put the security system out.'

Reece shifted uncomfortably, moving from foot to foot. 'It's getting sorted, all right? But, Dad, why would Billy Murphy's mum be snooping around our site? If it was one of the Murphy brothers, I'd understand. But a woman? On her own?'

With her eyes widening in disbelief, Candice angrily spat, 'Didn't you hear a word I said when I fucking told you how *dangerous* that bitch is?'

Dario, who had been silent until now, sat beside his grandmother and patted her back. 'Grannie, listen . . . maybe you just had a nightmare. You thought you saw this woman. She sounds scary enough to me.'

Candice's eyes narrowed as she scanned the three of them, with disgust written all over her face. 'You lot still don't believe me, do you?'

Gerard sighed. 'It's not that, Mum. I just think Dario's got a point. With everything going on, maybe it just ended up in a nightmare. I can get you some sleeping tablets, if you want? It might help you rest, perhaps. What do you think?'

Candice shook her head. Absolutely pissed off with this useless bunch of wankers, pure fury was burning in her eyes.

'Just get the cameras up and running. You lot are a fucking shower of shit.'

Before Candice could hurl any more abuse, Reece's phone rang. He glanced at the caller ID, then, putting a finger to his lips, he signalled for everyone to be quiet.

'Hello.'

'They have you under surveillance.'

'All of us?'

'Yeah. You, Dario, Gerard, all the cousins, their pubs, clubs, and even the barber shops.'

'Why?'

'Shit, I must go.'

The blood drained from Reece's face. 'We're being watched. All of us. Under fucking surveillance, again.'

Gerard rubbed his bristly chin. 'So, Billy Murphy grassed, did he?'

'I don't know,' Reece muttered. 'But they can't prove fuck all, so don't stress. We've just gotta lie low for a bit. Keep everything above board.'

Gerard threw his hands in the air. 'Lie low? The fucking clock's ticking! I can't believe you stood and watched that twat Jameson swallow the evidence. And you couldn't even retrieve it from his dead body, could ya? No wonder you didn't get a GCSE in human biology! Max and Moriarty will be in court soon. The bullets can be challenged by our lawyers in court, but there are no guarantees. So, it's the address we need. A simple poxy address. Without that, our lads are toast.'

Leaning with his hands on the back of the kitchen chair, his voice dripping with frustration, Gerard looked at Reece and growled, 'So what now, clever clogs?'

As Reece paced the floor, all eyes were fixed on him. 'It's not over. We've got a plan B.'

Gerard's grin was demonic. 'This had better fucking work, boy,' he growled.

Candice was staring into her coffee, her fingers gripping the cup. 'I'm beginning to wonder if I'll ever see me two grandsons again. It'll finish me off, if we don't get them out of prison soon.'

'I know, Mum, but we're doing our best. You know that.'

Candice looked up, not happy at all. The stress of it all was carving deep lines into her face. 'I know, but I just wish you'd go in harder and not be such pussies. Fuck the Murphys. Our boys come first.'

'Grannie, Billy Murphy's girlfriend was practically dead on arrival, and even that didn't make him pick up the blower. Maybe he values money over everything else.'

'Yeah, see . . .' Candice snapped, her eyes burning with frustration. 'You see, *we* don't worship money over everything else. For us, family comes first. That's why we're fighting to get our boys out of prison. And it just proves Billy's a psychopath, like his mother, Dorothy Ellis.'

Gerard rolled his eyes. 'Okay, so maybe Billy *is* a psychopath. But what's about to come next will make him think twice.'

'Have you even thought they might pull Jesse Murphy off the case?' Her voice rose as she leaned forward. 'They could move the witnesses to some place he doesn't even know about? And then what, Gerard? I'll tell you what it will do. It will right royally fuck us.'

Reece finally stopped pacing. 'Gran, then it'll be in Jesse's hands to *find* that address. He'll have to do what it takes to get it for us. And, believe me, Billy Murphy will be begging Jesse to get the address. Because as much as I want me brothers out of jail, this has just got personal!'

Candice's gaze drifted out of the kitchen window. The new development was speckled with luxury houses, every one of them occupied by a member of their family. But just beyond that were fields. Woods.

She had never lived in the country before. It had always been council estates, streets packed with people. Now, all that empty space felt like a fucking nightmare – like she was wide open to something dark waiting in the shadows.

***

Cas drove into the pikey site without a care for pedestrians. After what they'd done to Billy, he couldn't give two shits if he ran one of them over. Bronte was the only good thing that had ever come out of the place. But although no one would condone what she had endured of late, there were questions for her to answer, that was for sure.

As soon as he pulled up outside Benny's caravan, curtains twitched in the neighbouring vans.

Billy stepped out as bold as brass. Most men who had been through what he had would never return here, let alone stand there like they owned the place.

But Cas had seen him in action at Spud's gym. He knew precisely what Billy was capable of. All the Murphys could handle themselves. Even young Nellie could throw a punch, which really amused him. He liked her feisty ways. In that respect, she was much like her mother.

But today, Cas was ready. If any one of these pikeys tried to hurt Billy, he'd make sure they never got the chance again.

Reaching under his seat, he pulled out the gun he'd taped to the underside and slid it down the back of his tracksuit bottoms. Just as he stepped out of the car to follow Billy, Franklin and Archie appeared from nowhere, like two greedy rats.

Franklin's most distinguishing mark was his quiff, and yet even that was dishevelled.

By his side, Archie stood wide-legged, trying to look hard, but he couldn't hide the flicker of nerves in his eyes.

But to be fair to the men, they were giving it their best shot. Franklin glared at Billy. Then he gave him a smirk, suggesting that he had the upper hand.

'Brave,' was all he said.

Cas clenched his jaw but he decided to hold back and wait this one out.

Billy didn't flinch. 'I'm here to see your old man.'

'Like fuck you are. Turn around and fuck off.'

Franklin's gaze shifted to Cas, who was grinning from ear to ear.

'Did I fucking hear you right? Someone needs to tell you, ya cunt, that Elvis is dead, as you will be!' said Cas, now stone-faced.

Before Franklin could react, Cas grabbed a fistful of his quiff and rammed the gun straight into his mouth, shattering two of his teeth on the way.

'Now, Mr Presley, you're gonna back the fuck off and take your fat fuck of a brother with you, while we pay your old man a visit. Comprende?'

Franklin nodded, his eyes wide and unfocused, like a captured wild animal.

'Good,' Cas said, as he removed the gun and slapped the man's cheek. 'There's a good boy. Now, run along.'

Franklin suddenly clutched his mouth. His face fell a mile. Not only was there blood dripping between his fingers but two of his teeth dropped onto the ground.

'You heard him, Franklin. Go on, the pair of you,' Billy said, his voice cold. 'I need a word with your old man.'

Both men watched as Archie put an arm around his brother's shoulders, only for Franklin to shrug him off. Their bodies slumped in defeat as they dragged their feet back towards their caravans in silence.

'Cowardly cunts,' Cas muttered, as he followed Billy towards Benny's caravan.

The door was already open. Benny stood in the doorway, his face wizened from years of hard living etched into his skin.

'So, what brings you here, Billy?' His words were soft and hollow and carried the weight of a man who was just too tired to argue or resist.

Billy stepped inside.

Cas stared at the state of the man. He noticed his tatty long cardigan and stained shirt before he followed close behind.

Benny gave a slow nod of respect and gestured towards the sofa.

'I can't apologise enough, Billy,' he admitted. 'Because I know what they did was wrong. But me apologising for them nearly mullering you . . . well, it ain't enough.'

Billy nodded, his expression inscrutable, as always. 'At least it wasn't you, though, Benny. The Shipleys paid them to do it.'

Benny lowered his gaze in shame. 'Aye. It don't surprise me.'

'You knew?'

'That flashy-looking mush came here. I saw them having a meeting in Franklin's caravan. I warned 'em, Billy. Told 'em to stay away, but they're greedy boys, proper greedy. They always have been. To tell you the truth, alls I care about is me dear little Bronte girl. I wished at the time that woman *had* slit my throat. I couldn't bear it, Billy, seeing you getting mullered. It was wrong. It turned me, Billy, it did. It proper turned me.'

'Benny, do you know where she has been living?'

'Yeah, I do. Her friend, Rosie May, she's been having a bit of bother – got took sick – and my Bronte girl's been watching her little chavi.'

'How long has she been doing that for, Benny?'

'Since the day you two broke up. That's what, nearly five weeks ago? She said she was at yours to pick up her overnight bag when Rosie May called in a proper state, the poor malt. My Bronte's been there most nights, helping out, keeping her mind off you.' His eyes glazed over. 'She loves you, Billy. She never meant to cause no trouble.' His head dipped in quiet disappointment. 'Those two fucking boys of mine promised her she'd make a lot of money. It was supposed to be just one small job, and she'd have enough to treat you, for everything you do for her. She wanted to take you on a holiday.' Raising his hand, he shook his head again. 'Before you say anything, I know, Billy. I know she made a stupid mistake.'

Sauntering over to the side table, he pointed to the brandy. 'Want one?'

Cas shook his head, having spotted the label and knowing cheap brandy would burn his throat.

Billy also swerved the offer.

Benny sighed. 'Is everything all right? Why are you here, anyway?'

'Benny . . .' Billy took a deep breath. 'Bronte's in the hospital.'

Benny froze. '*What?*'

'The Shipleys threw her out of a van,' Billy said, his voice tight with fury. 'She was bound and gagged, with a fucking sack over her battered head.'

Cas clocked the way Benny's face blanched, the shock hitting him like a gut punch. His body swayed, and before anyone could do anything for him, his knees began to buckle.

'Whoa – steady, old man.'

Cas was the first to jump up from the sofa. He managed to grab Benny before he collapsed and hit his head on the coffee table. Easing him down into his armchair, he kept a firm grip on his shoulder. 'She ain't dead, Benny. She's hurt, but she's alive. We came to take you to the hospital to see her.'

Benny blinked, his breath coming in short, ragged bursts, as he tried to process what he'd been told.

Instinctively, Billy poured a generous measure of brandy and pressed the glass into Benny's trembling hands. 'Here. Drink this. And when you're ready, we'll take you to her.'

Cas's eyes flicked over the old man's tattered clothes once more, and for a moment, he felt sorry for him. As his gaze wandered around the caravan, he took in the small details – the framed photo of Benny and Bronte and another beside it, likely Bronte's mother. A stunning woman, she had been. His eyes lingered on the younger Benny in the picture, and he had to admit, the old man had once been a big deal. There was a bit of Paul Newman about him.

On the side table, Bronte's necklace and rings lay neatly beside a vase containing a few fresh flowers. The caravan was old and worn, but small touches – like a new rug and modern paintings – brought life to it. That was Bronte's doing, no doubt.

Everything Cas had seen and heard in that short time told him one thing – Bronte was a kind girl. Sweet. The lump in his throat tightened.

He wished his own daughter had been like that. But she wasn't. She was off somewhere, shagging the next rich fella, and she certainly wouldn't be giving a second thought to her old man. He could bank on that.

As soon as Benny pulled himself together, he stood up and slipped his bare feet into a pair of black shoes, not bothering to tie the laces.

'I appreciate this, Billy. You're a good man, a decent man.'

Billy smiled. 'Let's get going.'

But the second they stepped out of the caravan, they were surrounded.

Franklin, Archie, and two others blocked their path, all with the same menacing expressions.

Archie lifted his chin. 'Where the fuck d'you think you're taking me farver, eh?'

Still nursing his broken teeth and split gum, Franklin glared but said nothing.

Before Billy or Cas could answer, Benny pointed at them. 'You two are no sons of mine. Get your caravans off my site.'

Archie laughed. 'Oh yeah? And what's that wanker told you, eh? More lies?'

'Lies?' Benny snapped. His face twisted with rage. 'My Bronte – your little sister – is in hospital! Thrown from a van, battered. My dear little girl. And it's all your fault.'

Billy saw the flicker of confusion on Franklin's face. Then, suddenly, the younger man's hand fell away from his mouth, his jaw gaping in horror.

'How did the Shipleys know where she was, eh?' Benny's voice turned to a low snarl. 'Franklin – did you sell her to those men like you sold me precious horse for a few quid to that fucking poncy Lord Ashcroft?'

It was Archie who replied. 'No, 'course we never! So that's what Billy told you, is it? 'Cos that man's a liar.'

Shaking his head, Benny ignored Archie completely. His attention was locked on Franklin.

'What did you do?' he hissed, his eyes wild with fury. 'What did you do, Franklin?'

Franklin shook his head, but his expression said it all – he knew something.

Billy stepped forward, his voice dangerously calm, although he kept his anger on a tight leash. 'She was dying in front of me. They beat her so badly, she stopped breathing. She had a clot in her brain. She's alive now – but barely. I'm taking your father to see his little girl. So, like he asked – what the fuck did you do?'

Franklin's mouth hung open in shock. Slowly, he turned to Archie, then back to Billy. 'We . . . we didn't do anything. Reece came here. Said he wanted a favour from Bronte. Said he'd see her all right.'

The red mist descended. Billy lunged forward, and with a single almighty punch, he dropped Franklin to the ground.

Before Billy could land another blow, Cas, with the help of another man, dragged him back, but his eyes burned with rage as he spat through clenched teeth. 'You sold your sister to the Shipleys? Is that right?' His chest heaved as he fought to break free. 'You'd better run, you cunt, because when I come for you – and you, Archie – it won't end pretty.'

Scrambling to his feet, Franklin wiped the blood from his mouth. 'Billy, if you're going after the Shipleys, I'm coming too. I swear – I never knew they'd hurt her. I might be a cunt at times, but she's me little sister. I protect my family. It's what I do.'

Billy glared. 'You couldn't protect a fucking budgie. Don't stand there talking about protecting her while she's lying in a hospital bed, unconscious, with tubes and wires keeping her alive. You wanna fight the Shipleys? Be my guest. But that don't exempt you from what's coming to you after I take your father to see his daughter.'

He shook Cas and the other man off and was about to head to his car when Archie suddenly felt brave.

'*We're* taking our farver to the hospital. She's our sister.'

Billy was about to march towards Archie and give him a proper hiding, but Benny stepped in.

'No, you ain't.' His voice was ice-cold. 'Neither of you.' He took a deep breath and then he spat the next words out like venom.

'Now, get your caravans off my site. You're not welcome. I disown the pair of you.'

Cas helped Benny into the car before giving the pikeys his signature teasing grin. Then, waving like the lord he was – all but in name – he left the gathered onlookers with something to gossip over around the fire pit.

CHAPTER TWENTY-FIVE

When Jesse woke up with a banging headache, he quickly realised that he'd slept through to the afternoon. With the room spinning as he tried to get up too fast, he was forced to steady himself.

He groaned and rubbed his temples trying to recall what he'd done before he went out like a light. Looking at the alarm clock, it appeared that he'd crashed onto his bed without setting it and had then fallen into a deep, heavy sleep.

Grabbing his phone, he checked his missed calls. Several were from the station, including one from Redwood himself.

'Shit,' he muttered, yanking on his trousers and hurrying to the bathroom. Splashing cold water onto his face, which was covered in sweat, he scrubbed his teeth, in an attempt to look respectable at least for when he arrived at the police station.

A final look in the mirror had him sighing. But not from fatigue. It was his appearance. He looked dog rough.

His thoughts drifted to Billy. His brother must be exhausted. Realising that he didn't have time now, he decided that he would call him as soon as he reached the station. He was relieved in one respect that there were no missed calls from Billy, so he assumed there was no change in Bronte's condition.

***

When Jesse arrived at the station and walked past the custody suite, he noticed it was busier than usual for a late afternoon. There were a few well-dressed lawyers around. And men in handcuffs. But they didn't look like two-bit opportunists or street brawlers. Something big was going on, that was for sure. There were also a number of plain clothes coppers loitering in the background.

He carried along the corridor to the incident room, which was a hive of activity.

Melanie was the first to greet him. For a moment, Jesse was taken aback. She was actually wearing make-up, which was a surprise. What a beauty she was. He hadn't really noticed her before because she had always worked closely alongside Wesley, never once looking his way.

'Afternoon, Mel. Can't believe I slept in so late. As my mum would say, I must've needed it.'

'Hiya, Jesse. We've been – well, I've been trying to call you.'

Jesse stopped dead in his tracks and ran a hand through his unruly hair. 'Yeah, I noticed. I had a few missed calls. What's going on?'

Even as he asked, a knot tightened in his gut. He had a feeling they knew about Bronte.

Melanie glanced around to check that no one was listening, before she leaned in slightly. 'Jacob Kerns, who used to work here. You remember him, don't you? Well, he called the governor. He said your brother's girlfriend is in hospital after a rather vicious attack. Is that true?'

Eagerly awaiting his reaction, Melanie's attractive blue eyes widened in anticipation.

'Yes.' Jesse frowned. 'But why would Kerns call Redwood? Surely, he would go through formal channels, not speak to Redwood directly?'

Melanie grinned, knowingly. 'Kerns was an arse-licker. He was jealous when you came to work here. He didn't like the fact that you were so well off. And he was probably envious of your dynamic personality! We didn't like him.'

She blushed slightly, before adding, 'We like you, though, Jesse.' She flashed him a playful grin, which displayed her pearly white teeth to perfection. 'Plus, you're better looking than that old git.'

Jesse chuckled. 'So you weren't keen on him, then?'

'No,' she scoffed. 'He was a bit of a wank stain, if you ask me. Always acted like he was in his twenties, and his jokes were well inappropriate. The governor told him to stop, which got right up his nose. And listen to this. He didn't move purely for his parents – as he tried to make out he did. He was kinda pushed out by Redwood. I guess this is all new to you, isn't it. You were probably still finding your feet then.' She shrugged her shoulders.

Gently tapping his chest, she said, 'Speaking of Redwood – he wants to know why you didn't report it.'

'Fuck me, it's only just happened.'

Melanie tilted her head. 'Well, not really, Jesse. Look at the bloody time.'

He glanced up at the clock and cursed under his breath. 'Shit. It's late. Well, I was south of the river at the hospital with my brother all night,' he said, as he suddenly caught Shona giving him the side eye, which made him shudder.

'He might take you off the case, Jesse. Your position may be seen to be compromised. Just saying.'

Sighing wearily, Jesse managed a smile. 'Thanks for the heads-up, Mel. And, without sounding like a pervy wank stain – you look lovely.'

Her smile lingered as she fluttered her lashes and slowly returned to her desk.

Standing nervously outside Redwood's door, Jesse was about to knock when it suddenly swung open.

Redwood appeared in the doorway. With a pile of papers shoved under his arm, he looked flustered.

'Where the hell have you been?'

Jesse had never seen the man in such a flap.

'Overslept, Gov. I was—'

'In the hospital all night, yes, yes, I know. Well, come in!' he snapped.

Instructing Jesse to shut the door, Redwood dumped his papers on a table by the window and said, 'A huge chunk of the budget has now had to be allocated to a surveillance team. It's a bloody big one too, to watch the Shipleys. It all happened while you were out.'

Jesse stood there like a schoolboy being reprimanded by the headteacher.

'For God's sake, man, why didn't you tell me about this girl?'

Jesse frowned. 'Tell you what, Gov?'

'That your brother's girlfriend was attacked. Brutally, by all accounts.' Redwood looked exasperated. He was standing behind his desk with his hands on his hips and a scowl carved into his face.

'With all due respect, Gov, it happened late last night. I rushed to the hospital the second I got the call. I was there with my brother, and Kerns was already handling it. It happened on his patch. My priority was Billy. And, well, Bronte's like family, Gov.'

With the image of Bronte lying motionless in that hospital bed flashing through his mind, it sent a fresh surge of anger through him. Mirroring Redwood's stance, he planted his hands on his hips.

'But she's stable, thanks for asking.'

The second the words left his mouth, he knew he'd fucked up. But right now, he didn't care enough to apologise. Instead, he met Redwood's gaze with an unflinching glare as if the man himself was the enemy.

To Jesse's surprise, Redwood just sat down. He motioned for Jesse to do the same.

'Yes, quite. Sorry,' he muttered. 'I imagine that was difficult for your family. I understand she was in surgery – a blood clot?'

Jesse nodded. 'Yeah. They managed to remove it. Hopefully, she'll make a full recovery, but until she wakes up, we won't know if she'll be the same person.'

Resting his elbows on the desk, Redwood steepled his fingers.

'Have the Shipleys approached you, Jesse? Or your brother?' He watched closely, trying to read Jesse's deadpan expression. 'They will know by now that you're the lead on the Shipley murder case, so I have to ask.'

What he hadn't expected was the grin that spread across Jesse's face. It was unsettling, to say the least.

'Gov, tell me this. You've been trying to bring the Shipleys to justice. For what? Ten, twenty years? And yet, have you ever managed to break them? I mean, they run everything in North London. The clubs, the drugs, even the guns.'

Redwood's face tightened, his skin paling with anger. The softness in his expression vanished. It was replaced by something cold and challenging, but he knew the point Jesse was making, so he bit his lip and listened.

'You think putting them under surveillance will stop them? They'll know you've got a budget. And the second they get wind of it, they'll shut down all illegal activity until they get the nod that it's safe to start up again. You'll get fuck-all on them. Or . . .'

Redwood's nostrils flared, but Jesse didn't care. Not today. As much as he loved his job, he loved his family more.

His thoughts suddenly shifted to the custody suite.

'And those men downstairs – who are they?'

Redwood bowed his head slightly. 'They're Shipleys. Got them an hour ago moving money and some marijuana. So we've got them banged to rights. They're being processed now.'

Jesse narrowed his eyes.

'How much money? And what amount of drugs are we talking about?'

'I don't know yet, but I'll find out soon enough. That's irrelevant. They sussed they were under surveillance and got caught – so they're nicked.'

Jesse's grin widened. 'And how did they know they were under surveillance?'

'Well,' Redwood said, rubbing his temple, 'when we nicked one Shipley on one side of town and another on the other, I'd imagine they put two and two together.'

Jesse shook his head. 'No, Gov. I mean *before* they were trying to move their money and drugs. How did they know?'

Redwood sighed. 'I'm not actually sure they did. Could just be a coincidence and we got lucky.'

Shaking his head, Jesse let out a low chuckle. 'And you have no idea how much money, or even the weight of the drugs? Can you find out for me, please?'

Redwood's face tightened, his irritation obvious, as he snatched up the phone and called down to the custody suite.

'It's Redwood here. I want the details of the money and drugs confiscated in the raid.'

Jesse tried to hear what the sergeant on the other end was saying, but he was barely able to catch what was being said.

When Redwood finally replaced the receiver, his jaw tightened. 'Twenty thousand pounds and half a kilo of marijuana.'

Jesse frowned. 'No guns? No cocaine, heroin?'

Slowly shaking his head, Redwood muttered, 'No.'

The realisation settled in, wiping the contempt from his face and replacing it with something Jesse recognised all too well. Abject defeat.

'So their solicitors down there, who are probably on the Shipleys' payroll, will have every excuse up their sleeve to have them back on the streets by teatime. A kilo of marijuana? That's a slap on the wrist. And I'd bet my bank balance, they'll be able to account for every penny of that twenty grand.'

Jesse leaned forward, his voice lowering. 'Gov, it's obvious what the Shipleys are doing. No disrespect, but they played us. While we're dragging them in over a few pennies to them, a more serious transaction – guns, cocaine, something bigger – is probably happening right now, right under our noses. So while the surveillance team are slapping each other's backs, the Shipleys are clapping their hands. They'll clearly use every opportunity they have and will use the surveillance team to play cat and mouse.'

Redwood exhaled, rubbing his temple. 'Well, that's why I have you on this team. Like I've always said, Jesse, you have the ability to think like a criminal. That's why I'm reluctant to take you off the case. I need a man like you to catch these bastards.'

He leaned back in his chair and studied Jesse carefully. 'May I ask – what was the real reason you wanted to be a police officer?'

'That's easy,' Jesse replied. 'As a kid, I watched too many bad guys get away with things they should never have. Then I'd visit my dad, who is a good man, a decent man, serving time in jail. He had his face slashed inside, and it changed him. And what was the reason he was even there? *A bent copper.*'

Redwood nodded. 'Honestly? But was that the only reason you joined the force?'

Jesse met Redwood's gaze without hesitation. 'I wanted to go after the really bad guys. The kind of evil that walks the earth. Men like the Shipleys – who bully, terrorise, and who won't think twice about hurting women and children. The kind of bastards who should be put down like a vicious dog.'

'You can't take their crimes personally, Jesse.'

'No?' Jesse scoffed. 'Then where does the passion come from, eh?'

'I get it,' Redwood said. 'But if you take it personally, you'll mess up.'

Jesse smirked. He was unable to help himself. His mouth always worked faster than his brain.

'And what about you, Gov? You have a personal reason for wanting the Shipleys brought to justice, don't you? Tell me I'm wrong.'

Redwood narrowed his eyes. 'What do you know, Jesse?'

Jesse shrugged. 'I know people, Gov. I see the way you hate the Shipleys. You've been on their tail for years. But . . .' He smiled, knowingly. 'I don't know exactly why. Do you want to tell me?'

Shaking his head, Redwood muttered, 'Let's end this conversation.'

'No worries, Gov. Is there anything else?'

Redwood took a deep breath, coughing lightly, before meeting Jesse's eyes. 'You can bail out, right now. If they've threatened your family, if you're concerned, I can have you moved to another team.'

Jesse gave a slow nod. Then, his expression suddenly darkened. 'I can keep my family safe. Don't you worry about that.'

Watching the young, ambitious detective in front of him, Redwood considered himself very lucky to have Jesse on his team.

He smiled. 'Okay.'

'Gov, if it's just money and a bit of weed, can I deal with it my way?'

Redwood hesitated before throwing his hands in the air. 'Go on, tell me.'

'Get surveillance back on the clubs and pubs. Something is going down. They wanted surveillance earlier. As I said, they're probably patting each other's backs this very minute, knowing they're clogging up the custody suite and we're not out there watching the real deal.'

'Consider it done.'

Jesse left the office with a lot on his mind.

Someone had tipped the Shipleys off.

And it had to be someone in the team. But what about Kerns? Could he be involved? Why had he mentioned the Shipleys at the hospital? And, again, that niggling question. Why had he contacted Redwood directly?

Now, with his brain working at full pent, with all kinds of scenarios playing in his mind, it suddenly occurred to him that the most likely suspect was Redwood himself. He wouldn't rule it out. After all, the Shipleys had been the nemesis of the police for over twenty years. And in that time, their offences had been overseen by the present boss – Chief Inspector Redwood.

His thoughts drifted back to Kerns. Even though he himself hadn't been at the station for long, he had been made aware of how close Kerns had been to Wesley when they worked at the station together. Apparently, they were even drinking buddies. And that convenient transfer to the South East to look after his ageing parents. That wasn't him. He wasn't the caring kind. Not a bit of it.

Did he have a vendetta? Or was he in the Shipleys' back pocket? he wondered.

If his theory about Kerns and Redwood was correct, Kerns could have deliberately orchestrated a situation whereby Redwood had no choice but to transfer him to another police authority. By doing this, Redwood and Kerns would then be able to work with the Shipleys without anyone else knowing. Kerns could be Redwood's go-between. It was perfect!

It was so perfect that Jesse couldn't wait to get hold of Billy and sound him out on his theory.

At that moment, Melanie hurried over to him with a mug of coffee and interrupted his thoughts.

'Here, Jesse, I thought you might like . . . or rather need this.'

He smiled, now taking a closer look at her. She really was very attractive, and for the first time, her hair, which was usually pulled back tightly, was loose and wavy and framing her face.

'Cheers, Mel. Can we have a chat?'

Her face lit up, excitement flickering in her eyes. 'Yeah, sure.'

They walked over to her desk, which was set away from the rest of the team. She sat down and Jesse pulled up a chair and leaned in.

'What do you know about Redwood?'

Melanie's eyes sparked with curiosity, and she was almost in his lap, as she whispered conspiratorially, 'Why? Do you think Redwood's connected to the Shipleys?'

Jesse frowned. 'What?' *Blimy, was she thinking what he was thinking?* he wondered. 'No! Of course not. I just wondered if he had a personal vendetta against them, that's all. He's been on their case for years – every nicking, every raid.'

'I didn't know that.'

Jesse sighed and shook his head. 'No, sorry. I shouldn't have asked.'

She eased back in her chair, and her face softened. 'How's your brother's girlfriend?'

'I don't know yet. I'll leave early and head straight to the hospital to find out.'

'I'll give you a ride if you like,' she offered, an almost pleading smile tugging at her lips.

'Nah, it's fine. I've got my own motor out the front.' He shifted the conversation back. 'Now, what's the crack with the Shipleys? Who's interviewing them?'

'That's why we were trying to call you, Jesse.' She hesitated. 'I was waiting for you.'

The penny dropped. Wesley usually handled any Shipley interviews with Melanie at his side.

'All right. What have we got? I'm not going into the interview room blind.'

Melanie ran over the details and handed over the paperwork.

Jesse skimmed through it as they made their way to the interview room.

'There's not much, really. They were found with money and marijuana. We're interviewing Conrad Shipley, aged thirty-seven, who owns a bar, and his solicitor is Peter Levens. He's a bright spark.'

Jesse didn't bother knocking. He stormed into the interview room. Barely glancing at the solicitor, he turned on the tape recorder.

Jesse introduced himself and Melanie. Then, he said, 'For the benefit of the tape, I have in the room Conrad Shipley and his solicitor . . .' He glared at Levens. 'Your name?' he said, although he already knew it.

'Peter Levens.'

Levens peered up from his notebook. 'I hardly think you have enough to detain my client, Detective.' His tone was clipped, and his accent was as sharp as his designer suit. He carried an air of superiority, his beady, close-set eyes narrow and calculating, as he watched the detective at work with smug amusement.

Jesse wasn't in the best of moods, and when he looked at the man sitting beside his lawyer, he had to fight the urge to punch him in the face. The smirk, the self-satisfied arrogance, it made his blood boil.

Without breaking eye contact, he slapped the paperwork onto the desk.

'So, where did the money come from? Can you prove it was earned legally?'

His tone was so cold and matter-of-fact, it caught the solicitor off guard.

'My client can contact his accountant and provide proof of earnings.'

Jesse shot a hostile look at the man. 'I'm not a mortgage broker. I asked how he earned the money.'

'And, like I said, his accountant can verify that all the funds were obtained legally.'

Jesse tilted his head slightly. 'And the marijuana? That was obtained, grown, or supplied legally, too, was it?'

Levens gave a slow nod. 'Well, yes. They were found in possession of marijuana. Shall we finalise the paperwork so my client can be released? I know it will take bloody hours.'

'Released?' Jesse scoffed. 'Your clients were found with illegal drugs.'

'Who exactly, Detective?'

Jesse frowned. 'What do you mean, who?'

'Well, I represent two of the men arrested, and another three, I believe, are also being charged. But there was only one parcel of drugs carefully wrapped and most likely for personal use. So, Detective, who will be charged?'

Jesse clenched his jaw. The solicitor was pushing his buttons.

'And that, Detective,' the man continued, leaning forward with a smirk, 'is your conundrum, isn't it? Because they can't all be charged, can they? So what's it going to be – ip, dip, dog shit or eeny, meeny, miny, moe?'

Conrad then chuckled, his eyes glinting with mockery.

He wasn't a scruffy man. Far from it. He looked as though he'd just stepped out of a business meeting. *But his face looked like he was born at the wrong end of evolution.*

Jesse was barely keeping his temper in check. Turning to Melanie, he said, 'Mel, would you fetch us a coffee?' It was a sign for her to leave the room. He reached over and switched off the tape recorder, ignoring the uneasy glances from both the solicitor and his client.

'What is this?' snapped Levens.

Jesse smirked. 'I'm letting you go. I'm releasing all your clients.'

And there it was – the flicker of panic in the lawyer's eyes.

Rising to his feet, Jesse placed his hands firmly on the table. 'What's wrong, Mr Levens? Did you think I'd keep them here all night? That we'd drag out the process, tie up my team with paperwork in dotting the i's and crossing the t's? No, no. You can all go.'

Conrad shot a nervous glance at Levens.

'Oh, but we'll be confiscating your mobiles for a full forensic check. Other than that, you're free to walk.'

Conrad sneered. 'What's your game, Murphy?'

'I'm not interested in a poxy arrest that will end up with my team filling out useless charge sheets and wasting their time. I'm looking for a big nicking.' He winked. 'One that will drive me to carve a notch on my bedpost.'

'Are you threatening my client?'

Jesse smiled at Levens. 'Did that honestly sound like a threat? Because to me, I thought it sounded like a promise.'

'I know your game, Murphy. You think you're smarter than us. Well, you ain't,' hissed Conrad.

'Leave it,' said Levens, looking more than a little anxious. Detective Sergeant Murphy's initiative had clearly knocked the stuffing right out of him.

***

The custody suite was filled with confused men, except for the sergeant, who gave Jesse a nod and a wink. The surveillance team had already left and were back on the job – much to the shock of the Shipleys, who now found themselves without their phones. Their lawyers, clearly rattled, were frantically calling anyone they could, as they scrambled to reach the Shipleys' establishments and stop any illegal exchanges before it was too late.

CHAPTER TWENTY-SIX

Twelve hours later

Jesse arrived at King's College Hospital and went straight up to Bronte's room. He spotted Billy first, who was fast asleep in the chair beside Bronte's bed. His brother looked wrecked, exhausted, and unshaven. Yet he still gripped her hand even in his sleep.

But it was Bronte who caught Jesse's full attention. Her battered face was still, and her breathing was slow, but then he noticed a flicker of her eyelids. They twitched before slowly opening.

Blinking against the harsh light, Bronte looked around the room until her gaze settled on Billy.

Jesse's breathing went up a notch. He was about to wake Billy, but something held him back. Bronte's eyes were now locked on himself.

She didn't move, she didn't speak. She just stared as though she was seeing right through him. He managed a small, reassuring smile, but his heart was breaking inside – not because he loved her like Billy did, but because she was family to him, like a sister. And he knew, no matter how much Billy had tried to walk away from Bronte, he still loved her.

Jesse crept forward, his steps light, as if he was afraid to startle her. He reached out, his hand and gently covered hers. 'You're safe now, Bronte,' he murmured, the only words he could think of.

The quiet sound of his voice stirred Billy from sleep.

Jesse barely had time to move aside before Billy shot upright, the chair scraping against the floor. The sound that came out of his brother was something that Jesse had never heard before. It was a mix of pain, relief, and something raw enough to cut through the air like a blade.

Billy leaned forward, his hands now clutching the bedrail. 'Bronte?' he whispered, urgently, as if saying her name out too loud might make her disappear.

With sluggish, weak movements, she turned to face him. A tear slipped down from the corner of her eye where it landed on the pillow. 'I'm sorry.'

Fiercely, Billy shook his head. 'No, no – don't. Stop that,' he said, his voice cracking, as he fought to hold back the tears. He held her hand, hanging on to her, in case she might slip away into a deep sleep again. 'Jesse, call the doctor,' he said urgently, not taking his eyes off her.

Jesse didn't hesitate. He bolted from the room and headed for the nurses' station.

Bronte moved her hand towards her head, her fingers brushing over the bandages. Her lips trembled. 'Is it that bad, Billy? Am I scarred for life?'

Billy felt her fear as though it was a punch in the stomach. He reached out, his fingers gently wiping away another tear that rolled down her bruised cheek. Then he leaned in and pressed a kiss to her forehead. His voice was so soft, he could have been talking to a child. 'No, Bronte. You're not scarred. You're as beautiful as you always were.'

As her fingers trailed over her swollen cheek, her lips drooped into a sad, broken line. 'I don't feel as though I am,' she whispered.

Billy swallowed hard. 'That's only because you don't see what I see.'

He took a deep breath, his voice cracking. 'Bronte, I'm sorry . . . I'm so sorry. I wished . . . I just wished . . .' But the words stuck in his throat.

Bronte's pretty eyes blinked slowly. 'It's okay, Billy. It's not your fault.'

But it was. At least, that's how he felt. The guilt had been eating away at him from the moment he'd found out what they'd done to her. He tried to hold it back, but the tears came anyway, rolling down his face in silent, bitter waves. His head dropped onto the bed beside her hand, his shoulders shaking, as he let them fall.

Bronte had never seen him like this. Not Billy Murphy. Not the man who never broke down. No, not at all. He was like a man with a steel heart. With the little strength she had, she removed her hand from Billy's and ran her fingers through his hair. 'It's not your fault, Billy,' she whispered. 'It's not . . .'

Her voice faded so quickly that Billy's head snapped up. 'No! Bronte? Bronte!' He cried as he shook her gently, her body limp against the sheets. 'Wake up, please!' His voice cracked from sheer terror.

The door swung open, and to Billy's relief, a nurse rushed in ready to take over.

'S-She just – she just stopped talking,' he stammered, as he stepped back to let the nurse do whatever was needed to be done.

After checking the monitors, the nurse then placed a calming hand on his arm and offered a reassuring smile. 'She's okay, Billy, but she's exhausted. Her body's been through hell, but her recovery is looking good. She just needs rest and reassurance.'

Billy sat back. He nodded and swallowed hard. His nerves were shot to shit, but as he looked at Bronte's bruised face, he knew one thing for sure. He wasn't going anywhere.

He retook her hand and gripped it gently. 'I've got you,' he whispered. 'And I ain't letting go.'

As soon as the nurse left, Jesse entered the room. He could almost feel his brother's pain. 'You look like shit, mate. Shall I get you a coffee?'

Billy gave him a weary smile. 'The nurses have been good, Jesse. They keep popping in with drinks and food.' His gaze drifted back to Bronte, and his expression darkened. 'I fucked up, Jesse. Badly. Look at her. Look at her, Jesse. It's my fault. If I hadn't fucked her off that day, she would've been with me and not with some fucking pikey mate of hers.'

Jesse frowned. 'What happened, Billy?'

Billy let out a heavy breath. 'I'm still trying to get to the bottom of it. So I'm not really sure. But it seems as though Franklin gave the Shipleys the details of where she was staying. Apparently, she was looking after a mate of hers.' He huffed. 'Typical. She's such a good person. Always thinking of others before herself. I should've known she wasn't mugging me off.'

Jesse lifted his chin. 'Yeah, I thought the same. That ain't like Bronte.'

Billy shook his head. 'Those cuntish brothers of hers talked her into it, promising her a chunk of money . . .' His voice trailed off for a moment, lost in thought. 'She wanted money to treat me, Jesse. She wanted to take me on holiday. A fucking *holiday*, would you believe. She did it for *me*. And look at her, Jesse. Just look at the fucking state of her.'

'She's going to be all right, Billy.'

'I know. But what she must have gone through . . .' He turned his face away and smacked his forehead with his palm. 'I can't get it out of my head, Jesse. I fucking pushed her away.'

He looked up at his brother. 'The Shipleys ain't giving up, are they, Jesse?'

Pulling a chair closer, Jesse sat beside him. 'When Bronte's ready to leave the hospital, we'll take her somewhere safe, right? Most of the family are on a plane as we speak, off to Cas's villa. So that leaves you, me, and Cas. Oh, and our dad, Uncle James, Uncle Dylon, and Spud—'

'So, basically, all the women have gone, but the men are still here? Is that what you're saying?'

Jesse nodded. 'That's about the sum of it. And I gotta warn you, Billy – things will only get uglier.'

Billy didn't flinch. He slowly turned his head, his expression dark. 'Oh yeah, believe me, Jesse, it's going to get very fucking ugly. Whoever did this will die.'

Jesse nodded. 'I'm right with you, Billy. I gotta say, though, these Shipleys, they're crafty. They have spies in the camp. They knew they had a surveillance team watching them. Someone tipped them off, so they moved insignificant funds and drugs, keeping the surveillance team distracted. Meanwhile, a large shipment of cocaine arrived, and they were in the process of unloading. The bastards stored the drugs in beer barrels. Clever move – but not clever enough. Now we've got four Shipleys in the cells charged with importing a serious amount of Class A. A nice nicking. They were like rabid dogs screaming and banging on the walls. I tell you, it was a picture, seeing their snotty solicitor's face crumple. His face looked see through. I swear, when the charges were read out, he never made it to the bogs in time. I could smell the shit along the corridor.'

Billy momentarily grinned. 'Was the arrest your doing?'

Jesse gave his brother his lopsided, cheeky grin. 'Yep.'

'Ol' Redwood must be chuffed with you, then.'

'He gave me the option to move to another team because of, well . . .' He pointed to Bronte.

'You said no, though, right?'

'Of course, I said no. I want access to every name, address, and Photofit. I want to know everything there is to know about every single one of those Shipleys and their associates.'

Billy nodded, slowly. 'Good.'

'We can make a plan as soon as Bronte's out of the hospital,' Jesse said, with a small smile. 'Because let's be honest, you won't be able to think straight until she's better, will you?'

'I just need a couple of days, Jesse. Believe me, I'll be ready then to work out our next move.'

'Right, listen, I have to get off. They need me at the station. But I'll be back to give you a break. You need to sleep, Billy. You honestly do. You look rough, like you've spent the night in a tumble dryer.'

It brought a faint smile to Billy's face. 'And you look like you mistook a hedge for a bed.'

Jesse smirked, but his face turned serious. 'How was Benny when he saw Bronte? I bet it knocked him sideways.'

'Knocked him sideways? More than that, mate. He collapsed. He's in the room next door. The poor bloke thought he had lung cancer. It turned out he's got pneumonia. So, he's on a drip. A little bit out of it.'

'Do Franklin and Archie know?'

Billy shook his head. 'No. Benny's disowned them. And, anyway, they wouldn't dare step foot in here. I'll fucking kill 'em, if they do. This is all their fault. They sent the Shipleys to find her. They literally fed her to the fucking wolves.' His bottom lip quivered. 'Jesse . . . I don't know if they raped her.'

Jesse's hands flew to his mouth, his eyes wide. 'Fuck me, Billy. You don't think – Jesus, no.'

Billy shrugged, his face pale. 'I don't know, Jesse. I'd never ever forgive myself, if they did that to her.'

'Why would you even think that?'

'Her clothes are in a plastic bag in the locker.'

Jesse nodded. 'And?'

'Jesse, the zip on her dress was ripped, and her bra was torn, but . . . there were no knickers. I know Bronte. She never went out without underwear on. She didn't like to show off too much of her flesh. So . . .'

Jesse squeezed his brother's shoulder, his grip firm. 'Come on, Billy. You need to start thinking positively. Bronte's gonna need you to be strong, right? Not an emotional wreck. They may have binned the underwear.'

Suddenly, Bronte's eyes opened wide. She looked just like she was reliving a nightmare, and her breathing quickened.

'Bronte,' said Billy, as he gripped her hand. 'It's okay, baby, I'm here, I'm right here.'

Jesse watched as her eyes slowly fluttered shut as she drifted back to sleep. But that look of terror – the sheer panic frozen in her eyes – lingered like a shadow in the room. It was so haunting, he could almost feel it in his chest, a weight pressing down, and knowing his brother, he could guarantee Bronte's plight would be hitting Billy even harder.

'I'm heading back to work, Billy. You stay safe. I'm going to do some digging.'

Before he could leave, Billy grabbed his arm, his grip firm. 'I want everything on them, Jesse. Every single fucking thing.'

Jesse nodded. 'I'm on it, Billy. But promise me you won't do anything stupid. We need a rock-solid plan, and I need you to be safe. I can't lose you, Billy. I just can't.'

Billy's eyes held that familiar glint Jesse knew all too well. He raised a brow, already sensing what was coming. Then he saw it. His brother lifted his T-shirt to reveal the gun tucked into his tracksuit bottoms.

Letting out a short dry chuckle, Jesse shook his head. 'Just don't shoot yourself in the foot, for fuck's sake, Billy boy.'

Billy's jaw tightened. 'I'm done with being the good guy, Jesse. Look where it's got us, eh?'

Jesse met his brother's gaze, his voice low. 'I know, mate. I fucking know.'

CHAPTER TWENTY-SEVEN

It was late in the day when Jesse returned to the hospital. He was concerned that his brother wasn't getting any proper rest because he'd spent the past few days at Bronte's bedside.

Relieved that Bronte was at least stable and in good hands, Billy left Jesse to watch over her for a few hours while he returned to his apartment for a power shower. He needed to rid himself of the lingering smell of hospitals and the bitter taste of worry.

As soon as he stepped out of the taxi and paid the driver, he marched through the main door, where he barely noticed Clive, who was checking on the monitors.

The moment his eyes landed on him, the whole event came flooding back. The sight of Clive performing CPR, desperate to save Bronte, with tears streaming down his face, was something to behold. This man was worth his weight in gold.

'Mr Murphy,' Clive said, jumping up from his chair. 'How's Bronte?' His eyes searched Billy's face, hoping for good news. He could see the red rings around his eyes, the rough stubble on his chin, and the unkempt hair. They were all signs that the man hadn't left her side for days.

'She's going to be okay, Clive.'

Clive let out a shuddering sigh. 'Thank sweet Jesus.'

Wearily, Billy did the same. 'Well, thank you, Clive. Thank you.'

Before he could say anything else, his gaze shifted towards the glass entrance doors. His brow furrowed. 'Clive, whose old car is that parked out front?'

Clive followed his eyes to the tatty motor. 'Oh, sorry, boss, that's mine. I'll move it right away. I was in a bit of a rush, but I'll park it around the back, out of sight.'

Billy frowned but nodded. 'Yeah, do that.'

Clive assumed Billy was out of sorts for good reason. The whole ordeal had shaken everyone. He watched as Billy marched towards the lift, his shoulders seemingly heavy. Normally, his boss would have taken the stairs to keep fit, but not today.

As soon as he was out of sight, Clive hurried outside, moved his car to the rear parking lot among the gleaming high-end motors, and rushed back to his desk. He needed this job and wasn't about to give Billy Murphy any reason to sack him.

An hour or so later, the lift doors opened. Billy appeared, dressed in smart trousers and a crisp pale-blue shirt. His face was clean-shaven, and he smelled as though he owned a lime grove.

As he walked towards Clive, he beamed and tossed a set of car keys into the security guard's hands.

'Shall I put these in the safe, Mr Murphy?'

Billy smirked. 'No, Clive. They're the keys to the black Beamer around the back. If you want to park a car out front, park that one.'

Clive frowned, now, totally confused. 'Sorry . . . your black BMW? You want it parked outside?'

Billy chuckled. 'It's *your* BMW, Clive. All yours, mate.'

Clive's eyes almost popped out like a frog in a frying pan. 'Mine? Are you serious?'

'You saved Bronte's life, Clive. You deserve more than a car.'

'Mr Murphy, it was nothing. I like Bronte – she's a sweetie. And, if I may say, a better choice than that other girl.' He suddenly put his hands up. 'Sorry! Sorry! Not my place, not my business.'

Billy laughed. 'The thing is, I agree, Clive.'

His expression turned serious. 'Listen, if I pay you double, would you get your nephew to cover your shifts? I have another job for you.'

Clive didn't even need to ask about the other job. He just nodded.

'If I take you to the hospital, would you sit with Bronte for a while?'

Clive beamed. 'You can trust me, Mr Murphy. I was in the Army. I can handle trouble, no problem.'

Billy gave Clive a sharp nod. 'That's sorted, then. Call your nephew, and I'll take you there. I need to sort out a few things.'

Clive puffed out his chest. 'You're a decent man, Mr Murphy. You pays me on time, gave me a raise, and let me have time off – no questions asked – when my Pattie was taken ill. So, not that it's my business, but if you need some help, I can handle it meself.'

Billy stopped. Staring deep into the man's eyes, he was trying to figure out if the man really meant what he'd just said. But there was something there – a real glint of honesty.

Suddenly, Clive rolled up his trouser leg to reveal a long, ugly scar. Then, he pulled up his sleeve to show another nasty old wound. 'A tour in Bosnia and two in Northern Ireland,' he said, with a dry laugh. 'Four men, two knives, and a whole lot of Irish swearing. I couldn't understand a word of it, but at least they didn't kill me.'

Billy was intrigued. 'Clive, you saw what happened to Bronte, so understand this – whatever happens next is gonna be nasty.'

A flicker of excitement sparkled in Clive's eyes. 'Nasty? Nasty?' He grinned. 'Mr Murphy, I *breathe* nasty. That young woman is like a likkle ray of sunshine. She always stopped to chat with me. I never had no kids, but I'd want one like Bronte, if I did. So, like I says, if you needs me, Mr Murphy, you just say di word. I can make people beg. I mean, snot-flinging, piss-demselves beg.'

Billy was thoroughly enjoying listening to Clive, especially when he was putting on his Jamaican patois for effect. He grinned. 'No mercy, then?'

'Not a bit of it, Mr Murphy.'

***

Cas shoved the kitchen window open to let in a blast of cold air. The new makeover was all well and good, but the stink of fresh paint and polish clung to everything, and it was now making his nose twitch. That's why he hated hospitals too. The clinical stench was everywhere.

'Right, gentlemen, who's for a coffee?'

Walter Whistler and Dennis the Menace sat at the table, both meticulously dressed as if they were at a meeting with the CEO of the bank. Walter craned his neck over Dennis's shoulder to read the note.

'And this cunt Kenny Ruck didn't take our boys' message seriously?' Walter muttered with his famous whistle, while his fat fingers drummed against the table.

Cas poured himself a coffee. He was in no rush to join his team. 'Well, he got away, didn't he? Your boys might've thrown him in the van, but they didn't count on the fucker running off like an Olympic sprinter. Still, I've asked around. No one's seen him or knows who he's having it with. And let's be real, lads, he's got some serious fucking balls coming for me, especially now he knows I've got a firm behind me.' He smirked. 'Namely, your boys. Oh, and while we're on the subject – did they sort out Johnnie Booth's little problem with them Eastern European fuckers?'

Walter let out a dry chuckle. 'Nice little earner, Cas, that was. They set it up, just like you said. They waited for the cunts to swagger in, demanding their protection money, like they owned the place. Didn't even see it coming.'

'Go on,' said Cas, eager to hear the nitty-gritty.

'So, me boys dragged 'em outside for a *quiet word* – just them, a gun, and a cosh. And would you believe it? That big bulldog-faced Polack was carrying a fucking briefcase full of the night's takings. The bastard had been to all the local pubs demanding protection money.'

Cas laughed. 'Love it. Carry on.'

'So, me boys walked off with a nice little payday – twelve grand in cash, some gold chains, a couple of gold Rolexes – oh, and a promise. The bastards swore blind they'd fuck off and never come back. 'Course, they were left with a few broken bones and a headache to remember us by.' Walter grinned, his teeth yellow from years of smoking. 'And me, boys? They're buzzing. And they said to say, "Cheers, Uncle Cas." Now, they've got their own little racket running. And as for Johnnie Booth? Well, he's grinning from ear to ear.'

Dennis shook his head and smoothed his grey hair. 'See, Cas, since you've been off the scene, every fucker and their mother thinks you're out of the game. It left places like the local boozers wide open for scum like them Polacks to walk in and start throwing their weight around.'

Cas nodded, rubbing his chin. 'Well, come on, lads. I ain't getting any younger.'

Dennis shrugged. 'None of us are, mate. But that doesn't mean we run a fucking knitting circle. These young 'uns think they're hard, but they wouldn't know one end of a shooter from the other. Cowards, the lot of 'em.'

Cas nodded again, leaning in. 'Talkin' of cowards. This is why I wanted a word. You both know I've got my fingers in many pies these days. The business with young Billy Murphy, for example. I like the boy. He means a lot to me. He's got a problem, though. At first, I thought I'd keep an eye on things, but the more I thought about it, the more I realised this other firm's taken a right fucking liberty. And you know me. I don't like being mugged off.'

'What firm's this?' asked Dennis, clenching his fist.

'The Shipleys,' Cas replied, with an icy tone.

Walter and Dennis exchanged a look.

'They've always stayed in North London,' Cas continued. 'They never stepped on my manor. But now? Now, they've got the brass fucking balls to plant a load of marijuana in the basement of a building that I part own. A proper piss-take if ever there was one.'

Walter sneered. 'The fucking Shipleys. I'll give 'em one thing, though. They're a growing firm, although I've never liked 'em. Not one of 'em. But stepping on your turf? That's not on.'

'No, it fucking ain't,' Cas spat, his voice tight with anger. 'But it's more than that, lads. We reckon the Shipleys are responsible for beating Billy's girl half to death. You see, they want the address of the witnesses who saw the brothers Max and Moriarty kill that innocent couple. The young woman they murdered was pregnant. Anyway, Jesse is leading the case, so they've gone through young Billy to get it. You know how close those two are. Anyway, Billy basically told them to fuck off, and the next thing, they've hurled his bird out of a van. Hurt badly, she was.'

The air in the room shifted. The easy banter vanished. Both men leaned in, their eyes sharp, their expressions darkening.

'They beat up a young woman, you said?' Walter's voice was low and dangerous.

Cas nodded. 'Yes, Walter. They did. And I'll tell you this for nothing. They nearly fucking killed her.'

'Bleedin' hell's bells. So now we've got two problems: the Shipleys after an address and Kenny Ruck after revenge. By the way, does he know his missus is in Cyprus?'

Cas shrugged. 'I doubt it. She got a cab to the airport as soon as she could and jumped on a flight out there. I only texted her the address once she landed, so Kenny wouldn't know where my villa was. That poor cow was battered.' He gestured to the note on the table. 'Anyway, he's still out there, and as you can see, sending me threatening letters, like this one.'

Walter let out a wheezy laugh before breaking into a cough. 'My boys need to make sure that fucker understands what *back off* really means.'

Cas gave a slow nod. 'He's a bit screwy, though. Anyway, I reckon we've got a bigger problem with the Shipleys. I ain't having them taking liberties on my manor. I want to pay them a visit.'

Walter rubbed his hands together, and Dennis grinned, with that familiar wicked glint in his eye.

'But here's the thing. We can't do jack shit yet. Jesse tells me the cunts are under surveillance.'

Walter narrowed his eyes. 'Cas, do you trust Jesse Murphy?'

Without a second's hesitation, Cas replied, 'With my fucking life, I do.'

Dennis looked over the note. 'So what's he mean by: *If you don't pay up, I will take down everything you own*? *You'll have fuck all. And you'd better warn Billy Murphy as well. He needs to do as he's told.*'

Walter blew a ring of blue smoke. 'That's what I'm saying, Cas. This note – it stinks of something bigger. Kenny Ruck ain't got the brains to run a scheme like this on his own. He's always been a mad dog, but a mad dog on a leash. But the question is . . . whose leash?'

Cas leaned forward, his elbows now on the table. 'The Shipleys wouldn't bother with a loose cannon like Kenny. But think about it: if they needed some prick desperate enough, reckless enough to do their dirty work, he'd fit the bill. And if he's been inside with them, he's had time to get cosy.'

Dennis nodded. 'That's what I'm thinking. He's got nothing to offer, but he's got everything to prove. He'd be all in if the Shipleys promised him something – money, power, revenge. And by the looks of this note, he's already made his move.'

Cas clenched his jaw, his eyes flicking between them. 'If Kenny's gone crawling to the Shipleys, and they're using him as their attack dog, that means Billy ain't just a name on this note for the sake of it. They're coming for him too.'

Walter stubbed his cigarette out in the ashtray. 'The Shipleys will want to get to those witnesses, and believe me, they will do anything to get Max and Moriarty out of jail. It makes me wonder if those two brothers are holding the family to ransom over something to free them. But, anyway, we can't move on the Shipleys while they're under surveillance. So, what's the play, Cas?'

Cas exhaled sharply, while he rubbed a hand down his face. 'We need Jesse involved. He's the only lad who can keep us ahead of the game. He can keep an eye on who's under surveillance.'

Dennis smirked. 'And what if Jesse won't play ball? Don't forget he's a copper.'

Cas's lips curled into a knowing grin. 'Oh, he will. Because Jesse Murphy don't take kindly to people hurting his family. And if there's one thing I know about the Murphy boys, it's that when you push them' – he tapped the note – 'they won't roll over. They're fighters.'

***

Suddenly, the room fell silent. Cas looked up, Dennis cocked his gun, and Walter cracked his knuckles. The kitchen door creaked open and in walked Billy. Dressed in a Hugo Boss tailored suit, his expression was unreadable.

'Well, talk of the fucking devil.'

Billy shut the door behind him. 'Parked my car around the back,' he said, giving a polite nod to Dennis and Walter.

Walter eyed him up and down and grinned as he ran a hand over his protruding belly. 'Cor, he don't half remind me of meself back in the day.'

'Oh, fuck off, Walt,' Cas scoffed. 'You never had that much swagger. And you've got a face like a dropped steak and ale pie.' He smirked. 'Look at the lad. No comparison.'

Billy smiled and went over to the coffee machine to pour himself a cup of coffee.

'I bet he gets all the best-looking skirts,' Dennis mused, leaning back in his chair. 'Like me in me day.'

He wasn't wrong. Dennis had been the best-looking man out of the three in his prime, always pulling the top-tier girls. Even now, despite his years, he still held himself with that same upright confidence – not a wrinkle in his shirt, not a silver hair out of place. That was the problem, though – anyone who underestimated him based on his handsome face made a grave mistake.

The older Shipleys knew it well. One of the older brothers still wore the scar down his cheek as a permanent reminder. Most old-school villains knew the trio, and their firm was notorious for taking no prisoners.

'Right, Billy, take a seat and update these two.' Cas waved a hand in front of his nose and pulled a face. 'Fucking hell, Walter, you're wearing enough cologne to knock out a horse. Ain't your good looks working anymore?'

Walter cracked his knuckles again. 'Go on then, Billy. Ignore that comedian and tell us what's the latest.'

Billy nodded. 'Jesse reckons there's a fucking spy working for the Shipleys in the station. He wants to find out who they are so that he can feed them false information. Right now, he's doing his own digging. He's got three names so far.'

'He's a clever lad, eh?' Cas muttered.

Dennis and Walter both grinned. 'Yep, proper clever little fucker.'

'I've got a guard watching Bronte. All the women are at your villa. They're topping up their tans. Dottie's flying out there tonight. Spud says she had business to attend to, but she will be joining them soon. So now, it's just us left to worry about.' Billy's eyes narrowed, and his lip curled. 'Let the cunts bring it on.'

Both Dennis and Walter studied Billy closely. They'd never heard him swear much, but what was more alarming was the look on his face. It was dark. It was as though something had switched inside him, like a man who'd walked through hell and decided he liked the temperature.

Walter leaned forward, his smirk fading. 'Tell me, son . . . what's put that look on your face?'

Dennis, always the more observant of the two, folded his arms. 'Christ, I've seen that look before,' he muttered. 'That's the look of a man who, after this, ain't coming back the same.'

Billy's jaw clenched. 'They nearly killed her,' he said, his voice ice-cold. 'And now they're gonna fucking pay.'

Cas chose to say nothing. Instead, he just gave a slow nod of approval. He'd seen it before – that moment when a man steps over a line and knows there's no going back.

Walter rubbed his face. 'Well, shit. And here I was thinking we'd have a quiet retirement.'

Dennis chuckled, but there was no humour there. 'Quiet's overrated. Revenge, though? Well, that's a proper way to spend our time. Besides, I'm fucking bored. I think it's time we showed Kenny Ruck and the Shipleys what a real fight looks like.'

Walter stretched his fingers, his knuckles cracking like gunshots in the quiet room. 'Fucking retirement,' he muttered. 'Tried it once – hated every bloody second. Sitting around, drinking tea, playing golf? Nah, fuck that. I'd rather spend my golden years teaching a few pricks some manners.'

Cas nodded. 'Right, we need Jesse to get a list of every single one of the Shipleys' businesses.'

Billy frowned. 'What for?'

Suddenly, all three men burst out laughing.

'He's so green,' Walter sniggered, leaning back in his chair.

'This is war, Billy.' Dennis grinned and stretched his arms. 'And here's the plan: we're gonna take over their little fucking empire, hook, line, and sinker. It's what we do to liberty takers.'

Cas smirked, his eyes dark with intent. 'See, Billy, when they put their plants in my fucking building – sorry, *our* building – they took a liberty. That was a line they shouldn't have crossed. Now, it's my turn to step on *their* turf, and I'm taking the fucking lot.'

Billy sat there, mouth slightly open, trying to process what he was hearing. He wasn't used to this kind of business, not like them. But right now, he didn't care. If Cas and his firm wanted to bring the Shipleys down, he'd be right there beside them.

CHAPTER TWENTY-EIGHT

Ginty heard the strange ringtone and quickly realised that Carrie was obviously abroad. She ended the call right away. There was no way she was racking up sky-high charges. Frustrated, she tried Billy's number next, but her temper flared when it went straight to voicemail.

She was desperate to see the new apartment and wanted to measure up for curtains. Her neighbour had her hands on a load of knocked-off Next curtains, no less, and she wasn't about to pass them up if they fitted any of her windows. They were top quality, and it would have been criminal to say no at the price she was getting them for.

It was late, but she hoped Billy, or even Dottie, would be at the office. This time, instead of kicking off at the cab driver over the price of the fare, she actually paid without a fuss.

Arriving at Billy's office, she saw the Closed sign. And the door was locked.

After trying to catch Phoebe's attention, she finally banged on the window. Scowling at her, she barked, 'Open the fucking door!'

Phoebe turned off her computer, and then, rising slowly from her chair, clearly enjoying Ginty's frustration, she unlocked the door and opened it. 'Sorry, I was miles away. How can I help you?'

'What the hell d'you mean, *how can you help me*? I came to see me grandson, Billy.'

'Well, I'm afraid he's not in and hasn't been for a few days. How can I help?'

Ignoring her, Ginty glared at her phone and tried Billy's number again. It rang and rang, but there was still no answer.

Ginty stormed into the office practically shoving her out of the way. 'Why was the door locked?'

Phoebe looked momentarily stunned. 'Oh . . . er, well, I turned the sign round and locked the office while I went to the toilet and forgot to turn it back again and unlock the door when I came out.'

Ginty narrowed her eyes. 'And Billy ain't been in for a few days?'

Phoebe moved back to her desk and sat there staring at her computer screen.

The young woman's rudeness was doing Ginty's head in. 'So where *is* he, then?'

'I don't know,' Phoebe replied, with a shrug.

'You're supposed to be his fucking PA. How can you *not* know where he is?'

'I am his PA, yeah, but I'm not his wife.'

'Well, thank fuck for that,' Ginty snapped. 'Anyway, I need to see the flat. Sorry, I mean *apartment*.'

Phoebe slowly looked up from her screen.

'You'll have to come back.'

Ginty shook her head. 'No, I won't. And if you can't take me there, I'll take a cab.'

'I can't give you the keys without Billy's permission – that's not my job.'

Ginty had already forked out a score for the taxi, and it would cost her at least that to get back home. Suddenly, the so-called bargain curtains weren't looking like much of a steal. They would end up costing double. Calculating the profit or loss in her head, her eyes spotted a bunch of keys sitting idly by the coffee machine.

For a moment, she frowned. Staring more closely, they looked exactly like the set Billy had when he first showed her the apartment. In fact, she was sure of it. The four-leaf clover keyring Bronte had given him for good luck was still attached.

Casually, she slid behind Phoebe's chair, snatched up the keys, and dropped them into her handbag with a quick flick of her wrist.

Phoebe, on hearing the jangle, suddenly spun around. 'What are you doing?'

But Ginty wasn't about to answer to some jumped-up little bitch. Besides, she knew that the keys were always kept in a safe or locked in Billy's desk. Bronte or Billy had told her that when they took her to the apartments.

‘So, have you had anyone else interested in the apartments?’

Phoebe frowned. ‘No. Why?’

‘Just wondered.’ Ginty threw her bag over her shoulder. ‘Right, I’m off.’

The second the door shut behind her, Phoebe’s stomach dropped when her eyes flicked to the coffee machine. The keys had gone.

Her gaze snapped to the window just in time to see Ginty hurrying along the pavement, with her bag clutched tight.

‘Good riddance, you fucking old witch,’ she muttered.

***

When Ginty called the cab company, she was told it was now rush hour, and she would have to wait an hour. *Sod that*, she thought. Instead of standing around like a lemon, she decided to walk. She needed the exercise, anyway. Well, that was what her doctor kept telling her.

After a solid forty-minute trek, she finally reached the block of apartments. It wasn’t lit up all fancy, like in the photos, but, then again, Billy had told her that the building wasn’t finished yet. The final touches were still to be done, and, of course, there had been a delay with the building inspector – as bloody usual.

Still, she had waited patiently. Truth be told, she was proud of Billy’s achievements. He and Jesse were probably the first men in the family to go straight. And Jesse? Well, he was definitely the first copper. Of course, it went against the grain, but, secretly, she was proud of him. She knew Jesse wasn’t the type to nick his own mother over an untaxed motor. In fact, he wouldn’t nick any member of his family.

Her feet were killing her now, and she was desperate to sit down. Digging into her bag, she pulled out the keys and turned them over. She knew one was for the show apartment. If she could just get inside, she could have a quick sit-down and rest her weary legs.

She immediately noticed the door was ajar as she approached the main entrance. Hesitating, she hovered momentarily, before surmising that Phoebe had probably been here earlier and forgotten to lock up. It would be typical of the stuck-up airhead.

Stepping inside, she was met with darkness. The place felt eerie, and it was dead quiet, her every footstep echoing around her. Billy had described what it would look like when finished – with marble floors, plastered walls, and sleek chrome lifts.

Right now, though? It was still very much a building site – with plasterboards, planks of wood, and bags of God knows what littering the place.

Still, she could see beyond all that. She knew what a finished building looked like. Billy's apartment block, which he and Jesse lived in, was stunning. She had no doubt that this too would turn out the same.

As she climbed the stairs, a strange unease settled over her, and a feeling that she was being watched crept up her spine. It was probably just the fact that it was a building site with no builders, she told herself, shaking off any scary thoughts.

Reaching the second floor, she paused and stared at the door to what would soon be her new apartment. A sudden wave of loneliness hit her. It was as unexpected as it was unwelcome.

She glanced down the corridor. It was wide and spacious. Once finished, it would probably look like the hallway of some posh hotel, all lined with plush carpets and sleek wall lights. She could already picture the neighbours. Women with their Chihuahuas tucked under their arms, their noses in the air, and strutting about in designer outfits while clutching Chanel purses and car keys to some flashy motor.

Or maybe it would be the business types. The ones who barely looked at you, who were always in a rush, too busy to nod, and too self-important for small talk.

She stared down the corridor, trying to picture the couple across the hall hosting their fancy little dos, sipping gin and tonics, and nibbling on poncy finger food off silver trays. She wouldn't get an invite, that was for sure. But did she even want one? These apartments would be full of people who thought they were better than her. Who would look down their noses at anyone who didn't fit in, in their world.

And suddenly, she didn't want to step foot inside. She didn't want to measure up for curtains. Because all the fancy trimmings behind that door meant nothing when you had no one to share it with.

Her life growing up as a gypsy had been rough, cruel at times, but at least she had never been alone. Back then, the street had been full of her own kind, as in settled travellers, a proper community, where no one had to knock before stepping inside for a cuppa and a gossip. Those days were the best, the ones she'd never get back. The makeshift barbecues, the kids running wild, barefoot and laughing. The gossip traded over the garden gate. The homemade beer and the knocked-off gear that were passed around like treasures. The smell of a roasted pig spinning over a fire, with everyone singing and listening to stories late into the night. But it was more than that. It was who she was. She knew she was feared and respected. The knocked-off goods were always handed her way first. She had been the first port of call when it came to the fags and booze nicked off a lorry. She was someone back then. Maybe for all the wrong reasons, but she liked it like that. In fact, she revelled in it. Her new neighbours wouldn't respect her. They would be just like Phoebe, always looking down their noses at her. She chuckled for a moment, imagining their faces if she so much as said, 'Go fuck yaself.'

An unexpected tear trickled down her cheek before she could even stop it.

When she was younger, she used to dream of luxury – new carpets, fancy curtains, things she could show off. And now, she could have all of it. A kitchen straight out of a magazine, a bathroom fit for a queen. But standing there, looking at the life she had once wanted, she knew this wasn't it. It wasn't for her.

She didn't want some posh lonely flat. She wanted what she had lost. The old ways. The dealings. The people. She'd rather be in a caravan, a fire burning, voices raised in laughter, surrounded by her own. The council flat she was in now was actually okay, she realised. She got on with the neighbours and had a laugh with them. The problem was that it was full of black mould and not really fit for purpose. Maybe this was her only option.

Ginty sighed, rubbing her aching knees. Christ, her feet were on fire. If she didn't sit down soon, she would be crippled for the rest of the night. Just a few more steps – one short flight – and she would be at the show apartment. Gripping the handrail, she dodged the piles of plywood scattered about.

Then she thought she heard a noise. She froze and tilted her head to listen. Was that the sound of footsteps? Or was it just the creaks of an empty building? She held her breath, listening, but there was silence.

'You're being daft, Ginty. Get a fucking grip.'

She reasoned it was probably just the echo of her own steps. Still, something about the place gave her the creeps. If she didn't ache so much, she would have turned back. Sod the bloody curtains. But no, her ankles were puffed up like balloons, and her feet throbbed with every step. She needed to sit down.

Finally, she reached the third floor. There it was – the show apartment. A tidy 'welcome mat' had been placed in front of the door waiting for fancy buyers to wipe their posh shoes. Her fingers fumbled with the keys as she tried one after another.

'Come on, come on.' She tried to work out which keys she had tried before, but in her haste, she suddenly dropped them, which sent them clanging to the floor.

'Shit,' she muttered, under her breath, as she bent to scoop them up.

The minute she straightened up, she saw it. A big red drum at the end of the corridor.

'What the hell?'

She turned her head slowly, her eyes scanning the other end of the hallway. There were two more.

Her breathing started to speed up and become more laboured. She knew what those were. Her lads used to have one in her back garden.

Petrol drums.

Observing them more closely, her brain was working overtime. *Why the hell would Billy have petrol drums inside the building?* Her eyes flicked around looking for a reason as to why they were here. But there were no tools. No ladders. No workers.

Something wasn't right.

A prickle of fear crawled over her skin. She needed to go, and now. Yet when she turned to leave, her legs weren't having it. They were so heavy, swollen, and stiff that every step was like walking on pins.

Her chest tightened. Her breath came quicker.

'Move, Ginty. Move,' she said, aloud, as she stared at the petrol drums, red and menacing, there like a warning.

And suddenly, it hit her. She was not supposed to be here.

The surge of fear shot through her like an electric current. It sent adrenaline pulsing through her veins at a speed of knots. Now, very short of breath, she dragged her heavy feet to the stairs, very nearly losing her balance.

Then – footsteps. *Were there more than one set?* she wondered.

She froze, her heart hammering in her chest. They weren't hers. They were on the floor above her. And they were getting closer.

Someone was in the building. She was certain of that now. But then she heard more footsteps. So there must be at least two of them in the building.

A spear of dread sliced through her as a sharp, unmistakable scent filled her nostrils. Petrol.

Terror clamped around her throat, but she had no time to think. No time to hesitate. Her lungs burned as she forced herself forward, with each step a battle. A battle to survive.

The entrance doors were just ahead.

Almost there, she told herself, now desperate to get out of the building.

Then, just as she left, something caught her eye. It was no more than a flicker, but it came from the huge glass door and it made her eyes widen. She could see from the faint reflection that it was a man, but it wasn't Billy.

Her heart was beating out of her chest. She didn't turn around.

Instead, she yanked the door open and hurled herself outside, the rush of cool air slapping her face.

Fear took her breath away, but her survival instinct kept her moving.

To her utter relief, there crawling along the road was a black taxi with its 'For Hire' sign illuminated. Frantically, she waved her hand, and the driver pulled over. She climbed in and fell onto the seat.

'Where to, darling?'

'Away from here, and quickly, mate. That place is gonna go up in flames.'

The cab driver, who had no idea what she was talking about, pulled away.

Ginty was shaking from head to toe, her hands trembling so much, she could barely grip her phone. Her vision blurred as she tried calling Billy again. It rang and rang.

No answer.

She tried Jesse. Nothing.

Panic clawed at her chest, her breath coming in sharp gasps. In desperation, she dialled the fire service.

'Unless there's an active fire, we can't dispatch a crew,' the operator told her.

Her heart sank. 'No, listen, I saw all the petrol.'

BOOM!

The taxi jolted as a deafening blast tore through the night.

The driver slammed on the brakes and glared into the rear-view mirror.

Ginty instantly craned her neck. Her eyes were wide in horror, aware that if she hadn't got out when she did, she would be dead or at least barbecued.

Billy's building was in flames.

Red and orange flames roared from every window. They were licking the outside bricks, and black smoke was billowing into the sky like a beast unleashed.

'Holy fucking shit!' the driver shouted, fumbling for his phone. He called the emergency services and gave them the details of the address and size of the fire. As soon as he ended the call, he turned to Ginty, his gaze sharp and suspicious.

'How did you know?'

Ginty's heart pounded as she gripped the phone. 'Fucking hell, mate, do I look like I did that? No! I was in there checking out me new apartment when I saw all these petrol drums. I got out, flagged you down, and called the fire brigade, but that twat of an operator didn't take me seriously. And now—' She watched, helplessly. While the building was burning, all of Billy's hard work was going up in flames.

'Who would do this?' she said, utterly gobsmacked.

Her mind snapped back to the man she had seen. A shadow, a partial glimpse of a face – one she wouldn't forget in a hurry.

Suddenly, her phone rang just as the wail of sirens filled the air.

'Billy! Oh, Billy. Your building! The apartments . . . they're alight! The firemen are here now!'

'Slow down, Nan! What building? What are you on about?'

She inhaled quickly, trying to calm herself. 'I went to look at me apartment, but there were these petrol containers . . . like the ones I had at the old house. Loads of 'em . . . I could barely walk . . . but I got out, Billy. Just about. But listen. I heard footsteps. And I got sight of a man, just as I—'

'Okay, Nan, slow down. Are you telling me someone set fire to the building?'

'Oh, Billy boy, it's fucked, babe. The flames, they're enormous. They're licking the bloody sky!'

'Are *you* all right, Nan?'

'I'm alive, Billy, but your business – it's up in smoke. Oh, Billy, my heart breaks for you, boy.'

'Nan, just get away from there. Now. Go to my apartment, all right? Give the taxi driver my address. I'll call ahead, and security will let you in. You wait there. Got it?'

'I can wait for you, Billy.'

'Nan, did the man see you? Did you get a look at his face?'

'I think I did.'

Billy's voice turned sharp. 'Right. Nan, go to my apartment. Don't hang about. You hear me?'

'Yes, boy.'

CHAPTER TWENTY-NINE

Billy would never call Jesse at work. In fact, he barely used the phone unless it was for business. He always preferred to see people face-to-face. So when Jesse saw his brother's name flash on his screen, he knew something was wrong.

Answering immediately, he heard Billy's breathless tone and the words coming into his ear at a scatter-gun rate.

'Say that again, Billy.'

'The new apartments – they've gone up in fucking flames. I'm here now. The firefighters took forever to put it out. Luckily, no one died. Nan got out just in time.'

Jesse's stomach dropped. '*Nan?*'

'Ginty.'

'What the fuck was she doing there?'

'She went to measure up for curtains. Said the door was open, so she went in, saw a load of petrol containers, and legged it. But she mentioned hearing footsteps behind her. And get this: she caught a look of a man in the reflection in the glass door. She's still in a state. She's at ours.'

'Fuck!' Jesse gasped. 'So it was deliberate?'

'The firefighter I spoke to reckons so. He said the fire started almost simultaneously. It was like someone had lit it at the top and worked their way down. There was evidence of accelerants too. Jesse, whoever did this ain't stopping.'

'Is it salvageable?'

'Is it *salvageable*. No, mate! It's not! It's like a fuckin' crematorium, Jesse. The whole thing's gutted. The walls are blackened, the ceilings have collapsed. Even the steel has buckled from the heat.' Billy lowered his voice. 'It's gone, mate. Everything.'

Jesse clenched his jaw along with his fists. 'The bastards, the fucking bastards. Listen, I'm gonna check with surveillance to see if any of those Shipleys were anywhere near the building, even in the fucking area. I'll get back to you.' He paused and ran a hand through his hair. 'I dunno, Billy . . . maybe I should just leave the force. None of this is fucking worth it.'

'No, Jesse. No! We need you on the inside. You hear me? Because, believe me, I'm not done. I'm fucking raging. And we have the plan, which I told you about, after I left Cas's place, and just because they have burned down my properties, the plan hasn't changed. Jesse, I'm more determined than ever.'

Releasing a long drawn-out breath, Jesse continued. 'Right, listen, Billy. I'll be home, but it'll be very late. If we're going through with the plan, then I need to check out a few things. I need to know who the Shipleys have got on the inside.'

'Well, hear this, Jesse. Cas, Dennis, and Walter have a suspicion that this geezer Kenny Ruck is mixed up in all this. It's a long shot, but they could be right.'

'Kenny Ruck? Actually, Billy, that name rings a bell . . . Oh, I know. He came up on the recall list. He's missing, and there's a warrant to arrest him because he's being recalled to prison for failing to check in with his probation officer.'

'Well, they reckon he did time with some of the Shipleys,' Billy said, pulling a crumpled note from his back pocket. 'And the note he sent to Cas said . . . Hang on a sec, Jesse. I've got the note here.'

Billy unfolded it. 'It says: If you don't pay up, I will take down everything you own. You'll have fuck all. And you'd better warn Billy Murphy as well. He needs to do as he's told.'

Jesse frowned. 'That strikes me as—' He stopped abruptly and lowered his voice. 'I'll call you later, Billy. Got ears around me.'

Ending the call, Jesse slipped his phone into his back pocket just as Redwood approached.

'Jesse, how are we doing with surveillance? Anything to put on the board?'

Jesse was momentarily thrown off by Redwood's rough-around-the-edges appearance. The governor looked more knackered than usual. His hair looked greasy and his chin was full of stubble.

'No, Gov. Only the four men caught with the cocaine. They are being held in the cells, so, other than that, not at the moment. But give it time.'

'Time is budget, Jesse.'

'I know.' Jesse nodded. 'But we're okay for today, aren't we?'

Redwood sighed and rubbed his temple. 'Yeah. Just update me.'

'Will do, Gov.'

When Redwood left the office, Jesse clocked Shona and David scuttle out as if they had business of their own to see to.

But Melanie, on the other hand, wasted no time in easing herself over to his desk. She had clearly kept up with her new look. There was fresh make-up, sleek hair, and a perfume that was impossible to ignore.

'What did he want, Jesse?' She smirked. 'I saw him trying to blend in, but let's be real. He looks like a fish out of water here. He's not like one of us, is he. You'd never believe he was a PC when he started, would you. Still, he looks rough today.'

Jesse barely registered her words. His mind was still locked on to the fire, and the fact that Billy's hard work had just been reduced to ashes. In a few more weeks, the apartments should have been finished. Now? He imagined there would be nothing but a burned-out shell.

'Sorry, what did you say?'

Melanie pouted slightly. 'I was *saying*, the Governor looks rough, don't you think?'

'Family life, probably.' Jesse shrugged. 'The Shipleys' case . . . it might be grinding the old fella down.'

She lifted her chin. 'Redwood might even be rowing with the missus.' She grinned and leaned in as though she was divulging sensitive information. 'Have you ever met her?'

Jesse shook his head. 'No, I've never been to his place. I've never been invited. I bet it's a big posh gaff, eh?'

'Oddly enough, no. It's a detached place, maybe four bedrooms, but not grand or flashy.'

'And his wife? What's she like? Nice?'

Melanie hesitated. 'She's . . . quiet. Reserved. Sweet, even. But she's got a scar down her face – a nasty one. She could have been beautiful once upon a time.'

Jesse's eyes narrowed. As much as he had taken a liking to Melanie, he didn't like that comment, and he was getting a little bit fed up with her flirting. 'What do you mean, once upon a time?'

She leaned on his desk, completely oblivious to the fact that she'd just pissed him off. 'You know . . . before the ugly trench mark down her cheek, I bet she was a good-looking woman.'

Jesse's chair scraped as he stood up, the anger rolling off him in waves. He was already on edge, and Melanie had just tipped him over it.

'Beauty isn't on the outside,' he said, his voice edged with steel. 'That's just a fucking façade. Beauty is skin deep. A scar don't make you ugly.'

Melanie's eyes widened. She'd never seen Jesse snap before. She swallowed, flustered. 'Sorry, Jesse. Did I hit a nerve?'

The second the words left her mouth, she regretted them.

Jesse's voice dropped lower, his gypsy heritage accent thickening with emotion. 'Yeah, love, you did. Me farver has a scar down his face, and yet me muvver loves the bones of him. She says he's handsome on the inside, and that makes him handsome on the outside. And me muvver?' His eyes burned into hers. 'She got burned in a fire, which scarred her legs. And she's the most beautiful woman that ever walked this earth.'

He didn't break eye contact until Melanie looked away. 'I'm sorry,' she mumbled, but the damage was done.

Sitting down again, Jesse said, 'Yeah. So, think before you speak, next time.'

She nodded quickly before slinking back to her desk.

Jesse massaged the back of his neck. His head was already full of shit. Now, on top of everything, he had to figure out who the fuck had torched his brother's dreams. He'd make sure they paid for it, that was a given.

***

By nine o'clock in the evening, Jesse had memorised every single Shipley family member, every associate, their businesses, and even their wives. He'd gone through Companies House, checking for anything unusual. By the time he was done, he was thoroughly washed out. What didn't help was Melanie, who had spent the entire time trying to claw her way back into his good books. First, a coffee. Then, a heart-shaped doughnut. It was her way of saying sorry. Apart from serving her pussy on a platter, she was practically inviting him into her bed.

Melanie looked at her watch. Rising from her chair, she slid her arms into her lightweight denim jacket and sauntered over to Jesse's desk. 'It's late, Jesse. We should have left hours ago. Burning the candle at both ends and all that,' she murmured, winking, as she licked her lips.

Jesse fought the urge to heave. The one thing he couldn't stand in a woman was desperation. A bit of a chase? Fine. A bit of back-and-forth? Even better. But throwing herself at him like this? It was off-putting. If he pulled in a bar, that was different – it was mutual. But working with a woman who tried this hard? Nah.

Still, he had to rein in his distaste because, judging by the look on her face, she'd already clocked it.

'Yeah, I'm working hard, but a gang like the Shipleys shouldn't get away with what they do. And I'm sure, as sure as eggs are eggs, those witnesses will appear in court, and those two murderers will go down for a full life sentence.'

He watched as she nodded. Then he noticed her earrings. 'Blimey, those are nice. Diamonds?'

Suddenly, she touched her ears and blushed. 'Do they suit me?'

Here we go again, fishing for compliments, Jesse thought. But what really caught his attention was how the hell she could afford diamonds so large. 'Like diamonds, do you?'

She chuckled. 'Yeah, I do. They say diamonds are a girl's best friend.'

Jesse leaned in slightly to get a better look. 'They're proper twinklers. How much did they set you back?'

She touched them again, giving Jesse a coy smile.

'Well, he must like you, that's all I can say. Bet they cost an arm and a leg.'

For a moment, she looked embarrassed. 'Actually, I bought them myself – and to be honest, they're just cubic zirconia. But I can wish, eh?'

Jesse expected an indignant look. If he had said something like that to his sister or Dottie, they'd have bitten his head off. But Melanie hadn't.

'Nice. Right, I'll see you tomorrow.'

'You don't fancy a quick pint down the pub, then?' she said, as she lingered around his desk.

'No, I've still got a lot to do.'

Her face fell a mile, with disappointment evident in her eyes.

Jesse felt sorry for her for a split second, but he wasn't in the right frame of mind to placate her. As soon as she left and the office was empty, he threw the doughnut into the bin and sighed.

To his surprise, Redwood walked back into the office looking exhausted, his expression heavy with something that Jesse couldn't quite place.

'Working late, I see,' Redwood said, perching himself on the edge of a nearby desk. 'Those four downstairs – do we have enough evidence on them, Jesse?'

Jesse frowned. It was a strange question to ask. Typically, Redwood was the one barking orders, confident and sure-footed. But now? He looked worn down, almost hollow. *Was Redwood the spy for the Shipleys? Surely not.*

Jesse, being Jesse, went straight in, feet first.

'Gov, what's going on? You look – well, not yourself.'

Redwood sighed heavily, his gaze drifting to the ceiling. 'Burnout, perhaps,' he admitted, before locking eyes with Jesse.

Then, after a pause, he added, 'Anyway, I have to ask, Jesse. I've just been informed that a block of new apartments went up in smoke. Your brother's?' He stared, waiting for Jesse's reaction.

'Yeah.'

Redwood nodded slowly. 'The Shipleys?'

Jesse leaned back in his chair, the faint creak of its joints breaking the silence. His fingers drummed absently on the armrest. There was no point in trying to hide it. For some reason, he suddenly felt he could trust Redwood. It was as if they were on the same wavelength. There were only a handful of people Jesse felt that way about, and they were all family.

'More than likely,' he replied, finally.

'And your brother's girlfriend?'

Jesse bit his lip and nodded. 'Are you taking me off the case, Gov?'

Casting his eyes around the office, Redwood sighed. 'Years and bloody years, I've been in and out of this place. I started as a young man, fresh-faced, thinking I'd be locking up the bad guys, taking the scum off the streets.'

Jesse nodded, curious about where this conversation was heading. *Was he about to admit he was working for the Shipleys?*

'You know what my very first case was? Candice Shipley. A young woman – not the kind you'd meet at college or university, not in my day. She was feral, with a mouth like a sewer, and brutal with her fists. I was thrilled when I finally had her behind bars. I was patted on the back and we even celebrated down the pub. But then came the backlash – ripped tyres and a truckload of manure dumped outside my parents' house. And could I prove who did it? Not a chance. Back then, we didn't have mobile phones, ANPR, or half the tech we now have.'

'Bloody hell, Gov.'

'The Shipleys bred like rabbits – spreading like a disease. No thought, no restraint. Just mindless expansion at the expense of everyone else. Innocent people were crushed beneath them, lives shattered beyond repair. And all the while, as I rose through the ranks, I watched their empire evolve – growing smarter, more insidious.'

He sighed. 'You see, Jesse, they don't simply *commit* crime. That would be far too ordinary. No . . . they *own* people. The kind of people you'd expect to be untouchable. Ministers, high-ranking officers, lawyers, you name them. A great many names sit comfortably on their payroll. And the most amusing part? Not a single one of them would *dare* to refuse any request from them.'

Jesse released a sharp sigh before the words left his mouth. *He had to know.* 'And you, Gov? Have they got to you?'

'I like you, Jesse.' Redwood chuckled. 'Always straight to the point.'

'You mean straight in at the deep end with cement boots.' Jesse smirked. 'Sorry, I shouldn't have asked.' He shifted on his chair. 'But while we're on the subject – I think there's a spy in the camp.'

Redwood's smile faded. He shook his head with something that looked more like a laugh of resignation than humour. 'Oh,

Jesse . . . When I took you on, I could see straightaway you weren't the type to be bought. It's your background, you see. You've got money and are here for the same reason I am.' He swallowed hard. 'But they've gone too far this time. And it's only going to get worse.'

He leaned forward. 'I spoke to the surveillance team. They don't think any of the Shipleys left the manor. But there are so many of them, Jesse. And with their money and power, they don't need to do the dirty work themselves. They can pay their lackeys to burn down your brother's property, hurt his girlfriend, and do whatever else they choose.'

Jesse's jaw tensed.

'They will stop at nothing,' Redwood continued. 'And the sad truth? We don't have the budget to keep up. As for a spy in the camp?' He sighed. 'I very much doubt it's just one. There are probably a few. They're all over the place, and, again, it takes resources and funds to weed them out.' He shook his head. 'A minister. You know, the case I was assigned to? Well, that was linked to the Shipleys. The poor chap left his job.'

Now feeling comfortable to have this particular conversation with his boss, Jesse said, 'Can I ask you about Jacob Kerns? No one here really knows why he left. There are rumours, for sure. But something big must have caused him to get the push. Was he involved with the Shipleys?'

Redwood shook his head. 'No. I had him transferred, that's all. I tried to keep it hushed up at the time. And it obviously worked, if you don't know why he left here. But since you are clearly concerned that we have traitors at the station, I'll enlighten you. Kerns was removed because an officer here reported him for sexual harassment. Nothing was proved. It was a case of one person saying one thing and the other denying anything had taken place. You know the sort of thing. Anyway, Kerns felt it was impossible to stay here under a cloud of suspicion, so he asked for a transfer. Shame, really – he was a good copper.'

'Right. So I can cross him off my list. And Wesley? You had no idea he was bought?'

Once again, Redwood shook his head. 'Not a clue. Those bastards are clever, Jesse. They either use payoffs or . . .' His voice drifted off, his mind clearly taking him somewhere dark.

That's when Jesse noticed the glazed look in his eyes.

Redwood took a deep breath, and then he coughed. 'Violent threats and violent actions.'

For a moment, Jesse didn't know what to say. Obviously, this was wearing Redwood down, turning him into a shadow of his former self.

'Did they hurt your wife?'

Redwood's eyes widened in surprise, his head jerking back as if he'd been struck.

Instantly, Jesse regretted the question. 'Sorry, Gov. Cement boots again. It's just . . . Melanie said something, and—'

'Yes,' replied Redwood.

Jesse looked up in shock. 'Yes? They hurt your wife?'

'I can't prove it. No witnesses. Nothing said. No demands, no warnings. They dragged her down an alley and cut her face.'

Clenching his fists, Jesse's nostrils flared with anger. 'And they never admitted it? Never sent a note, a threat – nothing?'

Redwood shook his head. 'It was after I arrested Candice's father. He went to prison. Died inside. But, like I said, Jesse, they breed like rabbits.'

'I'm surprised you didn't leave or get a transfer.'

And that was when Redwood smiled. 'Jesse, I haven't seen *your* transfer request, have I?' His eyes darkened with understanding. 'You're a lot like I was. I wasn't going to let them win. And my Betsy – shy, sweet Betsy – she was adamant I stayed. She wanted me to bring them to justice. In fact . . .' His smile turned bitter. 'It was the first time I ever heard her swear. She said, "Prison is too good for those bastards. They need to burn in hell."'

Jesse nodded. 'She's right. People like the Shipleys don't deserve three meals a day in prison, living off the taxpayers. They're better off dead.'

Redwood's expression hardened. 'I agree. And between you and me, Jesse . . .' His voice wavered, slightly. 'Every time I see my sweet Betsy look in the mirror and run her dainty fingers down that scar – it breaks another piece of me.' He sighed again.

'That's why I need you to listen to what I have to say,' he said, his tone firm. 'It's evident the Shipleys want you to disclose the whereabouts of the witnesses. And from experience, they won't stop. First, the young woman – Bronte Penfold, I believe – and now your brother's property, his business. When will it end, Jesse? You'd be safer if you transferred.'

Jesse nodded. 'You're right. My family and I *would* be safer if I left or transferred.'

Redwood gave a tight-lipped smile and pushed himself up from the desk.

But just as he was about to leave, Jesse spoke again.

'But I'm not going. Not yet, Gov.'

Redwood stared at him. 'Jesse, we don't have the resources. I've just been told to pull surveillance with immediate effect. It's costing too much. Like I said, they breed like rabbits – well, more like rats – and we simply don't have the funding. Now, they'll run riot again, which leaves you and your family wide open. I've had decades of it, and as much as I believed you could make a difference, I'm beginning to think no one can. The law simply isn't enough.'

'Oh, Gov, I will take them down, one way or another.'

Redwood reached the door and turned back to face Jesse. With a slow, knowing nod, he smiled. 'My Betsy's sick, so I'm going away with her for a few days. The floor is yours, Jesse.' He pointed to the pyramid of the Shipleys on the board. 'Every one of those has a list of brutal and unforgivable crimes under their belts. Most have got away with it. I am probably going to retire soon, having spent the majority of my career bringing down this evil family and failing. Imagine, Jesse, just imagine. They destroy lives in one way or another, and we, the force, can't seem to stop them. But they must be stopped.'

Jesse nodded. 'I know, Gov, I know.'

As Jesse left the building, he had just one thought on his mind. Redwood could be crossed off his list of traitors as well as Kerns. The boss's heartbreaking story was totally convincing. Redwood deserved an accolade for what he'd been through.

CHAPTER THIRTY

Billy had only managed a few hours of sleep in the last few days, so when he walked into the private hospital room to see Bronte, even wearing a suit and having had a decent shave, he looked rough. It was in stark contrast to her.

Bronte was sitting up in bed and talking with Clive. Her voice, though soft, no longer sounded weak. And the colour had returned to her cheeks, despite the lingering swelling.

Billy paused to admire her. The shock of nearly losing her had put everything into perspective. That feeling of being mugged off weeks ago now seemed trivial. It was a clear sign of how much he cared for her, and now, how guilty he felt.

'Billy,' she said, a note of nervousness in her tone.

Clive hopped up from his chair. 'I'll fetch some drinks.'

'Cheers, mate,' said Billy, stepping aside for Clive to leave. With his hands awkwardly in his pockets, he moved closer to the bedside. 'How are you doing, Bronte?'

'Much better,' she replied, smiling gently.

He sat down and reached for her hand. 'I thought I'd lost you, Bronte. I'm sorry for not giving you the chance to explain. And for how I treated you just before . . . Well, you know what I mean.' He kissed her hand. 'If you want to call it a day, I wouldn't blame you.'

'No, Billy, there's no man out there for me but you. I love you, Billy boy,' she said, as tears slipped down her face. Suddenly, her bottom lip quivered, and the colour drained from her, as she averted her eyes and stared ahead.

'What's wrong, Bronte? Are you okay? Shall I get the nurse?' His voice tightened with worry.

Slowly, she turned to him, with more tears in her eyes. 'Billy, those men . . .'

He leaned closer, wiping away her tears. Hesitant before, he now pressed on. 'Who were they, Bronte? Did you get a look at their faces?'

Still holding her hand, he could feel how much she was shaking. 'It's okay, Bronte, you don't have to talk about it, but . . .' He paused, desperate to know if she recognised them. 'But if you know of them or . . .'

She shook her head, the weight of the world heavy on her shoulders. 'No. They grabbed me from behind and put a sack over me head,' she whispered, her voice trembling, as she stared blankly at the wall, unable to meet Billy's eyes.

When her shoulders slumped, and she slowly shrank into herself, it wasn't difficult to guess what had happened.

Instantly, he sprang from his chair and wrapped his arms around her, pressing soft, desperate kisses to her swollen cheeks. 'I've got you now, Bronte. I've got you, my girl,' he murmured, his voice thick with emotion.

He felt her bury her head into his chest, her body quivering with the overwhelming heaviness of despair. Every ragged, heart-wrenching breath echoed her pain, a silent testament to a horror that went far beyond a mere beating. The way her eyes stayed lowered, lost in torment, confirmed to him the unspeakable truth – they had raped her.

Slowly, she stopped crying, though a few sobs still caught in her throat. 'I have to tell you what they did.'

Billy wiped strands of hair from her damp face. 'No, you don't have to tell me. Not if you don't want to.'

'But, Billy, if I don't tell you . . . if I say it out loud, reliving it in a bad dream, or if I have a breakdown and everything comes out . . . I would feel dreadful. So I must tell you, Billy,' she insisted.

Slowly nodding, Billy sat back down and braced himself for those harrowing words. After taking a deep breath, he said, coldly, 'If those men raped you, I will hunt them down. I will kill them with my bare fucking hands.'

She nodded. 'You know I was a virgin when we got together, and, Billy, I swear to God, there has only ever been you.' She looked away, embarrassed.

'I know, babe, I know,' he murmured.

'How do you feel about me now, after . . .? I mean, I couldn't stand it if you looked at me like I was a dirty woman . . . But you have to know. They . . .' She put her hand to her mouth, finding it difficult to finish the words.

He grabbed her hand and pulled it to his cheek. 'I love you, Bronte. I always have. It won't change what we have.' Then, his tone reflected his anger. Thoughts of demonic plans were at the forefront of his mind. 'But it will change how they die.'

She looked into his eyes. 'So you don't hate me for it, Billy?'

'Hate you? Hate you for what those bastards did to you?' He sighed, a tear rolling down his cheek. 'I could never hate you.'

There was a heavy silence as they both absorbed the truth of it all.

After a sharp intake of breath, Bronte spoke once more. 'There was one man, a big man. He had two skulls, one on each hand . . .'

Now that she was opening up, eager to share any details she could remember, Billy nodded, gently. 'It's okay, babe. Whatever you can remember, tell me, no matter how small.'

'The other man had a really rough voice – as if he struggled even to speak. I don't think they were young. They sounded older.'

'What did they say? Can you remember?'

'It all happened so fast. I was coming out of me friend's house. I reached the corner of the road when I suddenly heard footsteps. Then, out of nowhere, a sack was shoved over me head. I screamed, but the man – he must have been really big – told me to shut up. He put a hand over me mouth and lifted me off the ground. A second later, I heard a van door slide open and I was thrown inside. Just at that moment, I heard another man's voice inside the van. He told me to keep still so that he could hold the sack tight and tie a rope around me neck to hold it in place . . .' She paused to take a few deep breaths before continuing. 'But I managed to rip the sack partly off. That's when I saw those tattoos on his hands. The man then punched me in the face, tied me hands together, shoved the sack over me head, and tied it tight. The door slid closed, and I don't know where I was taken, but, finally, when the van stopped and the door opened again, the other man climbed in. I think we were in the country. Everything went quiet, and there was a little light coming through the sack.'

She stared off into nothing, her voice on autopilot. 'I could hear birds, though. Sweet, sweet chirping birds.'

Billy could sense she was drifting away. 'And what happened next, love?'

She blinked a few times, her bottom lip trembling, but she steadied herself. 'They pinned me down and ripped off me knickers, and . . .'

'It's okay, love, you don't have to say it.'

'I – I thought they were just going to do that, and then let me go, but they didn't, Billy. They started punching me. I begged and begged and begged them to stop, but they didn't listen. They hit and kicked . . . and punched and kicked and . . .'

Billy could see the beads of sweat across her forehead and the panic in her eyes, as she relived the ordeal. Now, sitting on the bed, he pulled her close. 'It's okay, you're safe now, Bronte. I won't let anyone hurt you again.' Yet, even as he comforted her, his hands trembled with the promise of retribution. He wanted nothing more than to find those men who had shown her no mercy and make them pay.

After a few minutes of silent embrace, Bronte cleared her throat. 'Thank you for helping me farver. We all thought he was dying. He wouldn't go to the doctor's, but he's a lot better now. He popped in to see me. He was even singing your praises, God love him.'

Before either of them could say another word, the door opened, and a doctor, who was accompanied by a nurse, walked in. The doctor was studying his medical notes and smiled.

'Your latest scan shows everything is as it should be, so we can discharge you. I'm sure you're sick of hospital food by now.' He nodded to the nurse to take over before he left.

'I know that when you look in the mirror, you might feel you're not ready to go home, but I promise the bruising is only superficial. In a few days, it will fade, and you'll be your beautiful self again,' the nurse said.

'Thank you, nurse. That's so kind of you. You have been amazing. Thank you for everything.'

Billy frowned. 'Er, are you sure she can go home? I mean, she . . . er, she . . .'

'Yes, Billy. She's been through a lot, but Bronte is a strong girl and will recover better at home in her own bed. The sheets here are a bit starchy anyway. And you won't have to come back to visit your father because he's also being discharged today. I'll just sort out your medication.' She looked at Billy. 'Will you be able to take Bronte home? She's certainly not ready for public transport. She's still fragile.' Her lip curled, and her eyes darkened. 'I hope they catch the bast . . . I mean the men who did this.'

Billy smiled. 'Oh, they will.'

The nurse nodded and hurried out of the room.

'Clive was so kind. He's a genuinely nice person,' Bronte remarked.

'He saved your life, Bronte,' Billy replied.

Her eyes widened. 'What? He never said that.'

'No, that's just how he is.'

'Oh . . . I get it, now.'

'Get what?'

'Clive said you gave him a car. He was over the moon – he'd never had anything given to him before. You've made his year.'

'It's the least I could do, Bronte. Because he saved my girl's life. I swear to God, I've never seen anything like it. He knew exactly what to do.'

'Am I your girl, Billy, or are you just being nice to me 'cos I'm in 'ere, sick?' she asked.

'Of course, you are, if you still want to be.'

'Billy, that girl in the office. I saw you with her. Who is she?'

Billy waved his hand, dismissively. 'She was a secretary-turned-PA, but, to be honest, she's a pest, useless and irritating. First thing tomorrow, I'm firing her.'

He didn't have the heart to tell her about the project burned to the ground, which meant there wasn't any need for a PA or extra staff to help sell the new apartments. The office would have to stay open because it was for the property management business, including his own apartment block that he lived in. Hopefully, once the insurance company paid up, he could return the buyers' deposits and start again.

Bronte nodded and gave him her sweetest smile.

But Billy didn't return the smile. He was now in a quandary. At some point, he was going to have to tell Bronte that he had slept with Phoebe, but he couldn't bring himself to do it – not today.

***

Just before the nurse returned, Billy's phone rang. It was Jesse. Billy winked at Bronte and turned to Clive, who had just brought in a tray of refreshments. 'Stay with her. I'll take the call outside.'

Once he had closed the door behind him, he answered. 'Everything all right, Jesse?'

'No, no, it fucking ain't. Listen, Mum and Dottie are probably landing at Gatwick about now. Dad just called. Apparently, Ginty rang Mum and told her about the fire, and now they're on their way back. Dad couldn't stop her. The others are staying, but I fucking *knew* they wouldn't stick it out. Honestly, Billy, I'm surprised they even went there in the first place.'

'Okay, okay. Right. They need to stay out of the way. I wish they'd just stayed put, though! Damn it! I'm taking Bronte to ours. Clive and his nephews will keep her safe.'

'Just get Bronte settled, then you need to meet with Cas again, and, hopefully, by then, I will have worked out who the spy for the Shipleys is.'

'And what about Mum and Mottie?'

'Dad and Spud will have to stay with them,' said Jesse, now exasperated.

'Jesse, listen.' He lowered his voice and walked away from the door, in case Bronte could hear him. 'Bronte . . .'

'Go on, Billy, tell me.'

'She was . . .' He struggled to get the words out. 'Two men raped her, Jesse. They fucking raped her.'

'Jesus Christ. Poor Bronte. Those bastards are crossing the line! Big time!'

'Jesse, she said she couldn't see their faces, but when they tried to tie a sack over her head, she managed to pull it partly off, and that's when she saw one of the men's hands. They were covered with tattoos. Skulls, Jesse. Skulls. She also said the other man had a rough voice as if he was finding it hard to breathe.'

'Fuck me, I know exactly who they are. I've been memorising every fucking detail of that family. Every single one of the cunts. And that bastard with the skulls was nicked for raping a teenager. His name is Bart Shipley, Candice's son, Gerard's brother. And his sidekick and cousin Richie Shipley, had a tracheotomy six months ago after getting punched in the throat in a pub fight. It could only be those two.'

'Who is the head of this rats' nest?'

'Billy, in our office, we have a board where we add information. Anything we think is useful is added. But in this case, we have *three* fucking boards. That's how many there are. But the head of it all? I'd have to say it's Candice Shipley. She doesn't manage everything because her eldest son does, but she rules that family. So, listen. Get everyone safe. Let me do the digging, and then we can set the plan in motion.'

CHAPTER THIRTY-ONE

Sliding into the unmarked car, Jesse bit his bottom lip. He felt weird spying on his colleagues, but the idea that someone was feeding info to the Shipleys was just as disgusting to him and the ultimate betrayal. He was going to check them all out, starting with the one he least suspected from the beginning, merely to leave no stone unturned.

Seeing Bronte in that hospital bed and knowing those bastards had raped her as well as beaten her up lit a fire under him. And listening to Redwood in that heart-to-heart conversation earlier had given him every incentive to take down the Shipleys in any way he saw fit. He just hoped that when push came to shove, his boss would still have his back.

He could have easily looked up the address to guess the value of the property, but he wanted to see it for himself. Finally, he pulled up on the road, drove past the house, turned around, and waited. The house wasn't overly large, but it was a detached new build that a single woman on an officer's salary couldn't easily afford. It was possible that the house had been purchased from an inheritance or a break-up settlement – but, as far as he knew, she'd never been married. However, from what he could see, there was nothing glaringly out of place.

He wasn't even sure what he hoped to see. Maybe a glimpse of her home life, a sense of who she was. After about an hour, he saw a car pull up. But it wasn't her car. A well-dressed middle-aged woman got out and opened the rear passenger door.

Jesse couldn't take his eyes off the car. He noticed the woman gently assist a little boy, possibly aged five or six, out of the vehicle. It might have been nothing out of the ordinary, if it wasn't for the fact that the kid was sporting a distinctive cap, a blazer, and shorts. This was definitely not the unform worn by kids attending the local primary schools, so it was probably someone from a private prep school.

Still, he wasn't going to jump to conclusions. He waited to see what happened next. One minute later, the woman grabbed a school satchel from the back seat and led the child along the garden path and through the front door using her key.

Opening his notebook, Jesse checked the house number. Yes, it was definitely the right address.

Once the door closed behind them, Jesse double-checked the address. Surely, she hadn't given a fake one, had she? He had to know. Just as he was about to leave his car and knock at the door, he spotted another vehicle driving along the road. He lowered himself slightly in his seat but kept watching.

Sure enough, it was Melanie Sykes's car. She parked right outside and dashed along the pathway.

The front door immediately opened, and the babysitter, if that was who she was, had a face like thunder with her arms slapped across her chest.

Melanie stayed on the doorstep. She was gripping her handbag and waving her arms around. Both women were having a heated argument, that much was evident.

Then he saw Melanie storm off. But she didn't get back into her modest Fiat Punto; instead, she strode across to the detached single garage and opened the door.

Jesse was shocked when she drove out in an Audi TT, similar to the one that Billy owned. 'What the fuck?' he said, out loud, his body now covered in goosebumps. *Surely not?*

Melanie shot away, like shit off a shovel, and Jesse discreetly followed. He had to see what the hell she was up to.

He was confused now. Who was that woman Melanie had been arguing with, and who was the little boy? But something else came to him. Why was she driving a car way above her pay grade?

As far as Jesse was concerned, there were a number of questions that needed answering here.

Now convinced that Melanie was not who she presented herself to be at the police station, he was going to follow her and find out who she was seeing. He assumed she wasn't off to do any shopping because why would she drive so fast or even bother to swap cars?

Not one to be afraid, Jesse was surprised by how uneasy he felt. His neck burned, and his hands trembled. Suddenly, it hit him. Those Shipleys, with all the crimes they'd got away with, were pure evil. Even though he wasn't scared of most people, the thought of confronting the Shipleys in a dark alley made his stomach churn. And now, knowing his mum and Dottie were on their way back only made things worse.

He kept his distance, by remaining two cars behind, until she turned onto Shepherd Road. That was when he realised where she was heading. The Blue Boy was a pub owned by the Shipleys. 'You clever bitch,' he muttered, thinking that going to such a place, no matter who owned it, wouldn't implicate her in any crime. He clocked her park directly outside. Luckily, he found a spot three cars behind her. The road was busy, and yet Melanie had decided to park on double yellow lines as though it was her own parking bay. She didn't get out of the car.

Jesse had a clear view of her on her phone. Then the bar door opened and out stepped Richie Shipley along with Reece Shipley. They were two of the many faces Jesse had burned into his mind.

Reece hurried to the driver's side of her car and leaned in through the window. There it was. The cherry on the cake. Everything he needed to know. Melanie Sykes kissed Reece Shipley. Not a peck on the cheek but a smacker on the lips.

So Melanie was Reece's girlfriend. If that was the case, he could assume that the kid was his son. He closely observed her as she handed Reece a piece of paper. Then he saw him slide a phone from his back pocket and give it to her, while she handed him hers in return.

'Fucking burner phones. That bitch, that fucking bitch,' he muttered aloud, as his insides trembled with rage and anger churned in his stomach. 'You will pay, you fucking . . .' Taking a deep breath to steady himself, he pulled away.

He drove for about two miles before finally pulling over. He felt sick thinking that while she had been inside their Serious Incident Suite, she'd been listening to every conversation and reading every detail they had on the Shipleys – their arrests and what the force did and didn't know about them. She had been privy to everything they had on them except where those witnesses were. His full list of suspects had comprised of Redwood, Kerns, Hammond, Shaw, and Sykes. He had removed Redwood and Kerns. So there were potentially three further suspects to rule out. But he was pinning his expectations now on Melanie Sykes being suspect number one.

Suddenly, everything clicked. Wesley – Melanie was using him to get what she wanted. He had probably been overwhelmed by the money the Shipleys had thrown his way, building him up to lose small pieces of evidence here and there, and giving them the heads-up on surveillance. It made sense because when Jesse had looked into Wesley's past, he'd discovered that Wesley had debts that his wife had racked up with her constant spending, although they had been cleared. That was around the time his suspected affair with Melanie had started. He would bet his bottom dollar that she'd been in on it and was blackmailing him.

Jesse sighed to himself. Wesley had more than likely swallowed those bullets because he'd probably had enough of being blackmailed, or perhaps he had discovered that Melanie was part of the Shipley gang. The poor bloke probably never even knew they were reeling him in like a fish or that they would gut him like one too. He shuddered at the thought of her knowing all this while carrying on working in the office as if everything was normal.

Melanie's affection for him had been so fake, yet any man could have been swept off their feet by such a good-looking woman. She had been trying to seduce him, and if she had been his type, he might have fallen for it. Who knows what kind of pillow talk would have followed. He suddenly recalled how surprised not only Shona had been, but, in thinking about it, Melanie had been as well, when he told them that Wesley was a traitor.

After a full second, he rang Billy, to check in.

'Jesse, where are you? Is everything okay?'

'I know who the fucking plant is. It's a bitch who works on my team. I followed her to The Blue Boy and saw her kiss Reece Shipley. I had to get away from there, or I would have considered going through their bar like a fucking tornado.'

'I'm glad you didn't. Are you all right, though, Jesse? No one saw you, did they?'

'No. Listen, I'm coming over to your place. Who's there?'

'Bronte is resting in my bed. She's being fussed over by Ginty. She's like a fucking mother hen, speaking in her own gypsy tongue – a few words I haven't heard in a long time – and Bronte, bless her, is enjoying it all. I've got Clive and his nephew at the door, and every camera is set up, so we're safe. I want you here as well because I can't trust anyone.'

'Where are Mum and Mottie?'

'Spud and Dad are collecting them from the airport – they're safe. And Cas, well, he's itching to get the plan sorted. But are you sure this woman is the Judas?'

'Well, why else would she be snogging the face off Reece fucking Shipley?'

'Good point.'

'Billy, I'll admit to you, I'm nervous.' He knew he could trust Billy with anything he told him.

'Me and you both, Jesse. But I'm more worried about the family. I wish Mum and Mottie had stayed in Cyprus.' He sighed. 'But with Ginty updating them – though I can't blame her for doing that – they were bound to come home.'

It was then that Jesse realised his brother was much tougher than he was because he was more scared for the family than for himself.

With the weight of the world on his shoulders, Jesse drove to the apartment. He wanted to be around his brother, and even Ginty, who could irritate the life out of him, because he didn't want to be alone. He wouldn't have slept well in his digs in North London; he was still spooked. Seeing Melanie, all sugar and spice, and then discovering that she was a devious, underhanded cow had definitely stirred unrest in him.

***

Entering the apartment, Jesse found Billy sleeping on the sofa. Clearly, not wanting to roll over and hurt Bronte, he was probably still treating her like a china doll.

Ginty was asleep in the spare room, still snoring and sounding like a farm animal.

Jesse crept into his bedroom, not wanting to wake anyone up.

***

Early the next morning, having made a cup of tea for his brother, Jesse plonked himself on the edge of the sofa where Billy was now awake and with his feet up.

'I've got to go to work and gauge the situation,' said Jesse, shaking his head, still in disbelief. 'Are you having your meeting with Cas to finalise the plan to take out the Shipleys' businesses? I'll need a time and a place. Oh, and that reminds me, I need to email all the details of the Shipleys' businesses to myself before I forward them to Cas.'

Billy nodded. 'I'm going into the office first thing.' He raised his brows. 'To fire Phoebe.'

'Oh, I see. Does Bronte want her old job back?'

'Of course, she will, but I won't need a PA or office staff for a while – only for the current properties, and I can handle those for now.' He shook his head. 'I'm absolutely gutted.'

Jesse nodded. 'I know, mate, I get it.'

'Yeah, well, I can't lie around here all day. I need to take a shower, shave this monstrosity of a stubble off, and shake myself out of the depths of self-pity.'

'Don't be too hard on yourself, Billy. Fucking hell, it's been a lot.'

Billy's eyes shot to his bedroom door. 'At least I have Bronte. Fuck, Jesse, I really thought I'd lost her.'

'I know, Billy, I know.'

***

Feeling much better after a long hot shower and now wearing a well-pressed suit, Billy picked up his office keys and headed down the stairs of his apartment complex.

He felt so much happier knowing that Ginty was taking good care of Bronte, and Clive was doing a fantastic job of guarding the apartments.

Sure enough, when he reached the foyer, Billy was faced with two men, who were built like brick shithouses. They were Clive's nephews, Denton and Abel.

Billy paused at the exit. The street was quiet, and the breeze was welcoming.

He climbed into his Porsche and pulled away, the routine giving him a sense of control, even if it was fleeting. All the way, he rehearsed how he would tell Phoebe she was fired –if, of course, she was in the office. He hadn't personally heard from her, though Ginty had mentioned she was there when she collected the keys to inspect the apartment. It would have saved him the trouble if Phoebe had already handed in her resignation.

As he approached the back entrance, he scanned his surroundings. He wasn't going to step out and risk running into the Shipleys again. But everything seemed normal. The bins outside were overflowing from the neighbouring shop, and there were no suspicious cars parked nearby. He locked his car, unlocked the back door to his office, and stepped inside. Everything appeared as it should.

'Get a grip, Billy,' he muttered to himself.

Walking through to the front, he checked to see if there was any mail by the door. There wasn't. But when he turned around, he found it stacked neatly on his desk. It was a sign that Phoebe had still been handling things.

All he needed were the reference numbers from his insurance policies for his existing properties and for the new project. He had the fire and police reports. Now, it was just a matter of calling the insurance company. He knew it would be a mere formality. He had insurance for the full rebuild. With any luck, he could turn this disaster into something of an opportunity. Mistakes had been made on the drawings that had led to cost overruns. He wouldn't make those same mistakes again.

As he powered up his computer, something instantly caught his eye. His email inbox was already open. His stomach tensed. He assumed that he must have left it open the last time he was here. But that wasn't like him. He never left his email like this.

A strange sense of unease crept over him, a chill that had nothing to do with the room temperature. He shuddered and tried to shake off a feeling that was generating unease by the second.

Scrolling through his inbox, his heartbeat quickened. A few more emails from the insurance company suddenly jumped out at him. His hands trembled slightly as he clicked on them.

As his eyes scanned the screen, his brain felt as though it had just been nuked by something that at first sight didn't make any sense.

Shit! Every single insurance policy had vanished.

The building insurance, the contents insurance, *and*, for fuck's sake, the public liability insurance had been cancelled for all of his properties. Every sodding one.

The emails were cold and impersonal.

Sorry to hear you are leaving.
Your policy has been terminated as per your request.
We regret to confirm the cancellation of your cover.

Billy felt his stomach plummet. This had to be a mistake.

Desperately, he clicked on the trash bin, hoping to find something – anything – that explained what the hell had happened. Here, he found that deleted emails were untouched. Either the perpetrator had tried to cover their tracks, but in doing so, had forgotten the final, permanent deletion, or they were novices at using a computer.

Even so, his head throbbed with the realisation that he had been utterly outplayed.

There was no mistake. His buildings were uninsured. All of them.

His breathing came in shallow bursts as he lowered his face into his hands. And his shoulders sagged under the crushing weight of disbelief and betrayal. His empire – everything he had built – had crumbled beneath his feet.

He now owed thousands, and there was no way to repay those who had invested in the apartments.

All that remained were piles of rubble. And nothing – nothing – to protect him from what would come next.

The aftermath of the shock hit Billy like a freight train. He jumped to his feet as rage surged through his veins. With a thunderous roar, he tore the computer from its stand, lifted it above his head, and launched it across the office. Breathless, he watched as it exploded against the wall. His screams of frustration pierced the otherwise quiet morning. The sound was so unrestrained that a passing shopper nearly jumped out of her skin.

The weight of it all crashed down on him like a tidal wave, his legs buckling beneath him. He dropped to his knees, his breathing now becoming erratic and his chest heaving. And then, he sobbed. He sobbed uncontrollably, like a child. He didn't know how much more he could take. First, the beating. Then, the gut-wrenching fear that he had let Bronte down. And now, this –

the complete and utter ruination of everything he had worked so bloody hard for. And for what? To protect two scumbags, ex-junkies, in a witness programme – that's what.

'What the fuck is going on?' A shrill voice cracked through the air.

He barely registered it at first, but then he heard footsteps. Slowly, he lifted his head, his vision blurred from tears.

Dottie stood there, her arms wide open, her face a picture of confusion.

Billy didn't hesitate. He needed that hug. He needed her.

Saying nothing, Dottie held her son in a firm embrace as he clung to her. But while she comforted him, her senses remained on high alert, her eyes flicking over his shoulders and scanning the office for anything out of place.

Slowly, Billy pulled away, wiping his eyes and coughing to clear the lump in his throat. He shook his head, still trying to process it all. 'Someone cancelled the insurance on all of the properties including the new apartments,' he muttered.

Dottie, who moments ago had looked so calm and serene in a cream linen suit with a slight pink sunburn on her cheeks, abruptly took on the look of a cat being electrocuted. Her eyes widened. 'What? That can't be . . . How could anyone . . . Are you sure?'

Billy bit his lip and nodded, his hands firmly on his hips, as he glanced around the office. 'The only people with access to my computer – our shared computer – are you, me, and Phoebe. Oh, and Bronte, but we can rule her out.'

Dottie frowned. 'Well, it doesn't take a mastermind to work out who's done this, Billy, does it?'

'You're right,' he said, shaking his head. 'So either Phoebe made a serious cock-up somewhere, or somehow the Shipleys are behind this.'

Dottie sat at the desk where the remaining computer was still intact. She powered it up, her fingers moving quickly over the keyboard. Her eyes narrowed as she scanned the screen. 'Jesus, Billy . . . someone cancelled everything. All in your name.' She looked up, her expression darkening. 'This isn't a mistake or some admin error. The cancellation letters are official and properly worded, though they have a few spelling mistakes.

Someone has actually gone to the effort of writing formal requests to terminate every single policy.'

Billy paced the floor, his jaw tight. 'I don't get it, Mottie. Why would Phoebe do this? She barely knows us. There's no reason for her to hold a grudge, let alone destroy everything I've built. And if she was involved, that would mean the bitch knew the building was going to be fucking torched . . . In fact, not only that, but she also knew that Ginty was going there to check out the apartment.'

'Shit, Billy, she is a fucking psychopath. Tell me this: what do you *actually* know about her?'

Billy's face flushed with anger as he suddenly realised how little he knew about his own PA. 'To be honest, not a great deal.' Then, something clicked. His head snapped up. 'Hang on – she used to work for an insurance company.' He clicked his fingers, trying to recall the name of it. 'They sent me her work references.'

Dottie's lips pressed into a thin line. 'Then we can trace her.'

Billy glanced at the broken computer lying in pieces on the floor, his mind racing. 'Better still – we can go straight to the insurance company. It's only in Bromley. I want to find out everything they know about her because I am beginning to wonder if she is another fucking plant.'

Dottie nodded, already grabbing her handbag. 'Let's go.'

CHAPTER THIRTY-TWO

On the way to Bromley, Billy filled Dottie in on everything he knew up to now.

Dottie wanted to update him and divulge why she took a later flight, but she resisted that idea. She didn't want to add to his worries.

Finally, Billy drove into the Harper & Lowry Insurance car park, which was well signed showing 'Visitors Only'. The substantial towering glass structure gleamed under the June sky. He glanced up at the company name, which was etched in sleek silver lettering across the entrance. He'd hoped to own a building as grand as this one, but perhaps that was a fantasy. It certainly looked that way now.

Inside was even more impressive. The lobby stretched high with floor-to-ceiling windows, and a chandelier the size of a small car dangled above a sleek, circular reception desk. A starchy-looking woman in a navy blazer was perched behind it. Her long red nails tapped efficiently against a keyboard.

'Welcome to Harper & Lowry,' she said, smoothly, as they approached. Her smile was false, and her voice was high-pitched. 'Who are you here to see today?'

Billy took the lead. 'We're looking for information on a former employee. Phoebe Langston.'

The receptionist's polished smile didn't falter, but there was the slightest hesitation before she replied. 'I'm sorry, but we don't give out details on our employees, former or current ones.'

Dottie leaned in slightly. 'Well, you might want to when your CEO is informed that you have withheld information regarding a very serious legal matter.' She looked at the name badge. 'Ms Penwith.'

The receptionist's smile tightened. 'One moment. And would you please take a seat?' She gestured to the four steel-framed leather chairs lined against the wall.

Billy couldn't sit down. He paced the entire lobby, his mind running in circles, as he replayed everything that had led them here. The first time Phoebe had walked into his office, she had come looking to buy property. Instead, she'd ended up securing a job.

'Damn,' he mumbled, under his breath.

Dottie patted the seat beside her. 'Sit down,' she said, as she tried to calm him down while battling with her own raging emotions. In her mind, she was stabbing every one of the Shipley clan because she was convinced that this was their doing, and, oh boy, were they going to pay.

Reluctantly, Billy dropped onto the chair, exhaling sharply. He turned to Dottie, his voice low and frustrated. 'You know, she wanted to buy an apartment. That's why she came to the office. But she never brought it up again after she got the job. And I remember asking her to type a letter, and she wasn't very good at it. As a matter of fact, it was shit. Why . . . Why was I so fucking stupid?'

Dottie gave him a levelled look. 'Billy, why on earth would you suspect anything less of a young woman looking for work? If, of course, this is all her doing.' And she believed it was. She was more certain than ever now that this Phoebe trollop was related to the Shipleys.

Before Billy could respond, a voice interrupted them.

'Hello.'

A young woman approached them, her smile warm and pleasant. She had soft features, with dark hair framing her face, and an air of quiet confidence. She looked about twenty-five and oozed cuteness with wide Disney-like eyes.

'How can I help you?' she asked.

Billy looked her over, trying to place her, but there was no recognition. 'I need some information on a former employee. Phoebe Langstone—'

'That's me.' The woman tilted her head slightly. 'I'm Phoebe. How can I help?'

Billy's mouth fell open. His brain short-circuited, and it took him a moment to recover. 'Er . . . Look, I had a woman working for me who claimed to be you. I even requested references for her, and shortly after, I got them. But if . . . you . . . are Phoebe . . .'

'Yes, that is rather odd.' The real Phoebe crossed her arms, frowning slightly. 'May I?' She gestured to the chair.

'Yes, please do,' said Dottie.

'It's all rather odd, because I was called into my manager's office one day and was asked why I was leaving. HR had sent out references on my behalf, but I had never given notice. I was just as puzzled as they were. I assumed it was some kind of prank or mistake, but . . .' She shrugged, lifting her palms. 'Anyway, I *am* Phoebe. And I *do* work here.'

Billy felt his pulse quicken. Someone had stolen Phoebe Langston's identity, and they had got away with it – well, hopefully, only up until now.

Dottie leaned forward, her voice carefully modulated and even in tone. 'Phoebe . . . do you have *any* idea who could have done this? Who might have used your name?'

'No. But if someone did . . . I think *I'd* like to know who and why, don't you?'

Billy sat back, his mind racing. This wasn't just about fraud. This was personal. Someone had gone to great lengths to pretend to be Phoebe Langston. And now, he and his mother weren't just looking for answers. They were probably looking for a ghost.

'May I ask . . . what did she look like?' asked the real Phoebe, her voice tinged with intrigue and concern. She had heard of stolen identity cases, the way they could financially ruin a person, leaving them with nothing but wreckage in their wake.

Billy exhaled sharply, raking a hand through his hair, as he tried to recall every detail. 'Er, yeah. She's about five foot four, maybe five foot five. Long blonde hair – like bleached blonde, almost white. It fell to her mid-back, I think. And, sometimes, she wore it up in a bun.'

Phoebe frowned. 'Any other distinguishing marks?'

Billy bit his lip, concentrating. 'Her skin . . . it was like porcelain. Flawless. I'm not sure if that was make-up or what. And just beside her left eye,' he said, tapping his face, 'she had a beauty spot. At least, that's what she called it.'

The moment the words left his mouth, Phoebe's face drained of all its colour.

Dottie, ever perceptive, immediately caught the reaction. Reaching out, she gently stroked Phoebe's arm. 'You *know* her, don't you?'

Phoebe shook her head in denial, but the sheer fear in her expression said she knew something.

Dottie wasn't one to let things go easily. Not when the stakes were this high. She leaned in, her voice urgent but steady. 'Listen, this woman – whoever she really is – cancelled my son's entire insurance policies, and what is most concerning is that his most recent development was set ablaze. She's left him ruined and now penniless.'

Despite Phoebe's short gasp, Dottie pressed on.

'And not only that,' she continued, her eyes locking onto Phoebe's, 'she gave the keys to Billy's grandmother to check out an apartment – *knowing* it was going to be burned to the ground and the old lady with it.'

Billy's stomach churned. The fire, the deception, and Ginty seconds from being burned alive, it was all leading back to the fake Phoebe.

Dottie's tone softened, but the desperation was unmistakable. 'Please, Phoebe. If you know who this woman is, you *have* to tell us.'

Phoebe remained still, her fingers gripping the armrest of the chair so tightly that her knuckles turned white.

Sensing hesitation, Dottie played her last card. She blinked, took a deep breath, and carefully crafted the final words, lacing them with quiet, deceptive fear.

'Because we're all afraid for our lives.'

Phoebe let out another gasp. And for the first time since they'd met her, she looked like she was about to break down.

Billy sat forward. 'Phoebe, who is she?'

Phoebe swallowed hard. Then, in barely a whisper, she said, 'I think . . . I think I know exactly who you're looking for. But her natural hair colour is auburn.'

Her voice trembling as she spoke, Phoebe glanced over her shoulder and scanned the lobby as if she expected to see someone lurking in the shadows.

Leaning in to Billy and Dottie, she lowered her voice to a whisper. 'But please . . .' Her eyes were wide with fear. 'Please never let her know I told you. Because . . .' Her voice cracked and her lower lip quivered. 'She's so violent.'

Billy felt a chill creep down his spine.

'She was my friend,' Phoebe continued, barely above a murmur, 'until . . .'

The pressure was getting to Phoebe. Now, both of her hands were gripping the armrests of her chair.

Billy and Dottie waited, giving her the time she needed. Whatever Phoebe had been through, it was clearly still raw – and probably very recent.

'She used me,' Phoebe said, finally, her voice filled with the kind of regret that comes from betrayal. 'For years, she used me. For lifts to work, to go out drinking. She didn't drive at the time, you see. She—' Phoebe swallowed hard, her eyes shining with tears. 'She made me feel like I was her closest friend. I didn't see it. I didn't see what she really was.'

Billy and Dottie exchanged a glance but said nothing to let Phoebe get it out of her system.

'I was supposed to get married,' she said, her breath shaking. 'But she put a stop to that.'

A single tear slipped down her cheek. 'She slept with him.' Her voice turned brittle with pain. 'Not because she wanted him. Just because she could.'

Billy clenched his fists. He had met cruel people before, but this – this was something else entirely.

'And the final straw? The day I finally said *no* to her. That's when I saw who she really was. She went into a rage and . . .' Her breathing quickened, and her face reddened with a mix of anger and sorrow. 'She put me in hospital.'

Billy threw a hand over his mouth in horror. 'Jesus. I'm so sorry, love. Really.'

Always the sharp one, Dottie leaned forward. 'But why? What set her off?'

Phoebe swallowed hard. 'She wanted me to take her to see her father, who was in prison, you see.'

Billy blinked. 'Prison?'

Phoebe nodded. 'Her father was in prison, up in Manchester, at the time. But I had work. I'd already been late too many times because of her. I was on my final warning. I told her I couldn't take the day off.'

Her expression hardened with the memory. 'She didn't care, though. She turned up at my flat that morning. She had a baseball bat in her hand. I thought she was just going to threaten me with it, which she did, but then, out of nowhere, she started swinging it. I couldn't protect myself. She broke my ribs, my knee, and fractured my cheek bone.'

Dottie gasped. 'My God.'

Billy felt the heat rise in his chest, his jaw tightening. This wasn't just manipulation; this was psychotic.

'Did you report her to the police?' Dottie asked.

Vehemently, Phoebe shook her head. 'No. She's not the kind of girl you go to the police over. Her father is.' Her voice dropped lower. 'Well, he's a dangerous man. If I had gone to the police, he would've had someone take me down a dark alley and finish me off. I knew better.'

Billy felt for the woman. 'So, what did you do?'

'I disappeared.' Phoebe wrapped her arms around herself as if she was trying to make herself smaller. 'I moved out of my flat. I stayed with friends and house-shared. I felt safer that way.'

Silence fell.

Billy could feel his pulse pounding in his ears. He knew what was coming. He just needed her to say it.

But it was Dottie who spoke first. 'Phoebe . . . who is she?'

Phoebe hesitated, her fingers trembling. Then, finally, she whispered the name.

'Tandy Ruck.'

The room seemed to shrink.

Billy felt not only his temperature spike but his body go rigid at hearing the name.

Ruck.

It rattled in his brain like a warning bell. He knew that name. His voice was low when he spoke. 'Is her father Kenny Ruck?'

Phoebe swallowed hard and gave a slow, fearful nod.

She brought her thumbs to her mouth like a frightened child, her eyes darting around the lobby again. 'Please . . . please don't mention me.'

Billy did something out of character. Without thinking, he pulled Phoebe into a hug. It was a rare show of emotion that even shocked him. Usually, he was all business. He leaned close and whispered, 'She won't even know I've been here.'

When he pulled back, he noticed Phoebe's cheeks had turned pink, whether from the embrace or from relief, he wasn't sure.

But Dottie wasn't finished. She had spent two days in Cyprus with Grace Ruck – Kenny Ruck's wife. And she knew enough to ask the next question.

'Have you ever met her mother?'

Phoebe gave a small, sad nod. 'A lovely lady. A real shame that Tandy hated her.'

Billy frowned. 'Hated her?'

Phoebe gave a dejected laugh. 'Tandy hates everyone. Except her father.'

Rising from her chair, Phoebe was about to head back to her office. Suddenly, however, something made her hesitate. Spinning back to face the couple, her expression sharpened.

'You said she cancelled the policies before the properties were burned to the ground?'

Billy nodded, sensing a flicker of hope. Maybe Phoebe could shed some light on how to deal with an insurance company's red tape.

She took a step closer, her voice lowering. 'I can help you.'

Billy and Dottie exchanged a look.

Phoebe continued, her voice steadier now, fuelled by purpose. 'After what she did to me, I want to be able to help at least one person fight back against her. You'll need the IP address of the computer used to send the cancellation request. There will be a timestamp, and you'll need to prove that you didn't make the request.'

Billy's heart pounded. This was exactly what he needed – a way to prove he'd been set up.

'It's a long-winded process,' Phoebe admitted. 'And believe me, the insurance company will fight tooth and nail to avoid paying out. But I've been working in insurance since I left school. I know how these things work. And . . .' She winked. 'I know how to get them to pay out.'

Billy looked at her, a rare smile tugging at the corner of his mouth. There was finally light at the end of the tunnel.

'I was at the hospital when it happened,' he said quickly. 'I have witnesses, security footage. And my mum, who always has access to my accounts, was in Cyprus at the time.'

Phoebe's eyes flickered with calculation, her mind shifting into her natural problem-solving mode.

'You wouldn't happen to have security cameras at your office, would you?' she asked. 'Anything that could place Tandy at the scene?'

Billy ran a hand through his hair, letting out a relieved chuckle. 'As a matter of fact, I have.'

Phoebe's face lit up. 'Then you have a solid case for fraudulent cancellation of an insurance policy. And with the arson investigation . . .' Her voice trailed off, her lips curving into something close to satisfaction.

'Tandy Ruck is looking at prison for a very long time.'

She beamed, a fire in her eyes. 'And I can tell you one thing – she will die inside there.'

Billy knew she meant it figuratively, but he also knew Tandy. She was the kind of person who thrived on control, manipulation, and fear. In prison, she'd have none of that.

Phoebe smirked. 'But don't worry. She'll be with her own kind, soon enough. Oh, and if you want to find her, I know that every Friday at five, she gets her nails painted at Nettie's Nails in Sundridge Park. I saw her there recently as I drove past.'

Billy rose and went over to Phoebe to give her another hug. 'You diamond. Thank you, Phoebe, thank you.'

Phoebe blushed. 'I didn't catch your name.'

'Billy Murphy.'

'Call me, Billy, and we'll get that insurance sorted for you.'

CHAPTER THIRTY-THREE

Jesse rhythmically tapped a pencil against his desk while staring at the blank computer screen, his mind deep in thought.

Moments later, Melanie strolled in swinging her bag. Under normal circumstances, Jesse would have assumed a large Chanel bag that size was fake, because if it was real, it would cost thousands. And since Ginty could always get her hands on a fake Burberry, be it a bag or a coat, and earn her pocket money by selling them to all and sundry, he figured a copper on a basic wage would probably have one like that too.

But as his eyes focused on the bag, he realised it was more than likely to be the real deal. The stitching was perfect, and the squares didn't have kinks in them. This woman had money, and the more he saw of her, the more he hated her.

'Jesse, good morning,' she said, with a sickly smile.

It suddenly struck him. There was not much to like about the woman. Her voice was now becoming extremely irritating. Her perfume made him feel sick. And to top it off, her over-the-top make-up made her look like the whore she actually was. In fact, he saw her as worse than some street-corner prossie.

'Morning,' he replied, in a flat tone.

Melanie hadn't even removed her jacket when she launched into her questions. Under normal circumstances, he wouldn't have batted an eyelid, but things were different now. Now he knew she was in bed with the enemy.

'So, where are we? Are the Shipleys still in the cells? What else do we have on them?'

Of course, these were bog-standard questions for any copper to ask, but Jesse was now playing a game. He had to get it right.

Turning to face her, he gave her his trademark lopsided grin and followed it up with a wink. 'Well, the amount of cocaine they were caught red-handed with is enough, wouldn't you say? Fuck me, what else do we need?'

'Yeah, yeah, sure. So, the CPS is agreeing to charge them, are they, or what?'

Jesse couldn't believe what he was hearing. 'Charge them? Of course, they are! Fucking hell, the street value was in the millions. They're going down for a long time, and so that's another four of the Shipley gang off the streets.'

A thin smile crept across his face. 'And, believe you me, Mel, with your help and the rest of the team, I will have . . .' He jumped up from his chair and tapped the board, his pencil striking the photo of Reece square in the face. 'All of them! Starting with this fucker.'

He didn't take his eyes off hers, and he saw it – that slight, involuntary twitch, just to the right of her eye.

'Do you actually have anything on him, Jesse?'

The second the words left her mouth, Jesse caught it – the flicker of regret in her expression. He suspected that she knew she was pushing too hard.

At that moment, his private phone on his desk buzzed. Anticipating that Melanie might try to sneak a glance at the caller ID, he pulled himself away from the board, snatched the phone, and stepped towards the window, just out of her earshot.

'Jesse?' said Billy, who was on the other end of the phone. 'It was almost certainly Kenny Ruck who set fire to the building. And get this. His cunt of a daughter, Tandy, is involved as well. She fucking cancelled my insurance.'

'She did what?'

'It's right, it's all connected. Long story, but she's not Phoebe. I met the real Phoebe – the one who actually works in insurance. She's going to help me with my claim. But the long and short of it is this: Tandy Ruck blagged her way into my office, acting as my PA, all so she could get into my private records. And I stupidly gave her the fucking passwords. She cancelled the insurance just before the fire, Jesse. She fucking knew the place was going up in flames. The bitch even let Ginty go off to the apartment knowing what was about to happen.'

Jesse's jaw tightened.

'And now, get this,' Billy continued. 'The description Ginty gave me . . . it kinda fits Kenny Ruck. Also, she thinks there may have been another person in the building. That would make sense, right? How could one man lift those petrol drums up those stairs all on his own? And one more thing. Mottie remembered something. Grace Ruck's story about how fucking evil Kenny is. He burned down a house, years ago, out of temper. His old buddy's place. So, he's our guy. And after that note Kenny left Cas, I'm convinced he's working with the Shipleys. In fact, one of the Shipleys could have been inside the building helping Kenny set fire to it, couldn't they?'

Jesse could hear the exasperation in his brother's voice.

'This wasn't just payback for the way Cas treated him. This has to be the Shipleys and Ruck working together. But Tandy knows all the business details now, including Cas's involvement and how much of the property he owns.'

'Jesus!' Jesse looked over his shoulder to make sure Melanie couldn't hear him.

'But, Jesse, the real Phoebe, basically said I needed to prove I didn't cancel any of my insurance policies to the insurance company. So I need CCTV footage of Tandy, which I have, to prove she was the one who sent those emails that cancelled the policies. But the bitch and her father must be arrested. I want to kill the cunts, but if I did, the insurance claim wouldn't stand, the investors won't get paid out, and you know me, Jesse, I'm a fair man. So can you get on it? By the way, tomorrow, late afternoon, she will be in Nettie's Nails.'

Jesse's mind was already one step ahead. 'So some cunt burned down your business, and now you are not insured. Do you have any idea who did it?'

Billy immediately caught on that Jesse was in someone's company, and he wanted to spin a yarn. 'No idea at all, Jesse. Only that her name is Phoebe Langston.'

'A Phoebe Langston? Okay, I'll look into her, Billy.'

He ended the call and spun around – only to find Melanie standing two feet away.

'What's happened, Jesse? Has someone burned down your brother's business?'

Jesse nodded. 'Yep. And he isn't insured. Someone called Phoebe Langston, who worked at the office, cancelled the insurance policies.'

What struck Jesse as odd was Melanie's reaction. Suddenly, she didn't seem to know what to say.

Then he dropped a bomb. To see how Melanie would react.

‘The Shipleys! They want my brother to get me to hand over the names of the witnesses for Max and Moriarty’s trial.’

There. He had said it.

Her eyes widened, full of confusion. She clearly wasn’t prepared for him to admit it so boldly, but there it was. It was out in the open.

‘Oh . . . er . . .’

Jesse could sense the cogs turning in her head, the confusion playing out in her eyes, as she scrambled to piece things together. Finally, her brain caught up. ‘And his bird, Bronte?’ she casually asked. ‘I mean, do you think that the attack on her was linked to the Shipleys as well?’

‘Well, of course it bloody was.’

The room felt too calm, like a storm brewing.

‘What are you going to do, Jesse?’

He stared at her lips, which were coated in so much gloss, they looked almost plastic, they were so unnatural. Too perfect, like the rest of her.

She shifted, uncomfortably so. ‘Has your brother asked you for the address of where the witnesses are staying?’

‘No!’

She jolted at his sharp reply.

‘Really?’ Her tone lifted. ‘Even after his bird got bashed up—’

‘And *raped*, Melanie.’ Jesse’s voice was stone cold. ‘They fucking *raped* her.’

For the first time, he saw real shock flash across her face – but not the kind he expected. It wasn’t horror at what had actually happened. It was something else. She was obviously trying to process something in her mind. The slight tilt of her brow, with confusion creeping in, was a dead giveaway.

‘Sorry to hear that,’ she muttered, the words forced, distant, as if she was simply stalling, until she had time to process all of the implications.

Then she blinked, regaining her composure. ‘I still don’t understand why he didn’t ask you for the address? Fucking hell, Jesse.’

Jesse clenched his jaw. ‘My brother would never ask me to compromise my job.’

She shook her head. 'Even when his bird gets bashed, raped, and his new apartments are burned to the ground?' Without realising what she'd just said, she carried on, as if she was on Billy's side. 'Christ, fuck the job. Why are we hiding those two ex-junkies in witness protection? Well, if it was me, I think I would tell him, Jesse. I wouldn't want any brother of mine to suffer that loss over two scumbags.'

Jesse's blood turned cold.

As far as he was aware, no one other than Redwood and himself knew any details about the key witnesses to the Fairweather murders. Melanie certainly wasn't told they were ex-heroin users. And he hadn't mentioned the specific fact that his brother's new apartments had been burned down, only his business. *How did she know that Billy had been building a new apartment complex?* he wondered.

For the first time, Jesse knew for certain that Melanie was in cahoots with the Shipley family. She was the one feeding information to the Shipleys. She had to be because she knew way too much.

And now? Now, he just had to figure out what the fuck he was going to do about it.

'My brother will handle things in his own way. He's a lot stronger than those Shipleys give him credit for.'

Watching her almost twist herself inside out, Jesse was tempted to keep winding her up. He wanted to push her, to see how much more she would squirm under the pressure. But he had things to do. She could wait for now.

His top priority was getting Tandy arrested, or, at the very least, keeping her under surveillance to track down Kenny. But it wasn't his jurisdiction. He was based in North London. Billy's problems were all on South East London's turf. But that wouldn't stop him. He just needed to think of a way in.

The station was waking up now. Officers trickled in, carrying paper cups of coffee, some yawning, others already firing up their computers and settling into their routine.

'Mel, I need to pop out. The Shipleys are being taken to court first thing, and there's a dead drug dealer found just off the high street. Can you check that out?'

She tilted her head. 'Where are you off to? Anywhere exciting?'

'I need a word with Redwood.'

Melanie frowned. 'He's apparently off for a few days seeing to his wife.'

Jesse froze for half a second. He already knew that. But how did she?

'Did he tell you that?' he asked, keeping his tone neutral.

She nodded. 'Yeah, yesterday, just as he was leaving.'

So, she hadn't left the building right away, as he had thought. What had she been hanging around for? Then, again, Melanie liked to be in the thick of things. She'd probably been sniffing around the custody desk enquiring about the Shipleys. The sneaky bitch.

'Right, catch you later. And call forensics about the drug dealer. I want to know how he died and when.' *That should keep her busy*, he thought.

'Oh, er . . . okay,' she muttered, as if caught off guard.

Jesse grabbed his wallet and jacket, snatched up his keys, and hurried out of the room.

As soon as he got inside the car, away from prying eyes and ears, Jesse pulled out his phone and dialled Jacob Kerns. The line rang a few times before a gruff voice finally answered.

'Kerns speaking.'

'It's Jesse Murphy. We need to talk.'

'Oh yeah? Do we?' Kerns sounded sceptical, but his tone had a hint of curiosity.

'Yes, Jacob. This is serious – and a right good nicking for you.'

'I'm all ears, son. Carry on.'

'I need to meet you. I can visit the station or there's that coffee shop, Meg's Muffins, along the high street. Your call.'

'Seein' as what you're about to tell me is bound to be interesting, let's make it the coffee shop. But it's obvious you've been away for a while, mate. The place is called the Catwalk Café now. Anyway, it's your shout.'

'See you there.'

Jesse ended the call and started the engine. This had to be done right. One wrong move and it could all go to shit.

Driving to meet Kerns gave Jesse time away from Melanie to process everything that had just happened. Yesterday had left him uneasy, but today was different. The unease was gone. He was ready for the Shipleys.

The coffee shop was one of those old-fashioned places, with wooden beams, worn leather booths, and the aroma of freshly brewed coffee mingling with warm pastries. The morning rush was over, leaving only a few customers lingering over newspapers and half-empty cups.

Kerns was seated at the back. It was the perfect spot, away from the windows.

Jesse would have chosen it, too. He ordered two coffees and two slices of homemade cake before carrying them over to the table.

Kerns licked his lips when he saw the cake. 'Fuck the diet,' he chuckled, grabbing a fork and diving straight in.

Jesse sat down and took a slow sip of his coffee before getting straight to the point.

'Jacob, I spoke with Redwood about you. I wanted to know why you left. Well, he told me in confidence what happened. It seems to me you had a shitty experience. Is that right?'

Kerns froze, the fork hovering in mid-air before he placed it carefully back onto the plate. His posture straightened, and the easy smile dropped from his face.

'What's this all about, Murphy?' He leaned forward, his eyes narrowing.

'Here me out, okay? The harassment complaint. Did it come from Melanie Sykes?'

Kerns let out a long sigh before he finally nodded. 'Yeah. Look, mate, I'm a flirt, yeah – a bit of banter, the odd innuendo. But! I never fucking laid a hand on that girl. She ain't my type, anyway. But she and her goofy PC mate – you never met her – she left shortly after – made out like I was some perv. The claims were unfounded, but I moved. Joint decision.' He shrugged. 'But moving to South London has its advantages. My parents aren't getting any younger, and this way, I can see more of them.'

Jesse sipped more of his coffee as he took in what Kerns was telling him.

'So, what's this really about? Only, you mentioned a decent nicking.'

Jesse leaned forward. 'Kenny Ruck.'

Instantly, the older officer's expression shifted. His eyes widened, and a slow grin spread across his face before he rubbed his hands together.

'Cor, I'd love to get that bastard. Nasty, evil piece of work, he is. What've you got on him? Other than the fact he's breached his licence and there's a warrant out to recall him to prison.'

'Arson. A block of new builds.'

Kerns let out a low whistle. 'Oh yeah, I saw the report come in – definitely deliberate, I would've thought. And you have a witness, do you?'

'Yep.'

'Well, that's great, if we can find the bloke.'

Taking another sip of coffee, Jesse lowered his voice slightly. 'It's not a bloke. It's his daughter, Tandy. She gets her nails done every Friday – late afternoon. So she will be at Nettie's Nails at around four forty-five tomorrow. Follow her, and I'm sure she'll take you straight to him.'

Kerns smirked, wiping the crumbs from his fingers. 'Now, that really is a bloody good lead.'

'When you get him, nick her as well,' Jesse added, his voice low but firm. 'She's committed serious fraud. She cancelled the insurance on all of the properties, including the building that was torched to oblivion.'

Kerns's brow shot up to his hairline. '*What?* That's a fucking vindictive move. Hang on, the name on the report said Murphy. Any relation to you?'

Jesse held his gaze. 'Yeah. My brother.'

'He's upset a lot of people then, Jesse. First his girlfriend, and now this.'

Jesse sighed. 'Redwood said you're a good copper, one of the good guys.'

With a tight smile, Kerns replied, 'Not that it does me much good. The place is filled with bent coppers. And me? I've never taken a bribe, never looked the other way – and yet I'm the one who had to leave over a false accusation.'

Jesse wanted to tell him what he knew, but it wouldn't be productive – not yet. Instead, he took a few sips of coffee and a bite of cake before wrinkling his nose.

'Cor, this don't beat me mum's cakes.'

Kerns grinned, reached over to Jesse's plate, and popped the contents onto his own. 'Waste not, want not,' he said, as he wiped his hands on his paper serviette.

Then his expression shifted – serious now.

'I underestimated you,' he admitted. 'I saw you walk in that first day, in your flash suit, designer shoes, driving my dream car, and handsome with it. I thought, look at this fucking flash prick.'

Jesse raised a brow. 'S'pose I did look a bit of a dick.'

Kerns chuckled. 'Not half, mate. I never imagined you'd cut the mustard, but you're one of the good ones. I heard how you managed to nick four of the Shipley gang for transporting all that cocaine.' He winked. 'And thanks for the info. I need a decent arrest.'

'My pleasure. And treat the bastard with the fucking contempt he deserves. Shit in his hamburger before you feed it through the cell hatch, if you want.'

Kerns nearly spat out his coffee, laughing at that one. He pointed to the cake. 'I'll be shitting out icing sugar, at this rate.'

'Do me a favour, though. Let me know the minute the bastard pair are in your cells screaming their innocence.'

'It's the least I can do, Detective Sergeant Murphy.'

Jesse's face flushed with pride hearing those last three words. It was affirmation that a colleague had granted him the respect he now deserved.

CHAPTER THIRTY-FOUR

Jesse didn't bother returning to the station. Instead, he headed straight back to the apartment that he shared with Billy. This was going to be bigger than even he could ever imagine.

He had already emailed Cas everything. All businesses, even the cars belonging to the Shipleys. He chuckled to himself. The way Cas would boldly take over was madness in Jesse's eyes, but what did he know? Cas was old-school, a gangster through and through, with years in the game.

Just before Jesse reached his apartment, he spotted Cas's car pulling into the car park. Cas hurriedly stepped out of his Bentley Arnage and glanced around as if he was expecting to find Kenny Ruck in person about to take a potshot at him.

Jesse had to suppress a laugh. The way Cas dressed never failed to amuse him. However, today, he wore a pair of jeans and a pink polo shirt. A far cry from his usual Hawaiian shirts or sharp suits, but the casual look suited him.

Cas removed his sunglasses, gave Jesse a nod, and strode over.

Hurrying to meet him, Jesse noticed Cas glancing around again before speaking.

'I'm glad you're here. I hate talking on phones. Anyway, listen up, boy. Listen up. I've sorted a farmhouse out in the marshes at Romney. The place is full of farmers, old pals of mine. I've got the address for ya. Now, all we need is a time.'

Jesse took a deep breath, before shifting nervously from foot to foot. 'Are we sure about this, Cas?'

'Are you fuckin' kiddin' me, Jesse? I've gone to great lengths, spent a lotta money to get the Shipleys' businesses all stamped and signed by my solicitor. And I'll tell you this: he doesn't come cheap. Now, all I need are their signatures.'

'Okay, okay. It's just such a big job, and . . .'

'I get it, kid. You don't want blood on your pretty little hands. Well, you ain't gotta. That's what I'm here for, son. This ain't my first rodeo. It's just another day's work to me.'

Jesse hesitated, and then he nodded. 'No, I'm in, Cas. After what they did to me bruvver – and Bronte – and nearly killing Ginty – I want to be there.'

Running a hand through his thinning hair, Cas sighed. 'Okay, but you and Billy don't have to be there. I've got this.'

'Cas, have you spoken to Billy?'

'Nah, why? I've been on the blower most of the morning. Got a text from him to come over.'

'He knows who burned the apartments down. It was Kenny Ruck.'

Cas's face darkened, his jaw tightening. 'That cunt. And all 'cos I never fuckin' backed him. Now, all this.'

Jesse shook his head. 'There's more to it, Cas. Ginty reckons there may well have been someone else in the building as well. Since, as we suspected, Kenny's in with the Shipleys, it could have been someone from that family. Anyway, let's go inside.' He wiped the sweat from his forehead. 'My head's about to explode.'

As they walked through the lobby, Jesse politely nodded to Clive's two nephews, who were instantly on their feet until they realised it was Jesse.

'This is Cas. He's okay.'

The two men at the entrance eyed Cas as though they were manning an Army checkpoint, their expressions hard and unreadable.

'Fuck upsetting those two,' Cas muttered, as he reached the lift.

Jesse chuckled, though more out of nerves than amusement. At the end of the day, his job was on the line.

The moment they stepped into the apartment, they were hit with a wave of noisy chatter – a stark contrast to the quiet space that Jesse had left that morning. The scent of fresh coffee and expensive cologne hung in the air, and the plush sofas were now occupied by family, their voices overlapping in conversation.

'There he is!' Carrie called, hurrying over, her arms wide open.

Jesse barely had time to react before she wrapped him in a tight squeeze and then planted kisses on his cheek.

'Mum, why did you come back?' He pulled back. Then he spotted Dottie, and his stomach clenched. 'You two should've stayed abroad, or, at the very least, stayed far away with Dad and Spud. It's too risky! Those Shipleys are animals. Look at what they did to Bronte.'

Carrie's expression sobered. 'I know, love. But pretending I was having a blast in Cyprus wasn't fun, I can tell ya that for nuffin. How could I sit there sipping cocktails while my two baby boys are here facing those bastard Shipleys? Nah, sod that. I'm right where I'm meant to be. With my family.'

Jesse's stomach churned. 'Shit! You didn't bring Nellie, did you?'

Carrie scoffed. 'No, I'm not that fucking stupid. She's having a great time with Charlie and your aunts.' She turned to Cas, her expression softening. 'It's a lovely villa, Cas. Bloody massive. And as for that pool. Well, it was huge.'

Cas kissed her on the cheek. 'Thanks, love. But Jesse's right. You should've stayed. Still, you're here now.'

Jesse caught the way Cas looked at Carrie – there was a great deal of respect, if not admiration, for the woman.

From the moment Cas had first laid eyes on her – when her ex, Jimmy Carson, had left her for dead, battered and burned – he had seen her for what she was. A fighter. And even now, as the years passed, she still had that fire, that presence, that turned heads.

A door down the hall creaked open. Billy stepped out, his face as inscrutable as ever. He flicked his head towards the kitchen, a silent command.

Jesse and Cas followed without question, leaving the women to their conversation.

The kitchen, sleek and modern, was cool and still. As they settled around the marble table top, Ginty bustled in and reached for a chair.

Billy put up a hand. 'Gin . . . I mean, Nan, you don't need to be here. Not yet.'

She huffed, crossing her arms. 'Well, I was nearly blown up in that apartment! So I think I've got a right to be at this table discussing plans. I'm a woman with *experience*. You could do with my help.'

Ignoring Billy's frown, Jesse pulled out a chair for her. 'You're right, Nan.'

Billy's expression tightened further, but Jesse just winked at him.

Ginty scooted in closer, straightening up, as though she was head of the family. 'So, what do we know?'

'Billy told me you heard footsteps, possibly from two people coming after you in the building. And there was one man you saw. A reflection of him in the glass door. We need you to identify the bloke,' Jesse said. 'Could you pick him out in a lineup? Or from a photo?'

Ginty's brow furrowed. 'Well . . . I'm not too sure.'

Billy leaned forward, his voice low. 'Didn't you tell me he had a scar? From his cheek to his chin?'

Her eyes flickered with recognition, and then they widened. 'Yeah! Yeah, he did! I thought the glass made his face look distorted, but no – it was definitely a big jagged one. The ugly bastard.'

Cas tensed. 'Hair?'

'Yeah, he had hair,' she said, with a small smile.

Cas sighed, clearly frustrated 'I meant, what *colour*?'

She hesitated. 'Not sure, but I think it was reddish-blond. A bit like Dottie's.'

Cas exchanged a look with Jesse, his grip tightening on the table.

'That's the cunt,' Cas muttered. 'And I reckon you *could* easily pick him out in a lineup. Right?'

Ginty pursed her lips, considering the question. 'Yeah, well, if you put it like that, I suppose I could.'

'Right, Nan, that's a massive help,' Jesse said, nodding. 'And now, I want to talk to Cas alone.'

Ginty shot Cas a look, but all she got in return was one of those slow assessing stares that could make a person squirm. This was why people feared him. It wasn't just what he was capable of – it was the *way* he carried it. There was a darkness in his eyes, something cold and calculating, as if they alone could shoot you dead.

Satisfied that Cas had the boys' backs, Ginty rose to her feet with the grace of someone of extreme importance. 'If you need anything else . . .'

Cas smirked and winked. 'Being a witness is the best weapon we have, darling.'

With her head held high, as though she was walking out of a royal court, Ginty left the room, her exit only slightly blemished by the way she narrowly missed colliding into the doorframe on her way out.

Billy got up and shut the door behind her, before he turned back. 'So, what's next?'

Cas grinned. It was the kind of smile a man gives when he's just been served his favourite pudding. 'All the papers are signed, all the i's are dotted and the t's crossed. The farmhouse is sorted. An old mate of mine owns it. Rents it out to one of those Airbnb bollocks, but no one really stays there. Bit of a shit pit, to be honest. But a fucking *big* shit pit.'

Billy arched an eyebrow. 'Sounds . . . promising.'

Cas leaned back, clearly enjoying himself. 'Yeah, well, he bought the place back in the day when you could knock over a post office and use the cash to buy property. Not like now, what with taxes and fucking money-laundering regulations—'

Jesse chuckled. 'Yeah, I imagine the cameras don't help either, do they?'

Cas huffed. 'No, they're a right fucking pain in the arse. Anyway, we digress. So, the farmhouse – outside, it looks in good nick. Right out in the sticks, on Romney Marsh. The place is dead quiet. There's just fields, crops, and a fuck load of sheep. Got a few farmer mates out that way. And under those fields? Probably a graveyard, but let's not dwell on that.'

Billy frowned. 'Comforting.'

Cas waved a hand. 'Point is, out there, there's no cameras, no nosy bastards. Unless you *live* there, you'd have no reason to go. The coast road gets a bit of traffic, but it's dead quiet further back. No streetlights, pitch-black at night. So, when it's over . . .' He shrugged. 'No one will see our next move.'

Jesse watched him, shaking his head. Cas talked about all of this as though he was planning a weekend getaway, not . . .

whatever this was. Then, again, this *was* Cas's life – one that, as he'd say, *was a lot easier back in the day.*

'I've got two more lads joining the party,' Cas said, leaning forward. 'Bit like the Spartans downstairs. Frazer, the fucking nutcase. He grew up around guns, and to be honest, I wouldn't like to upset the cunt. He's not wired up right. But, funnily enough, he kind of looks like a copper.'

Jesse raised an eyebrow. 'Reassuring.'

'And then there's Bailey,' Cas continued. 'Now, he's shorter, but fuck me, is he fast. He'd slice your throat before you could even blink. But, stick him in the right gear, and he could pass as a copper, too.'

Jesse folded his arms. 'And you *trust* these men?'

Cas scoffed. 'Trust them? Fucking hell, Jesse, they'll get a decent motor, and a little business sorted, all in a night's work – I should coco.' He smirked at his own joke before shaking his head. 'Yeah, I trust them. Done a few jobs with me in the past. Mutual respect and all that.'

Billy rolled his eyes.

'Besides,' Cas added, 'they wouldn't dare fuck around – not with Walter, Dennis, and their lads keeping an eye on them. I gotta say, those boys were *raised* to handle themselves. They take no prisoners.'

Billy recalled the day Walter's sons and Dennis's son charged into Cas's place. As much as he wasn't afraid of a fight, he knew at that moment that they would have killed him without hesitation.

'So,' said Jesse, 'all I need to do is somehow, without making it obvious, give Melanie Sykes the address. Right?'

Cas nodded. 'Look, the Shipleys will know the witnesses were moved because their position was compromised before. And they'll guess they'll be a few coppers guarding the place, yeah? So, they'll turn up mob-handed. But you, Jesse, need to let this tart know there will be more than two coppers, so the Shipleys will bring backup. The more the merrier!'

Jesse frowned.

'It's all right,' Cas said, waving a hand. 'I've got two lads drinking in The Blue Boy who are keeping an eye out, in case we need to take one of the Shipleys hostage to barter with. Just a little insurance policy.'

Jesse still looked sceptical.

'Listen,' Cas continued, 'there's other shit in place as backup, which you *don't* need to worry about. It's all in a fucking night's work.' He winked.

Jesse sighed. 'Well, you *seem* to know what you're doing.'

Cas let out a laugh. 'That's why they used to call me *The Governor*. But getting mixed up with you lot – I think I've fucking softened in my old age. However, this, boys, well, this is *my* game. So, you leave the finer details to me.' He turned to Jesse, his expression turning serious. 'One thing you have to be cocksure about is this tart Melanie Sykes.'

'She's definitely part of their firm,' Jesse said, firmly. 'Like I told Billy – they're everywhere, lining everyone's pockets. Growing like a fucking tumour. And when you take one down, another just appears in its place.'

Cas smirked. 'Then we take the head off the hydra.'

CHAPTER THIRTY-FIVE

Jesse had arrived early, dressed in black trousers and a black polo shirt. He looked as though he was going to a funeral. Yet, in some respects, he probably was. All he needed now was the phone call from Jacob Kerns. The plan would be ready to execute once Tandy and Kenny were in those cells.

His stomach was full of butterflies – and a few angry hornets – because right now, this was nerve-racking. The weight of responsibility pressed down on him, making his breath quicken and his palms sweat.

While he sipped his coffee knowing that one more cup and he'd be bouncing off the walls, he stared at the clock, willing the time away.

At four forty-five this afternoon, Tandy Ruck would be on her way to Nettie's Nails. Well, he hoped she would be because everything depended on her keeping that appointment.

Shona breezed in. Tossing her bag onto her chair, she then placed a white cake box on her desk.

Jesse glanced up and forced a smile. He had to look cheerful and not let his anxiety show.

'Someone's birthday?'

Shona smiled, her lips lifting towards her almond-shaped eyes. He hadn't noticed before how pretty she was.

'It's mine, actually, Jesse. I thought we could all do with cheering up.' She looked at the floor and sighed. 'I suppose you heard. Dave and me, we've broken up. Always bloody arguing, anyway.'

Suddenly, it all made sense why David and Shona always seemed to be up to something. Because they were. They'd been secretly seeing each other.

'So I've treated us to cake. Would you like a slice?'

Jesse nodded, though his stomach was in knots with nerves.

'Go on, then. That'd be nice.'

'So, the dead dealer was murdered, then?' Shona asked, casually.

Jesse frowned. The dealer had completely slipped his mind.

'Fuck! Was he?'

'Yeah. Didn't Melanie tell you? Well, the coroner called, not that she needed to tell us, because it was obvious. He was stabbed from behind. The blade ended up straight through the chest.'

'Do we have a name?'

'Brett Hutchins. Apparently, they call him Northern Brett.'

'Fuck.' Jesse exhaled sharply, recalling the time when he had been at the cottage where Mia and Jim had been staying. So Mia and Jim's dealer was actually called Brett Hutchins. He'd heard Mia call the dealer Northern Brett.

As soon as he had powered up the computer, Melanie strolled in, her face beaming and her make-up even heavier than ever. He'd have to play along, as though he wanted her to win him over, but, mentally, he just wasn't there.

'Er, Mel,' said Jesse, 'what do we know about the dead drug dealer? Shona tells me he was murdered.'

'Yeah. He had a ton of cocaine on him. Stabbed clean through to his chest. He was known in the area for supplying drugs. I guess that's another lowlife off the streets.'

With a plate of sliced cake in her hand, Shona walked across to Jesse's desk but not before she'd shot a look of disgust at Melanie.

'Melanie, it's not our job to judge. The man's been murdered.'

Melanie eyed the cake in front of Jesse and didn't bother hiding her irritation.

'What are you – the teacher's pet?'

She realised a second too late that she'd said the wrong thing and tried to laugh it off.

'Mel, have you written up the report? I'd like to go through it.'

Melanie frowned. 'We could go through it together, if you like?'

Her irritating voice and lack of subtlety was getting on his nerves, but sticking to the plan, he deliberately bit his lip and smiled.

'No, I, have a ton of stuff I need to do for Redwood.'

'Anything I can—'

'No, you get on with your report,' he snapped, before turning his attention to his computer screen and getting stuck into his cake.

***

The day dragged on. By four forty-five, Melanie was still hovering nearby. So, when Jesse finally got the call, he was already on edge and beginning to perspire to the point that sweat was pouring off his forehead.

'Sorry, Mel, I need to take this,' he said, jumping up from his seat.

Spinning around, he walked towards the window before answering the call. He didn't even get a chance to speak before Kerns's excitable, high-pitched voice came through.

'Jesse, we got her! And we didn't even need to follow her to find that bastard Kenny, either. He fucking dropped her off at the nail place. So they're both in cuffs, in separate police cars.'

'Make their lives miserable, for as long as you can. You know what I mean. Don't let them use the phone, delay a solicitor – all the little things that'll piss the bastards off.'

'Jesse, listen, I appreciate this, mate. That Kenny's going away for a very long time.'

'I know. And so he should.'

'No, there's more, mate. I spoke with the fire department – they were doing their own investigation, and it turns out that there were petrol containers outside in a car park. And one had his prints all over it.'

'Good.'

'I ain't finished. He only went and smacked one of the officers in the mouth for trying to resist arrest. Now he's also charged with serious assault. He knocked my officer clean out. Broke his front teeth.'

'Thanks, Jacob.'

Jesse ended the call but he didn't put it away. A eureka moment hit him. Pretending he was still on the phone, he grabbed a pen and paper. Talking to himself felt a little weird, but he hoped that it was a smart move.

'So, the dead drug dealer *may* have given away the Davenports' address, you say . . .? Are you sure?' He paused as if listening for a response.

That was when he saw Melanie's ears prick up with interest. Glancing over at Shona, he put his hands over the phone and said, 'Be a doll, would ya, and grab us a coffee.'

Shona didn't think twice about it – she nodded, smiled, and left the room.

Jesse then glanced at Melanie.

'Listen, there's a problem. That drug dealer may have given away the address to the witnesses' safe house. Their handler's off sick, so I've got to meet them at the new place, settle them in, and fucking stop them from telling people where they are.'

He pretended to be back on the phone.

'Right, got ya.' He began scribbling down the address of the farmhouse in Romney.

'I've got it. You say you need to step up with more officers? . . . Oh, you already have five? . . . Fair enough. What time will they arrive? . . . Seven o'clock? . . . Great, I'll be there then.'

Melanie's eyes widened, but it was obvious to anyone in the room that excitement flickered in them. She looked as though she had just won the lottery.

Jesse pretended to end the call and turned to her.

'Okay, you say nothing, Melanie, because I'm trusting you to man the fort while I'm gone, okay? Come what may, we *must* keep these two witnesses safe. Max and Moriarty aren't getting away with this.'

'Yeah, yeah, sure,' she said, though her eyes flitted to the Post-it note.

Jesse grabbed his rucksack, swung it over his shoulder, and hurried out of the room. He made it as far as the coffee station when he spotted Shona holding two coffees.

'Sorry, doll, I've gotta dash – oops, forgot something.'

He turned back towards the office and stepped inside just in time to see Melanie hurriedly writing something down. She looked up, startled.

'Jesse, you forgot this,' she said, her face flushed, as she handed him the Post-it note.

He winked and smiled.

'I'd forget my head. Thanks, love.'

He took the note and bolted down the hallway and out to his car. As he climbed in, he quickly dialled Cas.

'She took the bait. Kenny and Tandy are in custody. We're good to go, Cas.'

***

Billy pulled his belt tight, securing it with a sharp tug. He crouched down and tucked his knife into his boot, the cold metal pressing against his skin. His gun slid easily into the waistband of his jeans.

Bronte stood still, watching him. As he turned to her, his gaze dark and unreadable, her heart rate picked up sharply. He cupped her face, his fingers gently touching the bruises along her cheekbone. His jaw clenched as he tilted her head slightly and inspected every mark.

'Oh, Billy, please . . . just come back to me,' she whispered.

He kissed her softly. 'I'll be fine, Bronte. But I can't live letting scumbags walk all over me. I tried to do things the right way and look where that got me.' His voice hardened. 'I'm done. No more being Mr Nice Guy.'

Bronte almost laughed, but fear stole the sound from her throat. Billy had always been kind to her, but he had a side that wasn't so soft. He could fight. He could handle himself. She'd seen him in action. But this was different. And she was terrified he might not come back.

'Bronte, I don't say it often, babe, but I do love you. Now, you just stay put. Ginty will look after you. All right?'

She nodded, a tear resting on her cheek. 'Please stay safe, Billy.'

***

Billy stormed down the stairs and into the lobby where Clive and his two nephews were waiting.

'Clive, I need you here. I want this block watched. I've got no idea what the hell's about to go down.'

'Mr Murphy, I should come with you.'

Billy shook his head. 'No, Clive. Watching the building – with *precious cargo* inside – is more important to me.'

Clive nodded, though he didn't like it. He'd never seen that look on Billy's face before. His expression had turned to steel – his lips tight, his eyes dark. It wasn't just determination. It was something colder. He had met his fair share of psychos back in his Army days, and they all carried that same look.

Billy marched out through the exit, but then he stopped dead in his tracks.

Jesse had pulled up directly outside.

Billy frowned. This wasn't part of the plan. Jesse wasn't supposed to get his hands dirty. He was meant to find the rat and feed back false information.

Yanking open the front passenger door, Billy leaned in. 'What the hell are you doing, Jesse?'

'I'm coming with you. Fuck the Shipleys, fuck the force – this is a fucking *war*, and you, my bruvver, ain't going to war without me. So shut up and get in.'

Billy was about to protest, but one look at Jesse's face told him that it was pointless to argue.

The second the door shut, Jesse floored it.

'All right, *Jenson Button*, slow the hell down! I'd like to get there in one piece – we only get one shot at this.'

Jesse smirked. 'I drive better when my foot's to the floor. So, Cas, is he already there?'

'Yep. And the lads are strategically placed, though I still can't picture old Cas as some fucking colonel leading a unit.' Billy chuckled, shaking his head.

Jesse grinned. 'Yeah, Cas's more a pint-and-a-packet-of-crisps kind of guy than a military strategist.'

Billy's smile faded, his voice dropping low. 'Listen, Jesse, there's two men – *you* know who I mean. Skull Hands and his sidekick, Breathless. *I* want them. They're *mine*.'

Jesse glanced at him, the humour now gone. He nodded once. 'Then let's go get 'em.'

Gripping the wheel, Jesse said, 'Billy, if I die—'

'Oh, fuck off, Jesse.'

'Nah, nah, hear me out. *If* I die, I wanna be cremated, all right?'

'Shit me, Jesse, you ain't gonna fucking die. I won't let that happen.'

'You're only bloody *two weeks* older than me, so it don't really count that you're me big bruvver.'

Billy laughed. 'I've *always* been like your big brother. Shit, how many fights have I had to pull you out of? How many times did I have to beg the teachers not to expel you?'

Jesse smirked. With his eyes fixed on the road, he sped along the M20 towards Romney Marsh.

The brothers fell into reminiscing, talking about the old days – finding that dead body in the newt pond, getting into scrapes, and, not forgetting, taking down Irvin Slade the Monster. They always had each other's backs, whatever was happening in their lives. Today was no different.

Billy leaned back, rolling his shoulders. 'Jesse, you got a tool?'

Jesse scoffed. ''Course I've got a tool. I've got a boot *full* of tools. Take your pick.'

Billy grinned, shaking his head. 'You really are a dodgy bastard, you know that? How you ended up being a copper, I'll never know.'

There was a moment of silence as Jesse felt his eyes welling up. 'If I'd never become a copper, all of this wouldn't be taking place. You wouldn't have taken that beating, your building would still be standing, and Bronte wouldn't be . . .'

'Oi, enough, Jesse. Just because you're a copper, it doesn't give anyone the right to do what they fucking did. Anyway, they will fucking regret it, believe you me, Jesse, they will.'

The look in Billy's eyes left no room to doubt him – none whatsoever.

CHAPTER THIRTY-SIX

By the time they reached New Romney, the heavens had opened and rain was coming down in stair rods.

Jesse manoeuvred through the narrow winding lanes, which stretched like a maze. A few skeletal scarecrows swayed in the downpour. Their tattered clothes clung to wooden frames, which were nailed to wooden fences. Faded warning signs creaked on rusted posts, likely to be leftovers from the previous Halloween. The whole place looked like a scene straight out of an American slasher film.

The sky darkened as the storm clouds thickened, and as they rolled low over the vast landscape, they added to what was already a depressing scene.

Finally, after what had seemed like hours of driving, the farmhouse came into view. It was an old sprawling structure with weather-beaten brickwork and a slanted moss-covered roof. Surrounded by a cluster of trees that looked out of place against the endless stretch of farmland, the property stood out prominently. The fields around it were meant for arable farming. Here, the trees stood like warriors, shadowy and unmoving in the rain.

Beside the large farmhouse stood an equally sizeable barn that had been converted into a four-car garage, its faded red walls slick with rainwater. A single dim light flickered above the doors that barely cut through the gloom.

Jesse pulled into the long gravel drive, the tyres crunching over the wet stones before he steered the car around the back and out of sight. The moment he killed the engine, silence settled between them.

Billy adjusted his seat belt. 'Do you feel that?'

Jesse nodded, gripping the wheel a little tighter. 'Yeah. This place ain't 'alf spooky.'

Grabbing his jacket from the back of Jesse's BMW, Billy chuckled. 'It don't spook me, but it sure as fuck will spook the Shipleys.'

Jesse shot him a sideways glance, a little concerned at how Billy seemed to be completely unperturbed. But why? Did he not realise that they might be walking into a potential bloodbath?

Before he could say anything, a voice barked from the back door of the farmhouse.

'Oi, get in here, you two daft bastards!' yelled Cas.

Instinctively, Billy reached for his knife as he made his way straight over to Cas.

Jesse, however, popped open the boot of his car and started to dig through the stash of tools. Grabbing as many as he could, he hurried inside.

The farmhouse smelled of damp wood and stale air, the flickering kitchen light casting long shadows across the walls.

'Here,' Cas said, tossing Jesse a towel. 'And what the fuck is that lot?' He let out a short laugh as Jesse dumped a pile of tools onto the table – an axe, hammers, wrenches, a crowbar, and even a pair of bolt cutters.

'Just in case,' Billy said, shaking the rain from his hair.

Cas picked up the axe and turned it in his hands with a smirk. 'Jesus Christ. Listen, Jesse, we ain't here to chop fucking firewood for a cosy night in.' He shook his head and reached behind his waistband, where he pulled out a gun. 'You ain't got time to make a meal of it – just shoot the bastards. Well, after the cunts have signed the paperwork, that is. Then, it'll be job done.'

Jesse took the gun and turned it over in his hand. He'd been on plenty of target practice sessions, but he was no authorised firearms officer. This weapon felt different from the ones he had used in his training: it was heavier. And for the first time since holding a gun, he really understood that this wasn't for a warning shot or negotiation. This would *end* a life.

He glanced at Billy, who was holding his own gun with ease, as if it belonged there. He didn't look hesitant. Didn't overthink it.

Billy met his eyes. 'Are you ready for this?'

Jesse tightened his grip around the gun. Ready or not, it was happening.

'Yeah,' he said. 'Let's get it done.'

Cas called the men into the kitchen. All but Frazer and Bailey, who were in the lounge. Everyone else was gathered around the long pine table, the air thick with anticipation.

Dennis and Walter sat on either side of Cas, their faces deadly serious. Behind Dennis stood Denny – a towering six-foot-eight brute – with Walter's son Ryan at his side. Ryan was already flexing his fists, his gold knuckledusters gleaming under the dim light.

Cas launched straight into the plan – no pleasantries, no wasted time. But before he could finish, the kitchen door creaked open.

Already on edge, Jesse nearly jumped out of his skin, his hand twitching towards his gun.

Filling the doorway, standing broad and grinning, was their Uncle James. He let out a gravelly chuckle.

'Don't look so bloody shocked, Jesse. This is *family* business.'

Before Jesse could respond, Cas's phone buzzed. The room fell silent as he answered, nodding as he listened.

'They're on their way. A van and a car. My man reckons it's Reece and Dario in the car, but fuck knows who's in the van.' He snapped the phone shut and looked around the table.

'So, are we ready, lads?'

There were a few nods and a couple of smirks.

Ryan cracked his knuckles.

Cas grinned. 'We've got Bailey and Frazer in the lounge. The pair of nutters even put on copper uniforms for the occasion.' He shook his head, chuckling. 'Gotta *look the part*, though.'

Billy exhaled, his fingers tightening around the grip of his gun. There was no turning back now.

His gaze flicked to the tools laid out on the table, his mind already picturing the damage he was about to inflict on two of the Shipleys, in particular. Bart, the bastard with the skull tattoos on his hands. And Richie, the wheezing scumbag, who could barely breathe.

His eyes settled on the bolt cutters.

No one, *nothing*, was going to stop him from making those two *really* suffer.

A firm hand landed on his shoulder.

'Listen, Billy,' James said, quietly, his voice measured. 'You don't *have* to do this.' His gaze followed Billy's to the bolt cutters. 'Because once you do, you'll have to *live* with it for ever.'

Billy's grip tightened around his gun, his knuckles white, his face pale. But his eyes burned with fierce intensity as he stared hard at James.

'Uncle James,' he murmured, lowering his voice. 'They *raped* her. They *beat* her. I couldn't live with myself if I *didn't* do something.'

James breathed in sharply. He remembered, as clear as day, the time Billy had beaten an older lad half to death on the front lawn of his house. He broke the bastard's jaw, and he wasn't done. If he hadn't jumped in and pulled Billy off, that boy would have died right there on the grass.

So, firsthand he knew what Billy was capable of.

And this? This wasn't just a fight, this was revenge.

Cas's phone rang again, cutting through the thick tension in the room. He answered, and within seconds, a wicked grin spread across his face.

'My man in The Blue Boy's just checked in. He says the van has six Shipley men inside. And the bastard driving?' He let out a low chuckle. 'He's just confirmed it's none other than fucking Gerard. The *head* of the hydra.'

A murmur rippled through the room.

While Billy's fingers flexed around the gun, Jesse took a few deep breaths, and even James gave a slow, knowing nod.

'But listen,' Cas continued, raising a hand, 'don't kill 'em. *Yet.*' His voice dripped with amusement. 'I want them tied up, with a pen in their hands, ready to sign the *deeds*, the *logbooks*, and everything else I've got in this briefcase.'

He patted the black leather case beside him, his eyes gleaming with anticipation.

Billy smirked. 'So we're giving 'em a choice, are we?'

Cas shrugged. 'More like an *opportunity* . . . to walk out of here alive.'

A chuckle rumbled through the group, low and knowing.

'*Alive?*' Billy's face darkened, thunderous with rage.

Cas tutted, shaking his head. 'Keep your hair on, ya *silly bollocks* – 'course not alive.' He smirked. 'Can't let a *perfectly* dug grave go to waste, can I?'

Hearing that, Billy nodded in satisfaction.

***

Cas and his men went into the musty old dining room, adjacent to the kitchen, where he had already set up drinks. There was plenty of time. They knew how long the Shipleys would take to reach this godforsaken place.

Around half past nine, two sets of headlights shone through the windows of the lounge. And a moment later, before another word could be said, the low rumble of engines echoed through the rain-soaked night. They didn't need to check. They heard Frazer's voice bellow from the lounge.

'The cunts are pullin' up now!'

Suddenly, the tension in the room increased exponentially, with everyone shifting into position.

'The van's opening up. The back doors are wide open,' Frazer continued, his voice carrying. 'Reece and Dario 'ave just got outta the car. 'Ere, they're only gonna *knock* at the fuckin' front door!'

Billy smirked, rose from the armchair, and rolled his shoulders. 'Well, let's give 'em a warm welcome, then.'

Before Cas or anyone could stop him, Billy hurtled down the hallway, past the living room, ready to rip the door off its hinges.

Bailey just managed to grab him.

'What the fuck are you doin', mate? They might have a gun! At least *I've* got me flak jacket on. Get back, you crank.'

A sharp knock rattled the door.

Bailey pressed a finger to his lips, his other hand resting on the grip of his gun tucked in his belt.

Jesse hurried up behind Billy, instinctively joining him behind the door, both ready to pounce.

Unbeknown to them, the rest of the men were already in position.

Bailey cracked open the front door just enough to get a look.

But Reece was faster. He forced the door open and rammed a gun straight to Bailey's throat, shoving him back into the house.

'Right, mate, we don't want any trouble. You just do as you're told, and no one gets hurt.'

Dario lingered on the doorstep, his eyes darting around, scanning the surroundings.

Inside, Reece shoved Bailey backwards. No argument. No struggle. Just a cold, forced compliance.

Bailey held up his hands in surrender, which gave Reece a false sense of security. He smirked and pulled the gun away from Bailey's neck.

'Good man. Now, you just do what I tell you.'

Bailey took slow, cautious steps backwards, passing the lounge door on the left.

That was when Frazer, who was an inch away from the lounge doorway, struck.

With one swift, brutal motion, he swung his samurai sword. The blade bounced off Reece's gun – but sliced off some of his fingers.

Reece let out a choked scream, stumbling back, clutching his maimed hand, as blood sprayed across the wooden floor.

Bailey had already ducked, expecting gunfire, but none came – only the sound of flesh being met by steel.

Dario's eyes widened in horror. The moment he realised what had happened, he spun on his heels ready to run back to the car.

But Frazer was too quick for him.

Grabbing Dario by the hair, he yanked him backwards, dragging him inside with ruthless strength. Before Dario could fight back, Frazer slammed the front door shut behind them.

Billy stepped forward, with his gun raised and a smile on his face.

'Ah, so you were the other fuck-up who burnt my new apartments to the ground, nearly killing my gran in the process.' He nodded to the fresh burns that coated the back of Dario's hand and the bandages wrapped around his arm.

But Dario didn't answer. His mouth gaped open in shock.

Billy then grinned from ear to ear.

And just like that, the real fun was about to begin.

Frazer left Dario in Billy's hands and returned to the lounge, where he peered through the net curtains. Outside, the men in the van were still clambering out, completely oblivious to the bloodbath that had just begun inside.

Bailey, who was in the hallway, had his hand clamped over Reece's mouth to muffle his screams.

But Reece wasn't coping well. His skin had turned a ghostly white, with sweat beading on his forehead and his chest rising and falling in frantic gasps. He was shaking, his remaining fingers gripping his ruined hand, but the blood – there was so much of it – was everywhere and spilling between his fingers and dripping onto the floor.

However, it was Dario who looked the most terrified. His breathing was shallow, his entire body as stiff as a board, as he stared at Billy. Not at the gun aimed at his head or at the violence that had just unfolded before him. But at Billy's grin, which was slow, sadistic, and full of something far worse than anger.

Billy tilted his head, letting the moment stretch and savouring the raw fear radiating from Dario.

'Relax, mate,' he murmured, his voice almost friendly. 'We're only just getting started. Now, tell me this: what's the fucking plan? Are your lot gonna storm their way in through the back door, or are they gonna politely knock at the front door, like your brother just did?'

Dario, for all his usual bravado, was stumped. This wasn't how it was supposed to go. He wasn't the smart one – Reece was. Reece not only had the brains but he was quick-witted with it. But now, Reece was on the floor bleeding out, while he was left trying to figure out what the hell to do next. One thing was clear – saving his own skin was priority number one.

'Y-Y-Yeah,' he stammered.

Jesse shoved his gun under Dario's throat, the barrel pressing hard against his skin.

'If you're lying,' Jesse growled, 'I'll blow your fucking head off.'

Dario swallowed hard. 'I swear, all right? They're coming through the back. We were told to secure the front.'

Billy's eyes darkened, his gaze locked in a trance.

'Are Bart and Richie with you?'

Dario frowned for a second, confused. Why was Billy asking about them? Then it hit him. *Shit.* Murphy's girlfriend.

He'd heard what Bart and Richie had done to her.

Now, Dario's heart was hammering so hard, he thought he would have a coronary there and then.

Before anyone could speak, Cas strolled into the hallway. He was grinning as though he'd just walked into a pub full of old mates.

'*Well, fucking well* – if it ain't the two *flash* cunts,' he said, shaking his head. His eyes flicked to Reece, who was now as pale as a ghost and clutching his mutilated hand.

Cas tilted his head, inspecting the damage.

'That his left or his right hand?'

Reece's bloodshot eyes bulged in horror, but he was too stunned to make a sound.

Bailey let out a wicked laugh. 'Relax, it's his *left.* I'm sure the cunt can still sign his name.'

Cas smirked, nodding. 'That's all right, then.'

Billy stepped forward. 'Cas, they're gonna storm the back door at any minute.'

Cas didn't flinch. He just chuckled.

'O' course they are, Billy.' Pulling out a cigarette, he lit it with steady hands and inhaled deeply. 'We've got it sussed, mate – don't you *worry*. Everything's in order.'

Blowing a smoke ring appreciatively, he nodded towards the two captives.

'Now, drag these two cunts into the lounge, would ya?'

Before they even got Reece to his feet, a thunderous *boom* echoed through the house. The back door had been kicked clean off its hinges.

Cas didn't even flinch. He was *that* sure everything was in hand. Instead, he took another slow drag from his cigarette and exhaled a long plume of smoke.

'Didn't your ol' man never learn how to use a fucking doorknob?' he muttered.

There was silence for half a second – then came the sounds of a few choice words, a scuffle, a few grunts, and the unmistakable thud of someone hitting the floor. It was followed by the loud clicks of a few guns being cocked.

Cas smirked, still unfazed. 'Right. Get these little scrotums trussed up like two fucking chickens, would ya?'

Flicking ash off his cigarette, he glanced at Frazer.

'Oh, and, Frazer, can we *maybe* leave the samurai sword alone for a minute?' He sighed. 'I *hate* having to do clean-up jobs.'

Hearing the commotion from the kitchen, Billy pulled his knife from his boot and bolted, his heart pounding with raw, unfiltered rage.

He *wanted* to see Bart's and Richie's eyes as they died. He *wanted* to watch the life drain out of them as they screamed in pain.

But the moment he burst into the kitchen, he froze.

Cas clearly had everything under control.

The room was locked down. Polythene sheeting covered the floor. Every man from the van had a gun pressed firmly against his skull.

Cas stood calmly as if he'd been expecting this exact scenario all along.

Billy's eyes swept the room and then he saw him – Bart. The fat, ugly bastard.

But Billy didn't see Bart Shipley as such – he saw only Bronte trembling, terrified, and pleading for them to stop.

And just like that, the *red mist* came down.

With a snarl, Billy lunged forward.

Bart barely had time to flinch before Billy's blade sliced viciously across his face.

James, who had been holding his gun steady, jumped back in shock. He hadn't expected that.

Bart let out a choked, guttural scream, his hands flying to his face as he tried to hold it together – literally. A deep gash ran from his temple to his jaw, the flesh peeling away, and blood spilling between his fingers.

'You *bastard!*' Bart howled.

'*Bastard? Bastard?*' Billy roared, his entire body shaking with fury. 'Yeah? Fuck you! You fucking RAPED my girl!'

Hearing that, Bart gasped and staggered backwards.

But there was something about Bart that made Billy's blood boil.

Even with half his face hanging off, he was still laughing. Not with his mouth, but with his eyes. And that was the last mistake he was ever going to make.

Billy grabbed the bolt cutters from the table and swung them hard.

The heavy metal cracked against Bart's skull, sending him crashing to the floor and now barely conscious.

But Billy wasn't done.

He smashed the cutters into Bart's mouth. The force knocked his teeth loose – some clattering to the floor, others lodging in his throat.

Bart gagged, choking, his body convulsing as blood and saliva bubbled at his lips.

The room erupted into chaos. Shouting. Screaming. And the men with the guns forced the Shipleys to their knees.

Gerard was crying like a baby, and Richie – pathetic, wheezing Richie – was begging for mercy, pleading for them to let him go.

But Billy didn't hear *any* of it.

All he could hear was Bronte's voice – soft and broken, begging for her rapists to stop.

With a final, brutal motion, Billy *rammed* his knife between Bart's legs again and again.

'And *that's* for raping my girl,' he snarled.

Bart let out a strangled, inhuman wail, clutching what was left of his bollocks, as his body convulsed in agony. His eyes rolled back, his face twisted in pure suffering. 'Please, please, have some mercy,' he cried.

'Mercy denied, you cunt.'

Billy spat out those words, his chest heaving. Ignoring the fact that his hands were covered with warm sticky blood, he stabbed the ugly brute in what was left of his face.

While the blood pooled on the plastic sheeting, Billy watched with satisfaction as Bart agonisingly bled to death.

Richie stared in horror. Wide-eyed. Pale as a corpse. His body shuddered violently, a man already drowning in terror before the first wave hit. He knew. He knew exactly what was coming.

'I'm sorry,' Richie sobbed, his voice fractured, barely human. 'I'm so sorry!' Snot streamed from his nose, mixed with the saliva and tears, which soaked his chin. As his body convulsed in terror, he looked up at Billy and pleaded with him for compassion.

Billy didn't look at him. Didn't hear him. Instead, he heard her.

Bronte. How she would have cried, screamed, and begged.

His knuckles whitened around the hilt of the knife. With a single, fluid motion, he struck. The blade punched into Richie's arm – first one, then the other. He twisted viciously, feeling muscle and sinew grind against steel.

Richie's screams tore through the night, high-pitched and raw, sounds ripped from the depths of suffering.

Billy reached into his pocket and pulled out a plastic bag. He had dreamed of this moment. He had lived it in his head a thousand times. Every detail burned into him.

With a savage yank, he pulled the bag over Richie's head and sealed it with two thick cable ties. He clinched them tight with a sharp, brutal tug.

The room held its breath.

No one moved. No one dared.

Richie bucked – his body jerking, convulsing, and fighting for air that wasn't there. His hands clawed at the polythene, but he was powerless. The bag clung to his face, moulding itself to every contour. In short order, his screams turned to muffled whimpers.

But Billy wasn't finished.

Before Richie could draw what breath he had left in him, Billy stabbed him again. This time through both hands. The blade split tendons and shattered bones.

Richie shrieked, the sound barely making it past the polythene prison that was sealing his fate.

With practised ease, Billy yanked Richie's arms behind his back and bound them together, the cable ties slicing deep into the flesh.

Richie crumpled face down onto the floor, his whole body convulsing once more, like a broken marionette.

Every man with a gun to their head watched in horror. Their mouths hung open. Their bodies were locked in place, rigid with the primal fear of prey watching a predator feast.

Billy stepped back, his chest still rising and falling, but now in slower and more measured breaths. He didn't look at Richie anymore. He just waited.

Waited for the moment the last of the fight drained from his body.

Waited for the suffocation to take hold.

Waited to watch him take his last breath of air.

Richie had nothing left but time.

And Billy was going to make sure he felt every fucking second of it.

Breathless and now covered in blood, Jesse grabbed his brother and yanked him back.

'Leave it now, Billy. Come on.'

Billy was still seething like a caged animal.

For a second, Jesse thought his brother would shrug him off.

But it was James who took control. He gave a single nod – an unspoken order – to Billy.

At last, Billy allowed his brother to pull him away.

This was going to be a long night.

Cas clapped his hands together, grabbing everyone's attention, as though this was all just another night at the office.

'Right,' he said, stretching. 'Let's get the kettle on and the table set – for *torture* or *admin*.' He chuckled as he glanced around the room. 'What do ya say, Gerard? Fancy a bit of *dentistry*? Or maybe you'd rather show off your *writing* skills?' He smirked. 'Because you and your lot have taken a *right royal fucking liberty* with my family. And now? Now, it's time to *pay up*.'

Denny grabbed Gerard by his hair, lifted him off the ground, and forced him onto a chair.

Gerard glared, curling his top lip in disgust. 'You can *fuck off*, Cas.'

Shaking his head, Cas laughed.

'Yeah, I could fuck off. You're right. But, see, the thing is . . . I don't want to.'

He leaned in slightly, his voice dropping to something almost casual, almost friendly.

'I want your *signature* on that fucking paper.'

Gerard tried to push himself to his feet, but Denny shoved him straight back down onto the chair again.

'No, you don't, Gerard. You piss-taker.'

Gerard spat onto the floor, his breathing heavy, his demeanour defiant.

'I ain't signing nuffin,' he growled. His eyes flicked between Cas, Dennis, and Walter. ''Cos I *know* you lot. I know how this ends. I *won't* walk out of here alive.'

Cas nodded. 'Yeah, you know us well.' He leaned forward and rested his hands on the table. 'But see – here's the thing.' His voice was calm. Measured.

'It's the difference between a *straightforward* bullet to the brain . . . or us cutting you up, bit by bit.' He tapped the table, almost casually. 'And trust me, mate, I *came prepared.*'

He reached into his leather holdall and pulled out a roll of polythene and wire cutters and then tossed everything onto the table with a smirk.

'Got me plastic sheets, got me Marigolds. So really, Gerard, it's *your* choice. Ain't that right?'

Gerard's jaw tightened, his pulse hammering against his throat.

'Oh, and before you make up your mind,' Cas continued, his smirk turning colder, 'I'll be dismembering your two boys first. And you? You'll sit there and watch them scream. I can even order in the popcorn, if you fancy it.'

The room fell silent.

Gerard's breathing was ragged now, his fingers curling into fists.

Cas tilted his head, still smiling.

'So . . . what's it gonna be?'

CHAPTER THIRTY-SEVEN

Carrie closed the passenger door slowly, careful not to make a sound, before Dottie pulled away.

'I told you this isn't your fight, Carrie. Fuck me, Spud will go mental when he discovers we're both not there.'

'Look, Spud and Sunny are both shattered, bless them. They're asleep. And anyway, I'm not letting you go alone. It's always been me and you, Dottie, ever since we were teenagers. A strange kind of friendship, maybe, but a friendship all the same.'

Dottie smiled. 'And you, Carrie, have been the family I never had. Remember when we first met? You said you'd love to live on my side of the main road, and I knew then you wouldn't have lasted a day with my mum and dad. Evil bastards, they were.'

Carrie laughed. 'I remember it well, Dot. I said I hated living in my house because it smelled of dogs, and you said yours reeked of bleach. But now? I wouldn't have changed it for the world.'

Dottie was silent for a moment before she suddenly let out a laugh. 'I fucking made sure I changed mine.'

She had never laughed about it before. In fact, she rarely spoke about it. But whether it was a degree of nervousness for what they were about to do or simply that so much time had elapsed since their teenage days, it didn't seem to matter anymore. They both roared with laughter.

'Yeah, I guess I might have gone a bit over the top,' Dottie admitted.

'Over the top?' Carrie laughed. 'You fucking slit their throats, or something like that! The worst I ever did was slam my bedroom door, stick two fingers up, and swear under me breath. You went and killed yours in the dead of night!'

Dottie chuckled again. 'Well, when you put it like that, I guess we are different.'

'Not so different that we don't have each other's backs. You were there when I really needed you. You were like fucking Lara

Croft on speed. You saved our babies that night from that bastard.' Carrie paused. 'Do you ever feel guilty about killing Albert?'

Instantly, Dottie shook her head. 'No. Not at all. Why? Do you?'

Carrie shook her head too. 'Funnily enough . . . no, I don't.'

'Not even when you look at Ginty?'

Carrie frowned. 'I suppose I don't associate Ginty with her sons or even the past. Mentally, I've moved on because – dare I fucking say it – she's been good to the kids and to me. I think she's realised that bullying people gets you nowhere. Being kind always stands for something.'

'Ginty raised monsters—'

Carrie quickly interrupted her friend. 'But she knows that now. She's disowned Jimmy, and she's lucky she took the rap for murdering Irvin and Danny Slade or one of us would have killed her.'

Dottie stared ahead. But it was almost impossible to see the road. The heavens had opened, and the rain was pelting their windscreen.

'Candice raised monsters. And she's probably still one herself.'

The jovial tone turned serious. 'Dottie, I'm so worried. Our boys – this fucking evil family. What if . . .?'

'Carrie Ann, listen, and listen good, all right?' Dottie's voice was firm. 'Cas has lived that life for thirty to forty years, and he's still standing. His firm is still going strong after all these years in the business. And then there's Walter's sons and Dennis's son, who are in it too. They have their own men as well, but, more than that, Carrie, they have more arsenal than the Queen's Guard. Cas won't let our boys get hurt.'

Carrie chewed on her thumbnail. 'I fucking hope to God you're right, Dot.'

***

Candice sat at her small kitchen table staring at the photo of all her sons and grandsons, especially her two favourites Max and Moriarty. The two never missed coming to see her each Sunday, always arriving with flowers and a gift.

A glance at the kitchen clock showed that the time was five minutes to ten.

Taking a large swig of brandy, she hissed through her teeth, as the burning sensation hit her throat. Then, taking a long drag of her cigarette, she blew a stream of smoke up to the ceiling.

Flicking ash into a homemade pottery dish, a trinket Max had made for her when he was five, her eyes lingered on the tiny, imperfect edges of the dish, which was in stark contrast to the material world she lived in now, where everyone wanted the best on offer.

With a quick glance at her phone, she waited for the call to confirm that the witnesses had been silenced.

Then her thoughts became distracted. A rustling sound was coming from somewhere near the back door leading into the kitchen.

Her body tensed, her fingers tightening around the cigarette. For a split second, she wished she hadn't downed so much brandy. The warmth in her veins turned to ice as doubt crept in. Was she hearing things again?

The slow creak of the door sent a jolt through her. She held her breath, the hairs on the back of her neck rising. And then – that face.

Dorothy Ellis.

The image hit her like a fist to the chest, just as it had the other evening. That woman was here! She hadn't imagined it.

Her mind took her back in time. To Holloway Prison. That look – the raw, silent accusation – still haunted her. It clung to the edges of her mind, creeping into her sleep and poisoning her quiet moments.

Maybe her son and grandson were right. Perhaps she was seeing things.

After all, Dorothy Ellis's face had been the pinnacle of her nightmares.

She didn't turn around. Instead, with her hands shaking, she lit another cigarette, the flame flickering as her fingers trembled. About to pour herself another drink, she decided instead to abandon the glass and gulp straight from the bottle. But the burning sensation in her throat did little to steady her nerves.

This time, she heard the back door close – ever so quietly – but close it did. There was someone in her house.

Instinct kicked in. Her eyes darted around the room searching for a weapon. There was just one within reach – the wooden knife block on the counter. Springing to her feet, ready to lunge for it, she—

'I wouldn't do that, if I were you.'

The voice was slow. It was menacing. And it was followed by the unmistakable click of a gun being cocked.

Candice froze in mid-stride, her breath caught in her throat. Slowly, carefully, she turned around to put a face to that voice. Not that she needed to.

Dorothy Ellis wasn't that reckless teenager anymore. She was a woman now – strong, poised, and carrying herself with a confidence that matched the steeliness in her eyes. Eyes that spoke a thousand words, each one dark and dangerous.

That stare.

It was the same one she had witnessed the day she killed Ellis's best pal Billy Cardel. The same cold, merciless look that vowed I will hunt you down and kill you.

In all her years, she had never feared another person – man or woman. But Dorothy Ellis?

Dorothy Ellis. The Devil's daughter.

Her body betrayed her before her mind could catch up. Her shoulders sagged, and the strength drained from her limbs. She collapsed onto the chair, unable to hold herself against the weight of pure, unshakable fear.

'What do you want?'

'Candice, I haven't come for a chat or to bargain with you.'

As fear crept up her spine and tingled through every follicle on her scalp, Candice knew what her fate would be. She was going to die.

Why else would Dorothy Ellis be here?

'You stupid cunt,' Candice spat, forcing her voice to sound steadier than she felt. 'My grandsons will be back any minute now, and they won't be alone. And you, you silly tart, I bet you didn't know this place has cameras everywhere.'

Dottie smiled. 'Yeah, I know there are. But, right now, Candice? Not a single one of them is working.'

'And as for your boys? Hmm . . .' She tilted her head, almost mockingly. 'See, they chose to fuck about with my boy. My Billy. And no one hurts my son. No one. Because you know what I'll do, don't you?'

Candice curled her lip, baring her teeth. 'My boys will fucking annihilate you and your fucking kid.'

'Hmm,' said another voice. 'And that's what you believe, is it?'

Then Candice saw her.

A second woman had entered, moving silently. At first, she thought it was one of the cleaners. They all had that long, sleek black hair and that Spanish vibe about them. And for a fleeting moment, she thought she was saved.

Surely, Dorothy Ellis wouldn't do anything with a witness present, would she?

Relief flooded her, her shoulders dropping just slightly. 'Thank God you're here, love,' she said, the weight of her fear momentarily lifting.

But the woman didn't move.

She folded her arms and studied Candice with a cool, unreadable expression.

'And this is Candice Shipley, is it?' the woman asked.

Still holding the gun steady, Dottie smirked. 'The very one.'

'Dottie, I just called Billy.'

Dorothy didn't take her eyes off Candice. 'And?'

Carrie let out a heartfelt sigh before she turned to Candice, her lips curling at the edges. 'Apparently, he was in the car with Jesse. They were watching the Shipleys being dragged to their graves. It took a while for Gerard to sign all the papers, and as for Reece . . .' She paused, tilting her head slightly and watching Candice open and close her mouth like a fish out of water. 'Reece eventually signed over everything. But Jesse said it was lucky he's right-handed.'

Candice's face drained of all colour, her skin taking on a sickly, lifeless grey. Her breathing came in sharp, ragged gasps, as if she couldn't get enough air. The realisation finally hit her: the address Melanie Sykes had given them was fake. It was a trap. A fucking trap that she had insisted they fall into. And all because she wanted Max and Moriarty out of prison, come what may. This was all her own fault.

'My son—' Her voice cracked before she shrieked, 'Is he dead? Tell me! Is he dead?'

Carrie didn't answer immediately. She let the silence stretch, let Candice's fear settle deep into her bones. Finally, she nodded. 'Not just him, Candice. They're all dead. All except for Max and Moriarty, who will go to prison for a very long time.'

Something in Candice broke.

All the years of bravado, of sitting on her pedestal, surrounded by the empire she'd built with her sons – it was all gone. Now, the room felt smaller, the walls seemed to close in, and her world was reduced to nothing but an empty, meaningless shell.

Carrie reached into her pocket and pulled something out. With a smirk, she held it up.

'Oh, Dottie. You wanted these.'

Candice barely lifted her eyes. She just sat there, as if she had already died.

Dottie lowered the gun and stepped towards the table, her movements slow and deliberate. She tilted her head, her eyes never leaving Candice's stricken face.

'You know what, Candice?' Her voice was calm and edged with something far more dangerous than rage. 'You took something very precious from me. Billy was my friend. She cared about me. She was going to be there when my baby was born. When I needed her most.'

Candice barely breathed, her trembling fingers curling into fists against the table.

Letting out a humourless laugh, Dottie shook her head. 'And once you ended her life, I made a vow that one day, I would end yours. Believe me, you nasty piece of work, I've always wanted to make you suffer. I wanted to drag it out, to let you feel every inch of pain before I killed you. But looking at you now?' She leaned in slightly, watching Candice's face twist in sheer agony. 'This is better.'

She gestured towards the woman who once thought herself untouchable but who was now crumbling before her eyes.

'You've lost the people closest to you. Your sons. Your grandsons. You're alone. And that? That is torture enough.'

Reaching for the brandy on the table, Dottie slid it towards Candice. Her voice dropped to a whisper, cold and deliberate. 'You will die, Candice Shipley. And I will be the one to kill you. But I won't hurt you physically. In fact . . .' She smirked. 'You might even feel euphoric, knowing you will die, because you probably would have ended it yourself, now knowing my boys got to yours first. That they slaughtered your legacy. The truth is, Candice, I don't even have to pull the trigger.'

She nodded towards a bottle of pills she'd placed beside the brandy.

'Down the fucking lot,' she said, her voice like ice. 'Do yourself a favour. At least, this way, you don't go out undignified.'

Unexpectedly, Candice looked up, with a flash of defiance. It was as if someone had dosed her with cockiness, a final desperate grasp at control.

'I don't believe you,' she said. 'Prove it.'

Dottie tilted her head, her smirk unwavering. 'I get it, Candice. I'd be the same. I'd want proof before I ended my own life.' She nodded towards the phone on the table. 'So call them.'

Candice didn't need to be told twice. Picking up the phone, she gripped it so tightly, her knuckles turned white. She dialled Gerard's number first. It rang once. Then silence.

Dead.

Her breathing quickened as she frantically tried Reece's number.

Dead.

She felt the first real stab of terror in her gut, deeper than before. Her mind screamed at her that this wasn't happening, that they were fine, that something was wrong with the signal. But the truth was already sinking in, poisoning her from the inside out.

Dottie stepped back slowly as she watched the horror settle on Candice's face. 'Go on,' she said, arms crossed, her grin widening. 'Call the others. I think you'll find that no one is answering. That's because they're being buried in some mass grave right now.'

Candice's body trembled.

They never turned their phones off. Ever.

She had drilled it into them – always call, always check in. And now, as her glassy eyes flicked towards the clock on the wall, the inevitable hit her like a sledgehammer.

Ten o'clock.

They should have called by now.

They were dead.

Her breathing came in shallow, uneven gasps. She reached for the pills, but her body was shaking so uncontrollably that she found it impossible to remove the cap off the bottle.

Carrie went across to the table and helped her.

Candice dearly wanted to know what was in that bottle. She was desperate to know what it was that would finish her off. But her eyes were so filled with tears, she could barely see the label. Then, she thought: *what the fuck does it matter*?

Her gaze lifted to the framed photo of her boys, the last thing she'd ever see, and with one final, shuddering breath, she tipped the pills into her mouth, and swallowed them down with the last of the brandy.

Dottie and Carrie stood there in silence. One minute, two minutes, three minutes, they watched, as Candice's body slumped forward onto the table, with no discernible movement following that.

With a final intake of breath, Candice left this life almost peacefully, as if she had accepted the inevitable in those final moments.

Dottie gave Carrie a slow nod.

'And that was the real head of the hydra,' she murmured. 'She always has been. Because behind every successful man is a clever bitch.'

CHAPTER THIRTY-EIGHT

Early September

For Grace Ruck, this would be her first visit to Croydon Crown Court. She had come today to see her husband get his just desserts. Kenny had already been convicted for so many offences that she knew he would be given another long stretch, which would see him residing in the nick until well into his seventies.

It was the icing on the cake when her husband looked up at the gallery and saw her. And saw him! The expression on his face when he saw Cas with his arm around her said it all.

She was in her element. This was her moment – and she was going to make the most of it.

Ever since she had returned from his villa in Cyprus, Cas had been her rock. For the very first time in her life, she felt alive. And she intended to make up for lost time – with someone she really liked. Was it love? Not yet, but the signs were promising.

***

Three weeks later

Billy sat in the gallery in the same courtroom that Grace and Cas had been in a few weeks ago. He was flanked by Dottie, Bronte, and the real Phoebe.

Slightly further away, Grace, who was next to Cas, was silent but watchful.

The moment Tandy was called to the witness stand, there was a quick wave of mumbling before silence settled over the room. She stalked forwards, taking her place as though it was a throne and turned her gaze on her mother – a glare so venomous it was a wonder she didn't drop dead on the spot. Her mother would have been pinned to the wall if those eyes could throw spears.

Then, her gaze turned towards Billy. And it sharpened.

The fury in her eyes wasn't because he was there. No, it was because he was there with his arm slung protectively around

Bronte. To Tandy, Bronte wasn't competition. She wasn't even a person. She was nothing. A shadow. How dare he?

Billy had to blink twice. For a moment, he didn't recognise her. The bleached blonde hair was gone, replaced by her natural auburn. But it wasn't just the colour – it was everything. The shine, the gloss, the perfect image she used to wear like armour. It was all stripped away. Her skin, once flawless, was blotchy and broken out. She looked haggard. Cheap. Dowdy.

But beneath it all . . . dangerous.

He didn't know that she'd been spending a fortune on beauty treatments, desperate to look like the girl she'd once been. None of it had worked. Now, standing there, her face twisted in fury, she wasn't the polished goddess she thought she was. Instead, she was a monster.

Beside him, Phoebe shuddered.

Billy felt it instantly and tightened his grip on her hand. He leaned in and whispered.

'She's down there. But you're up here. With us.'

Phoebe nodded. 'I know,' she whispered back. 'But she still makes me nervous.'

The side door creaked open. Jesse appeared like a shadow sliding through the gap. Without a word, he dropped onto the bench beside Phoebe, pressed his leg against hers, and took her free hand in his. His fingers were warm and sure. He kissed her cheek.

'All right, darling? Sorry I wasn't here earlier. Jacob Kerns, the arresting officer, was just giving me the low-down,' he said, softly. 'They're going to read your witness statement soon. Don't be alarmed. And, no doubt, the bitch will glare at you. Let her. Don't flinch. Don't react. She can't hurt you now, babe.'

Phoebe breathed out slowly. She was still shaking, but now, she felt a little steadier on hearing those wise words of support.

Billy watched the two of them for a moment with a warm feeling inside. Phoebe had met Jesse when she'd helped Billy with the insurance paperwork after the fire. She'd taken to the cheeky brother instantly – and it was reciprocated immediately by Jesse.

And now, here they were, supporting each other.

The prosecution read the statement aloud to the judge. A man who had presided over thousands of cases in his career. Yet, despite all his experience, it was clear he was still struck by this one: a young woman carrying out a plan of meticulous cruelty, with a cold disregard for life, namely, Ginty Carson. He wasn't buying any excuses. And he wasn't accepting the defence's plea for sympathy. And certainly not the claim that she'd been acting under her father's orders. And he'd said as much in his summing up to the jury.

Also in the gallery, Ginty sat beside Carrie, her chin tilted high when the judge mentioned her name.

'A defenceless lady,' he said, his tone grave, giving the following sentence a sense of seriousness. 'Who could have perished in what would have been a terrible way to die.'

Carrie elbowed her, stifling a giggle. 'You? You old bat – defenceless – my arse.'

Ginty nudged her back. 'Shut your trap.'

The judge leaned back in his chair, his expression unreadable, as he instructed the jury to retire and consider their verdict. Not that there was much to decide.

The evidence was overwhelming – stacked high and damning.

Without her mother's purse strings, Tandy hadn't stood a chance. No top-notch lawyer in a sharp suit and silk tie to spin her story into something sympathetic – even believable.

All Tandy had managed to have was a drippy duty solicitor who could barely string two sentences together and a barrister who spent most of his time digging for gold up his nose instead of dismantling the prosecution's case.

It was over. She just didn't know it yet.

The gallery slowly filed out into the crisp afternoon air as the courtroom emptied. The chill called for a light jacket or cardigan despite it being late September. People gathered in small groups, some lighting their cigarettes, others stretching their legs.

Phoebe stood just outside the doors, as pale as chalk.

Carrie and Dottie noticed straight away and hurried over to her.

'It's over, darling,' Carrie said firmly, resting a hand on Phoebe's shoulder. 'She ain't getting out anytime soon, believe you me. She won't.'

Carrie glanced at Jesse.

'Why don't you take her home?'

Phoebe shook her head quickly. 'No . . . no, I want to see this through. I want to watch her get her comeuppance.' Her voice shook, but her eyes were hard. 'And what she did to Ginty – well—'

Carrie cut in. 'Never mind Ginty. That one can fight fire with fire.' She gave Phoebe's arm a gentle squeeze. 'Anyway, tomorrow night's a big one. You're coming, ain't ya, Phoebe?'

Phoebe glanced up at Jesse and smiled softly. 'Well, Jesse invited me . . . and I'd love to.'

Carrie was warming to the young woman. *Sweet enough*, she thought. Good enough for her Jesse.

A little further along, Cas slipped his arm around Grace.

'I get it, Dol,' he murmured. 'It's hard. She's your baby, and as much as she's a cow . . . she's still *your* cow. Ain't that right?'

Grace smiled faintly but shook her head.

'The thing is, Cas . . . I'd love to agree with you. I really would. But the truth is, we never had a bond. As much as I tried, she never let me in. She was a cruel little cow from the age of six. That bitch made my life a misery.'

Her voice was steady, but her eyes were distant. 'She's her father's daughter, all right. Through and through.'

She sighed, her shoulders easing just a little.

'At least I won't have to worry about either of them anymore. He's never getting out, and I should think she'll be away for a long time.'

Grace smiled again, this time with something closer to peace.

'I feel relieved, really, Cas. Relieved.'

***

Redwood stepped out of the courts. He was looking immaculate in his suit and wearing a grin which encompassed complete satisfaction. He caught Jesse's eye and nodded.

After giving Phoebe's hand a quick squeeze, Jesse left her with his mother before walking up to his boss.

‘Gov,’ Jesse said, his voice low but steady. ‘All right?’

Redwood’s grin widened. ‘Couldn’t wait for this day,’ he said. ‘And now . . . Now I can finally relax.’ His expression softened. ‘Even my Betsy’s changed. She was brave, sitting in that courtroom, watching the trial of Max and Moriarty. When the judge sentenced them – thirty-five years each, with another ten for the burglary, I saw her smile.’ He paused, and then he added, quietly, ‘She never told me, Jesse. Never said who cut her face. But the way she looked at those men in that courtroom a few weeks ago . . . it told me everything I needed to know.’

Redwood clamped a firm hand on Jesse’s shoulder.

‘And I have you to thank for that. You’re a good copper.’

Jesse beamed. ‘I want to be, Gov. I really do. Because when I saw those Shipleys get sent down, it gave me a buzz that was better than any drug I’ve ever had. And I want that buzz again.’

Redwood chuckled, giving him a conspiratorial wink.

‘Well, you’ve got what it takes. Kenny Ruck is back where he belongs. Tandy, no doubt, she’s going away, and again, thanks to you, Melanie Sykes is too. It seems to me you have a nose for it, son.’

‘Well, Wesley’s wife told me during the reinterview,’ Jesse began, his voice low and deliberate, ‘that after their row, the night he was killed, Wesley got into Melanie’s car. We confirmed it on the ANPR, and once we joined the dots, it was easy to link her to the Shipleys. Finding out her son was Reece Shipley’s was the final nail in her coffin.’ He shook his head, a cold glint in his eye. ‘Another rat behind bars.’

Redwood glanced off towards the street. ‘I wouldn’t like to be her. A copper in prison? She’ll find it hard.’

‘Still, she was in a position of power. And she abused it,’ said Jesse.

‘I’m glad you’re on my team. As I say, Jesse – you’re a good egg.’ His voice lowered. What he said next was said with some feeling. ‘And as for your methods of ridding London’s streets of scum . . .’

He smiled, but the smile didn’t reach his eyes.

‘Let’s just say they’re questionable.’ Then, with a grim tilt of his head, he added, ‘But I don’t care. You get results.’

Jesse gave him a half-smile, but inside, he knew what Redwood was really saying.

And in that moment, Jesse knew for sure. Redwood understood. He knew exactly what had happened to the Shipleys – their sudden disappearance, their permanent silence – and he would never breathe a word of it.

Redwood would never grass – not on him.

An usher suddenly came bounding out. 'Mr Murphy, the jury is about to read the verdict.'

***

Everyone rushed back into the courtroom and quickly took their places in the gallery. The atmosphere was heavy and tense.

The first thing they noticed was Tandy's demeanour. The cockiness that had clung to her like a second skin was gone. Sheepishly, she stood up, her hands clasped in front of her and her head down. But it was too late for regrets.

The jury had heard it all. The statements, the witnesses, the truth of who this woman was, and what she was really all about.

The jurors were certainly not fooled. Nothing went unnoticed.

As the foreman stood, the courtroom held its breath. The question was asked.

'Have you reached a verdict?'

The silence, the pause, was almost for effect.

'Yes, your Honour. We find the accused . . . Guilty.'

There was no cheer, no shout of relief. The gallery remained composed, mostly out of respect for Grace. But the feeling was electric.

The judge took a moment, his eyes remained fixed on Tandy. As he spoke, his sharp yet deep voice cut through the air.

'I sentence you to eighteen years.'

For a split second, Tandy froze. Then, the mask slipped. Her eyes widened with fury, her lip curled back like an animal baring its teeth, and the words exploded from her mouth – vile and venomous.

'You old cunt! I hope you fucking die!'

The room recoiled, but the judge didn't flinch. He brought the gavel down hard.

'Remove her,' he ordered, his tone cool and final.

The guards closed in, grabbing her, as she thrashed and snarled.

And just like that, it was over.

***

Saturday night

Even though Luanne's party had been delayed, it didn't detract from the fun everyone was having. The party was already in full swing when Billy approached his grandmother's table.

Luanne cupped his face in her hands and kissed his cheek.

'You know what, my Billy boy? I still remember the day your aunt and I walked into your mum's flat ready to take over – seeing as she had you and Jesse, dear little babies on her own. You were so beautiful.' She chuckled softly. 'But she was doing just fine, really. And the lungs on you, my boy! You were a strong-willed baby. And there was your bruvver Jesse, right by your side – both of ya – the talk of the town.'

Her eyes shone with pride. 'I've always wanted my two eldest grandbabies to have the right girl on their arm. And look at you – handsome, clever. The pair of you.'

Luanne glanced across the room and pointed to Bronte, who was sitting next to Carrie. 'She's the right girl for you, Billy boy. That little beauty there, the one who don't take her eyes off ya.'

Jed leaned in, smirking. 'She's yours now, Billy boy. Stop bein' so polite, lad, and do what you gotta do. I'll have a word with the DJ.'

Billy smiled, kissed Luanne's cheek, and whispered, 'Thanks, Nan.'

He could see she was welling up, and when he glanced over at his grandfather, he saw the old man discreetly wiping a tear from his eye.

As Billy made his way across the room towards Bronte, it was as if everyone suddenly knew what was about to happen – everyone except her. She was still in deep conversation with Carrie, completely oblivious to what was going on around her.

Then the music cut out. Silence filled the room.

Bronte turned, confused, her smile fading for a moment. As Billy got down on one knee, she spotted a small velvet box in his hand.

She gasped, her hands flying to her mouth, as tears welled up in her eyes and spilled over her cheeks.

'Will you do me the honour of being my wife?' Billy asked, as a nervous smile spread across his face.

For a moment, it was as if the whole room held its breath.

Bronte was speechless, until the realisation sank in. Then she flung herself at him, nearly knocking him over.

'Yes! Yes, oh yes! I'll marry ya, Billy! I will!'

The room erupted – cheers, laughter, and applause filled the air.

Jesse was the first on his feet. Running over, he scooped Bronte up and spun her around as she laughed through tears.

'I've got another sister! Look at that, eh?' he said, kissing her cheeks. He set her down gently. Then, he turned to Billy and pulled him into a tight, fierce hug.

Billy grinned as they slapped each other on the back. 'You'll be next.'

Jesse glanced over his shoulder at Phoebe, a mischievous glint in his eye.

'I'm workin' on it, Billy boy.'

Everyone wanted to congratulate the newly engaged couple, but Billy had another surprise – one that he'd promised himself he would do a long time ago. It was born out of nothing but respect.

He headed towards Benny, who was beaming from ear to ear.

Ginty, who'd been spending the last few months in Benny's caravan, was smiling too. She was enjoying the party with some of her own people – and not forgetting Benny.

'Billy boy,' Benny said, holding out his hand. 'I couldn't be more proud, son. You make my girl so happy, and you've made an old man happy too.'

Billy dismissed his hand and pulled the old man in for a hug instead. 'Benny, remember when you made that joke about me buying you a state-of-the-art caravan?'

Ginty was by Benny's side now, earwigging as usual. But this time, she was smiling, a tear rolling down her cheek. 'Go on, Billy, tell him,' she said. She was genuinely pleased for Benny – because she knew exactly what Billy had done.

Billy held up a set of keys. 'Well, I'm marrying your daughter, and you *are* getting that caravan. In fact, while you've been here tonight, the beast of a van has been delivered.'

Benny stood there, his mouth wide open. 'Are you serious, mush?'

Ginty nudged him in the ribs as more tears rolled down her cheeks. 'It's beautiful, Benny. I mean, proper fucking nice. I helped Billy choose it, didn't I, Billy boy?'

Billy smiled. 'There is a condition.'

Benny stayed frozen, gobsmacked, his face full of wonder. 'Anything, Billy.'

But Billy didn't answer.

Instead, Ginty jumped in. 'I'm moving in an' all.'

'You promise, girl?' Benny squeezed Ginty's hand.

'You try and keep me away.' She grinned. 'I love van life, me. I'm not one for a posh apartment.'

Billy smiled awkwardly, feeling slightly embarrassed by all the appreciation directed his way. He wasn't one for over-the-top displays of emotion.

His gaze drifted across the room. Taking it all in, he could see that Jesse was as animated as ever. He was laughing loudly, with his arm around their mum, Carrie, and trying to get her to dance. They were both beaming, full of life and utterly enjoying the celebration.

And then his eyes found Dottie.

She was standing quietly in the corner, watching from afar, with a smile that stretched from ear to ear. She'd always done that – holding herself back and letting others take centre stage. Even now, after all that she had sacrificed, she stood back and allowed the Murphys to make the fuss. Letting them have their moment while she simply watched.

Not intruding. Not wanting to take anything away.

Billy's chest tightened, something fierce and grateful rising inside him.

Without thinking, without worrying how it might look, he strode over to her and took her hand.

'Come on,' he said.

And then he did something completely uncharacteristic – he pulled her on to the dance floor.

The music picked up as he swirled her gently into the dance. He wanted her to feel part of this new life he was building with Bronte. She deserved that. More than anyone, she deserved to feel like she belonged in this happiness.

As he danced her around the floor, he caught sight of his other mother, Carrie, across the room. She nodded slowly, a knowing smile on her lips. There was pride in her eyes . . . and he saw something else.

Understanding.

Carrie looked on, with tears in her eyes. She knew what Dottie had sacrificed. She knew how much her best friend had carried quietly for years. And now, as Billy's mother, in every way that mattered, it was Dottie's turn to shine.

And Carrie, with grace and heart, was letting her.

Billy's throat tightened, but he held the emotion in and smiled down at Dottie as he danced her across the floor.

For the first time in a long time, it felt like everything was exactly as it should be.

Printed in Great Britain
by Amazon

62950853R10214